THE SIDEKICK

Benjamin Markovits is the author _____
named a *Granta* Best of Young British Novelist in 2013 _
won the James Tait Black Memorial Prize for *You Don't Have To
Live Like This*. He lives in London and teaches creative writing at
Royal Holloway, University of London.

Praise for *The Sidekick*

'[*The Sidekick* is] about how some people succeed and some fail in
their professional and personal lives and perhaps about how America
is failing. Whether or not you are interested in basketball, this is what
draws us in. Much of the novel is set in the 1990s but *The Sidekick*
has the melancholic and sour feel of Biden's America and proves why
Markovits is one of the best American writers of his generation.'
Jewish Chronicle

'Markovits always surprises and illuminates [and here] he has created
a subtle drama of relations between black and white, between star
performer and amiable, envious sidekick.' Lisa Appignanesi

'Exquisite . . . Somewhere in a golden triangle between Frederick
Exley's *A Fan's Notes*, Richard Ford's *The Sportswriter*, and David
Shields's *Black Planet* comes Benjamin Markovits's warm, humane,
and tragic *The Sidekick*. I hadn't known, until I picked it up, that
I was hungering for this kind of classic American voice; I hadn't
dreamed that it could be informed with so much gentle savvy about
male friendship, and the dynamics of race, sports and the media.'
Jonathan Lethem

'Markovits's sharp portrait of sporting ambition and its toxic fallout
kept me gripped.' *A Life in Books*

'I loved – loved – *The Sidekick*. Really terrific. So funny – I was laughing out loud – and poignant and intimate and true-ringing and beautifully paced.' Asher Price, author of *Year of the Dunk*

'Markovits draws domestic fraughtness excellently. The novel's strongest points are in its scenes of the mundane everyday of suburban American life, imbued with a bittersweet nostalgia . . . a refreshing take on the classic American novel.' *Lunate*

'The strong tang of sports jargon, of technical vernacular and slang, of tactical insight all serves the text, provides a compelling kind of music, a rhythm. I could smell the gyms, could hear the squeak of basketball boots on a polished floor . . . Markovits's achievement is to write into that resonance all the detail and pitfalls, all the heartache and exultation, not just of sport itself, but of contemporary American life.' *Caught by the River*

THE SIDEKICK

BENJAMIN MARKOVITS

faber

First published in 2022
by Faber & Faber Limited
Bloomsbury House
74–77 Great Russell Street
London WC1B 3DA

This paperback edition first published in 2023

Typeset by Faber & Faber Limited
Printed in the UK by CPI Group (UK) Ltd, Croydon, CR0 4YY

A CIP record for this book is available from the British Library

ISBN 978-0-571-37153-2

10 9 8 7 6 5 4 3 2 1

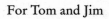
For Tom and Jim

1

I was a big slow fat kid but one thing I could do was shoot free throws. That's because my dad put a hoop over the garage door for my ninth birthday. He thought it might help me lose weight.

We had just moved to Austin after my mother got a job at the university. Dad was always hanging around—he used to pick me up from school. "Tell me if you notice anything different," he said, as we walked down the middle of the empty road to our house. Trees arched over us, late October Texas weather, bright yellow and blue. It took me a few minutes to find it. I was staring at the yard, the front porch, the picture window. But then he pointed up.

"Rawlings All-American" was scribbled in shiny cursive across the fiberglass board. It looked great, it made our house look like any other American house. Then he clicked open the garage door and came out again with a fresh basketball sticking out of the jaws of a cardboard box. I tore at the cardboard with small fingers. The artificial skin of the ball felt tacky to touch, almost sticky, like lizard skin. I had to get a pump to pump it up.

The first time I threw it at the rim, two-fisted, like a life preserver over the side of a boat, I got lucky. The brand-new nylon net made the little sound it makes, like corduroy pants on a fat kid, rubbing at the thighs. After that I was hooked. I've heard gamblers start like that, but it was also just something for us to do after school. We were both a little bored and lonely. Pounding the ball against the cement driveway, pushing at each other, sweating into our shirts, calling fouls and complaining, counting scores, joshing about it at the dinner table afterward.

One Saturday morning, my dad took a can of green paint from the garage and measured out fifteen feet, stepping out heel to toe in his

1

size-13 Rockports. Then he got down on his knees to paint a line. The green was Celtics green—he grew up in Philadelphia but hated the 76ers and liked to piss people off.

"This is the most important shot in basketball," he said, while we waited for the paint to dry. "The free throw. There are no variables, nothing is moving, you got no excuse."

After lunch, I tested it underfoot. Dad handed me the ball, but I was too weak to shoot from that kind of distance. It ended up bouncing to the back of the garage, with the lawnmower and the summer deck chairs, garbage pails and coils of garden hose.

"I can't do it," I said. But he chased down the ball and passed it back.

"Try again."

The same thing happened. "I told you, I can't do it." In that whiny voice I used that I should have grown out of.

"Try it like this," he said, "Rick Barry style," and flipped it to me underhand.

"Who's Rick Barry?"

"The greatest shooter who ever lived."

And the truth is, underhand works. Sometimes adulthood reaches back across the unlived years to touch you on the head and say, *This* is who you're going to be. Pay attention, kid; it starts *now*. Pretty soon I could make four five six in a row like that, holding the basketball like a pot by the sides, and swinging it lightly back and forth, getting the feel of it, letting go.

Eventually I learned to shoot normally, too. I had a decent old-fashioned set shot like my father. He learned it by watching Dolph Schayes.

My house was less than a ten-minute walk from school. Kids started coming home with me—nerd kids, the kind I could beat. Anyway, I was a pretty big sixth-grader, I used my butt. Dad took a back seat. He watched us from the porch or the picture window but didn't get involved. I never lost weight but I used to take money off my friends in free throw competitions. Money or Halloween candy. They laughed at me and I took their Reese's Peanut Butter Cups; everybody won.

Sometimes they stayed for dinner and Dad let us watch a ball game afterward, while my sister sat at the kitchen table and did homework and complained. I called out, "This is math. What we're watching is really just math in action."

My friends and I argued about three-point shooting percentages and the cost of turnovers. We came up with formulas for measuring the *totality* of a player's performance. It got to the point in high school where my father said, "Why don't you quit talking, and try out for the team?" And I thought, why not? By sophomore year I knew that I wanted to be a sportswriter and figured doing time on the JV would look good on my résumé. It might help me understand what I'm talking about. All this stuff is easier if you don't really care.

I had become one of those kids with a clear idea about his future prospects, and if other kids wanted to make fun of me, that was fine with me. Because I knew that childhood is short-term. What you go through in high school, what makes you popular or happy, doesn't count for much at any other period of your life, and the kids who think high school is the best time of your life, those are not people who live happy or successful lives.

But actually, I had a pretty good time. I liked my friends; we'd survived middle school together. At lunch, on the round blue cafeteria tables, we used to read out the box scores while playing cards. What a bunch of nerds. In Hollywood movies they make the nerds look like outsiders desperate to get with the in-crowd. But the truth is, nerds are pretty exclusive, it's not easy to sign up, you have to be funny and smart. What I mean is, we looked down on everybody else, too. Trying out for the basketball team was like a joke on the whole system. If Brian Blum can make it then what the hell.

———

The last bell rang and while everybody zombied out to the parking lot, human life-forms parasitized by backpacks, I pushed against the foot traffic to the gym. Already I had this weird feeling that something had been set in motion.

About forty boys were getting changed in the locker room. Mike Inchman was supposed to come along but he bailed at the last minute. "I've got bar mitzvah practice," he called out, waving a hand. You could hear the showers going when I walked in, everything smelled of BO and deodorant.

I stood around for a minute, waiting for a spot on one of the benches to clear, but nobody made room. My fourteen-year-old body was the kind of body you want from your two-year-old son, pale pink and soft, and I never liked getting changed in front of other kids. I was a tough kid, I could take it, but I didn't like it. None of these people were my friends. My gym shirt was a man-size Fordham University T-shirt, because Fordham is where my dad went to law school, before dropping out and switching to accounting. It was deep purple and made me look like a grape. Underneath the logo it said, FUTURE ATTORNEY.

Afterward, since I didn't have a locker, I dragged my backpack to the court, but there was nowhere to put it except against the wall, with all the other bags, and you worry, maybe somebody's going to steal it. I had a Mattel Electronic Football handset inside, which I wasn't supposed to take to school.

When I'm nervous I try to make people laugh.

"I'm Brian Blum," I said and started shaking hands. "Remember the name. If you're looking for a lawyer. Hi, I'm Brian Blum." The kids were just waiting around like sheep. Then the whistle blew.

Coach Caukwell stood in the middle of the court, bouncing a ball. He was an old football player and wore shorts with pockets, a short-sleeved collared shirt that said PROPERTY OF BURLESON HIGH SCHOOL BASKETBALL, and a whistle on a string around his neck. His arms looked like legs, he had light black skin and a shaved head. His voice was quiet, though; he was hard to hear. The whistle didn't work so to get our attention he cocked the basketball and threw it against the brick wall over our heads. It made a noise like a car backfiring. So he started again.

"My name is Coach Caukwell," he said. "I don't like to shout."

There was something in his mouth, he seemed to be chewing, you could see his tongue pushing up against his cheek. But the gym was quiet now. Cathedral light came in through the high windows. You could see dust in the air, and for some reason I felt happy just to be there, to be scared, to be in the middle of my childhood with all those other kids.

The first thing he did was make us run. He kicked open the double doors at the back and let us out into the sunshine. When he stepped outside he spat; he was chewing peanuts, I could see shells on the ground. Then he put his hand in his pocket and pulled out another fistful. This was Texas in mid-September. The grass had spent all summer dying, the ground was like a parking lot, cracked and dusty. Walking outside was like walking out of a refrigerator. Kids started blinking, but at four o'clock the sun had a kind of red haze around it, the skies looked scuffed and dirty. Everything looked colored in.

Burleson High is one of these fifties yellow-brick low-rise municipal buildings you get in Austin, set in a few acres of ground. The perimeter roads are mostly residential, but there's no sidewalk. We were supposed to run four times around, a little over two miles. Coach Caukwell stood by the back door with a clipboard and asked your name as you ran past.

About halfway through the second circuit I stopped to puke. I was at the back of the pack, but already kids were starting to lap me. I could hear somebody laughing, somebody saying, "Chicken enchiladas." There was a pile of red ants on the ground, bright little fuckers like armored vehicles, and when I threw up on them they got busy. Sweat stung my eyes but I couldn't see straight anyway. My heart kept beating in my ears.

I felt a hand on my back, this black kid leaned over. "You all right?" he asked, and I said, "Terrific," which is what my dad would have said, and he straightened up and started running again. He had long legs and a kind of high butt. I followed him for about thirty yards, and then he was too far ahead. My mouth tasted like vomit. This was my first interaction with Marcus Hayes.

Then the temperature dropped fifteen degrees. A dark cloud rolled up, you could see it walking toward us in the sunshine, on rainy legs. Either I ran into it or it stepped over me—suddenly the element thickened, the plug had been pulled, I was pushing through heavy atmosphere. By this point I was on the third circuit; some of the kids had already finished. A few others gave up. But the rain cleaned me up, I didn't mind. My T-shirt put on a couple pounds of wet, it dragged lower than my shorts. The ground was too dry to get muddy, instant streams filled the cracks, I could hear my socks in my sneakers. My head cleared, too, and I stuck out my tongue.

Coach Caukwell stood in the shade of the tall gymnasium wall. When kids came past, he said, "All right, son." A gust of air-conditioning blasted through the open doors, but I kept going, shivering, on empty guts.

By the time I finished the fourth circuit, he had already split the boys into teams, they were running layup lines. A heap of dirty towels lay on the floor. I wiped my shoes on them, dragging thin flannel along the shine of the wood, and got into a line. Something hurt in my chest, a sharp delicate pain, and I couldn't figure out what. Someone passed me the ball and I squelched toward the basket and laid it in. Then the penny dropped.

"Does anybody else have nipple chafe?" I said, following the boy in front.

"Say what?" he said.

"From the wet shirt."

He turned around, laughing. "You hear that? Brian's got nipple chafe."

Kids were cracking up, but I thought, what the hell. Let them laugh. Coach Caukwell looked at me, shaking his head.

There were forty boys, most of them never made the team. Caukwell told us, "Today is just the first cut. I'm gonna put a list on the locker room door at seven a.m. with about twenty names on it. You can come back for the second cut in the afternoon."

In those days Burleson was fifty percent minority, mostly Latino. But there were all kinds of kids. Kids who wore Lacoste shirts and New Balance running shoes, kids in Harley tank tops and Chuck Connors. There was also the puberty divide. It came late for me. I had pimples, which I picked at until they scabbed and bled, but no soft stubble. Some boys had sprouted like plants in the dark, all pale and thin. You saw a lot of unshaved mustaches. A couple of kids had started hitting the weights, they couldn't scratch their noses without flexing their biceps. Also, you could smell us. After a day in school, wearing old T-shirts, running around in wet sneakers, squeaking on the hardwood, the noise and stink, if you looked at us from above, which is what Coach Caukwell had to do, you might think, somebody turned over a rock, and this is what wriggled out.

In elementary school, kids called me Brian Bum. It's Blum! I said, Blum—like the flower. That didn't help. What I mean is, there was also a lot of frustration working itself out. Not just for me.

Marcus Hayes had a short flat Afro that made him look taller than he was, which was only five ten. A couple of kids could dunk already. I saw Marcus touch rim but he didn't stand out in other ways. He was basically a shy kid, he ran hard but didn't like to make eye contact, he didn't say much. I kept talking the whole time.

For the last half hour Caukwell let us scrimmage. He stood leaning against the wall with the clipboard in hand and just watched. By this point I was pretty gassed, I was getting pissy, too, whiny and kid-brother-y, which happened to me sometimes, on the edge of tears. Stop it! Stop it! That's what I wanted to say. Kids kept pushing me around. I kept calling foul, foul! If I missed a shot I called foul, if someone stole the ball I called foul. Come on, man, they said, and I said, honor the call, you gotta honor the call—and because the coach was there, they let it go.

But even my teammates froze me out. I pushed my ass under the basket, swinging my elbows and shouting, Pass! pass! pass! Why don't you pass? I wanted something to be happening that wasn't happening and there was nothing I could do except complain about it. Then someone passed, hard, and caught me in the face, and I was leaning over in the sudden dark and felt a trickle of warm and wet flowing out of my nose.

Caukwell came over and put his arm around me. "Somebody get some paper towels," he said, still chewing nuts, and pulled me to the sideline. "Keep on playing," he told the other boys.

Blood filled my hands, so I wiped them on my T-shirt and lifted the soaking cotton against my face. After a second the tickle came back and I had to wipe again.

I couldn't see straight either and kept squinting against the drip of sweat. It felt like I was swimming in saltwater with open eyes. I leaned against the wall; my knees felt wobbly.

"What's your name, son?" Caukwell asked me.

A kid gave him some crumpled paper towels from the bathroom and he handed them to me. Coach was one of those big guys who is so big that everything he does is gentle, like he constantly has to restrain himself.

"Brian Blum."

"What are you doing here, Brian Blum?"

"What do you mean, what am I doing?" I said. "I'm trying out for the basketball team."

He pushed his tongue around the front of his mouth to clean his teeth. "You having fun, kid?"

"It's not supposed to be fun."

"What's it supposed to be?"

I didn't say anything, I just stood there.

"I saw you running out there," he went on. "And I thought: the kid's not fast, but he keeps going. He's proving a point. I think you can tell yourself tonight you proved that point. You showed up."

"I'm not proving a point, I want to make the team." But I couldn't look at him.

"Why do you think those kids don't pass you the ball?"

"I don't know."

"How come you keep calling fouls?"

"Because they keep fouling me!" The whine was back. "I mean, this whole thing is . . ."

"What?" Caukwell asked me.

"I mean, you're not . . ."

"What?" he said again.

"It's pointless, the whole thing is pointless. Even if they honor the call, they just give you the ball back."

"I don't understand."

"I mean, there aren't any free throws. This whole thing is point-less without free throws. The free throw is the most important shot in basketball. Of course, they're going to keep fouling, because it doesn't matter, all you do is get the ball back. It's just . . ."

"It's just what?"

"It's just a dumb way of testing who should make the team, if you don't have free throws."

I looked up at him now and could see him thinking, what kind of fish have I got on the hook here? He stretched his neck from one side to another—there were too many muscles in his back to keep all of them happy. Then he pinched his nose and sniffed. "All right, Brian."

"All right, what?"

"Call me coach, not what. And get back out there."

Practice was almost over anyway. A big black railroad clock, high up on the wall, showed two hands aligning . . . almost six. The bus had dropped me off for class at seven a.m. Eleven hours later I was still there. But the fight was gone, even my whining was used up. Nobody noticed as I walked back on court. When the kids started running one way, I ran after them. Not hard enough to catch up, just sort of hanging around.

Well, I tried, I thought, just at the point where I had stopped trying. Eventually Caukwell blew his whistle. "All right, fellas," he called out. Sneakers stopped squeaking; a ball slipped out and bounced slowly to the wall. You could hear the boys breathing and the hum of the air-conditioning, like a factory noise. "Line up, line up," he said. He could raise his voice when he wanted to. It filled the gym. "Everybody's shooting free throws. When you miss, you can go home."

So that's what we did, forty kids standing in a long snake. The first kid missed and Caukwell gave him a pat on the back, and said, "What's your name, son?" and the kid said, "McGinley," and Caukwell wrote down his name on the clipboard and told him, "Check the board in the morning." The second kid made his shot, it hit the front of the rim and rolled in, but when he started to leave, Caukwell called him back. "Son," he said, "you need to listen. Get to the back of the line. You're still in it."

At that point, when I figured out what was going on, my hands started to sweat again and I tried to dry them on my legs. There were about twenty kids ahead of me . . . It's funny, when you're young, you think, every stupid thing matters, every little chance, it counts, it changes everything, but what I didn't realize is that it would.

Mostly I was worrying, should I shoot it underhand, which everybody's going to make fun of me for, while the line got smaller in front of me. About half the kids missed and went home; the rest circled back. In my small scared heart I wanted all of them to miss.

Marcus Hayes stood in front of me and reached down nervously to rub his hands against his socks. Then someone passed him the ball and he stepped up to the line and made his shot; I saw him clench his fist. Then he passed me the ball. I leaned over and touched it to the floor, bent my legs quickly like a frog about to jump, and flipped it underhand into the air.

Somebody said, "Granny style! He's doing it granny style," and kids started falling over, laughing the way kids do, trying to laugh, forcing it, so they could join in the joke, as the ball slipped through the net.

Coach Caukwell shook his head, and I went around to the back of the line behind Marcus Hayes.

In the end, it was just the two of us, Marcus and me. He made five or six in a row, but it didn't matter, eventually he missed—and walked away without looking back. Then it was just me, and a few other kids who had stuck around to watch, and Coach Caukwell.

"Where'd you learn to shoot like that?" he asked.

"From my dad. He says the free throw is the most important shot in basketball, because people make free throws more than they make any other shot." Then I said, "How long do you want me to keep going for? I can keep doing this all day."

He stood under the basket, feeding me the ball.

"Keep going," he said. But then I missed and the ball bounced away into a corner and the whole thing was over. For a second, I thought, somebody must have taken my backpack, but there it was, sitting by itself against the wall, and I was almost too tired to bend down and pick it up. When I walked outside, the heat had risen again and the sun going down was shawled in dark cloud—super vivid, and Dad pulled up at the curb and pushed open the door. Sometimes when he worked at home he stayed in pajamas all day and just pulled on pants when he walked out of the house. It embarrassed me, seeing him like that; but nobody else noticed, we were in the car. He turned his headlights on as the first fat drops of rain hit the windshield.

"How'd it go?" he said.

2

Mel Caukwell died a couple of days ago; he was sixty-six years old. ESPN flew me down to Austin because my editor thought Marcus Hayes might show up to the funeral, and maybe there was a story there.

I hadn't been back since my sister's wedding. When my mother passed in 2007, my dad started living with me in Hartford. But he never sold the house in Hyde Park, and then when my sister needed another bedroom (after Troy was born), she moved back in. Anyway, they were still living there, so I had a couch to sleep on. My bosses would have paid for a hotel but I prefer couches.

Various things emerged about Coach Caukwell that I didn't know. He was born in Homewood, outside Birmingham, where his father worked for equipment services at Samford University. As a kid, Mel used to shoot around at the Pete Hanna Center while his dad mopped the floors. Later he played defensive back for Alabama. He got his degree in physical education then spent five seasons on the Dallas Cowboys practice squad, playing special teams, too, before tearing his ACL. Football teams are big organizations, they carry an extensive payroll, and guys at the periphery, like Caukwell, drift in and out. These are basically the kind of assets you use up. Their knees go, their mental health breaks down, they have problems with money or the law or pain medication, and after a few years you replace them.

For Caukwell, it was only his knee. After retiring, he worked in security, sometimes as a bouncer at the Red Zone in Dallas, a bar and gentleman's club, where some of the Cowboys like to hang out. That can't have been fun for him, not just the contrast but the kind of place it was. He started a teacher prep program at Denton and passed the state exams. Later he moved to Austin, where his sister lived, and eventually got the job at Burleson, teaching Health classes and coaching basketball, because Burleson already had a football coach.

Another injury (he took a helmet to the nuts at Alabama) left him infertile, which maybe explains why he never got married. The *Statesman* obituary described him as a "long-time bachelor"—funny they still use that word. But he "was a father figure" to a lot of his players, especially his nephew Lamont, who I used to play with.

Caukwell's death got picked up by the AP, just two lines. The only thing he's famous for now is being the coach that cut Marcus Hayes from the varsity sophomore year.

His funeral was at the Corinth Baptist Church in East Austin, near Oakwood Cemetery. I caught the early flight out of Logan and drove there straight from the airport.

My plane was late and I worried I might miss the service. Traffic thickened as we crossed I-35, and then there was nowhere to park. The curb was lined with cars, including a Hummer and several SUVS with tinted windows. A security van blocked the entrance to the parking lot. Come on! I thought, give me a break, when a man in a black suit with one of those curly cords reaching around to his ear waved me along.

The first space I found was three blocks away, outside a coffee shop. One of those mushrooms of eastside gentrification. Beards and babies. So, I got out and ran, or jogged and then walked and then ran. It was February, but in Austin you could feel the spring coming. Possum haw berries along the chain-link fence, which stretched north and south on either side of the cemetery, showed like spots of blood against the yellow-white grass. I could taste blood in my mouth by the time I reached the church.

It was a modest brick building, like a barn, with a few square windows blanked out by office blinds. The big double doors were shut,

but the handle turned—and as soon as I opened them . . . felt the concentration of people. Plush red carpeting like cheap red wine stained
the floor, the walls were bare, except for a few scattered crosses, but
the pews were full, and the heat and noise were like the heat and noise
of a basketball gym on a Friday night. Strip lights overhead, cavern-
ous echoes, and the pastor, a tall black man in a bow tie, stood in the
glare with a microphone in hand. A casket lay on a trestle table beside
him, raised up on the stage.

I hadn't really thought about anything all day. Just wake up and get
to the airport, remember your ticket, remember your wallet. Sitting on
the plane, I finished a piece and filed it. Then it was just . . . sign for the
rental car, hit the highway, find a place to park. But Coach Caukwell
was dead and lying in a box, I hadn't seen him for twenty years, and
in that time the muscle mass had probably declined, the bones had de-
calcified, the vertebrae shrunk, otherwise you couldn't fit him in that
box. Only when I caught my breath, standing and blinking at the back
of the church, feeling the burn in my chest, the heat in my armpits, the
sweat on my neck, did I remember why I'd come.

The pastor's forehead shone under the lights. He looked like an
ex-basketball player, they have a certain stiff grace. When he walked
around the stage you could see all his joints in operation.

His voiced sounded overeducated, a little finicky. There was some
call-and-response but not much singing. The passage he chose was
Romans 6:4: "We were buried therefore with him by baptism into
death, so that as Christ was raised from the dead by the glory of the
Father, we too might walk in newness of life."

Now my dad is a Passover-Hanukkah-Rosh Hashanah-Yom Kippur
kind of Jew. At New Year in Hartford, I buy a Golden Delicious from
the ShopRite, we cut it up in the kitchen and smear it in a plate of hon-
ey, and say L'shana tovah. But synagogue is only for Yom Kippur, and
sometimes I come along with him and sometimes I don't. It depends on

the state of our relations. When we're fighting, I come. Afterward he always complains about the rabbi. These days they sound like Christians, you can't tell the difference. I don't even know what that means. This is the kind of argument we get into.

So now I know. Pastor Rencher (that was his name—you could see it pasted all over the church, tacked to the brick wall, and next to the double doors, like the headline act on a nightclub flyer) liked to walk and talk. "All of us dream about getting a new car," he said, striding front stage. "But mostly we end up with somebody's castoff, some secondhand lemon, where you have to close your eyes just to drive it out of the lot, you have to have *faith* . . . But sometimes, sometimes, you step into a new car, and it has that smell, right, that new car smell . . ."

I wondered how well this guy actually knew Caukwell and decided, not well. Maybe this was his sister's church. Coach sometimes talked about his sister. But I also remembered a Sunday practice in March, a week before the first round of the playoffs. It was a mild sunny winter morning, a little like today. Coach made us run and afterward he treated anyone who could stick around to lunch. It was the first time I'd hung out with a black man on the weekend in what you might call an out-of-school situation. Caukwell took us to Popeyes, and I got a chicken sandwich to go and a soda and fries. Then we sat on a curb in the parking lot in the sunshine.

Coach didn't like to talk much about his life but sometimes offered glimpses of a private personality. "Preciate y'all's coming out here on a Sunday," he said. "Giving up your time. When you could be in church."

A few of the kids laughed, and Caukwell said, "Instead you got to play ball with me." Nobody talked much when he was in this kind of mood; you just waited, and eventually he went on: "My sister sometimes says to me, come on out to . . . wherever. Always trying somewhere new. *We got some good church.* Only one thing I give my money to. And his name is three letters long. 'I. R. S.'" He wiped his hands on his knees and stood up. We squeezed into his car, an old Buick LeSabre with a bench front seat, and he drove us back to school, where my dad picked me up.

"What is that new car smell? Why does it smell so good?" Pastor Rencher kept circling and hovering. "Because nobody else has messed it up. Not even *you*. Not even you have messed it up. Eating those potato chips when you drive. They're good—I know they're good. I eat 'em, too. Leaving old letters in the car. Bills. Receipts from the drive-thru. I'll deal with that later. That's what you tell yourself. I'll deal with it later. One of these days . . . one of these days . . . I'm gonna get *cleaned up*. Smell like new. Like that new car."

He stopped and looked at us. He stopped fidgeting. "And you ask yourself what it means to walk in newness of life." And then angrily, in wonder: "You ask yourself what it means. *You* know what it means. *You* know."

I lowered my head and saw: grease prints on my tie, a spare tire, old shoes, beaten up by too many Northeastern winters. Salt stains on the black leather, a gap in the seams, you could see my sports socks sticking out. There was a call-and-response thing going on, and every time Rencher said, *Newness of life*, we had to repeat it. So I called out with everybody else, *Newness of life*, and thought, I need new socks.

"When you die, you start over," he said. "Everybody gets a clean slate. Everybody gets that new car."

The church smelled of overdressed people. The heating system was running, it was a mid-sixties February day, and the human animals gave off a lot of heat, too. I pulled at my tie and loosened the knot.

"But what happens to that old car, that old car you leave behind?" he said. "People get attached to those old cars. They keep the license plates. I've got on the wall of my study the license plate of the first car I ever bought, a 1972 Datsun Bluebird . . . in George-town, when I was in seminary. People get attached to those old cars, they don't want to give them up. You bring 'em to the dealer, because you want a part exchange, am I right? You want to get something for that old car. Maybe you drove your kids to school in that car, or baseball practice, and those kids are grown up now, they have their own kids. But that old car is your *life*. And you know what the dealer says, right? He walks around it and he kicks the tires. He tells you to turn the key in the ignition, he listens to the noise the engine makes. He's got that look on his face, like he smells something bad. And you know what he tells you, right? It's not worth anything but scrap money, I'll have to break it up for parts. But I tell you what, because I'm a nice guy I'll give you fifty dollars. I'll give you a hundred bucks for it. Ten years of your life. That's what he gives you for it."

Then he lowered his chin to the mic, he lowered his voice. "But not this dealer. You know who I'm talking about. Not this dealer."

I couldn't help it, there was a lump in my throat. The woman sitting next to me had short hair and pearls around her neck; maybe she was fifty years old, her chest sloped away from her like a baby she had to hold in her arms. She was moving from side to side and kept bumping into me, so I bumped back. We had been going like this for five or ten minutes.

"Every man's life is touched on by greatness," the pastor said, in a rising voice, "because every man's life is touched by Jesus. But Coach Caukwell was more blessed than most . . . he spent his life as a shepherd of young men, but among his flock was the GOAT. Stand up and be counted, Brother Hayes!"

Cameras flashed and a tall black man, filling out his dark suit (he'd gotten fatter since retiring), half-raised himself and lifted a long-fingered hand. His high forehead glittered in the lights, with the cornrows pulled back tight, and then something strange happened, people were already standing up, but they started to clap. There was a feeling of blessing, just his presence blessed us, raised the occasion, and we blessed him back by applauding. I put my hands together, too, and felt the sweat on my palms. I hadn't seen him in three years, not since his last championship parade.

Afterward, we filed out into the sunshine. Marcus Hayes was surrounded by people, I couldn't get near him. Just to make the journey from the church and across the road and along the central avenue of Oakwood Cemetery, he got in a car—a black Lexus sedan—and the security van trailed him through the cemetery to the graveside. I walked with everybody else. It was three o'clock, and the sun had dropped a quadrant and sent level rays in our direction. You had to blink and squint, and the procession proceeded in a kind of thin glitter toward the heart of the afternoon, as if somehow we were heading into the bright past.

To transport the coffin the last few yards, six men gathered by the hearse. Marcus was one of them. Lamont, Coach Caukwell's nephew, was another—I recognized him because he looked like Coach. They lowered their heads to accept the burden and marched in step as well as they could.

It's a tricky business, and sometimes they looked like rowers who had caught a crab. In his playing days, Caukwell weighed two hundred and sixty-five pounds, but the old man must have been lighter. There was also the weight of the box. Around the grave, three or four Astroturf mats had been laid down, in case of rain, but the ground was hard. The pallbearers walked on either side of the hole, staring frontward, then they shifted the weight from their shoulders to their hands, turning a little, and setting the box down gently into a hydraulic lift. Someone pressed a button; it made a sound like an old refrigerator. By inches and degrees, Caukwell approached his destination.

In practice, Coach sometimes lined us up against the wall. If we were wasting time, fucking around. He lined us up against the wall and picked up a basketball and stood looking at us. The first person to fidget or speak or blink or whatever, and Caukwell cocked his arm and threw a fastball at the kid's head. He never hit anybody—it's not hard to duck, but the ball went Boom! against the bricks. After that, we'd go back to work.

Well, we were all lined up now.

3

My dad dropped me at school early so I could get to the gym and check the list. He wanted to come in but I wouldn't let him.

Another clear-skied Austin September day. Still cool outside, but the air-conditioning was already turned on, and you could hear it humming, because the corridors were empty. Empty schools are funny places to be; everything shines, everything echoes.

All night I had dreamed about showing up at the gym's double doors and seeing my name at the top of the list, and thinking, I can't believe it, I made the team. But the dream kept recurring in slightly different forms, and inside each version I could remember the previous dreams, and I knew they were dreams and not real, and part of what I felt each time was: This is really happening now. This one counts.

I could see the gym at the end of the corridor. Two glass panels glowed with the light behind them, but when I walked up to the doors, there was nothing on them—they were blank. No sheet of paper fluttered under a piece of tape. I stood there for a minute, staring at the paint, then switched my backpack, which had forty pounds of books inside, from one shoulder to the other and headed to class.

It was lunchtime before I had a chance to go back. Marcus was standing there, reading the list; he wore parachute pants and those red-and-black Air Jordans, and a green IZOD polo shirt buttoned up to the neck.

"What's your name?" he said.

"Brian Blum."

And he pointed his finger at it. "Top of the list."

I looked at it for a moment, waiting to feel what I was going to feel. "It's alphabetical," I said. "What's your name?"

And he pointed again: Marcus Hayes.

"Congratulations. We made it."

"First cut," he said. "I'm going for varsity."

For some reason, neither of us moved, we just kept staring at the sheet, reading the names. Gabe Hunterton. Ben Silliman. Isaac Brown. Lamont Melrose. Blake Snyder. Tony Chua. Josh Ramirez. Coach Caukwell's handwriting was weird and tiny, like he could barely get the muscles of his hand around the ballpoint pen and had to make very small motions with tremendous effort.

"Where'd you learn to shoot?" Marcus said.

"My dad taught me."

"Next time, I'm gonna beat you."

Other kids came up and leaned over; a woman pushed open the doors, then pulled a cleaning cart behind her, with a mop handle sticking out that caught on the frame, and when the doors shut again, Marcus had gone.

I turned around, too, and started running. We only had a half hour for lunch and I wanted to get to the cafeteria to tell my friends. They were all sitting around the table, fucking around, like there was nowhere else in the world you'd rather be, even if you pretend like this is the last place on earth . . . Mike Inchman, the DeKalb brothers, Max Strom and Andy Caponato, never any girls, and I dumped my packed lunch on the blue Formica and announced: "I made the cut."

"What does that mean?" Mike said.

"I have to go back this afternoon."

Frank DeKalb was a senior and the editor of the school literary magazine. Even though he was two years older than the rest of us, and in the process of applying to Swarthmore under their Restrictive Early

Action program, we all treated him like his brother Jim treated him, like somebody you could make fun of in a friendly way. Frank had scoliosis. He wore a back brace that was visible under his shirt and meant that he always sat up extremely straight and turned his whole head when he moved, giving you his full attention, as if he were a very upright principled guy, a little stiff, which is also basically what he was like. I asked him if he wanted a story for the magazine about the basketball tryouts, and he said, "Write something and we'll see."

This turned out to be my first published piece. My dad framed it and hung it in the kitchen. He said he was prouder of that than he was of me making the team, which I don't think is true. The lit mag was called *Excalibur* (our school mascot was a knight for some reason) and came out once a month, on the kind of cheap glossy slightly hard paper you find in D&D adventure modules. Frank was also my first editor, and a good one. He pushed me to turn the story into something more than just a series of impressions, he wanted me to talk to some of the other kids, about when they started playing and what it meant to make the team; it was also important to interview the kids who got cut, and for this I needed Coach Caukwell's permission.

What I didn't know at the time was that I'd found my subject. This is what I wanted to spend my life writing about, natural selection, the way people get measured. All the stuff we don't like to think about, which is that everything we do we do on a scale, which can be graded, and some people are better and some people worse, but there's actually always somebody better. And not just what we do, but who we are. Like, for example, some people are more attractive than others, that's obvious, but not just more attractive, also more lovable. There's a scale for that, too, and how do people put up with the fact that what we like to think of as our unique characteristics are really just a series of grades. If we're unique it's because we possess a large number of midrange qualities to different degrees. These are obviously the thoughts of a high school nerd, a grade-obsessed nerd, who hung out with a bunch of other nerds and couldn't get a girlfriend, but I don't know that I've outgrown these thoughts.

One of the kids I interviewed was Marcus Hayes. His mother was a nurse at Seton Medical Center. His parents were separated. His dad worked in Killeen at Mission Auto Repair (he specialized in German cars) and used to play football for Cisco College. He was a linebacker, but Marcus looked more like his mom, who ran track for SMU, that's where he got his athletic talent. The article was called "Making the Cut."

A few of the sophomores made varsity—Isaac Brown, for example, who was later recruited by Ole Miss—but Marcus wasn't one of them. JV was good enough for me. We were teammates.

Marcus loved the piece. Frank sent a student to take photographs of all the kids who featured heavily, and he was one of them. He wore Dockers and loafers without socks, and his IZOD shirt; his hair was freshly cut, with a low fade, and he brought the magazine home to his mom and later I saw it framed in *his* kitchen, too. He already had a sense of himself as somebody who was going to end up in newspapers, and this was his first confirmation.

4

I hadn't seen Marcus in three years. When he won his fourth championship, there was a parade down the streets of Boston and I drove up with my dad to watch it. He always got a kick out of this kind of thing.

After the parade, which ended with a rally at the Garden, speeches, jokes, video montages, all of it about as much fun as a forced smile, the team threw a party at the clubhouse restaurant, and invited certain members of the press. Including me.

By this stage our professional relationship had clouded or covered over much of our personal history. I was another sports reporter, one of the people he used or manipulated or had to defend himself against. His rules were pretty clear-cut and you played by them or he didn't play—refused to answer or even acknowledge your questions at a press conference or pick you out among the scrum of reporters that surrounded him in the locker room after or before a game. He had his guys, and through them he released the information he wanted to make public.

For years I was one of his guys, and then I wasn't.

A few months earlier referee Pat McConaughey had been sentenced to fifteen months in federal prison for betting on the games he officiated during the 2006–2007 NBA season. The general impression being, this was the tip of the iceberg. That McConaughey had not only bet on his own games, but had manipulated the outcomes to cover the spread—that he worked for a gambling syndicate, which made hundreds of millions of dollars from these interventions, and that the illegal activity stretched well beyond the previous year and probably dated back to 2002 or 2003. The period in question included two of Marcus Hayes's four NBA titles, and even though there was no suggestion that any players had benefited from or in any way participated in the point-shaving scandal, McConaughey was a first-tier ref who officiated in several Finals—including the classic game six comeback against the Lakers in 2005, where Marcus scored fifty-three points (and shot twenty-five free throws, thirteen in the fourth quarter alone) on the way to his first Finals MVP.

If you were one of Marcus's guys, you didn't write about Pat McConaughey, you let it lie. At that point nobody had proved he did anything worse than bet on his own games, but I wanted to write a piece about the complicated influence of NBA officials, their weird lives and often intimate relationships with some of the players. McConaughey grew up in the same Philadelphia suburb where a lot of NBA refs came from, and next door to the neighborhood where my dad grew up—their high schools used to compete against each other. I thought I had an *in* into this world, it was something I could write about. Guys went to the same schools, the same bars, they knew the same coaches, and helped each other get jobs.

What really interested me wasn't the idea of some widespread conspiracy of illegal activity, but something subtler and totally legal, the power of referees to change a game not for money but from other kinds of bias or sympathy. Just the fact that this was difficult to measure didn't mean it didn't happen. McConaughey used to play golf on the same Florida course designed by Tiger Woods, where Marcus was a part-owner. When McConaughey's sister got cancer, Marcus visited her in the hospital; he signed balls for kids from the Sacred Heart School in Havertown, P.A., where Pat went to school. Are you telling me that when Marcus goes hard to the hole in game six of the NBA Finals, and there's contact and the ball rims out, these factors don't at least wet the lips of the guy blowing the whistle?

I didn't mention Marcus Hayes or any particular games, but I wrote the piece, and after that, Marcus shut me out. So I brought my dad to the after-party to smooth the waters.

For my father, this is still one of the great nights of his life. Security guys and front office guys exchanged awkward but basically happy high-fives in the hallways, the floors were sticky with popcorn and spilled booze, streamers lay like autumn leaves on the ground. There's an office next to the clubhouse lounge with leather sofas and chairs, and Marcus Hayes and a couple of suits were sitting inside, away from the scrum, smoking cigars. I recognized Bob Storey, the owner, and Terry Andaluz, the GM—you could see them through a glass panel in the door.

At the other end of the lounge, somebody had rigged up a stage with a karaoke machine, and when we arrived Damon McElmore and Andrea Boroni were singing a duet, "Summer Nights," from *Grease*, where Boroni took the part of Travolta and McElmore played Olivia Newton John. (McElmore was a fresh-faced first-year guard from Murray State with a little goatee; Boroni had the kind of big-man's body that might have been stitched together by Dr. Frankenstein.) Stacey Kupchak, a beat reporter for the *Globe*, had pulled off his tie and was waving it around to the music.

It took me a few drinks before I could face that office door. My father is not a drinker, the only thing he likes is champagne, but that's what there was—an iced bathtub full of celebration-edition bottles of Krug Grande Cuvée, with a green-and-white banner draped around the sides of the tub that said, *2008 NBA Champions*, and the team slogan underneath, *History Repeats Itself*.

Waitresses came around with glasses on a tray but you could also just take a bottle and swig from that. Dad went in first, and Marcus called out "Mr. Blum," and sat up in his chair, he tried to get up. But the leather was soft and deep, he was happy and bone-tired, slack from end-of-season slackness, drunk already and fell back. "Hey, Baby," he said, when he saw me, which is what he used to call me, or Bee-Bee, for my initials, and this time managed to escape the chaise lounge and put his arms around me.

He was still wearing the oversized goofy team shirt they printed for the parade, which had the same logo as the bathtub full of Krug. It smelled of sweat and alcohol. Normally he left the house in a fresh Armani suit and Hermès tie. His cornrows looked sticky to touch, but I gave his head a rub (and felt the loose hairs; he always let it grow after the season was over) and he bent his neck to the collar of my jacket. He was three or four inches taller than me, but I'm a pretty big dude, it's not like some of the reporters who cover these guys. I'm fat and out of shape but you don't have to adjust your sense of scale, I'm in the picture.

"All you need now," I told him, "is one for the thumb."

"Listen," he said. "My mom's here, Pop, too. Make sure they don't have to talk to each other."

So I drifted away and looked for them. Marcus had mixed feelings about his mother. Selena was young when she had him, just a sophomore at SMU, which meant she was still pretty young and didn't mind at all being Marcus Hayes's mother. I saw her on the dance floor in something gray and fluffy, I think they call it tulle. It showed a lot of arm and leg.

My dad was watching me watch her. He said, "If you got it . . ."

Then I saw Marcus's father by the champagne bathtub—an old black man in a soft cap. When I went over to him, he said, "Travis is here."

"Where?"

And he pointed. "I'm worried he might have brought something to the party."

Travis was Selena's son by her second marriage, Marcus's half-brother. He had a history of minor brushes with the law: speeding tickets, a DUI, they stopped him once and found a two-ounce baggie of weed in the glove compartment and a few pills. (Marcus paid the legal costs.) Don had no one to talk to and kept shifting his attention from Travis to Selena, until my dad came over and they shook hands and I went to get them both a plate of food from a table laid out with cold cuts and fried mozzarella balls and sushi and potato chips and soft white rolls. This is how the party went on.

I ran into J. P., too, Marcus's wife.

Her face was flat, kind of vague-looking but also like, I'm in control, and she wore big flat sunglasses, even inside; there was a woman from Nike she got along with, who hung out with her at public events, made sure she had somewhere to sit and introduced people to her so she didn't have to approach them herself. Her name was Angie and when you talked to J. P. you sort of addressed yourself to Angie.

"He did it again," I said. You say this kind of thing to these people, it's like talking at a wedding, you can only say the obvious thing.

Angie said, "Even after all this time I still can't watch. My husband watches for me. If I'm not working, I stay in the kitchen, I make dinner, the kids do their homework, and at halftime he comes in and eats and tells me what's going on, and then he goes out again. That's all I can do."

"I don't worry about him anymore," J. P. said.

Her real name was Josephine Patrice, she grew up in Natchitoches. Before she dated Marcus, she dated a couple of other players—she used to be one of the Celtics Dancers. When young guys came into the League, she showed them the ropes. Agents liked to deal with her, they thought it was a good thing if J. P. took you in hand. She upcycled till she got to Marcus.

"If he loses," she said, "it puts him in a bad mood, but we have a rule, you don't take your bad moods home."

"Does that work?" I asked.

"I don't know, he always wins."

You couldn't see her expression under those glasses, and it was too loud in the clubhouse to keep a conversation going. Everybody sort of realized this and gave up.

At one stage, Bob Storey walked over to the stage, and someone shut off the karaoke machine and passed him a mic. He had a fat red face and thin blond hair on top of it, big shoulders, he looked like the chair of the Chamber of Commerce in Bedford Falls. He was having a good time and it didn't make him nervous to talk because everybody always had to listen to him anyway. So he talked, he thanked people. He talked about the city of Boston and Celtic basketball and Marcus Hayes, and Marcus stood around with everybody else, still smoking a cigar and smiling and clapping like everybody else.

Afterward they got the dance floor going again. It was seven o'clock on a summer evening, but the clubhouse was windowless, bright with artificial light, and it felt like two in the morning. Marcus can't dance but he danced anyway, first with J. P., it was something they went through, like a wedding dance, then with his mom; he was touching all the bases, this part of the evening was mostly for show. There was a DJ now, sitting on a high stool in the corner, messing around with whatever they mess around with. People came up to him and made suggestions. He wore big furry headphones and nodded the whole time like he could hear. Somebody must have suggested "Only God Can Judge Me" and Marcus started singing along.

"Nobody else," he said, "nobody else" but didn't really know the words.

I danced for a while, I cleared a little floorspace, then went to sit with his dad on one of the fold-out chairs. We stared at happy people and the music was loud enough we didn't have to talk. Everybody looked the way they look on these occasions, sweaty and like they're fighting for their lives in some thick substance. I said to Don, "Your boy done good," and he said, "What?" and I said, "He did it again," and Don lowered his ear to my mouth, and I repeated myself, and he nodded.

"Listen," he said, "if you get a chance, maybe you could put in a word. There's a business opportunity I want to discuss with Marcus. I've been talking to some people about sausage." When I looked at him, he added, "Sometimes it works out better if the idea comes from somebody else."

A few hours later I ended up following my father into a limousine and stumbling somehow into one of the seats and feeling the deck sway underfoot as the car with its tinted windows pushed through traffic toward Beacon Hill. The sun had set but the streets were still twilit gray, people were eating outside, crowding the sidewalks, and we stopped on a side street, and I stumbled out again. A door in the wall opened onto stairs, it was the back entrance of some private club, the kind of club with oil paintings on the walls and gas fires and chesterfields in front of them, and I followed more bodies to a landing and through a door to a private room, where the long oak table was laid with platters of lobster and steak and oysters and *frites*. Joe Hahn was there, Marcus's lawyer, Coach Steve Britten, a couple of other players. I nodded at Stacey Kupchak, the Celtics beat reporter, who looked like Vizzini from the movie, what's his name, Wallace Shawn, bald and crinkle-eyed. There were several women around the table, I started eating.

At some point in the evening Marcus had put on a suit. He wore Ferragamo moccasins with gold buckles and no socks, I noticed this when we went up another set of stairs. We were in another room, playing cards. The gas fire was lit, my dad was still there. "I thought you were mad at me," I said to Marcus.

"What should I be mad about?"

"Nothing."

"What should I be mad about?"

"Nothing."

"I'm not mad at you," he said. "This man, this man," he pointed at my father, but I don't remember what he said.

Two weeks later, in the *Globe*, Stacey Kupchak broke the news that Marcus was retiring. He had nothing left to play for or prove. There was a long interview, which should have been mine.

5

Sam's Bar-B-Que, one of these eastside institutions, had set up in the church parking lot. There were beef ribs and sausage, brisket and mutton, potato salad, mac 'n' cheese, yams and baked beans laid out on temporary tables, with a white paper tablecloth underneath. Food had to be covered; flies hovered already. People said, we're so lucky with the weather.

The pastor let Marcus Hayes use his office, this is what he told me. "A man like that always has business to conduct, there are no days off." We talked briefly about basketball and I asked him where he played. He gave me a shrewd look.

"Southwestern," he said. "Div three."

I saw one of the security guys walk past carrying a plate of food and a bottle of Shiner Bock into the church. So I followed him, through the double doors and along the red-wine-carpeted central aisle toward the stage. You had to climb up to get to the office; the door was behind the altar.

Inside, French blinds blocked out most of the sunshine. Cigar or cigarette smoke filled the air, and the walls were covered in signed certificates like a dentist's office, from Georgetown Baptist Seminary, etc., and photographs of the congregation at different festivals and occasions, including pictures of forty or fifty people sitting down to a meal on a bright sunny day on tables covered in paper tablecloths in the middle of the parking lot.

I recognized some of the people, like Joe Hahn. Steve Henneman was there, too, executive vice president of basketball operations for the NBA. The man sitting behind the desk in the pastor's office chair, and spinning restlessly on his feet, wasn't Marcus Hayes, but Taffy

Laycock, the Seattle businessman, who at that time owned part of the Supersonics and various other sports-related enterprises.

But there were other people hanging around as well, too many to count. Jerry de Souza, Marcus's golfing buddy, and his personal trainer, Brad Weldt. Ted Myers, the Nike rep, who used to coach at Grambling and still looked like a coach, in loose chinos and an old sweatshirt. Amy Freitag, Marcus's long-time assistant, poured out coffee from a ridiculously large bright red thermos into crinkly little plastic cups. She asked me if I wanted one and I said yes, because it's my policy to say yes in any social professional situation to anything offered. Marcus himself sat in a leather armchair next to the desk, with his long legs kicked out; he looked like he was asleep. His face had the faint sheen and puffiness of the recently fat man.

"Is somebody going to wake him up?"

"Is that you, Brian?" Marcus didn't open his eyes.

"Take off those glasses and maybe you can see."

"I take them off when there's something I want to look at." But he took off the Oakleys anyway. And underneath what you saw was something like his father, a big gentle black man. He sat up, too, with some difficulty. "I had an early flight, I didn't sleep."

"Join the club." And I turned to everyone else. "You know, the first time we met I beat him in a free throw shootout."

"Why you make that stuff up?" Marcus said. But other people came in, they wanted to pay their respects. Old teammates, including Lamont, Caukwell's nephew, and for them Marcus pushed himself out of the leather chair and gave them the ballplayer's hug—where you clasp hands first and pull the other man toward you.

"He talked about you all the time," Lamont said. "I mean, senior year—that was the only time he went to state. I don't think it bothered him but he wanted to win that one."

"Me, too," Marcus said. "I can tell you everything that happened the last five minutes."

"He said, for someone like me, I only get one chance."

"Every play."

"He was real proud of you." People came up to talk to him but they didn't want a conversation, they just wanted to say their piece. Marcus was just the chorus. "He said, I never saw anyone work harder for what he got than Marcus Hayes."

"He coached us right."

"I don't know," Lamont said. The piece was over. "Uncle Mel didn't know a damn thing about basketball. He was a football guy."

And then you got passed along, Amy was good at that. She gave you a cup of coffee or asked for your personal details, and a few weeks later, you might get an autographed picture in the mail, or a Christmas card, if it was Christmas.

But I didn't want to hang around all day. "Marcus," I said. "I'm writing a story on Coach Caukwell. Maybe you could give me some time."

"It's a funeral, take the day off."

"That's what I'm here for, to write the story."

"I thought you were here for Coach."

After a moment, I said, "That, too."

"I'm flying out tomorrow morning." He lay back again and stretched out, with his glasses on. "Where you staying?"

"At the house. Betsy lives there now."

"How's your old man?"

"He's all right. Trying to lose weight. He moved in with me a couple of years ago."

"Give Amy your number. We'll try to work something out. Say hi to Betsy for me."

And that was it. I was dismissed, he had other business to attend to, other people to deal with. He's like the uncle with a piece of candy. When you get the candy, you're supposed to leave him alone—that's what it's for. So I left him alone.

————

Lamont and a couple of other guys were clearing one of the tables away when I stepped outside. I figured you may as well help so I helped. It was covered in paper plates of food and stained with sauce and bits of mac 'n' cheese and meat rinds, soda cans and crumpled plastic cups. They set it down in the grass and walked back toward the parking lot.

"Most of this stuff can probably go in the trash," I said.

But it turns out they weren't clearing up, they were making space. At the far end of the lot, away from the church, a wooden pole stuck out of the ground with a backboard and hoop. A few loops of net hung from one of the rings. The pastor had parked his vintage maroon Saab 9000 under the hoop, but I saw him get in the car and turn the engine on. People were standing around, he edged his way out, leaning on the open window, and talking—eventually he gave a little toot of the horn. Then he parked across the lot next to the caterer's truck.

"What are we doing, are we playing ball?"

"You want to get in on it?" Lamont asked.

"Isn't it . . . I mean, this is a funeral."

"You think Coach is gonna mind?" He had his uncle's solid jawline and blank bald forehead, and the same way of looking at you like he's waiting for you to say something stupid.

"What about the pastor?" I said.

"He's playing, too."

And in fact Pastor Rencher, when he got out of the car, disappeared into the church for a minute. Five or six guys were taking off their jackets and ties; they laid them over the backs of fold-out chairs. A little crowd gathered, too. They stood on the bit of lawn between the lot and the street. Across the road, over the chain-link fence, you could see the cemetery stretch out flatly under the sunshine.

Caukwell's sister was walking up and down, in a fret. "If I wasn't wearing these shoes," she said. She wore red high-heeled shoes and a tight black dress, which moved with her and showed her long legs. "I can't play barefoot on this tarmac. Lamont gonna step on my feet."

The pastor came out with a cheap rubber basketball. "It's a little flat, but it'll serve."

Lamont said to me, "You gonna play?"

"I haven't played in fifteen years."

But I took off my jacket anyway and pulled the shirt-ends out of my belt.

"Let me warm up, give me the ball."

Somebody passed it to me and I shot from about ten feet. I always hated shooting with those rubber balls; they stick to your hand, and the ball banged off the rim and skittered away across the parking lot.

"Close enough," the pastor said.

After that, he split us into teams; his spiritual authority seemed to carry over. We started playing, Lamont checked the ball and I gave it back to him. It was me, Gabe Hunterton, Ben Silliman (who I also went to Hebrew school with), and Josh Ramirez, against Lamont and Pastor Rencher and a couple of other guys I didn't know. We were banging and bricking, it was old man basketball, shooting from the hip, breathing heavy and cursing, a lot of shits and fucks. Rencher could still play but he was taking it easy. Just once he sort of moved into space and went up for a fifteen-footer, with a funny kind of motion, bringing the ball up fast and hard to the side, and centering it high above his head before releasing—the kind of shooting motion you develop when you play against people who can play. The ball ended up in the grass because it slipped through the rim without touching anything.

"Did it go in?" he said. "Did it go in? I don't have my glasses on."

"It went in."

Mel's sister kept walking up and down, rubbing her hands on her thighs, like a kid who has to pee. "It kills me I can't play."

Gabe said, "I've got a pair of running shoes in the car." In high school, he was like a Southern cracker, a big Texas kid who lived out of town and wore cowboy boots and drove an El Camino. Now he had skinnied up—I think he worked in Dallas for the McKesson Corporation; they sold medical supplies.

She said, "Will they fit me?"

"What do you wear?"

"Size 9—I got my daddy's feet."

"You can try 'em." So that took a couple of extra minutes, too. I said to Lamont, "I don't know why I stopped doing this. This is more fun than the rest of my life."

"See how you feel tomorrow."

The shoes didn't fit but they were close enough. Mel's sister's name was Jackie and she knew how to play—she had big hips and didn't mind swinging her elbows, and guys got out of the way. She could finish with either hand. She caught me in the neck once and this was her apology, "You gotta bring some to get some," which is what Coach used to tell us. After that we started trading Caukwell-isms. *Knucklehead. Bonehead. Been playing with yourself last night*—if the ball slipped through your hands. We tried to keep score but there were too many arguments. A lot of water breaks, too, except a bunch of the guys drank beer.

Lamont said, "The only way you get Mel to church was to kill him."

"That's not so," but his mom was laughing.

At one point I looked over at the church. The office was on our side of the parking lot, and I could see a hand pull down one of the blinds. It was Marcus, you could recognize him by the Oakley shades, and he watched us play for a minute then let go of the slat.

Afterward, Pastor Rencher handed out his card. I told him I lived in Connecticut but his company had offices there, too, he said. They sold insurance. It was a three-block walk to the rental car, which gave me a chance to cool off. What always happened every time I played, I went over in my head the shots I missed and tried to count up the ones I made. I hadn't done this in fifteen years but did it again anyway. Then drove to my sister's house, which is really the house I grew up in.

6

The first high school game I ever played was against Copperas Cove. Marcus wanted to show up early before school, to get some shots up, and persuaded me to come along. Coach Caukwell agreed to open the gym, so my dad dropped me off at a quarter to seven.

Sunrise in Austin in late October is almost eight o'clock. We didn't know how to turn on the lights. The basket came down from the roof, and behind the stanchion was a tall rectangular window made of small subway-style panes of glass. It cast a kind of bright shadow across the court. Just the bounce and echo of the ball made me feel nervous. A cold front was moving in but the heating hadn't come on yet. I could see my breath. Marcus warmed up by running suicides while I practiced free throws. Then we took turns feeding each other jump shots, from elbow to elbow, along the baseline, and afterward moving along the three-point arc.

"Do you think I'm gonna start?" he kept asking. "Coach say something to you?"

"I don't know, Marcus."

"He better start me. That's all I'm saying."

"Or what? What are you gonna do to him?"

No answer. And then, a minute later, "He better start me."

In the end, I just let him shoot, while I rebounded and passed him the ball. Then the bell rang, and when I got my backpack to go to class he was still moving around the gym, chasing his own misses.

Copperas Cove is about an hour away. The bus that drove us there was just an ordinary shitty school bus, with peeling leather seats and stuffing coming out of them and gum on the window. I didn't know anyone on the team except for Marcus. He took a seat by the window and I followed and sat down, but then he put his headphones on and before we even left the parking lot fell asleep.

You take 183 North the whole way. The landscape you go through is just really not there. Grass and trees and telephone wires. I pulled out my homework, some of the kids listened to music, some of them played video games. Coach Caukwell sat in front with the driver. After about forty minutes he stood up in the aisle and started talking to us; we had reached the outskirts. The sun was setting, against the window on my side of the bus, but if I squinted a little I could see single-story houses in small yards with chain-link fencing around them, broken sidewalks and a few stumpy trees.

Caukwell took out a crumpled piece of paper from his pocket. He tended to mumble when he made speeches, not like he was nervous but like he didn't see any reason to raise his voice, unless we wanted to *give* him a reason. "First game of the year . . . I want to try out a few different things . . . I might change my mind . . ." And he read out the names on the list. "Tony, Josh, Gabe, Marcus—Brian," and for a second I thought I was one of the names. "Take off Marcus's headphones."

"It's not the headphones, he's asleep."

"Well, wake him up."

So I pushed him a little, and then pushed harder.

"Is he awake?"

"Not yet."

"Do you know how to wake somebody up?"

"Yes."

"So wake him up."

Eventually Marcus opened his eyes, and Coach started again. "Tony, Josh, Gabe, Marcus—nice of you to join us," he said. "I know you've had a long day. Breon." And he folded up the paper again and put it in his pocket.

Marcus whispered, "What's he doing? What's he reading out?"

"I don't know," I said. "The starting lineup."

Lamont called out, "Uncle Mel, Uncle Mel," and Caukwell looked at him, stony-faced. "You mean you not gonna play me?"

The kids around him were cracking up.

"Do you want to call me uncle?" Caukwell said to him.

"That's what you are, aren't you?"

"Is that what you want to call me on this bus?"

"Do you have like a different name for everything we driving?"

"What do you think you should call me on the bus?"

And somebody said, "Coach, call him Coach," and Lamont said, "Uncle Coach?"

"No. You are not starting, Lamont. Your ass is riding the pine. Does that answer your question?"

And the kids were still laughing. He punked you, he punked on you. Lamont didn't seem to care. We pulled into the high-school parking lot, which was huge, like a Safeway lot. Everything was flat. You could see nothing for miles, just cars and empty parking spaces and a few houses and those stadium-style lights over the football field. Sunset going on, a clear sky, a bit of moon. Caukwell stood in the bus aisle, looming, as solid as a tree. He said, "I'm only going to say this once. We come here to play basketball. We did not come here to shoot our mouths . . . or engage in anything extracurricular . . . with the fans or with the players or with the refs. What we're going to do is go in, warm up, kick their butts, and go home, and that's all we gonna do." He added, "I don't care what they say to you."

And then we filed out into the cold, stiff from sitting, but also, like a bunch of boys let out after a long ride, kind of high and lighthearted and scared as hell. Even before we went inside you could hear the noise from the gym; it was full and warm and bright under the lights.

You had to walk across the court to the visiting locker room. The floor shined and creaked; the boards were old, and the gym was so small the bleachers came right up to the sidelines. It had a low roof, too; people in the top row almost had to duck under the ceiling. Some kids in the crowd started chanting "Burleson Sucks," and the sound followed us down the corridor as we disappeared into the locker room. I didn't see any black kids in the stands. It was a very white place, and even kids like Breon and Lamont who normally make a lot of noise and like to mess around kept their heads down.

The locker room benches were so close to the showers you figured anybody leaving their bags on them would end up with wet bags. The whole place smelled of drains. Coach Caukwell said, "Take your stuff with you, you can give it to Kia." Kia was actually Gabe's cousin and the team manager and scorekeeper and the only girl on the bus but nobody ever acted like that was a thing, partly because of Gabe's personality. He was the kind of kid you didn't piss off.

We put on our uniforms and walked out into the noise again. Kia sat at the scorer's table, next to the bench; she soon had a pile of backpacks under her feet. Coach Caukwell said, "Where's Marcus?" and I said, "Maybe he went to the bathroom."

"What do you mean maybe?"

"I think I saw him go."

"Well go get him."

Marcus was finished by the time I knocked on the stall door; I heard the flushing sound. But he didn't come out and eventually I knocked again. I could smell the stink of it.

"You okay?"

He didn't answer for a second, so I said, "Everything all right?"

"Yeah, I'm fine."

"Coach Caukwell told me to get you."

"Tell him I'm coming."

"*You* tell him you're coming." And then: "Did you just take a crap?"

"It helps me relax," he said. I was still talking to him through the stall door.

"How relaxed do you want to get? Open the damn door. It's game time."

He opened the door and came out. But he looked funny; there was sweat shining on his forehead, under the hairline. I could hear the music coming out of his headphones, extremely loud.

"You okay?" I said again.

"I'm fine." But his hands were shaking when he stuffed the Walkman in his bag; he had trouble with the zipper.

As we walked out through the double doors and into the gym, just for a second I put my hand on his back. I was holding one of the doors for him. There was a gap in the bleachers and one of the students called out—I don't want to write what he said. He called me an N-lover, and somebody else laughed. Maybe it had nothing to do with putting my hand on Marcus's back. The whole thing happened quickly and Marcus just kept walking, and afterward he never said anything about it either.

But that's what it was like all game long, that was the atmosphere. Copperas Cove didn't have any black players. We had five, including three starters. The refs were white, too. For the first quarter, Coach Caukwell went up and down the sideline trying to bend their ears, but afterward, in the huddle, he said to us, "I think y'all know by now we not gonna get the calls, so I don't want to hear any bitching and moaning. Just shut up and play. If they want to play streetball we can do that, too."

Then Gabe knocked down a couple threes, and Lamont came in and picked up some offensive boards. When he smacked the glass you could hear the contact of his hand, even over all that noise.

Marcus couldn't hit a shot, he was too keyed up. Something else I noticed: when we practiced in the mornings before school, he used to hop a little on his jump shot but not much. He liked to keep himself under control. But in the game, with his juices flowing, he'd rise up two feet in the air, nobody could touch him. But his release had too much lift, he shot long and flat, and at halftime, Coach Caukwell told him point blank, "Marcus, you need to stop shooting."

We were sitting on the slat benches by the dripping showers.

Marcus couldn't make eye contact. His leg had a loose wire in it that kept humming. Then Coach said, "I want you to take number seven. Pick him up full court. Make him feel you."

Seven was Cyrus Millhouse, their six-four point guard who went on to play for Vanderbilt, and even made all-SEC his senior year. He was a dominant high-school player, because nobody who was big enough to guard him could keep in front of him. He had like thirteen points at halftime, six or seven boards, three assists; the score was 29–29.

Caukwell said, "Nobody gets showered after the game, nobody gets changed. When the whistle blows you get your bags and walk out. I don't care what happens, nobody says nothing to nobody. I'll make sure the driver has the engine running."

Then the horn sounded and we ran back on stage.

The first time Cyrus took the inbounds, he tried a little left-right shimmy at his own free-throw line and Marcus picked his pocket and strolled in for a layup. The second time, Cyrus used his ass. He kept backing and shifting, like a truck in reverse, working his way up court from side to side, but then Marcus "pulled the chair" and Cyrus almost fell over. Another pick, another layup. After that, they let someone else bring the ball up.

These days Cyrus Millhouse is a scout for the Bucks; sometimes I run into him and we talk about Marcus. He remembers that game, too. He says, it's the first time I was ever really guarded, when I even knew what that meant.

But it was still a close game, and with about a minute left, Copperas Cove started fouling. Breon missed the front end of a one-and-one, and then they came down and scored on a put-back, and the lead was four. Then Gabe missed another, and the lead was two. Coach Caukwell looked at me at the end of the bench; I hadn't played a minute all game. There were thirty seconds left.

"You want to shoot some free throws?" he said. I was sitting on my hands to keep them warm. "Get on out there. Just remember to check in."

"Should I shoot it . . . underhand?"

"What are you talking about?"

"I mean, do you care if I shoot it underhand?"

He looked at me, and what he said next sounds angry but wasn't; somehow it calmed me down. "Brian, I don't give a fuck."

So that's what happened. Nobody even guarded me the first time around. Gabe threw me the ball and I put my head down and swung my elbows and hung on. Eventually the whistle blew and I could see again. Then I had the long walk down court to the free-throw line.

I had to wipe the salt out of my eyes but my palms were sweaty too so that didn't help. Getting fouled, swinging my elbows, feeling their hands on me, had activated my fight or flight response. But I bent down anyway, bounced the ball twice between my knees, rose up, and spun it two-handed toward the basket.

Because of the adrenaline rush the ball banged hard against the backboard and because of the spin it went in. The noise dropped and in the relative quiet I could hear somebody say, "Jesus H. Christ." One of the referees. Then I made the second one, too.

That's all we needed. Cyrus heaved a three-pointer at the rim, which rattled out, and Gabe picked up the rebound and threw the ball in the air. The horn sounded. The building was like a balloon with the air leaking away. It was just another Friday night, after eight o'clock, and a couple hundred kids suddenly had time on their hands; they had to get home. But Coach pulled us into a huddle anyway, by the side of the court. He said, "Remember what I told you. Shake their hands and let's get out of here."

So we lined up at center court, and they lined up, too. One of the kids called me a faggot, I don't know what they said to anybody else. But Coach grabbed Lamont by the neck and we followed him to the bench. Kia stood there, surrounded by bags. Somebody must have said something to her, too, because Gabe had to be restrained—this time it was Breon who held him back. "It's just the usual bullshit," he said. "Just a bunch of crackers." Then somebody came out of the stands to go after Breon, and Coach had to separate them.

"What did I tell you? What did I just say?"

But we got our bags and walked out. Caukwell in the rear, I was a couple of steps in front of him. The other coach was standing by the door, I guess to keep order, but Caukwell as we went past said something under his breath. Then we were outside, in the cool October air, and I could feel the heat of the running engine as I got on the bus.

"What did I tell you?" Caukwell was still steaming. I don't know who he was talking to. "You think you get through life running your mouth?" Breon maybe, who had sat down stupidly in the line of fire, two rows from the font. "You need to be smarter than that. Don't talk shit unless you got someone to back you up."

"You backed me up," Breon said.

"First and last time."

And then we were driving away, out of the lot, through the small-town Texas streets, the stop signs coming back, the chain-link fences, the low houses with the lights on now, people having dinner, and then out onto the highway, where the noise of the road softened the mood again, an hour from home. I was sitting next to Marcus on one of the bench seats. He had his headphones on and his face against the cool window—there was nothing to see out there, just dark country. Everybody stank from the game, the whole bus, with the heating on now, but Marcus still smelled of sour guts.

I said, "Cheer up. We won," and he looked at me and lowered the headphones around his neck.

"We won," I said again.

"Don't act like you did something 'cause you didn't."

Then he put his headphones on and turned back to the window.

It was almost ten when we pulled into the lot at Burleson; my dad had waited for me in the car. "Well," he said, as I shouldered my bag into the back seat. "You stink like you played. How'd it go?" And I knew that if I told him it would make him happier than I could bear to see.

7

Betsy came home in parent mode, and we didn't really get to talk until the kids went to bed. She made dinner, chicken pot pie—the kids didn't like the pastry, so she just served the stew part over rice and put the rest of the pie in the oven so we could eat it later. In her own way, she's an efficient woman. The house was a mess but she knew where to find what she needed, and everything that had to happen happened the way she wanted it to. But something was missing, too.

After a day at work (she was a project coordinator for the Sierra Club), I can understand she didn't care much what she looked like. She had two children, she was almost forty years old, but her attitude to her appearance had turned into my attitude to my appearance, and it didn't used to be. Her red hair had grayed or faded, it was frazzled, too, about shoulder-length, and she pulled it out of her eyes with a ponytail. But she wasn't very careful and loose strands of hair sprayed around her face like static.

When Troy didn't finish his plate, she finished it for him. She didn't like throwing food away, but she'd also put on weight, and she said, when she forked another dollop of chicken mush into her mouth, "This is why I need to lose twenty pounds."

If I didn't know her and hadn't grown up with her, if I met her for the first time now, I'd think, you're a middle-aged woman, which is of course what she was. She looked like our mother.

At the airport, I'd managed to pick up some Celtics gear, a softball-sized basketball for Troy and a cap for Albert. Albert said thank you, he had reached the age of politeness, and put it on the table, and Betsy said, "Why don't you try it on?" so he tried it on. "Look at you," she said and he said thank you again. And his mom said, "Stop being so polite."

44

"What should I be instead?" he asked her.

This seemed a reasonable question. He had gotten glasses since I saw him last, black-framed Woody Allens. They hid his face the way a kid like that wants to be partly hidden. But with Troy it was easier to break through. I played catch for a minute, throwing the ball into his little kid-gut, so he couldn't help but catch it, and praising him afterward. Then I got bored and picked him up and put him on my head.

Betsy said, "Watch out for the ceiling fan." All the rooms in the house had a ceiling fan over the light fixture.

"What does he look like?" I asked.

"He looks like a kid on a head."

"No, I mean, happy or sad."

"He looks worried," my sister told me. But when I put Troy down again, slinging him over my shoulder and letting him slip down my back, he said, "Again." So I figured introductions were made.

Greg came home around eight o'clock and opened a bottle of beer. He gave me one, too. Betsy poured herself a glass of wine and wandered back and forth from the bathroom to the kitchen, to check on the kids. She said, "Troy wants to show you something, he wants you to come look," so I took my beer into the bathroom and looked. Albert was sitting in the bath, too. He had his glasses on, he was reading a book.

"What'you reading, kid?"

He looked at the cover before answering. *The Mystery of Cabin Island*.

It was one of my old Hardy Boys. "That's one of my old books," I said, and then, like a dumbo, "Don't get it wet." So Betsy stepped in. "Be careful," and we had to go through the whole thing, "I am careful," and so on, and I had to watch. Eventually I said, to break it up, "What did you want to show me?" and got down on my knees to make eye-level contact with Troy. He had the new ball in the bath, and when he pulled it underwater and let go, it sprayed upward in a little fountain.

Albert said, "You're making me wet."

In the kitchen again, Betsy said, not really to me or Greg but just out loud, "Greg can take them out of the tub. He always puts them to bed," and Greg disappeared. I said to Betsy, "They're not exactly interactive," and she said, "What do you mean?"

"I mean, in the bath."

"It's usually better when they don't interact," she said. "That's probably true for all of us."

It was nine o'clock before we sat down to dinner, under the yellow lamp. Betsy laid out the green rose tablecloth we used to eat on as kids. "What's the special occasion?" Greg said, and Betsy didn't answer.

Mostly we talked about Dad. His medical conditions. He was on warfarin for the blood clots and had to shoot up with insulin before every meal. There were other pills in his pillbox I didn't even know what they were. He was a heavily medicated individual. In the old days, you just got old, now you became a walking pharmacy. Greg mostly stayed out of it. He was my age, a little younger than Betsy, a lawyer for Planned Parenthood, blandly handsome, a good guy — one of those very sweet, very mild men and my sister was clearly incredibly frustrated by him. He overpraised her cooking and after dinner she said, "Greg can clear up. I'm going outside on the porch to smoke a cigarette. Come talk to me," she said.

"I wish you wouldn't." Greg finally showed a little backbone. His voice was level, he said it like he said everything else. "Albert's going to wake up one of these days and see you. He can smell it from his room," but she ignored him.

"You coming or not?" she said to me, after taking a pack from her overcoat by the door.

"You're not very nice to him," I told her.

We sat on the porch steps, it wasn't really warm enough. Across the road, you could see the corner of the park, and under the streetlamps, the playground, the jungle gym, the blue curve of the slide, and then the basketball court on the field below, pale in the artificial glow—the weirdly heartbreaking silhouette of an empty net hanging from a rim leaning off a pole. Beyond that, Waller Creek, and the thicker traffic moving along 45th Street.

"Yeah well," she said.

I started picking at the dirt under my nails, in the light from the hallway coming through the glass in the front door.

"That's a disgusting habit," she said.

"It's disgusting to have dirt under your nails."

And she looked like she was going to say something else but didn't. Then she said, "How's Dad?"

"You're changing the subject."

"I didn't know there was a subject. Okay, let's talk about your hygiene."

"That's not what I meant."

"I know what you meant but I don't want to discuss it."

This shut us up for a while. I felt like, if you're going to play the big sister, fine, but you start the conversation. Finally, she asked, "What does he do all day?"

"He sits around. He watches sports."

"That sounds depressing."

"What do you think I do all day?"

"At least it's your job."

"Does that make it better?" And I laughed.

A car went by, the kind of Volvo station wagon the neighborhood used to be full of, but now you saw a lot of SUVs and upmarket sedans. There was an intersection at the corner, with four-way stop signs, but the streets were wide and quiet. Not many sidewalks; front yard trees leaned over and cast their shade in the road. I liked being a kid here and it seemed like a place where, if you had a house and kids, you should be happy, too.

"You doing okay?" my sister asked.

"Eh," I said.

"I know I owe you something for taking on Dad. It's my turn and I want to do my bit but not now. Now is not a good time for me."

"Dad is fine," I said. "He keeps me company, he gives me something to worry about."

"Well, I've said what I wanted to say. It's too cold to sit out here anyway." And Betsy stood up, pushing against her knees.

Greg had gone to bed when we came back in. The table was cleared, the chicken pot lay drying on the counter. Betsy said, "Let me just make up the sofa," and when I tried to help, she said, "Please." So I watched her move the coffee table and pull out the mattress and get sheets from the hall and unroll the comforter and eventually got bored and figured I might as well use the bathroom and get out of her way. The door to my old bedroom was open. Troy liked to sleep with the hall light coming in, and I could see his crib under the side window and another bed that looked recently slept in, with sheets and blankets and pillows tangled up in each other. Maybe Betsy sometimes used it if Troy had a fever, or maybe she just slept there anyway. But this wasn't my business so I took my toothbrush to the bathroom and did the usual song and dance, drying my face afterward on one of the kids' bath towels. When I came back out the sofa bed was made.

"I can't pretend you're going to get much sleep," Betsy said. "The kids have to be out of the house by eight o'clock. Greg usually leaves around seven thirty, but he's quiet, he doesn't make much noise."

"It's just nice to be here," I said, and she said, "If you say so."

I can't sleep anywhere on the first night anyway. Not in hotels either, where you have to kick out the tucked-in sheets and the place stinks of air-conditioning and cheap carpeting, and there's a TV, and you think, I'll just see if something's on and you lie there in the flickering glow with no real reason to turn it off.

The house you grew up in casts a weird spell. I could hear the dryer in the utility room, and a clock ticking (even the cheap Ikea clocks, battery-powered, turn out to be audible in darkness), and from time to time the soft breathing of the heating vents. Austin in February, especially after a sunny day, gets cold at night. The heating came on and off, the furnace started to rev and then suddenly relaxed again, and after a minute the chill crept back, and you waited for the next surge of hot air. When I closed my eyes I could feel the faint glare of the streetlamp coming from the park across the street, but it was only ten o'clock, bedtime for people with small kids who have basically given up on the idea of an evening.

For some reason the pastor's corny phrase, newness of life, kept running through my head, like sheep jumping fences as I tried to sleep. New cars, new car smells . . . and then I woke up, because my phone had just pinged, and rolled over in bed to check it.

The screen said, "Let's go, Baby. I'm outside." And I looked out the window and saw a black Lexus sedan with the lights on hovering in the road.

8

Marcus kept bugging Coach Caukwell about playing varsity. "Coach, Coach," he'd say at the shootaround before practice. "When you gonna bring me up?"

"Bring you up?"

"Promote me."

"Promote you?"

"You know what I mean. Make varsity."

"Just keep on doing what you're doing," Caukwell told him. "But better."

My dad still dropped me off before school to meet Marcus in the gym. I told him, in games and scrimmages, you jump two feet in the air every time you shoot, but that's not how you practice. In practice you just kind of hop a little, it's a totally different motion. He didn't like to take advice, especially from me, but the other thing about Marcus was, he also listened, he thought about what you said in his own time and if he agreed with you started making corrections. So now even in warm-ups he jumped as high as he could and that meant for at least two or three months his shooting got worse. I used to beat him at H-O-R-S-E all the time, it drove him crazy.

Sometimes we played pickup on the weekends, too. Marcus lived just south of MLK Boulevard, at the edge of the Burleson district, on East 17th Street—a few blocks from Oakwood Cemetery. I'm talking about old Austin, before gentrification, when the Eastside was still the black part of town. He lived with his mom in one of those manila-brick apartment buildings, on the corner of Chestnut Avenue.

You could bike from his house to mine in about fifteen minutes. There's a public court in Shipe Park, next to the creek, but Marcus never wanted to play there. A lot of neighborhood kids went to Shipe, along with a few old-timers, guys who wanted to swim afterward; nobody good. So he made me bike over to Eastwoods Park, near campus, another ten minutes away. Mostly because that's where Isaac Brown and some of the varsity guys liked to play.

Waller Creek runs through Eastwoods, too, but it's greener and shadier, more treed in. It's close enough to student dorms that frat-boy types sometimes walk over on Saturday afternoons. Not real basketball players but big guys, who played high school football and still lift weights five times a week. On a sunny weekend, you might have ten, fifteen bodies hanging around on the sidelines, watching. It wasn't easy to get in a game, you had to know who to talk to, you had to wait your turn. The varsity players tended to stick together. They were good enough, once they got on, to hold court for most of the afternoon. That's the way it worked—winner stays.

So when we got there, we dumped our bikes spinning in the grass, and Marcus moved along the sideline, asking, "Who got next? Can we run with you?" Sometimes when they saw me they said no, a fat pale-faced kid wearing cargo shorts and a "Weird Al" Yankovic T-shirt . . . Sometimes only Marcus got to play. He didn't look like much either, just a short skinny black dude, real young-looking, with a flattop. But anyway, you had to wait.

Live oak trees branched out over the side of the court. The grass was patchy in the shade, there were those public park garbage cans next to the benches, overflowing, attracting bees and flies. A few cars drove by but other than that the only sounds were the sounds of squeaky sneakers and hard rims, a ball banging on concrete. After lunch could turn into early evening without anybody noticing.

The first time we played the guy who had next was this skinny grad-school type in jean shorts, who had a dick-ish voice. A Quentin Tarantino type of white guy—*Reservoir Dogs* had just come out. Marcus said to him, "Can we run with you?" and he looked at us.

"You want to run with me?"

"They said you got next."

"They did, did they?" That's the kind of guy he was. I don't know if he thought he was being funny or if this is how you should talk to kids.

"I mean, do you got next?"

"Oh I *got* next, I got it."

All this time a game was going on, people calling out the score. The rule was, you played to twenty-one and then whoever lost had to get off the court, and whoever had next had to find four guys to come on with. On sunny days, on busy days, there was next and there was next-next and there was next-next-next. That's how it worked.

"Well," Marcus said, "can we run with you?"

"You any good?"

And Marcus checked out the action. Isaac Brown was out there, and a couple of other varsity guys, Terence Triesman-Smith, who played wing, and the starting point guard, John Linehan. Then there were a few other kids I didn't recognize.

"I'm better than them," Marcus said.

"What about your friend there?"

Marcus looked at me. "He's all right."

Anyway, Tarantino let us run. In the pause between games, some of the varsity kids wanted a water break. "I been kicking ass since two o'clock," Terence said, and Isaac started messing around on one of the rims, just dunking, and trying different stuff. People were watching, making watching noises. Isaac had this body like one of those plastic figures, like he was made of some harder material than the rest of us. Now he was trying to palm two basketballs, one in each hand, and dunk them both. He had everybody's attention. I mean, it was kind of amazing, he was just a fourteen-year-old kid.

But Marcus couldn't stand around while this was going on. So he tried to dunk, too. His ball didn't have any grips so he borrowed mine and slammed it against the bottom of the rim. There was an audible *boing* noise, like in the cartoons, and he fell on his butt. It didn't matter, he got up and tried again. People were laughing at him and cheering him on at the same time, but Marcus even then could concentrate out other people. Until Terence came back from the water fountain and we started to play.

The varsity kids had winners out and scored before we knew what was going on. Then the grad-school guy insisted on bringing the ball up. He had a high dribble; he was a real ball pounder. His socks were these sports socks with the three-color stripes, and he wore them pulled up on his hairy white-guy ankles, along with Converse All-Star sneakers. The whole thing was like a style thing for him. He liked talking the talk, too.

"Get who gets you," he said.

Linehan was guarding Marcus but Marcus wanted to guard Isaac Brown. This caused a certain amount of confusion. Also, Isaac was just too big. He was a lot stronger than Marcus, too, and kept posting him up. There's a reason he made varsity. He pushed Marcus under the basket and Linehan threw him a lob and Isaac elevated and laid it in. I don't like the word but that's what he did, he just moved a little higher on the vertical plane than anyone else. And there's nothing we could do about it.

Isaac was actually a pretty nice kid. But clumsy. Not just like, he didn't know his own strength, but like, it didn't really bother him if you ran into his elbow. His one basic decision in life was, I'm not going to apologize for being bigger than you. Other people had to get out of his way and Marcus wouldn't get out of his way.

He caught an elbow in the mouth and one in the neck, where afterward he couldn't breathe. But Marcus was too proud to call foul. He knew that kids disrespect kids who call foul, so instead he preferred to get beaten up, which is what happened. I can't even remember the score. Tarantino could play, he had a funny little hook shot that high-school-age kids were not in a position to respond to. And he sweated a lot, I mean, really sweated, so that reasonable people would not want to touch or get near him, and picked up a lot of rebounds. But we lost anyway, it wasn't close. And then when you lose it might be an hour before you get back on. You have to walk up and down the sideline again, and say, You got next? Can I run with you?

That was my first experience of the Eastwoods Park pickup scene. I don't know why Marcus wanted me along. But still on Saturday afternoon he used to bike by my house and leave his bike in the yard and ring the doorbell and ask, Is Brian home? He never wanted to come inside, he waited on the porch. My mom sometimes brought him out a glass of water. And then when I came out, he said, "Let's go to Eastwoods," and for some reason I always said, "Okay."

Playing basketball at Eastwoods involved a lot of sitting around and watching other people play. Marcus liked to shoot on the empty side of the court when he wasn't in the game. It's a little nerve-wracking. You've got to be ready to clear out, which is fine if you make the shot, but if you miss and it bounces the wrong way then suddenly ten guys are coming down on you like a herd of buffalo. So Marcus always made me get his rebounds. Sometimes I shot a little, too, but mostly I was too nervous. Marcus, I said, I mean, come on, Marcus, let's just—I mean, let's just, *Marcus* . . . When I was a kid I was one of those kids who used my friends' names a lot.

The rest of the time we just hung out. One thing I learned, Marcus liked science fiction—his dad had all these old Bantam paperbacks lying around the apartment, the ones that say .45¢ on the back cover, and Marcus used to read them just to get a little space from his dad, when they were stuck with each other in Killeen. His view of the world was kind of like a science-fiction novel, where everything's normal but at the same time not quite right, and there are some pretty basic details missing. So, for example, I remember we once had a conversation about wiping your ass. He wanted to know if I wiped my ass sitting down or if I stood up afterward to wipe it like that. Except instead of ass he probably said butt.

"What do you want to know for?"

Three in the afternoon and we're waiting to get in a game. Even Marcus feels bored.

"I don't want to know, I'm just curious."

"Marcus, that's the same thing."

"No, I mean . . . I don't know what other people do. What do you do?"

"I sit down."

"Every time?"

"Yes, Marcus. Every time."

"But, I mean. Can you reach everything?"

"Everything I need to reach, I can reach."

Sometimes the stuff he said, it's like he was setting you up to make fun of you, so I never knew how seriously to take him. But that doesn't mean he was never serious. Maybe if you live with your mom, if you're a teenage boy, if that's your main experience of family life, there are certain things that don't get discussed.

But also, he was just a weird kid. The stuff he liked to talk about was stuff like, if you're eating a piece of pie, how big are your bites? What do you mean, Marcus, I don't understand. I mean, and he tried to explain himself, like, should you take a lot of little bites, and have a lot of bites, or just a few big ones, where you have a whole mouthful every time?

I don't know, Marcus. It depends on how hungry you are.

And then he thought about that for a minute. I don't think it depends, he said.

Whole afternoons could go by like this, watching basketball, waiting to get in a game.

9

"Is that what you're wearing?" Marcus said as I got in the car. When he texted I just picked up what was lying on the floor, the same clothes I wore to the funeral.

"Is the answer to that question ever no? I was in bed."

"Brian, it's ten o'clock on Saturday night."

I looked at my watch. "More like eleven. Where are we going?"

"To a titty bar."

"I don't want to go to a titty bar."

"Tough shit," he said.

I could hear soft jazz leaking from Marcus's ears. Somehow the saxophone gloomed me out. Our headlamps lit up arching trees and grassy front yards, quiet neighborhood streets, and then we merged onto I-35, and it was a highway world, cars coming and going at a slight elevation, where the flat city spread out vaguely below and away from the noise.

"I want to talk to you about Mel Caukwell," I said, but with his headphones on it was easy for him to ignore me.

Ten minutes later we arrived. The Palace is a men's club on East Ben White, just where it runs parallel to 71. I shit you not, this is one of the dark corners of the universe. Austin is not really that kind of late-night town. You can hear good music if you want to, you can get drunk, but you have to put up with women wearing clothes. The architecture was Austin hacienda-style from the seventies—beige and red bricks, and tiled roofs, and the whole thing looked less like a palace than a motel. There was a furniture discount outlet next door. Somebody had planted a row of firs outside the parking lot, to block out the highway ambience. But when we got out of the car, you could still hear trucks going past, putting in easy empty miles.

Also, I was cold. When Marcus texted, I ran out without a coat, and under a clear sky, even Austin nights feel like winter.

I said, "What's your name?" to the driver.

"Radko."

"What's that, Russian?"

"My father's from Kiev." But his accent sounded Sunshine State.

"Come on," Marcus said. "Enough chitchatting. Let's see some titties."

The bouncer at the door just nodded us through. He looked weirdly like John C. Reilly. After that we went past a security cordon and up some stairs. Most of the people sitting around in the VIP room, which overlooked the main stage, had the look of people sitting around and thinking, what the hell are we still hanging around for, until Marcus came back.

It was all the same guys from the funeral. Joe Hahn, the lawyer, sat there scrolling through his phone. Over the balcony and half a story below, on the main stage, women contorted themselves around upright poles like firemen in no particular hurry, while the PA system played "TiK ToK", *Don't stop, make it pop*. I couldn't really hear the words. There was something almost private about the whole thing, because it was just ongoing and you couldn't always pay them attention, but they continued anyway, though maybe the atmosphere was different on the floor.

Jerry de Souza was flirting with the waitress. He lettered in golf at Texas when Marcus and I were freshmen there, one of those tall lanky guys people instinctively like.

"After a week I almost gave up," she told him. "I almost brought her back to the pound. It was worse than when Jenny was born, because at least with Jenny I could nurse her back to sleep."

She wore cowboy boots and a little red uniform skirt, and that was it.

"You gotta stick with it," Jerry said. "I have three now, a King

Charles Spaniel and a Cocker, and this mutt I picked up because she was taking their food, but she didn't have a collar. But she's smarter than the boys, put together . . ."

Steve Henneman was trying to pop a Nicorette from the pill pack, next to Ted Myers, who seemed especially miserable. Ted sat with a beer between his legs, and his legs together, looking at the large flat-screen television on the wall. It was almost midnight in Austin, but only ten o'clock in California, where the Suns had a three-point lead on the Kings, midway through the third quarter. For him this was just an evening to get through.

"What took you so fucking long?" Taffy Laycock said.

"Brian had to get dressed."

Taffy was the richest guy there, which meant he could get away with stuff other people couldn't. He was basically a software engineer. In grad school, he figured out that you could use the Internet to broadcast local sports radio across the country. So he dropped out and started a company. Later he sold the technology to Yahoo for a billion dollars. Now he did what a forty-something nerd who everybody bullied in high school *would* do when he got rich: hang out with celebrities, buy sports teams, and lift weights.

Marcus looked me over and said, "You need to cut your nails."

"Not you, too."

"What do you mean?" he said.

"Betsy was on my case about that tonight as well."

"Well, you should listen to your sister." Then he said, "You look like a loser, you look like someone who doesn't give a shit anymore."

"Some things you can't hide."

So he called over to one of the women sitting around. Not all of them were naked. "Kyla," he said, and people squeezed over, Kyla started moving her ass along the booth. Another girl came with her, they must have had one of those, where you go, I go, party arrange-ments. People got up and sat back down.

At the same time, the waitress with the dog problems said to Marcus,

"What are we drinking, Mr. Hayes? How about your friend?" and Marcus said, "What kind of gin you got? I mean, like sipping gin?"

"Let me just find out for you."

When she moved, you could see she had to keep her posture upright with muscular effort, almost like a dancer or a woman riding a horse, to look the way she wanted to look, so she didn't look like a woman getting dressed or going to bed but like someone on show.

"Kyla," Marcus said, "I want you to meet my friend Brian Blum, the famous sportswriter."

She was a light-skinned black woman who turned out to be a sophomore at UT majoring in Communication and Leadership. Her hair was straightened; she wore braces on her upper teeth.

"How do you know Marcus?" I asked her, and she said, "I really don't. I just met him this afternoon. On Saturdays I do a shift at Sam's Bar-B-Que," and then I realized why she looked familiar. She was standing behind one of the fold-out tables in the church parking lot, wearing a Sam's apron and dishing out meat and beans from the hot-plate-heated metal trays.

"I don't understand."

"You don't understand what?"

"How this kind of arrangement is made."

"What do you mean?" She stiffened a little.

"I mean, did Marcus like, just ask you out?"

"I didn't even talk to him, it was the other guy, Radko. He said Marcus was having a get-together tonight and did I want to come along. So I said, I need to call my boyfriend, so I called him. And my boyfriend was like, Marcus Hayes? You definitely need to go. Maybe he'll join us later, he's a night stocker at Lowe's, they get off around two. This is my friend Quinn," she said, pulling her arm. "She got my back."

Quinn was white, Irish-looking; she had my mother's red hair, which went down to her waist, and the kind of pale skin that goes red easily, like somebody slapped her or she just came out of the shower.

But apparently this is what happened to her when she drank. They were doing tequila shots, and she offered me one, and I drank it and that was enough, not to make me drunk, but just to slightly change the direction of the evening.

"Have you ever been to the Palace before?" she asked me.

"I have never been to the Palace before. I will never go to the Palace again."

"Don't you like naked women?"

The waitress arrived with a bottle of Monkey 47, and Marcus told her to pour me a glass, so I drank that, too. "You're supposed to sip it," he said.

"Why, when it tastes like poison?"

"Come on, Baby," he said. "You need to get with it."

"Why does he call you baby?" Quinn asked.

"He likes to exert power over people by giving them nicknames."

But Marcus wasn't paying attention. He had decided to bug Ted Myers instead, because Ted wasn't talking to anybody or drinking but just watching TV.

"Why Communication and Leadership?" I asked Kyla.

"I want to work in the food industry, but not like making food, more from a business point of view."

"Teddy, Teddy," Marcus said. "I want to talk to you, come talk to me."

And Teddy turned with his sad eyes patiently.

At the same time Taffy Laycock was trying to get into conversation with Quinn. He sat opposite us, not in the booth but on one of the chairs, and leaned forward with his elbows on the table—everything he did, every physical movement, he had to negotiate around the constriction of his muscles against his shirt. Quinn said she wanted to work in sports management. She played volleyball for UT; maybe she'd go into coaching. One or the other. I noticed that even sitting down she had an unusually tall presence; her upper body was very long.

"You seem very occupied by something on your phone," I said to Kyla.

"I'm sorry," and she looked at me in a friendly way. "I'm not usually like this. My boyfriend keeps texting, he wants to know what's going on. Radko said I'm not allowed to take pictures so I'm just trying like to describe what's happening."

"What *is* happening?"

"He's not like what I thought he would be."

"What did you think he would be like?"

"I mean, he's just like . . . a fun guy, he wants to have a good time. I know a lot of guys like that."

"What did you think he would be like?" I said again.

"You know, kind of intense. More like, reserved."

"He is both of those things."

"I own a . . . I don't know how to say this in a normal way," Taffy said, "I own a number of . . ." and he put on a stupid English voice, "sporting clubs, and there are a lot of opportunities for somebody who wants to work like you do in those fields, at a high level, especially someone with firsthand experience of that kind of competition."

"What clubs do you own?"

"The Seattle Supersonics. The LA Kings."

"Is that the hockey team?" she said. "I don't understand why there's a hockey team in LA."

"We sell out every night."

"I don't know. I guess as a matter of like fact hockey is something that people want to do and watch but I never saw the point of it."

"What's so great about volleyball?" Taffy asked. He was getting annoyed.

"Spiking," Quinn said.

Marcus was trying to get Ted to tell him which of the girls he liked. I mean, which of the girls on the stage, which had maybe a dozen poles with girls dancing around them (some of them were unoccupied).

Ted didn't want to talk but Marcus made him look. They stood up to survey the field. It's one of the things Marcus liked to do, to make people do stuff they didn't want to do, just because he could. The girls were maybe thirty feet away. All you could see was movement and skin and hair.

Marcus said, "We need to get some more women up here. I want you to pick the women."

"Marcus," Ted said. "I'm fifty-two years old. My women-picking days are behind me."

"Don't you see anything you like?"

"Sure. Whatever you want."

"I want you to choose one or two."

"Marcus."

"If that's too hard, just like, three or four, if you can't decide. As many as you want."

"I don't want any."

"Don't you think these are attractive women?"

"They are obviously attractive young women."

"So pick some," and Marcus called the waitress over. He said, "The stage is a little far away, do you think you could ask some of the ladies to join us," and she said, "Sure, who do you want me to ask. Let's see who we got performing." She leaned over the rail. "Right now we've got Erica, Christi, Ceylon, Jennifer, LaShawna, Monique, and Tricia performing. You can just point."

"Come on, Ted," Marcus said and waited. I saw the whole thing happening while trying to talk to Kyla at the same time. Marcus said to the waitress, who wasn't wearing anything where you could pin a badge, so I didn't know her name, "Joe's going to give you two thousand dollars and when that's used up just let us know." And Joe stood up, he was still on his phone, and pulled out his wallet. And Kyla said, "How do you know Marcus?"

"We played basketball together in high school. I mean, we were on the team."

"Oh really?" and she laughed. "I guess you're a pretty big guy."

She looked at me expectantly, maybe she wanted me to say some-thing. Her face was long and pretty, she had a strong chin, the braces in her mouth made her top lip push out a little. One thing I didn't like, her eyebrows looked painted on, and her eyelashes were thick-ly mascaraed, which made her look like she just got out of bed or something. I say I didn't like her eyebrows but that's not really what I mean. Who cares what I like or don't. I just mean, it's one of those things that women sometimes do to themselves that makes me want to look away. Otherwise she was obviously pretty and you had the feeling she was a nice person pretending to be something else.

But the truth is, I was more interested in Quinn. She was talking to Taffy Laycock. So when Kyla finally said, "So you're a sportswriter. That sounds like a fun job," to break the awkward silence, it was a relief when Taffy stopped talking to Quinn and suddenly said, "You wrote that piece about the Hall of Fame speech."

"What piece?" Jerry de Souza had decided to join the conversation.

"Jordan's Hall of Fame speech," Taffy said. "You wrote that piece about it in *Slate*."

"I write for ESPN."

Marcus was listening now. "What did you say?"

"He said it was like a racist thing, the reaction against him. Every-body saying like, what a vulgar speech, what a son of a bitch. So that's what he's really like, when your point was . . . white people don't know what competition looks like, on the inside, even though they watch all these black guys play, they don't know what it really means to compete. To play hard."

"I don't think I put it in those terms. I don't think I talked about white people. I talked about audiences."

"It's the same thing. That was your piece, right?"

"Probably."

"He took a lot of shit for that speech," Marcus said. "A lot of bull-shit."

"He looked fat though, right?" Taffy was needling him. "He looked like he was wearing a whole other suit of clothes under his jacket and tie. He looked like he just put all of his clothes on at once."

"He still kick your ass," Marcus said.

"He'd just have to sit on me."

And then the dancers showed up, and the sequence of events started to blur. There were two of them, and the waitress introduced them: Monique and Christi. She also brought another bottle of Monkey 47, but Marcus wanted to cut it with ice and grapefruit juice. "I like to keep hydrated," he said.

"This stuff is too good to waste on grapefruit juice," Taffy told him.

"I waste what I want to waste."

"No, but it's like a . . . faux pas, it's like . . ." And Marcus looked at him.

"Are these the women you picked?" he said to Ted, and Ted kind of shook his head. But Marcus said again, "Are these the women? Because otherwise we'll get the ones you wanted, that's what we paid for," until there wasn't anything Ted could really do except nod. Marcus said it loud enough so the women could hear. Afterward, he turned to them graciously. "By particular request of this gentleman."

If you pissed him off, he took it out on everybody.

There was a small stage on the balcony, just a single pole, and a disco globe spinning around at the top of the pole, and that's where they started dancing. Monique wore a G-string and nothing else, but Christi had put on some clothes, a man's shirt, a tight pair of jeans, with nothing underneath it turned out, and while they danced Monique slowly took them off. That was the routine, button by button. They were so close now you kind of had to watch. It was almost rude not to, like, these people are making this effort right in front of you. But Marcus said to me, "There's something I want to talk to you about. Remind me later."

"I'm not sure how much *later* I've got in me."

Afterward, Marcus tried to get Teddy to have a lap dance. For some reason, Teddy was his whipping boy tonight, he couldn't do anything right, he couldn't get away. But Teddy finally stood his ground.

"I can't sit down anymore," he said. "Not with my back."

"I've seen you sit down. You were sitting down five minutes ago."

"Marcus," and Teddy looked at him. He was using the voice he used to remind Marcus, there is a better side to you, you have a better side. You are a person capable of respect. I'm older than you, I've been in the game a long time. "Nobody wants to sit on my lap and dance."

"They get paid to do it," Marcus said.

"Well, they can do it to somebody else."

And somehow it worked. He shifted his attention. "Come on, Brian, come on, Baby," he said. It was my turn now. But he addressed the ladies also, I mean, the two women. "I apologize for my friends," he said. "They have no manners. All they want to do is watch TV."

But they didn't know what to say. When you're naked, it's hard to just stand there, you have to do something, you have to keep moving. The music kept going relentlessly and if you just stood there somehow the illusion was gone. I mean, the illusion that we were all sexy people having a party, the kind of party you see in a movie, where debauchery is taking place, and the good times are rolling, and this is the place everybody wants to be, but the illusion was already pretty weak to begin with.

"Come on, people," Marcus said. "Let's give these women something to do."

So Jerry de Souza offered up his services. "I mean, sure."

Quinn volunteered, too.

"Are you serious?" I said to her.

"Why not? I always wondered what the big deal was."

"You crazy girl," Kyla told her, in her you-crazy-girl voice.

She had to scooch out, so Quinn could follow, because there wasn't room in the booth, so I gave up my chair and Quinn sat down and

one of the women came over. The chairs were deep and softly up-
holstered and forced you to lean back, so the dancers could straddle
you—it put them in a position of control.

Marcus said to me, "Smile. We're having fun."

"I want to talk to you about Mel Caukwell."

"Come on," Marcus said. "Stop working me."

"It's my job, that's why I'm here."

When the lap dances were over, Joe Hahn glanced up from his
phone. He looked like a guy at a conference, killing time between
seminars. He said to Jerry, "Did that do anything for you? Was she
getting through?"

"Was it embarrassing?" I asked him.

"I almost creamed myself," Jerry said. "That would have been embarrassing."

Kyla was still on her phone, staring at the screen and moving her
thumb with incredible rapidity across the interface, when Quinn re-
joined her in the booth. "Move over, girl. Are you texting him? What
are you saying?" she asked, and Kyla said again, "You crazy."

"Are you telling him what happened?"

"No way. He talks about you enough already."

"What do you mean? Is that what he's into?"

"Come on, Quinn, all guys like that kind of thing."

"What kind of thing?" Her voice was very level, a little deep, she
didn't really have an accent, and for some reason it made me think,
cool to touch, like glass.

"Anyway," Kyla said, "you don't have to think about what people
think about you."

"What does that mean?"

"White girls can just be like, whatever. If you want to be skeezy,
you can be skeezy."

"Who even says skeezy?"

"You do, that's one of your words."

"Guys are skeezy, girls are—"

"What? Girls are what?" Kyla said. "Thank you. That's what I'm saying."

"I don't even know what we're arguing about," Quinn said.

At a certain point, when I'm drunk, it's like I don't even think I'm there, I'm just for some reason receiving information. Which doesn't mean that at the same time I wasn't thinking: What are you doing with these people? Go home, sleep on your sister's sofa bed, say hi to her kids in the morning.

Taffy wanted to talk shop. He was one of those guys who even in the presence of attractive women secretly prefers talking business with men. Anyway, for some reason, he latched on to me.

"The game is changing," he said. "The smart organizations are starting to bring in math and computer grads from MIT. Those kids are really running the show, the coaches answer to them. And the smart players know it, the really smart players. Marcus would clean up. All the advanced metrics we get are telling us this is his kind of league. Three-pointers and foul shots, that's all that counts."

Kings–Suns was still on TV, and this distracted him for a minute. During a time-out, he asked, "Has Marcus talked to you?"

"About what?"

"He said he was going to talk to you."

But then the game came on again. Quinn said to me, "You don't look like you're having a very good time."

"You're the second person who said that to me tonight."

"Well, it's your face."

"What's wrong with my face?"

"It doesn't look happy."

It occurred to me, this was an intimate thing to say. Up to that point most of my conversations had been surface-level, I was skating on ice. "This is just a job for me, I'm working overtime."

"You have a funny job," she said. "What exactly do you do?"

"I'm a sportswriter."

"Don't you like being a sportswriter?"

"It's a job." The opportunity was slipping away. Then the game ended and Taffy started looking around, and I had twenty seconds to think of something to say to Quinn that would make the conversation look deep enough he might decide to leave us alone.

"Your hair is the color of my mother's hair."

"I don't know what the right thing to say to that is," she said.

"I mean, was or . . . she's dead now."

"I guess it still is anyway, right?"

"No, we cremated her."

"You're really good at talking to women," she said.

But it didn't matter, Taffy started talking to me anyway. He reached over and poured another shot of gin and filled my glass, too. "Something interesting is going on right now. The whole culture is changing. It's like *Moneyball* all over again, except basketball is more interesting than baseball. It's a lot more fluid, it's a lot more surprising that this kind of computer analysis works. We can isolate pretty much anything on the court right now. Pick and roll efficiency, usage rate, real plus minus. I'm telling you . . . it's like . . . everything human turns out to be measurable. There are things going on that guys like you should be writing about."

Maybe he was drunker than he looked. Marcus was watching him. He said, "What should Brian be writing about?"

"I don't get much practice," I told Quinn. "Mostly I talk to men. Tall men and short fat sportswriters. Did you like having a lap dance?"

"I wanted to see what the big deal was. I wanted to like, imagine I was a guy, and this was happening to me."

"So what's the big deal."

"Women are very beautiful, don't you think. They have beautiful bodies."

"I guess," I said.

"Don't you like naked ladies?" she asked again. "Are you gay?"

"No. No. But that doesn't mean . . . if you're my age, if you're not married, if you look like me, if you even . . . make the least comment, or look at somebody or whatever, people think you're a creep. I'll tell you something that pisses me off. I don't expect women to be attracted to me, obviously not. But that doesn't necessarily mean I'm attracted to them. When a pretty girl walks past and turns away as if, like, she has to hide herself from me, because I can't help but . . . I'm not making much sense. Just the basic assumption that a guy wants to . . . or is attracted to . . . which is not always the case. Most of the time I don't want anything to do with anybody, and that includes pretty girls."

"Oh," she said. "Does that mean you want to talk to me, or you don't? I'm trying to figure it out." And she laughed.

"What?"

"Do I count as one of the pretty girls?"

You forget what it's like to talk to twenty-year-olds, to really try to explain yourself. All these conversations have possibilities, these are people who still think of their lives as places where things might happen. When I was twenty, that's what I felt, and if there was a girl in the room, somebody I liked, I thought, uh oh. Concentrate. Make a few jokes but don't be a jerk about it. It's like, for people at that age, their personality is like a shop window, where you put these interesting things in the window, to get people's attention, instead of what it is now, just these tendencies you're stuck with.

"Anyway, girls like tall guys," she said. "It doesn't matter what they look like. Some girls just won't go out with somebody who's shorter than them. They just won't."

"That's good to know."

After a while, after another silence, she said, "I wasn't supposed to drink tonight. I get pretty bad cedar fever and alcohol interacts with my medication. It makes me kind of spacey."

"Do you want a glass of water?" I asked.

"No. I want to keep drinking."

Henneman had disappeared downstairs. I don't know what he was doing, maybe hanging out in the bathroom, but he came back now and said, "What's the plan?" and I pressed the glow button on my Timex. It was two in the morning. I had been up since four, almost twenty-two hours. Marcus had a suite at the Four Seasons and someone suggested heading back there. He had a six o'clock tee-time but could sleep on the plane afterward, he didn't care. What about me, Jerry said, but didn't really mind. I noticed when no one was talking to him he sometimes closed his eyes. There was a question about whether we could bring the dancers along—Radko had ordered a limousine.

Kyla kept trying to get through to her boyfriend. He could meet them at the hotel, she said. It was really a question but nobody answered. People had basically stopped responding to her and I could also tell that in spite of that she wanted to come along. Henneman asked me, "Has Marcus talked to you yet? We'd like to coordinate some kind of announcement," but all of these conversations were taking place with other conversations going on at the same time, and the music was really too loud.

Quinn touched me on the elbow. "Are you coming?" Maybe she was one of those girls who finds it amusing if she realizes a guy is attracted to her, and even if she's not attracted back goes along with it for a while. Or maybe she actually liked me.

"I'm pretty tired," I said, and Marcus said, "Come on, Brian. We're just getting started here."

But I don't like being bullied. "I'm going home." When I said it, I realized I didn't want to but it was already too late. Marcus said, "Come on, Radko. Let's put Baby to bed," and everybody filed out, down the dark sticky stairs, through the lobby, and out into the parking lot, where the highway noise replaced the music from the PA. The limo was waiting out front, but Marcus and Radko headed over to the Lexus, and I got in the back with Marcus, on the soft cool leather upholstery, and the almost-silent powerful engine revved into gear.

"What about the others?"

I could see Quinn through the tinted windows standing around with everybody else. She had a trench coat and a yellow handbag and looked as tall as the men. The way she stood, you could tell she was an athlete, but it also gave the impression of somebody sensible, she moved efficiently and had to duck her head to squeeze into the limousine, along with Kyla and Jerry and Taffy Laycock, Monique and Christi and Steve Henneman and poor Ted Myers. They were going somewhere with her, things were going to happen that I had nothing to do with.

"Jerry will take care of them," Marcus said. "It's what I let him hang around for."

I-35 was almost empty, but Radko kept the needle at seventy, he didn't push it. I guess that's what you pay him for if you're Marcus Hayes, not to drive the way you do. Marcus said to me, "Brian always needs his sleep."

"It's two in the morning."

"You got something to go home to? You got anything better to do?"

"That's not really my kind of party," I told him.

"You don't like that redhead girl? I thought you liked her."

"Which girl?"

"You know who I'm talking about, Kyla's friend. She had a lap dance. You didn't notice?"

"She's twenty years old."

"You asked her? So you did notice."

"How come you don't want to talk about Mel Caukwell?"

The only thing you can do is push back, it's what he respects.

"I said everything I got to say at the funeral."

"You didn't say anything. If it wasn't for him, we wouldn't be sitting here now."

"Yeah, well."

"When I saw the coffin, it was like . . . I can't believe he fits in there. Do you know what I mean?"

But Marcus didn't answer.

Eventually I said, "He was the first grown-up black man I ever knew."

"Congratulations."

"He meant something to me. I thought he meant something to you."

We rode in silence for a while and I thought the conversation was over. Radko in the front seat must have heard the whole thing. But all I could see was the back of his crew-cut head, and unless he checked the mirror, it didn't move. I closed my eyes and Marcus said, "Two years ago, Mel got in touch with one of my representatives. He needed some money for a hip replacement."

"Didn't he have health insurance?"

"I don't know; he said he didn't, or not enough. Anyway, there are things the insurance didn't cover—he needed to make some changes in his apartment. Like the bathroom."

"So what did you do?"

"What do you think I did? I gave him the money. It was fifty thousand dollars. Later it turned out some of it went to other debts. He used to go to the race track, he lost a lot of money."

"How do you know this?"

"When people want things from you they tell you things they think you want to know. I mean other people, when they heard what I gave Mel Caukwell."

"Maybe he thought you owed him."

"If he wanted to play the ponies, he should have said. I don't care what he needs the money for."

"Maybe he was ashamed."

"Maybe he was," Marcus said. "Anyway, that's not what I want to talk to you about."

We came off at Airport Boulevard and crossed under the highway again, toward 45th Street. It's like traveling along a computer circuit, where what you come out at, once you leave the circuit, is reality, trees and sidewalks and houses, actual neighborhoods. Even in the dark you could feel the green of the park. Radko pulled up outside the house, behind the Honda in the driveway, and let the engine idle. I was going to get out but Marcus didn't move and even though I'd known him for more than twenty years, we had a relationship that pre-dated everything that had happened to him, somehow in his presence you still waited to be dismissed.

"How's your sister?"

"Not great. I think she's heading for a divorce."

"What's wrong with her husband?"

"Nothing, except she doesn't like him anymore."

"Your sister is a woman of strong opinions, I respect her for that."

"Much good may they do her."

And still I waited.

"How's your dad?"

"Fine. Overmedicalized. He has type 2 diabetes, and they've got him on warfarin, too. He gets headaches all the time. Sometimes he calls me into the bathroom after he goes because there's blood in his shit and he wants me to look. This is one of the side effects."

"What's wrong with him?"

"He's old, he's fat, and he's lazy. Most days he doesn't leave the apartment. The last time he got on a plane to see Betsy he ended up in the hospital with a thrombosis so he doesn't do that anymore." Then I said, "He used to love to watch you play. It meant a lot to him. Every night we sit around and watch basketball on TV, but he says it's gone downhill since you retired. Everybody in the neighborhood knows that we know you—I mean the guys at the grocery store, the other people in the building."

"Did Laycock say anything to you?"

"He talked about the new NBA."

Marcus took off his sunglasses and looked at me. Not that I could see him any better; the only light came from the streetlight across the road, by the playground and swimming pool. Sometimes, when we were kids, I'm talking about senior year in high school, we walked across the park to play basketball after school and held court until dark, because he let me play with him, and there was nothing anybody could do by that point to stop him.

"I don't want you to write about Mel Caukwell," he said. "I'm asking you as a personal favor."

"Okay."

"Laycock's going to move the Sonics to Austin. It's all official but you can't say anything till the season's over—I'll let you know. I'm coming back, I'm going to play for them."

"Why are you telling me?"

"I want you to write about it," he said.

And that was that, he put his shades on, and I stepped out into the cool of the early morning. The quiet powerful engine of the Lexus eventually went silent as it drove away, between the arched trees, down the neighborhood street. He was heading back to the hotel, people were waiting for him to get the party started or keep it going, people including Quinn. But I walked as softly as I could up the porch steps and into the sleeping house and pulled off my clothes and lay flat on my back on my sister's sofa bed with the ceiling fan suspended overhead. Maybe this is my chance, maybe I can start again. These are the thoughts that make your heart race at three a.m.

10

Marcus invited me once back to his place after school. He said his dad was coming down for the weekend. It must have been Friday, because we didn't have practice. Sometimes Coach gave us the day off if we won on Thursday night.

At lunchtime I called home and asked Dad if it was okay, and he said sure. So at four o'clock, when the last bell rang, I met Marcus outside the gym and we lined up to get the bus. The cold white morning had turned into a warm blue sunny afternoon. Everybody had too much stuff on their laps, backpacks and clothes, and the bus made stops outside the Walgreens on Guadalupe and on the corner of Shipe by the swimming pool, two blocks from my house, before continuing onto Airport. It was like a weird science experiment, where the concentration of black kids increased with each stop. Then we passed under I-35 and drove through Patterson Park and got off at the 7-Eleven on MLK, because Marcus wanted to get a Big Gulp.

Those things always give me brain-freeze. But I filled a 32 oz. plastic cup with crushed ice and A&W, picked up a pack of Ho Hos at the checkout, and we walked toward 17th Street, eating and drinking. It's not a nice walk, even in the sunshine. MLK is a four-lane road and there's nothing really on it except some parking lots and apartment buildings, separated from the road by chain-link fencing. At a certain point you cross the tracks. I was also a little nervous or shy. Marcus and I tended to interact with a basketball between us, talking about basketball, playing basketball, but this felt different.

The previous night we beat Lanier, which put us in shooting distance of the District playoffs. Even though Breon rolled his ankle in the second quarter, and Gabe was in foul trouble most of the second half. What happened was this. After Gabe fouled out (there were five minutes left, we were down two), Coach Caukwell turned to Marcus in the huddle and said, "We need you to take some shots, we need you to score." By that point in the season Marcus had become more of a defensive specialist. He didn't like to shoot unless it was a layup, because he didn't like to miss. The truth was, he'd lost confidence. When Coach turned to him he just sort of kept his head down.

"Marcus," Coach said again. I always made a point of getting off the bench for every huddle and standing around like an idiot with everybody else. Marcus looked up.

"What'd I just tell you?"

"Shoot," he said.

"So what are you going to do?"

"Shoot it."

And that's what he did. I don't want to take all the credit but those zero-hour sessions in the gym were paying off. He hit a jumper from the top of the key, which was basically a panic shot—Coach told him to shoot, so the first time he touched the ball he rose up and shot, but it went in anyway. A few plays later he banked one in after a hard two-dribble drive to the left block, over a forest of arms, which is when I realized that nobody could really get in his way unless he let them. Then he hit a catch-and-shoot three from the corner. That was the ball game—we won by four, he finished with thirteen, but after the game, for the first time all year, he wanted to talk to kids on the bus ride home like everybody else, and I sat on the bench where we normally sat together on my own. Then the next day he invited me to his apartment after school.

Because his dad was in town, and I think he wanted me to tell him about the game.

In the parking lot outside his apartment building, he pointed to a brown two-door sports car with one of those nostril-like race-car bumps on the front hood and a tailfin at the back, I don't know the technical terms. Just looking at it you could almost hear the engine rev, but it also looked like something that maybe wouldn't start in the used car lot.

"That's my dad's car," Marcus said. "Pontiac Grand Am."

"Nice car."

"He'll probably sell it next week. That's what he does."

His mom's building was three stories high, covered in half-dead ivy, with big Gothic bronze-colored letters spelling out SU CASA APTs bolted into the brickwork, which the ivy climbed around. Marcus had a key to a metal gate, which opened onto a tiled windowless communal stairwell, and I followed him up the stairs.

The closer we got to his apartment the less we talked.

His dad sat on the couch watching TV. The lights were on, even though it was a sunny day; the curtains were drawn. There was a kind of bar area with a kitchen on the other side of the living room, where his mom stood by the sink, and she said, "Turn off the TV when they come in."

"It's almost over."

"He's got a friend here, show some manners."

"You said he got home at five o'clock."

"What's that got to do with anything?"

"He's late."

"So what?"

"I bust my ass to get down here and he's late, and he brings another kid over."

"I'm sorry," his mom said, and she came out from behind the bar with an apron on. "Marcus's father is somebody I can't control so I stopped trying. You boys must want something to eat."

"We stopped at the 7-Eleven," Marcus said.

"That's why you late," his father called out, but he was still watching TV. She walked over to the box and turned it off. Mr. Hayes had the remote but the battery must have been dead; he kept pushing at it with his thumb but nothing happened. If he wanted to turn the TV on he had to get off his ass. The room felt suddenly quieter and eventually he quit pushing buttons, he just sat there with his hands on his knees and looked up.

"Hello, son," he said.

"I thought maybe you had practice." His mother put her arm around Marcus and kissed his head. She was still as tall as him.

"Coach canceled because we won last night."

This was my chance to say something but I was too slow.

"You going to introduce us?" she asked.

"This is Brian. Brian, this is my mom. This is my dad."

"Call me Selena," she said, and I noticed that underneath the apron she wore heels and a dress; she was still a young woman, in her early thirties.

"You going out tonight?" Marcus asked her.

"I got a date," she said, in the voice she must have used with her son all the time, like they were pals together. "But don't worry. Dinner's in the oven, all your father has to do is take it out."

"Can't even spend one night at home with your family," he said.

"I spend every night at home with my family. This is your night."

"Yeah, well."

But he didn't make eye contact. He just looked at the blank brown screen of the RCA, which was six feet away from him, against the wall.

"You don't want me hanging around anyway. I thought you needed space."

"I need something," he said, but the fight had gone cold.

He was still an angry presence in the room, and I didn't want to look at him. Of course, at the time I had no idea that he was actually going through a transition of some intensity, from lazy disgruntled maybe even depressed but still basically virile middle-age to gentle elderliness, and had to come to terms with the fact that his old girlfriend and the mother of his son was still a sexually desirable and active woman who looked after herself much better than he ever could.

Also, she was using his arrival to rub it in.

This is what happens when you invite your friends home from high school—you're inviting them to a show they're not really old enough to see or understand. Anyway, Marcus took me to his room, and I said to him in an undertone, "What am I supposed to call him?"

"What do you mean?"

"Your dad, I don't know his name."

"Don. Mr. Hayes. I don't know. Don't call him anything. You don't have to talk to him."

There was a computer in his room, one of the old Apples, dusty and bulky, and for a while we played games on it, stuff like Donkey Kong and Hard Hat Mack. All the time I was listening out for what was going on in the other room, but there wasn't anything to listen to. Just silence.

I said, "Where does your dad live?"

"Killeen."

"Where's that?"

"I don't know."

"You never been there?"

"Sometimes he comes down and we drive up together but it's not like, I mean, I don't have to read the map. It's not that far, it takes about an hour."

"How much do you see him?"

"Enough," he said.

About half an hour later his mom put her head around the door. "I'm going now. Marcus, look up. Look at me when I speak to you, I need your attention for two minutes."

"What?"

"I'm turning off the oven now, it's Friday-night chili. It'll stay hot for a while, otherwise turn it on again for a few minutes. Or eat it like it is, you know where the Fritos are. I don't want you hiding out in your room all day with your friend playing on that thing. Your dad comes down to see you."

"*You're* going out."

"That's so you two can have some time together, without me getting in the way. Anyway, that's my choice."

"What about my choice?"

"You don't get one here. Listen to me, Marcus. Listen to me." (He had started up the game again.) "I don't want to hear about it afterward."

"Hear what?"

"Like, when I come down he just hides in his room. I don't want to hear it. I hear enough crap from him anyway."

"Okay."

"Okay, what?"

"Okay, like, I'll do what you want me to do, or be like what you want me to be, I don't even really know what that is, but I'll do it."

"I'm sorry, Brian," she said, in a different voice. "When you get divorced, that's one of the things that happens, everybody sees your business."

After she left, after a few minutes, he turned off the computer and we went into the living room. I just kind of followed him. His dad was watching TV again, and Marcus said, "Okay, Dad, what do you want to do?"

"What are you talking about?"

"Mom says I have to like do something with you, so what do you want to do?"

"She isn't here now, we don't have to do what she says. This is boys' time. We can do what we want."

"Well, what do you want to do?"

"I want to sit here and watch TV."

It was the six o'clock news and he had the volume turned up high. You had to shout over it. Soviet troops were leaving Afghanistan. Marcus said something, and his dad said what, and Marcus said, "Brian and I are gonna go shoot hoops." Outside the window, which was over the kitchen sink at the other end of the room, you could see the sunny day going pale, the blue sky wasn't blue anymore, it looked thin.

"Come on, Brian," and I followed him again. The ball was in the coat closet by the front door.

"All right, all right, hold up," and his dad got off the couch and turned off the TV. We waited while he put on his shoes, which he kind of shuffled into, and then sat down again to pull them all the way on and tie the laces.

"Do you know this guy your mom is going out with tonight?"

The stairwell felt like it was halfway outside, because the door at the bottom was really just a metal gate, which let the air in.

"I don't know. No. Maybe it's not a guy, maybe it's one of her girlfriends."

"She said she had a date."

"Sometimes she says that stuff just to piss you off."

The nearest hoop was five blocks away, in the parking lot of the Corinth Baptist Church. There was a high school with a full court, which was closer, but they locked the gates after hours, and we couldn't get in. The sun actually set while we were walking, you could see it casting shadows across the gravestones of Oakwood Cemetery. It slipped moment by moment behind the trees, which didn't offer much sound protection from the big tangled mess of the interstate on the far side. Traffic was close enough you could hear it, a lot of people going home on Friday night, heading north to neighborhoods like Hancock or Hyde Park, where I lived, or out of town to the suburbs, like Pflugerville and Round Rock. It was dumb, I should have brought a coat. Marcus had the ball and it rang hollow on the concrete sidewalk in the cold.

When we got there, after warming up, Mr. Hayes said, "How about I take you both on?" He had a funny little short-arm push shot, which barely got over the rim. Whenever he missed, he said to whoever got the rebound, "Give me another, come on, give it to me." He missed a lot, I kept passing him the ball.

"Dad," Marcus said. "We're gonna kill you."

"Let's see about that."

He took the ball first and backed his way in against Marcus, butt-first, pushing and elbowing and turning from side to side. I just stood around. I felt like, this isn't my fight. Anyway, it was too cold. Marcus kept reaching and his dad kept slapping his hand away; you could hear the slap. "Come on, Brian," Marcus said. "Come on." But his dad was already too deep. He spun, hooking Marcus with his left hand, and laid the ball in with an easy flip. This put some bounce in his step and he clapped his hands.

"My ball," he said, so I passed him the ball. "Winners out."

"That's a hook," Marcus said. "That's a foul."

"You feeling me? You feel me now? I'm teaching you a lesson here. This is what fathers do."

Then they went at it again. The parking lot had loose gravel on the surface, which skittered around. "Come on, Brian," Marcus said again, and so I vaguely tried to get in the way, and suddenly felt the grown-man weight of his father against me, when he turned, still pounding the ball, and Marcus slipped past and picked it clean on the half-dribble. I could feel the fat on his father's back and hips, I could smell him, too, the smell of a guy who had spent the morning working and then an hour in the car and then a couple of hours sitting around in his ex-wife's apartment, where maybe he didn't want to shower or clean up, because it wasn't his apartment and anyway what did he care. When Marcus tried to drive past him he stuck out a forearm and pushed him back hard.

"That's a hand check," Marcus said. "That's a foul."

"Come on, son. You're better than that."

"This isn't football. You have to know how to play."

"I know how to *teach* you how to play."

And so it went on. Marcus passed me the ball and told me to shoot; his dad was already breathing heavy, standing under the basket, waiting for the rebound. The first time I shot I missed; my hands were still cold, they felt like baseball gloves. Nobody could score. Marcus wanted to win too bad, it was like that first game against Copperas

Cove, he was too hyped up. Also, we could barely see the rim. The sun had set, and the gray light had a weird rich depth, like color by Technicolor. Our breath misted on the air, there was a streetlight by the cemetery fence that cast a distant glow. But after a while I got the feel of the space in my head, it was like mentally arranging the furniture, and the truth is, what are we talking about, eight-foot dink shots against the backboard. I should make those with my eyes closed. Mr. Hayes had just planted himself under the basket. Half the net was torn away and when the ball went through it hit him in the face.

"Brian can shoot," Marcus said, giggling. "You can't leave him."

But his dad was just too tired. We beat him pretty easy. I don't think he even cared by the end.

"Come on," he said. "It's getting dark, I don't want nobody to get hurt. Let's eat, I've had a pretty long day."

Marcus wanted to keep playing, he wanted to go one-on-one. "Come on, Dad," he said. "You're just chicken."

But Mr. Hayes had turned into the grown-up.

"We can play in the morning," he said. "We got all weekend." And then, because he couldn't help himself, "We can straighten out that jump shot." Which is when I should have said, he knocked down three straight last night to beat Lanier, he didn't miss. But I didn't say anything.

"You don't know this guy your mom is going out with?" Mr. Hayes said.

"I told you, Dad. She just likes to piss you off."

"I'm not just talking about tonight. I'm trying to look out for you, I want to know who she's got hanging around."

I followed two or three paces behind them in the dark, but I could hear every word. The high school cuts through 17th Street, so we had to walk around it, past Paquito and Alamo. Sidewalks faded in and out so we walked in the middle of the road. In those days most of the houses were still little ranch houses, with driveways and a bit of front yard. Brick siding or limestone, furniture on the porch. Most of the lights were on inside, it was Friday night, dinner and TV time. Telephone poles grew right next to the curb, leaning like trees. They talked around me like I wasn't there.

"If you was here you wouldn't need to ask me," Marcus said. He sounded different around his father.

"Is that what you want? Did you tell your mother that?"

"I don't tell her nothing she doesn't need to know."

"Maybe she needs to know that."

"*You* have to tell her."

"I tried, Marcus. I tried."

After the heat of the game, in the cooling down, this is how they talked. But they also walked in silence.

"So you won last night," his father said at last. We were coming up to Chestnut Avenue, where the traffic thickened after MLK. I could see the ivy of Su Casa apartments in the flash of headlights.

"Yeah, we won."

"Who'd you beat?"

"Lanier."

"How many points you score?"

"Thirteen."

"That all?" and he opened the gate to the stairwell. I guess he had a set of keys.

When we got back to the apartment, I said, "Maybe I should call my dad."

"Don't you want to eat?"

"I don't know, it might take him a while to get here."

"Where's he live?" Mr. Hayes said. "Westlake Hills?"

But he was kidding me and I didn't get the joke. Afterward, he took the chili out of the oven and Marcus got a bag of Fritos and we sat down. Mr. Hayes said grace beforehand. It's the first time I ever sat at somebody's table where they said grace—I already had a spoon in my mouth. But when he started with "Bless us O Lord and these thy gifts," I closed my eyes and felt dumb. The chili was warm not hot but that didn't matter, everybody felt hungry. A few minutes later the doorbell rang, and I said, "I guess that's my dad," but Mr. Hayes had to go downstairs to let him in. I almost followed but he said, "Finish your food." I looked at Marcus but Marcus had his face to the bowl, he wasn't talking. Then we heard our fathers coming up the stairs.

They looked in their own way like brothers. Two big men, over-weight and overaged, as if even getting older comes from laziness or sloppy habits—men who look like . . . not everything has turned out their way, but maybe it doesn't matter anymore. My dad wore dirty chinos and no socks in his loafers. Like Mr. Hayes, he some-times struggled to put on his shoes. But he also looked happy, he liked company, he liked talking to people. All day long he sat around at home sometimes doing accounts but also watching TV and feeling, I don't know what he felt, like a dripping faucet. Waiting for his kids to come back from school, so the second part of his working day could begin, where he made us a snack and drove us to music lessons and bugged us about homework, until Mom got home and started cooking. He said, "Hey Marcus, I hear you're the big star."

"What's that?" His father answered for him.

"Marcus was Mr. Clutch last night. This is what Brian tells me."

"Is that right? Is that right?"

Mr. Hayes's voice when he was smiling sounded like soda over-flowing or a bad radio connection, it had a kind of static in it. He offered my dad a bowl of chili, there was plenty in the pot, but I said, "I guess I'm finished already. Maybe we should just go home."

So that's what we did. On Monday at school Marcus didn't say anything about the visit so I took my lead from him and didn't men-tion it.

11

When Marcus and I were kids, Austin was a college town and a football town. Now it's one of the fastest growing cities in America. The culture has changed, it's whiter, richer, less Southern. The demographic moving in is basically a basketball demographic. Laycock was a businessman, he wanted to make money. The city had promised him a stadium, although there was still a bond vote coming up. Until then the team could play in the Erwin Center, where Marcus played in college. It seated almost 17,000, which put it at the bottom end of NBA stadia in terms of capacity, but still in the ballpark. If taxpayers voted down the new bond, who knows what would happen. But Laycock figured that if he brought playoff basketball to Austin, nobody would vote it down.

I quoted him for the story, too: *Marcus Hayes Is Coming Home*.

None of my pieces ever got so many hits. By the end of the month, my agent had a deal with HarperCollins for the book, and for that, Marcus had to sign off, he had to grant exclusive access. For weeks I waited around to get his signature. First, he was in China on a shoe tour, then he was training hard in LA, trying to get in game shape. Nobody could reach him; everything shuts down in August anyway, I mean, my publisher and agent, the literary types. So the deal was on hold. Meanwhile, I had to rearrange my life.

At the end of August I packed a few suitcases, put a bunch of crap in storage, rented out the apartment and drove west. My dad refused to fly because of the DVT, even though the doctors had cleared him; but it didn't matter, we made a road trip out of it. We didn't need any furniture because my sister said we could stay with her and help look after the kids. By that point Greg had moved out. Well, she kicked him out. She said she'd rather live with us. "It's either you or get a dog," she said. "That's what I promised the boys. And I don't want a dog."

It's a two-day drive if you drive all day; we took three.

I own a Corolla, the trunk size is not really adequate. We had to fill the back seat with luggage. Not even suitcases but just stuff we couldn't fit anywhere else. Like, how many shoes do you really need to take? We put them in paper grocery bags. It feels weird locking the door for the last time. You think, did I leave a coffee mug in the sink? Does it matter? But it's also like, when you get in the car, and everything you actually need is in the car, and you can really go any-where in the world or at least America (even if the place you're going is your hometown, and the person you're going with is your father, who you still live with), you feel light, you feel happy, you feel like, fuck everything, who cares, I'm basically okay, which is what I felt.

Of course, we argued most of the time. The plan was to reach Knoxville by dinnertime, where my dad had a fraternity buddy. I said, Dad, this guy does not want to see us, he does not want to put us up. Of course he wants to. He'll be excited to see *you* again. Steve reads your stuff all the time, he told me so. You're famous. Dad, I said, Dad . . .

Steve turned out to own several furnished apartments in Fort Sanders, near the university. That's actually where we stayed the night, in one of his student rentals—because the semester hadn't started yet, he had a lot of empty units. He brought sheets and tow-els from his own house and took us out to dinner. And, in fact, it's true, he had read my article and wanted to discuss Marcus Hayes.

My dad said, "Brian is writing a book about him, he signed a six-figure deal."

"Well, I still have to get access."

"He requested you specifically, you're the only reporter he trusts."

The poor guy had to listen to all of this, maybe he got a kick out of it, I don't know. Dad also talked about Betsy. My daughter is having a temporary break from her marriage. I'm moving back just to help out; she's got two small boys. Since I'm retired anyway. And Brian has the book to write. After fourteen hours on the road, when you just want to go to bed, you don't even bother to correct him. The waiters started putting chairs on the tables.

On the drive the next morning, we argued about Greg.

"There's something going on that I don't understand. Every interaction I had with him was pleasant—he was the kind of guy, if Betsy was in high school, I would have been happy for him to escort her to the prom."

When my father took the wheel, he pushed the seat back so far it was almost like he was sitting in the row behind. He laid his forearm on the window frame; to check the mirrors he adjusted his eyes. The impression he gave was of expertise and control.

"She never dated guys like that in high school."

"Yes, well."

"Probably because that's not the kind of guy she likes."

"Somebody who respects her, somebody who treats her like a serious person."

"He bores her."

"You don't know what you're talking about," my father said. "At her age, in her position, who has time to be bored. When she gets home from work, it's put food on the table, wash the clothes, brush the teeth, get the boys to bed. Go to bed yourself so you can do the whole thing again tomorrow. If this life bores you, you should sign up for a different life."

"Maybe that's what she wants to do."

"This is not a realistic option. When you have kids. That *is* your life. And by the way, what she's signed up for is not rock and roll. It's living with you and me. I think, after a few months of us, she may reconsider."

"Listen," I said. "I don't even really disagree with you. But I don't want you to show up at the house with false expectations. What you said to your friend about a temporary arrangement—that's not the sense I get from Betsy. The sense I get from her is, this has been a long time coming."

We stopped at the Arby's just after the exit to Lebanon and picked up sandwiches to eat in the car. They're even good cold the next day, we bought enough for two meals. The weather was summer hazy, and sometimes you could see a storm cloud waiting for you at the highway horizon, a sort of stain on the air, which you slowly approached and then entered, the light changed, rain slashed the windshield, and then you emerged again. We passed Nashville and Memphis and crossed the border into Arkansas. From time to time we got gas and switched seats. My dad had a 2-liter bottle of Diet Coke, which he nursed the whole trip—the sound of the built-up carbonation releasing every time he twisted the cap was one of the sounds you get used to in the car. It slowly flattened as the miles rolled away beneath us but my dad drank it anyway.

Outside of Texarkana we saw a sign for Red Roof Inn and pulled off. You have to pass Hope to get there—after a while, everything becomes a topic of conversation. You can fill the hours just reading out the exits. By this point it was almost eight o'clock, sunset poured through the windshield. I was driving and the rich red light, which I had to shield my eyes from (lowering the flap only helped a little), was a vivid reminder of cosmic forces. There's large-scale machinery out there that can make you feel the pressure of its thumb whenever it wants. The motel had a pool next to the parking lot, and after checking in, I dug a swimsuit out of the trunk and padded barefoot across the day-hot asphalt to the water. My dad joined me, but in his clothes; he lay back on one of the lounge chairs and I stepped down the concrete steps.

Even in the water you could hear the highway; it didn't matter, I let it trickle into my ears. Everything seemed to be floating—my hair spread out, and something, a vein maybe, in the red of my eyelids crawled around like a microscopic organism on a slide. The place I had lived for the past five years was behind me; the place I was going was the house where I grew up. I could feel the chlorine on my skin and almost sense in the trembling water the stress on the landscape caused by cars and trucks. For some reason the phrase, "All of these arrangements are temporary," ran through my head. When Marcus Hayes goes anywhere he takes his own jet.

My dad and I shared a bedroom—these motel rooms all have two queen beds. The air-conditioning dripped and smelled of cigarettes. In the morning, we breakfasted on cold roast-beef sandwiches in the car and continued on. Austin appeared around lunchtime, you could see the treetops rising over the line of the elevated highway. After three days on the road, where America basically seems a country of concrete inhabited by commuters, it takes a little adjustment to stop at stop signs again and see the world at a pace where people can live in it. Dad had the wheel and pulled in behind Betsy's Honda. He sat there for a minute then pushed open the door. The temperature must have been a hundred degrees. Just the heat made a noise, like a pulse, like a great heart beating. We were home, like nothing had happened to us in twenty years, and Dad was picking me up after basketball practice.

12

Marcus grew five inches between the end of the basketball season in late February and the beginning of junior year. It was like one of those nature documentaries where they photograph a plant over several months, and you can actually watch it flower—as if growth were a kind of real-time movement, like opening your hands. Maybe this is why he spent that summer in such a bad mood. His back hurt, and there was an ache in his knees that nothing could touch, not stretching or running or resting. He felt hungry all the time.

The other reason is that Selena got a boyfriend—I mean, Marcus's mom. She started hanging around with one of the ambulance drivers at Seton Medical Center named Tony Diaz. Whether this was the guy she went out with on the night Marcus invited me over, I don't know. Anyway, Tony spent a lot of time at the apartment, because ambulance drivers work crazy hours and he was going through a divorce and didn't have anywhere to live, after his wife kicked him out. Also, he had two kids, a fifteen-year-old son from a previous relationship, and a six-month-old daughter. His wife kicked the son out, too, a kid named Harvey, and so Marcus had to share his room.

At the beginning of the summer I got my lifeguard certification and did a few shifts at the pool. All I had to do was get out of bed and walk across the road—that was my commute. The city paid five bucks an hour and I spent most of the money on ice cream at Amy's Ice Cream, which was a five-minute bike ride from the park.

Sometimes Marcus showed up at my house when I was working. He'd drag Harvey along. They rang the doorbell and my dad might answer the door and tell them, he's on shift.

Marcus didn't like swimming and never brought his swimsuit. Dad told him, you can borrow one of Brian's but Marcus wasn't the kind of kid who borrowed other kids' clothes. Harvey never had a swimsuit either but didn't care. He just walked into the pool in his shorts and T-shirt and figured, after a half hour in this heat I'll dry off anyway. Also, he was kind of overweight and didn't feel any need to take off his shirt in public.

I only saw the situation from Marcus's point of view, and from Marcus's point of view it was obviously annoying to have to drag this kid around with you just because your mom started having sex with his dad. But it can't have been a picnic for Harvey either. Most of the time he actually had a better time than Marcus. He didn't really swim much, but waded around in the kiddy section and somehow there were always kids who wanted to splash him and he let them splash him and sometimes carried them around on his back. I think, if you were a parent whose child was being played with, you'd think, is this kid okay, and you'd watch him for a while and decide, he's just a nice lonely kid.

From where I was sitting in the lifeguard chair I could see over the chain-link fence to the court and the creek beyond, which was bordered by reeds and thick bamboo growing out of the creek bed. Sometimes guys lost balls in the creek and had to tiptoe down to retrieve them from the mud. But it's also amazing how often the court was just empty, just a square of bright concrete in the three o'clock sun. Sometimes when my dad answered the door Marcus asked him if he could borrow my basketball, so while Harvey jumped in the water in all his clothes Marcus walked around by the side of the park to the court and played by himself.

It turned out Harvey liked D&D, although he actually preferred more sophisticated iterations of the basic premise like Battle Tech and Ringworld. Or so he said. But since we already had a campaign going (Dungeon-Mastered by Frank DeKalb), Harvey joined in and we even persuaded Marcus to make a character. Frank said, this is the last summer I'm going to hang around you losers playing this stupid game, because he was going to Swarthmore in the fall and expected to come back afterward a changed man.

I tried to explain it to Marcus. There's this world, and it's a fantasy world . . . people have swords and armor, certain people have access to magic, there are monsters and treasures, and the idea is, you adopt some character in this world, like a character in a book, and act it out. I don't understand, he said. What don't you understand. Why anyone would want to do that. Well, because, and I tried to explain again. The character you adopt can do cool stuff, stuff that you as an ordinary human being in a pretty average world cannot do. Like what? Like, for example, if you're a thief, climb sheer walls. Or if you're a magic-user, emit from your finger a ball of fire and direct it at your enemies.

But you can't actually do any of those things.

Of course not.

You just like, imagine that you can.

That's the idea.

Why do you want to imagine doing stuff that you can't do?

I don't understand.

But he just repeated himself. Why do you want to imagine doing stuff that you can't do?

I don't understand. I mean, I don't understand what it is you don't understand.

We looked at each other for a minute; everybody was in my bedroom, either sitting on the bed or on the carpet on the floor, and there were bits of paper all over the carpet, dice, pencils, open books, and a large half-finished bag of Lay's potato chips. Frank DeKalb had the chair at my desk, which had casters and a seat that you could spin around in. It gave him the impression of natural authority, which was his right and role. Harvey was on the rug, along with Andy Caponato and Frank's brother, Jim. Mike Inchman and I had the bed, which I made up only when kids came over, because it was kind of disgusting. I think Marcus was standing.

Why would you want to imagine doing something you will never be able to do?

Because, I said, because . . . this is what humans are like.

I mean, why not imagine doing stuff you can actually learn how to do?

Like cast fireballs?

I don't want to cast fireballs, he said.

The only part he got into was the ability scores. What do you think my dexterity is? he said. Do you think I have like a nineteen dexterity? Nineteen is the top score for elves. No, I said, because in real life you're human. Eighteen is the maximum. Frank said that eighteen means that if there were 216 people in a room, that's how the odds play out, you would be the most dexterous person in that room. No way I'm eighteen, Marcus said. What about a thousand people in a room? What about a hundred thousand? What do you think my strength is? I bet I'm stronger than all of y'all.

I hate to break it to you, Marcus, that's . . . I mean, I'm sure you are. I mean, we're all a bunch of nerds.

He spent hours on the floor, trying to roll the perfect character. Mike explained that the point of the game isn't really to be the best at everything. It's to be a character, to have flaws and make that fun, just to enjoy sucking sometimes, and developing that . . .

Why would you want to do that, Marcus said.

Harvey thought the whole thing was funny as shit. He was one of those kids who once he started laughing couldn't stop, until everyone else started laughing, too, and then got tired of it and annoyed. But Marcus couldn't stand it after a while.

He said to me once, "I think you like Harvey more than me."

We were shooting around in the park; for once, Harvey wasn't there.

"What are you talking about?" But my heart skipped a beat.

"Whenever he come over, you always want to talk to him."

"That's 'cause you bring him over. If you don't want me to talk to him . . ."

"He's just always around," Marcus said. "I wake up, and it's like, what are you doing in my house? And then I come around here, and I have to bring him along, and everybody's like, Harvey's a great guy."

"It's just . . . he's not always trying to win."

"What do you mean?"

"He's just, easy to get along with."

"I don't always have to win."

"Marcus."

"I just don't like losing."

"Marcus, come on. I'm not even talking about basketball."

"Then what are we talking about?"

"Anyway, I don't think Harvey really cares what anybody thinks about him. If you don't want me to talk to him I won't."

Another time, they came over and I wasn't working and Marcus wanted to bike over to Eastwoods Park. Their bikes lay in the grass in the front yard; maybe it was eleven in the morning. Not cool, but also like, when you have your finger on the volume control and begin very gently to turn it up. Harvey said, "All you ever want to do is play basketball."

"What do you want to do?"

"I don't know. Something else. Watch TV."

"Where you going to watch TV?"

"We can watch at Brian's house."

We stood on my front porch, with the screen door on the latch behind me. Mom was at work and Betsy, because it was the summer and she never got up for breakfast, was in the shower.

"Brian doesn't want to watch TV."

"How do you know what Brian wants to do?"

"Because I know. Because I've known him like a hundred times longer than you have."

"Well then, what does he want to do?"

"Play basketball."

"Why don't you ask him then?"

"Okay, let's ask him," Marcus said. "Brian, what do you want to do?"

"I don't mind playing basketball."

"Told you . . ."

"That's not what he said . . . He said he didn't mind," but it didn't matter, because I got my bike out of the garage and put a basketball in my backpack, and we biked over to Eastwoods.

When we got there the court was full. Ten or twelve guys sitting on the benches or on their basketballs by the side, waiting to get in a game. Eastwoods Park is pretty shaded but it still gets too hot to play in the afternoon, so sometimes late mornings are the busiest time of day.

Isaac Brown was there, along with a few other varsity kids, John Linehan, Triesman-Smith, and they were holding court. Miles Drachsler was one of them, this big Addams family kind of white guy, with high shoulders and hanging arms. He once asked my sister on a date, or to come out to some party somebody was throwing, and when she said no, he said, Ookaaay, in that drawn-out way, like it was funny and surprising. Talking to him was like having a conversation with a Magic 8 Ball. He was a pretty good basketball player, though; he got a lot of offensive rebounds.

The guy who had next was this skinny black guy wearing jeans and no shirt. He had a bandanna, too, like Rambo. I learned later he used to play for Burnet when they went to the State Championships and lost. I don't think he was the star or anything but he was on the team. After a while if you go to the same park long enough you learn vague things about people.

Marcus went up to this guy and said, "Can I run with you?" And the guy looked him up and down.

"Sure."

"How about my friends?"

"How many you got?"

"These two."

"I'm not taking the fat kid."

"Forget it then."

"You playing or what?"

"Not with you."

Harvey said, "Really, man, I don't care. I don't even want to play."

"You playing."

"Leave him alone, Marcus," I told him. "He doesn't want to play."

"What's this got to do with you?"

"What are you trying to prove?"

"I'm not trying to . . . Fine. Forget it. Fuck both of you. I'm just trying to stand up for him."

"He doesn't want standing up for."

"I don't even know which kid he meant was the fat kid," Harvey said.

"Fuck you, too, then." But I didn't really care.

Anyway, he sat out and Marcus said to Rambo, "Okay then. I changed my mind." For a while I couldn't tell if I was included in this mind-change but it turned out not, because when the game ended and Rambo started warming up on court, I counted the guys who went with him and there were five, including Marcus. So I sat on my backpack next to Harvey and watched.

Sometimes in these games you get a weird class-conflict vibe; it wasn't necessarily a race thing, because Isaac Brown was black, so was Triesman-Smith. But the varsity guys played like varsity guys. They had that attitude and ran sets, pick-and-roll actions, high-low screens. When Linehan brought the ball up court he called plays. And the guys they were playing against were just five random guys. Rambo wore one of those key chains you hang from a belt loop. Another guy on their team was this bald but not very old white guy. Maybe he was on steroids, he looked like a weight-lifting type;

they played skins and his back was covered in acne and acne scars. The last of the five was a skinny long-armed kid, but a real kid, like eleven years old, who always hung around the park asking, who got next, until someone took pity, and said, all right, you can run with me. Whenever he got the ball he shot.

It shouldn't have been close, and it wasn't close, until Marcus took over. Rambo was quick but couldn't make a layup—he had a sort of crazy dribble, which was hard to predict, and got to the rim and missed and cursed like he had never missed before. Every time. But he played hard defense, fouled a lot, and the varsity guys liked to pretend they didn't need to call fouls. The white guy could rebound at least. The kid tossed up threes until everyone stopped passing him the ball. In other words, what you had was a lot of guys who were pissed off about things in one way or another expressing their anger and resentment through basketball. And what they were up against was a well-coached group of smoothly efficient high-school players for whom all of this was just a practice drill.

Except one team had Marcus Hayes and the other didn't. It was around this time that I realized he was taller than me. We stood back-to-back one day by the chain-link fence that ran the circumference of Shipe Pool. Which means he must have been about six two. It was like, someone had given him a new car to play with, or his dad had slipped a few hundred dollars in his wallet and said, go have some fun. What I mean is, he had a new toy, and the toy was himself. At six foot two he could get his elbow to the rim. Obviously, he couldn't guard five guys at once, but he always had more energy than everybody else and covered a lot of ground. When Isaac Brown picked up a rebound and tried to lay it back in, Marcus came from the top of the key and pinned it against the metal board.

One of the things I've always liked about pickup basketball is the public celebration. If a guy does something like that everybody responds, the guys on the sidelines waiting to play turn into commentators and audience. Did you see *that*? Did you *see* that? Jesus.

When he came down I thought he might break his leg, because he landed on the white dude's shoulder, but the guy sort of caught him and Marcus managed to slide off.

Linehan was a hard, quick son of a bitch but it got to the point where he couldn't bring the ball up against Marcus. Drachsler ended up doubling back to set picks, just to release him from his own half-court. A lot of little things like this were happening. Marcus was a total disruptor and eventually his teammates realized, maybe we can beat these guys. A new kind of intensity set in. In pickup basketball the stakes on the one hand are, who gets to keep playing that afternoon, but also every game is like a test of how good you are in some absolute sense. So even though it doesn't really matter it matters too much.

Anyway, they were losing sixteen-six when Marcus hit a three. Next play down he blocked that shot, and then Rambo found him backdoor for a layup and it was sixteen–eleven. Triesman-Smith missed a jump shot from the elbow but Drachsler tapped it in. Now the varsity guys just needed a three to win it. Marcus hit another jump shot but his foot was on the line, and Linehan said, "That's a two," because he was a real court lawyer and good enough to make it stick. Then Brown tried to post up Marcus, who dug his heels in and suddenly pulled the chair—when Isaac fell down, Marcus picked him clean.

What happened next I'll never forget. He pushed up court past Linehan and Triesman-Smith. Drachsler had tracked back but Marcus took off anyway and suddenly it was like Drachsler had stepped aside because Marcus was hanging on the rim. Everybody went crazy: 18–15 and Triesman-Smith missed another three, because he was rattled and wanted to put an end to it. Then Marcus came down and there were three guys waiting for him at the three-point line, Brown and Linehan and Triesman-Smith, but Marcus pulled up five feet away from them and knocked down a thirty-footer and the score was tied. I heard Linehan say, "Happy birthday."

The guys on the sideline were all standing up, even Harvey. The feeling we shared, that this is where the center of the action was, in the trapped heat and dappled sunlight under the live oak trees, on this half-size public court, was strong. And, in fact, it's true, we didn't know it then, but what we were watching was like that old JFK joke about the White House dinner—at which Kennedy had assembled the greatest collection of American talent since Thomas Jefferson dined alone. Marcus Hayes was dining alone, except it wasn't the White House, it was a park in Austin on a Tuesday morning, just before lunch, in the noise shadow of I-35. Then Linehan hit a three-pointer, and the varsity won anyway, and we went home. Well, back to my place, because I had a shift at the pool that afternoon.

13

Albert must have heard us drive up. He opened the front door but left the screen on the latch and stood with his face against the mesh looking out. "Do I get a hug from the big guy?" Dad said, but Al only looked at him.

Betsy walked up behind; she had Troy in her arms. "Make eye contact. It's your grandfather. You remember him."

"It's okay," my dad said. "I need the facilities anyway. Give him a minute," and he pushed past her to the bathroom down the hall.

I was hauling suitcases on to the porch but stopped and opened the door and picked up Al whether he wanted me to or not. This involved propping the screen against my butt. I turned him upside down and shook him out, like I was looking for loose change.

"I don't think he likes that," Betsy said. "Anyway, you're letting the mosquitoes in."

The way she stood there, holding her three-year-old boy like a baby for protection, reminded me of that scene in a Western where the cowboy rides up to the log cabin house in the middle of nowhere, and the woman comes out to see what's going on.

"Well, he better get used to it. Right, Al?"

And when I set him on his feet he said, "Okay, Uncle Brian."

"In the meantime, you can help me with some of this stuff."

The screen door clabbered behind us, and when we walked out to the car together, he took my hand.

It's too hot to stand outside in Austin in August, whatever needs doing you have to do quickly. I gave Al one of the shoe bags to carry. The junk in the car, the empty soda bottles and candy wrappers on the floor and on the seats, all that could wait.

When I brought the last load up the steps, Betsy put Troy on the ground. "Let me help you," she said. And then: "She says, when it's too late." And then: "I'm sorry, this is totally meaningless, this is because it's nice to see you," because there were tears running down her cheeks. "You forget that your kids have actual feelings about your brother," she said. "You think it's just another one of those things you force on them."

The house I grew up in is a small three-bedroom house, which meant that Betsy obviously kept her own room, which had the big double bed in it she didn't need anymore. But the boys had to move in together, and Dad and I were going to share. At least that was the initial plan. Troy's room, which was my old room, was also the smallest, and Betsy thought the boys should go in there. But Albert raised a stink and Dad said, "Let him win this one," and Betsy said, "He wins all of them. I let him win all of them. Eventually he has to stop winning or we'll all go crazy."

Then Troy kicked up a fuss, when he saw us moving his bed into Al's room. In the end we agreed on a compromise arrangement—he could sleep with his mom, which it turned out he was mostly doing already. But in his own bed. So we moved his little Ikea race car into Betsy's room, where there wasn't really space. "This is pointless," she said, sort of supervising and sort of protesting. "He just climbs in with me anyway. I like it."

"I don't think that's a long-term solution," my dad told her.

"There are no long-term solutions. There are only short- and medium-term solutions. Medium-term is anything over a week at this point."

My old bedframe was in the garage, and just locating it and making room to carry out the relevant pieces of wood was a two-hour job, which Albert helped me with. Then trying to bang the pieces together again, finding the Allen wrench, twisting the bolts. Dad offered to sleep permanently on the sofa in the living room. "I don't sleep anyway," he said. "I watch TV. I wake up at five in the morning to use the bathroom. Brian is thirty-five years old. He doesn't want to sleep with his father."

But Betsy put her foot down. "I'm not turning the house into a dormitory. If this is going to work it's because we keep up certain standards."

Meanwhile, Troy had a playdate with a friend of his from day care, which Betsy had totally forgotten about. "I didn't know when you were coming, I couldn't just totally suspend my life . . ."

"Nobody asked you to," I said.

"The mom is one of the moms I like. They live out by Deep Eddy. The plan was to take them swimming."

"I can drive him, if that's of any assistance."

"Dad, I don't think you want to spend the afternoon hanging out with this woman."

"Why not?"

"Dad, don't adopt positions that are totally implausible."

"Those are my favorite positions."

"Why don't we all go, why don't we all go swimming," I said. But Albert point-blank refused. For some reason, he doesn't like swimming anymore, Betsy said. The water is cold, it's too cold. The water at these pools is not cold, it's like lukewarm, it's like piss temperature.

Don't be disgusting, that's disgusting. And so the long day wore on. In the end Betsy and Dad took Troy, they went in Betsy's car, and left me and Albert at home to sort out the house. There were still suitcases in the hallway, mattresses leaning against the wall. Dishes in the sink. Dad had to park in the road so that Betsy could back out, so he got out of one car and into the other. All of this took time, but when the Honda disappeared at last through the arches of live oak shadowing the neighborhood street, Al turned to me and said, "Finally, peace and quiet," and I tried to figure out if this was something his dad said, or if it sounded more like Betsy.

"Let's get out of here," I told him.

"Where are we going?"

My old basketball was in the garage, along with everything else. It just needed pumping up. "To the park. To shoot hoops."

"I don't want to play basketball. It's too hot."

"I'll buy you an ice cream after." So that's what we did.

This became something of a habit. Albert had recognized what other kids before him had recognized, a way of escaping domestic life. I'm just going out to shoot hoops. Sometimes he just messed around in the driveway, so Betsy had to park her Honda in the street, if she didn't want to hear the ball bouncing off the windshield. The Rawlings backboard my dad had put up over the garage door almost thirty years ago was mostly eaten away with rot. The rim leaned down at an eighty-degree angle, which made it easy to shoot at. I could lift Albert up over my head and hold him there long enough to dunk. Sometimes while playing these games with him I was aware of my sister watching us from the living-room window.

For complicated reasons, which were partly financial, Betsy had decided to take Al out of the Montessori out past Barton Creek and send him to Lee, the local elementary, where I used to go. Private school is one of the things she argued about with Greg, part of their general disagreement about the life they were living. Anyway, she didn't want to pay for the Montessori, now that Greg had moved out along with most of his salary, and she didn't want to sit in traffic all day, driving Albert to and from. So, in addition to all of his other life changes, come Monday morning, he had to face a new school.

So if I, his uncle, could spend an hour with him in the driveway or the public court passing a ball back and forth, saying, well done, when the ball went in, I was happy to do it.

Al's best friend from kindergarten was a kid who lived three blocks away on 48th Street—just the other side of the park. He was already going to Lee, which is another reason Betsy thought it would be okay.

His name was Noah and they had a good time together, but Noah also liked to make Al feel like, you're a little bit worse than me at everything. At least, everything to do with sports, racing, throwing, jumping, biking. Shooting hoops. Anyway, it's how their friendship worked. I saw enough of these interactions after school to judge what was going on, but you have to tell yourself, they're just kids, this is what kids do to each other, and maybe in his own way, Al fought back. Who knows.

Noah had an older brother, who started at power forward for Burleson High. This kid's name was Zach, he was about six five, and Noah probably thought: that's what I'm going to be when I grow up. If I'm lucky. And because Zach was obsessed with the fact that Austin was getting its own NBA team, Noah couldn't talk about anything else.

Al had to be able to hold his own in these conversations, which should have been easy for him, because his uncle happened to be writing a book about Marcus Hayes; they were old friends. But Noah refused to believe him. No way your uncle is friends with Marcus Hayes. No way. They were shooting around in the driveway, and Noah was basically pushing Albert around. I stood on the front porch watching, and Al called out, "Is it true? That's what you said. Aren't you writing a book about Marcus Hayes?"

"It's totally true," I said, feeling like, score one for the nephew but also like, you know, a bit of a schmuck.

"Isn't he a friend of yours?"

"That's right. He even lived with us for a while. In this house."

"No way," Noah said. "I mean, no way."

"Absolutely way," but I could see the kid thought like, whatever.

"Why don't you invite him over then? To shoot hoops?" Noah said.

"Maybe I will."

"Come on, then. Call him now."

And I thought, you twerp.

———

But the truth is, I was having a hard time getting hold of Marcus Hayes. That was one of my problems. His old coach at Texas, Todd Steuben, he was really the assistant but recruited Marcus out of Burleson . . . anyway, he left Texas and after a stint in the NBA took the job at UCLA. So Marcus spent his summers working out at Pauley Pavilion. A lot of ex-Bruins were in the League, a couple of All-Stars, the competition was high-level, guys like Taylor Johns and Demme Franklin, plus all the young guns coming up who wanted to prove themselves against NBA talent. So at the end of August I put the wet heat of Austin behind me for a couple of days and flew to LAX, where it was just as bad.

Getting in touch with Marcus involved negotiating with middlemen, a lot of people whose job it was to run obstruction. I called his agent, Sheldon Fitch, and left a message with his assistant. I called Ted Myers, the Nike rep, with whom I'd always had a human relationship. But he was on vacation in Hawaii. And so it went.

The scrimmages at Pauley were closed to the media, but sometimes if you play it like an ordinary civilian, a dad or a janitor, you can just walk in. Coaches aren't allowed on court with the players until the practice season officially starts at the end of September, so there's this unofficial quality to the summer workouts that makes them hard to police. I put on shorts and high-tops and my Burleson varsity shirt, which was one thousand washes and twenty years old, and nobody stopped me. A fat, six-three thirty-five-year-old guy is probably just an ex-player, even if he looks like me.

Pauley's a nice arena, you realize when they're empty just how spacious these places are. Like airport hangars. There were guys playing on the main court and pockets of guys warming up on some of the side baskets. But people also lined the sidelines, watching.

Marcus Hayes wore compression sleeves on his legs. He had long gray shorts and a gray Longhorns T-shirt that hung over his waist so you couldn't see his stomach. Also, he'd let his hair grow and looked a bit like one of those dudes you see in the park shaking out the kinks, talking trash. Because that's what he did, pounding the ball, making guys wait while he dribbled up court. I guess he was still getting into shape, and because Marcus was Marcus, they let him play his way in. Which doesn't mean he wasn't under attack. When you're Marcus Hayes everybody wants to say they did this or that, especially these college kids, where maybe it's their first real contact with royalty, where afterward they can brag, I blocked Marcus Hayes.

In fact, that's what I saw. Marcus came off a screen at the top of the key and drove hard to the hole. But when he planted, something was missing. His leg didn't buckle exactly, but the thing that's supposed to happen, where he's suddenly at the rim, didn't happen. So when he laid the ball in, some college kid, a light-skinned dude, maybe six nine, pinned it against the glass and started whooping.

Marcus said, "Count it," and the kid said, "What do you mean," and Marcus said, "Goal tend," and because he was Marcus Hayes, the score was now whatever it was, six–five. They were playing by ones and twos.

"Aw, c'mon man," the kid said and kept talking about it all the way down court. Marcus was guarding him but got stuck on a back screen, which nobody called out. Somebody tossed the ball at the rim and the kid was there to throw it down. He sort of bounced into the air and then kept bouncing after he landed. "That's how we do," he said. He was having a good time. "That's how we do."

Somebody told him, "Just shut up," and Marcus said, "Give me the ball."

I knew the kid; his name was Jabari Moore, he was a prospect, if he filled out. In college you can get by on talent, but he had an NBA body, and if he put in the work, the scouting report said, he might turn himself into a useful energy guy off the bench. If he learned to shoot, he could be something more, maybe a 3 and D guy, a third or fourth option on a good team. That can make a nice career for you, if you put in the work, and you're willing to accept it, but he was at the stage where he really didn't understand how severely limited his talents were.

So Marcus said, give me the ball, and had to pound and spin his way up court because Jabari kept hounding him. Marcus used his ass to keep the kid at bay, he wasn't quick enough anymore just to blow by. Just after half-court, he curled off a high screen and took two steps, with the kid on his hip, and fired from twenty-five feet and knocked it down.

"Eight–six," he said. "Keep talking."

After that he hit two more three-pointers. I don't think either of them touched rim. Ten–six, twelve–seven, game over. But it was hard work, and Jabari was just a dumb . . . I mean, it shouldn't have been so hard.

Then somebody said, "Excuse me, you can't film in here. You need to give me your phone."

"What are you talking about?"

I had my phone out, set on video, holding it out like I was trying to see the screen, in the soft atmospheric light that filters down from the complicated roof of the windowless arena.

"Sir," he said. The kid was just some college kid, working a summer job. "You need to give me your phone. Don't make me be like an asshole about it. I don't want to have to call security."

"I thought *you* were security."

"Come on, man. Look."

"This is a public university. My tax dollars paid for this building." Which totally wasn't true, I never paid taxes in California. Sometimes you say this stuff because it seems like the kind of stuff you should say. It's stupid, and you feel stupid. You feel like, everything would turn out better if you treated this like a human interaction. So I said, "Marcus Hayes is an old friend of mine. I'm a writer, he wants me to write a book about his comeback. Go ask him."

But it didn't matter because by that point security had come. One of those fat-nosed white guys, where his face is like any other muscle, almost expressionless. Suddenly I called out, "Marcus, Marcus, it's me, Brian Blum. Hey Marcus," and for a second the ball stopped bouncing and from a distance of thirty feet the guys on court stood around to see what was going on. It's hard to tell but I think Marcus recognized me, he looked at me with a certain detached amusement. These are the things you're willing to let other people do for you, if you're in his position.

"Marcus," I said, "It's me," while the guy took my arm and I shook it off but walked out anyway into the corridors, past the weight rooms and the ticket concourse. There was construction going on outside, which was maybe why they let me through in the first place.

I was staying at the Marriott in Pasadena—that's where the magazine always puts me up. Hotel life depresses me, just the time you waste thinking, should I go out and see something, or should I stick around the hotel. It saps your energy, which includes the energy to get the hell out. But there's nothing to see in Pasadena anyway. The Rose Bowl. Also, my platinum status gave me access to the lounge, free drinks, fruit slices, muffins, bags of popcorn, so that's where I spent most of the afternoon.

At one point, Fred Rotha stopped by to say hello. He's another one of those NBA reporters who actually lives in LA but takes pity on out-of-towners.

"Did you make it into Pauley? Did you see anything?"

So I showed him my phone. Even if you magnified the image, Marcus Hayes looked like everybody else. When his jump shots fell, the net seemed to blur and swallow, but it was hard to tell if the ball went in.

"What am I supposed to do with that?" he asked me. Fred had a piece to file on "the comeback" but all he had was a bench guy for the Bruins saying, "He looks sharp. I just can't believe I'm playing against him."

I liked Fred. Everybody did. Even in the hotel lounge in Pasadena he wore his dad's tweed jacket and a totally generic blue tie. Fred got paid two hundred thousand a year. Everybody read him, including front office guys. If it wasn't the NBA he'd be covering the White House for CNN. But when success happens to you, you've got to maintain some kind of act that is different from that success. Because you don't want to be the guy acting like two hundred thousand a year. So Fred played up the old beat reporter thing, which I basically respected him for—the spiral notebook, the chewed-up pencil, cab receipts coming out of his pockets.

"I tried to squirrel my way into Pauley but they wouldn't let me in."

"That's because they recognized you," I said.

"So what did you see?" He ignored the implication. "How does he look?"

Something told me I should keep my powder dry on all this, because if you're writing a book about Marcus Hayes, you need every scoop you can get. But I like to talk.

"He looked heavy, he looked old. What you see in that video is after he got blocked by Jabari Moore. He tried to plant on a layup and nothing happened. It's like he was jumping on sand."

Fred looked at my phone again, I replayed the clip.

"All those shots went in?" I nodded my head. "At least he can shoot. That takes legs, too."

"It looks different to me, his release, the whole thing. He used to get up on his jump shot, too. But now it's more like a quick-trigger. Jabari is long but he doesn't know how to fight through picks."

Fred kept tapping the screen, freezing each frame, to see what was going on. Part of what he's known for is real-time analysis. But he didn't say anything and eventually passed me the phone again.

"So where are you with Marcus Hayes?" I asked. This is how we talked to each other, this is the language. Like, everybody has this complicated private relation to these people, which we have to digest and eventually make sense of. "What's the piece about?"

Fred had been looking at all the players under contract, who the

Sonics were taking to Austin. Last year they finished 36 and 46, which was a big step up on the previous season, mostly because of Jean Mmeremikwu. He had different nicknames because his last name was hard to pronounce, and his first name was French, so Americans either got it wrong or sounded stupid saying it. Fred made a point of calling him Mmeremikwu, like, what's your problem, it's not a big deal. But people also called him Mickey. His father was Nigerian but he grew up in Marseille and only started playing basketball when he was fifteen. His real love was soccer, that's the kind of piece people wrote about him. He was six ten with a seven-five wingspan and could go baseline to baseline in two dribbles.

"What really worries me," Fred said, "is Marcus going up against that guy in practice every day. Mmeremikwu's a killer, he's going to run him off the court. If there's a power struggle in the team, and there's *going* to be a power struggle, I don't see how Marcus can keep up with him. He just won't have the energy."

"Is that what you're going to write?"

"More or less. But I wanted to see him play first."

The lounges in these hotels always pipe in soft jazz and easy-listening pop. There are heavy-leaved plants in large pots that have to be watered daily and give off a faint scent of spritz. The upholstery is totally sound-absorbent. That's the atmosphere in which you conduct these conversations.

Fred said to me, "You look a little beat."

"I flew in yesterday. I've been running around, trying to get people to answer my calls. My publisher needs Marcus to sign one of these access agreements for the authorized biography. Blah blah blah. They're totally meaningless, but that's what they want. If he changes his mind, he can change his mind, and there's nothing anybody can do. But the whole book was Marcus's idea in the first place, that's what I told the publishers. So they want proof."

"Congratulations, by the way. I've been meaning to write you."

"Yeah, well. I don't know."

Sometimes almost in spite of these collegial relationships, where what you share is a nerd interest in unimportant facts, something human passes or gets communicated. "What's up?" he said.

"Don't you ever get sick of playing handmaiden to these people?"

"What do you mean?"

"They put balls in hoops, that's what they do. But we chase them around the country for eight months a year trying to persuade our readers that it matters."

"I know what you mean. I miss my kid."

"How old is he now?"

"Three next month."

"One of my nephews is three," I said, but that wasn't really an equivalent response. "None of this would bother me if we actually got to write what we think about these people, but we're basically in the PR business."

"I hate to tell you but I write what I think. This is the dumb stuff I think about. I'd rather cover these guys than Congress. At least these guys are good at what they do."

"Maybe," I said.

That night I got a call from Joe Hahn, Marcus's lawyer, who told me to stop by the house on my way to the airport in the morning. My flight was at noon. I'll give you breakfast, he told me. What do you like? Pancakes, oatmeal, egg-white omelets? I've got a personal chef these days, my wife tells me I need to lose twenty pounds, but you can eat what you want. Joe's accent was still the accent he grew up with, in Saginaw, which is one of those cities where the government is starting to tear stuff down. Just because nobody wants to live there. Anyway, that's what he sounded like, pure Michigan, so when he talked about egg-white omelets it was hard to tell who he was making fun of. Me or this life he led. I said, toast is fine.

I can do toast myself.

He lived on Foothill Road, between Santa Monica and Sunset, in a modest six-thousand-square-foot ten-million-dollar house that looked like a Ramada Inn. The street was lined with palm trees, the grass had been recently crew cut, the hedges were shaped like fresh pears. When I rang the doorbell I could hear the clanging echoing through marble halls—it was nine o'clock in the morning, and the smell of freshly watered lawn rose in the air like mist from a perfume bottle. Already I could feel the heat of the day in my armpits. I felt like the kind of guy who gets turned away by the guy making ten bucks an hour to turn such people away.

Actually, his teenage daughter opened the door. The air tasted filtered and the kid said, "Hello? Can I help you?" She had been well brought up.

"Is your dad around? I think he's expecting me," and a voice from the back called out, "Kimmy? Who's there? Is that Brian? Tell him to come in," and she said, "Please, follow me."

"Did you have a good summer?" I asked her.

"Yes, thank you."

"Shouldn't you be at school?"

"It's Saturday!"

"That's no excuse."

"It's not an excuse, it's a reason."

There was just a little eye contact, before her hair fell across her face. Then she handed me over and disappeared wherever in a house like that kids go.

Joe's office was really the kitchen table. He even had a phone on it, and part of it was covered in papers. He said, "We've got seventeen rooms in this house, and it doesn't matter, I always end up here. It drives my wife crazy, she says there's nowhere to eat, so I said, that's a fixable problem. Just get a bigger table, so that's what we did."

Behind him a wall of glass exposed the swimming pool, which was designed to look like it had been carved out of natural rock. Ferns and ivy overflowed into the water, and to walk dry-footed across the lawn a sort of trickle of paving stones had been set irregularly into the grass. You had to look closely through the tropical border to see the high metal fence.

I said, "Where is she?"

"Who?"

"Your wife."

"On Saturday mornings she sings in this Anglican choir. It's like a cult, but it makes her happy." Then he said, "Can I get you something to drink? I make my own coffee. It's better than the coffee other people make."

"First you can tell me what the hell is going on," I said. "Does he want me to write this book or not?"

"Let's have coffee and we can talk about it."

"I don't want coffee, I have a plane to catch. The coffee at the Marriott is fine with me. I want a signature on a piece of paper."

"I thought your flight was at twelve."

"It is."

"So sit down and chill the fuck out and let me make you a cup of coffee."

And that's what he did. It was a whole production, I don't want to go into detail. He made me sit through it because the machine was too loud to permit conversation. After it was over, in the fresh quiet, he handed me a small cup and waited for me to say something about it, so I said, "It tastes like coffee."

"You're a real charmer."

"Yesterday they kicked me out of Pauley when I tried to watch him practice."

"It's a closed session."

"He asked *me* to write this book. I flew down here, at some personal cost. Every time I go out of town, arrangements have to be made, about who looks after the kids . . ."

"What kids? You don't have any kids."

"I'm living with my sister, she's going through a divorce . . . I upend my whole life and move to Austin so I can write this book, and the publishers won't even pay me until I get some kind of assurance that Marcus is going to play along."

"I'm sorry to hear about your sister," he said. The madder I got, the quieter he became.

"Marcus saw me at the gym, he let security take me away."

"Let's not worry about what Marcus did or didn't see or do. He's very focused right now on what he needs to be doing, which is getting himself ready for the season."

"You forget, I've known him a lot longer than you have."

"I don't think making this personal like that is going to help anybody."

"Then why did he ask me to write the book?"

For a second, Joe looked at me, he didn't say anything. Then he said, "He wants you to do it but he wants to make sure you're going to do it right."

"What does that mean?"

Then Kimmy came into the kitchen and opened the fridge, like she was sneaking around.

"What are you eating?" Joe called out.

"I'm not eating, I'm just looking."

"You just had breakfast. Have a piece of fruit."

"I'm not hungry for fruit."

"Have an apple."

"I can't eat apples." And she grinned to show her braces.

"I'll cut it up for you."

"Dad," she said and closed the fridge and walked out.

"How old's your daughter?" I asked.

"I'm not talking about her."

So we sat in silence for a minute. He looked at the papers on his desk, he had something to occupy him. I mean, he actually started working or whatever it is that lawyers do. After a while, you think, this is stupid, I'm not going to play these games. So you always lose.

"Why'd he ask me to write the book if he didn't want it to be personal?"

"There's personal and there's personal."

"So what does Marcus want?"

"The right kind."

"I don't know what that is."

"Yes, you do. And if you don't . . ."

"What?"

And he stopped what he was doing and looked up. "Come on, Brian. This is a beautiful story, don't make it complicated. A kid like Marcus Hayes, who grew up the way Marcus grew up . . . single mother, there are a lot of different men around, not all of them nice. In the end he gets taken in by another family, a nice white middle-class family, so he can finish high school. I don't need to tell you any of this. Anyway, he makes it to the NBA, he wins titles, he wins MVPs, he makes a ton of money and retires. And now he wants to come back for one more run, so he can bring NBA basketball to his hometown."

"I don't understand why he wants to come back."

"I just told you."

"I don't understand why he quit in the first place."

"Brian," Joe said. "Is what I just described not an accurate description of events?"

"It's fine. So you write the book."

"He asked you. For what it's worth, I advised against it. I said, Brian Blum is one of those reporters who thinks the real story is always something unpleasant."

"You're talking about the gambling piece again. Pat McConaughey."

"I'm making a general observation."

I looked at my watch, I had a plane to catch. But time never passes the way you want it to . . . there was no great urgency. It was half an hour to the airport from Beverly Hills and only nine o'clock. Joe saw me look and said, "There's plenty of time."

"So what happens now?"

"Are you going to write something about the workouts at Pauley?"

"I was there for like five minutes before they kicked me out."

"Are you going to write something?"

"I might."

"We look forward to reading it," he said and walked me to the door.

14

I didn't see as much of Marcus junior year, because Caukwell promoted him to varsity. On Friday nights, the JV game tipped off right after class; it was really just the warm-up act. We finished around six, and most of the guys showered and went home. But I hung around the gym afterward because I'd started writing a sports column for the school newspaper. So I watched him play like everybody else, from the bleachers.

Marcus had a breakout season and Burleson spent most of it in first place. Then, just before the playoffs, Isaac Brown quit the team and transferred to McCallum. I mean, he actually left the school because of Marcus, who just abused him in practice. Caukwell tried to put a stop to it, he tried to contain it. In scrimmages, he made them play together. But what Marcus did, since he often had the ball, was drive deep into the lane and then suddenly whip a pass to Isaac under the basket. That was Isaac's weak spot, he had hard hands. Marcus didn't even have to say anything when the ball bounced out, he just ran back on D. But the next time down he'd do the same thing again.

It got to the point where Isaac wouldn't even get in rebounding position, because he didn't want to drop another pass. I heard all this from Caukwell years later; he thought it was funny. Most coaches have a soft spot for guys who are totally ruthless. Especially ex-football types. But at the time it must have been a real problem, Isaac was his second-best player.

Various things were going on in Marcus's home life. The reason Selena moved from Dallas in the first place is that she broke up with her married lover, who was a patient-care technician at Baylor. That's why she ended up at Seton Medical, to make a clean break. But later that year, over the summer, she moved back to Dallas and eventually started living with the guy, who had gotten a divorce. Who knows when they actually resumed their relationship, maybe they never completely fell out of touch. Selena needed and received a lot of male attention. Tony, Harvey's dad, was basically living with her at the time. He also had a new baby with his former wife and a house in Taylor for which he still made mortgage payments.

But Marcus never talked to me about all this.

A few weeks before the playoffs started, we biked over to Eastwoods and Harvey tagged along. Sometimes he liked to stand on the sidelines and comment on the games, like he was Brent Musburger. "What a rebound by Marcus Hayes! Flying through the air! Head and shoulders above the crowd!" Loud enough so everyone could hear.

Afterward, when we got on our bikes again, Marcus said to him, "Why are you such a loser?"

And Harvey said, "What are you talking about?"

"You let all those people laugh at you."

"They were just laughing."

"Because they're thinking, what a loser."

"You know what, I don't even care what people are laughing at."

"That's good, because it's you."

"Whatever."

On the way home, we saw a piece of garden hose lying in the road. Then we realized it was a rattlesnake. Harvey got off his bike and picked it up—he held it limply in his hand, because it was dead.

Marcus said, "You crazy, man. You one crazy kid."

"It was obviously dead."

"Maybe it's just asleep."

And Harvey put his knuckle to the snake's head, and said, "Wakey, wakey!"

"You're crazy," Marcus said again.

"Do you want to touch it?" Harvey said.

"No way."

"Come on, touch it. It's like, super dry." He stroked its back like he was stroking fur. "It's kind of cool."

"No, thank you."

"What are you going to do with it?" I asked.

"Give it to my stepmom. For a necklace."

And he hung it around his neck. It was only four or five feet long, just a baby rattler, and you could see where it got run over by a car. Part of the middle was squished flat.

"For real?" Marcus said; he was laughing. He actually had a nice laugh, totally kid-like and almost silent.

"No, dipshit," Harvey said and threw it down the curbside drain. We went as far as Red River in convoy, mostly on neighborhood streets, then I headed north alone and they crossed under the highway to the east side. I watched them bike off together.

Shortly after that Harvey and his dad moved out, back to Taylor, where Tony was trying to patch things up with his wife. I didn't see him again.

Burleson faced Lockhart at home in the first round of the playoffs, and Caukwell let me into the locker room before tip-off — so I could write about the game.

There was a shower area, with three or four stalls, and an open doorway to the main room, which had two tiers of rusty gray lockers running along the walls. The atmosphere was, like, urinal and humid. Even the wooden benches felt slick to touch. I noticed a smear of some white pasty substance on the floor tiles. Marcus was actually in one of the stalls, taking a shower, and when he came out again and put a towel around his waist, you could see how skinny and muscular he had become.

"What the hell's that?" I said, pointing at the mess.

"I threw up."

"I mean, what *is* it?"

"Bounty. I didn't like my energy flow so I had a couple candy bars. Don't write about this," he said.

But when the game started, Marcus seemed fine. Lockhart had this short barrel-chested point guard, who was strong but not that quick. John Linehan just hounded him up court, so that the Lockhart kid had to use his butt to keep him off the ball, and constantly shift direction, like a sailboat tacking against the wind. Marcus played two guard for us. At one point in the second quarter he slipped his man and timed it so that just as the barrel-chested kid reversed field Marcus picked his dribble off the bounce and strolled in for a dunk. All on his lonesome; nobody came near him. He cupped the ball against his wrist and swung his arm midair from his hip to over his head. For some reason they call this rocking the cradle. Everybody went nuts.

After that Lockhart advanced the ball by committee. It was a three-man job, and their bigs had to come back to set screens.

We were up nine at the half. Marcus had seventeen points and something like eight rebounds. He picked up a lot of defensive boards by swooping in after the shot and jumping over people—he liked to keep the ball in his hands and afterward push the pace. Even as he caught the ball, his body was turning . . . and midway through the third, he landed hard on nothing and ended up in a heap like the witch in *The Wizard of Oz.* Caukwell ran out to help him off the court, but Marcus pushed him away and limped back to the bench himself. Then he sat for the next few minutes. At the end of the third, our lead was down to two, and Marcus used the break to run up and down the sideline, warming up. For some reason, Caukwell let him back in the game. He didn't think you could run on a broken foot.

And when Marcus walked out again to start the fourth, everybody stood up, three or four hundred kids . . . who roamed the hallways with him and sat through class together, who wasted their lunch hours in the same cafeteria . . . rose to their feet and began to stamp the bleachers. Later, Marcus got used to this kind of thing. Maybe it's no big deal, when you've had the Boston Garden call your name in a single voice, to feel the heat of admiration fill Weizenkamper Gym at Burleson High. But Boston hadn't happened yet, and Marcus was just a sixteen-year-old kid. He didn't look up or even react, but there must have been a certain amount of internalization going on. All right, all right, you're getting there. That view you have of yourself, which you've been clinging to, maybe isn't total self-delusion.

He couldn't really run and let Linehan bring the ball up; mostly he hung around the three-point line, looking for kick-outs. The first time he caught the ball, he head-faked and planted (I can't imagine how much that hurt), took two hard dribbles and knocked down a fifteen-footer. Which kept the defense honest; I don't think he drove again. But his presence was enough, and we hung on. Triesman-Smith had a hell of a game, too. After the final whistle, Marcus started hopping to the bench, and somebody had to lend him a shoulder so he could make it to the locker room. Then Caukwell personally drove him to the ER, with Selena in the front seat and Marcus stretched out by himself in the back.

The X-rays showed a broken metatarsal, and they put him in a cast—it's not the kind of thing you operate on. But his season was over, and two days later Burleson lost to LBJ, with Marcus sitting big-white-footed on the bench.

15

Even after the season finished, I used to see Caukwell because he taught Health and Driver's Ed. One day after class he asked me to wait for him, and kids were like, ooh, Brian's in trouble, what did Brian do now. Brian didn't do nothing, Caukwell said. Run along and mind your own business. I just need to ask him a question.

You didn't want to mess with Caukwell, which is why, even when he was teaching a class of thirty bored kids, he never raised his voice or even spoke all that clearly, but just kind of mumbled and expected everybody to pay super-close attention.

"Walk with me," he said.

The lunchtime rush was on, but he took the first exit into the outdoor air—onto a pebbled concrete patio behind the school, with a few picnic tables where kids could eat their packed lunches.

Caukwell sat down and put his Health textbook and leather briefcase on the metal picnic table. If the breeze picked up you could see it in the little shadows of the leaves, and then feel it on your face.

"How's Betsy doing?" he said.

My sister had graduated the year before. "She's all right. She's at Oberlin now. I think she's having a good time. When she calls she talks to my mom. Nobody tells me anything."

"Worst driver I ever taught," he said. "Bar none."

"She loves driving."

"That's the problem." And he didn't say anything for a while. I sat down and waited. You could hear the kids in the hallways on the way to lunch; some of them came outside, saw Coach Caukwell and kept going toward the football field.

"I'm asking because I thought you might have a spare room," he said eventually. "Marcus's mom is moving back to Dallas this summer. But he wants to finish his education here."

"I don't understand."

"I thought maybe he could bunk with you."

"Oh."

"You guys are friends, right? I thought you were tight."

"We hang out sometimes. I mean, sure."

"Maybe you could talk to your dad about it."

"Did Marcus—I mean, did he ask . . .?"

"I'm just trying to work something out. His situation is a little up in the air right now. Talk to your dad. And your mom. Your parents are people I don't need to worry about, I know that." He wanted to say something else, but didn't. "All right, Brian," he said. "Go get some lunch." But then when I was walking away, he said, "Tell your dad to call me, if he wants to talk it over."

The first thing I thought, when I got back into the air-conditioning, was like, whatever . . . this is kind of funny, because I was in school mode, where everything is kind of funny, and about to have lunch with Mike Inchman and Max and Andy and Jim DeKalb (Frank was already at Swarthmore). I had to stop by my locker, and they were sitting down already when I got to the cafeteria, at the same blue table we always sat at, by the window overlooking the scenic parking lot. You'll never guess what Caukwell just said to me, this phrase kept running through my head. So when I actually saw them, all I had to do was open my mouth. "You'll never guess . . . he wants Marcus Hayes to move in with me next year. He can sleep in Betsy's room, that's what he said," and I looked across the cafeteria and saw Marcus with Breon and Triesman-Smith, the other black kids on the team, and for some reason the fact of it suddenly hit me. Marcus was still on crutches, which he rested against an empty chair.

But I asked my dad anyway when I got home—half-expecting, even hoping he would say, forget about it, there's no way. But he took it as a realistic proposition.

"We can make a real difference in this kid's life," he said. And for some reason I felt like, what about me. I mean, like other people were taking over my friendship with Marcus, and leaving me out.

"That's so patronizing," I told him.

After school, I always ate a pair of Eggo waffles and watched *The Bob Newhart Show*, so this conversation was taking place against the background noise of the television and the whole seventies stage-set of their sitcom apartment.

"He hasn't had the advantages you've had."

Dad was staring at the TV, too.

"What advantages? I spend the whole time chasing balls for him."

"I don't think you're thinking about this seriously." Then he sat down with me and watched the show. I thought it might blow over unless I pushed it but then at dinner Dad brought it up again.

Mom said, "What do you think, Brian? Is this something you want?"

I realize that my mother hasn't played a big role in this story so far and that's not because I didn't love her. She was my mom, you can't describe your mom. (Her name was Eileen.) She worked in the vice president's office at the University of Texas. Her job title was something like, senior administrative associate.

"I don't know, Mom. It's just something Coach Caukwell asked me to ask you about."

"But is it something you want? It's a big deal, having a strange kid in the house, looking after him, being responsible for him."

"He's not a strange kid, he's my friend."

And my dad chipped in, "If Brian wants to help out a friend, I don't think we should discourage him."

A few days later, Marcus came out of the cast and we started shooting hoops again before class. One morning I asked him, "Coach Caukwell said you're moving to Dallas?"

"Well, my mom is."

"He said, maybe you'd want to live with us."

It was easy for Marcus not to talk because all the time we were talking we were also shooting basketballs, concentrating on that, chasing them down, while the echo of the balls was like a soundtrack or background music that meant nobody had to say anything.

"Where would I sleep?" he said eventually.

"In Betsy's old room. Except maybe when she came back for Christmas, or stuff like that."

"I guess at Christmas I'll stay with my mom."

And that was that. At this point the adults took over. Caukwell must have contacted Selena, who stopped by our house twice that summer. Once to just like check it over while the arrangements were being made. And once to deliver her son unto us and say goodbye.

She came on a Saturday morning, just after breakfast, but dressed to the nines, like she wanted to make an impression. Red high heels, a slinky summer dress, bright makeup, heavy earrings. She could hardly move in the shoes and the dress though at the same time, like, you could see her moving.

My mom had been cutting bamboo, which sprouts like grass in Austin backyards. She liked to do the yardwork early, before the sunshine went vertical and the heat of the day set in.

So when Selena clicked up the porch steps and rang the bell, Mom was just sitting down to a second cup of coffee and a piece of toast, in Dad's old Fordham T-shirt, with her hair sticking to her neck and forehead. She had totally forgotten that this thing was happening this morning. I think she thought, who the hell is this, and said, "Can I help you?" when she opened the door.

"I'm Marcus's mother," Selena said. "I just come to introduce myself."

I was sitting in the kitchen and could see them through the arch to the living room, which was also the front room, where the TV was. Our house isn't very large. When Selena walked in you could smell her perfume.

"Hi, Brian," she said. "It's nice to see you again." And maybe it was a sign of her nervousness that she reached out and shook my hand.

That was the first visit; I don't remember much else about it. "I really just come to say how grateful we are." That's the kind of thing she said, and the kind of thing we said was, "It's just nice for Brian to have a friend around, now Betsy's gone." And my mom showed Selena Betsy's room, like a real estate agent. "This is where Marcus will sleep. He'll have to share the bathroom," and everybody laughed, and Selena said, "That's all right, he's used to having woman's things around," and we all laughed again, like sitcom people.

At one point she turned to my dad, maybe because she figured, he must be the breadwinner. She said, "I don't have much I can give you."

"For what?" he said.

"For room and board . . ."

My dad is good at these interactions, maybe it's one of those things you learn by not being a great success. "Please," he said. "Let's not hear any more about that, okay? Marcus is welcome here."

After she was gone, my mom said, "I don't understand that woman." She could form sudden and passionate judgments and aversions. "I just don't understand her. Leaving her son for another woman to look after him."

"Mom, he's seventeen. I don't know how much looking after he needs."

But you couldn't talk to her. "Parading herself like that. Who's she trying to impress?"

It didn't occur to me that she felt threatened, or ashamed, in her dirty T-shirt and uncombed hair.

"She impressed me plenty," Dad said.

The next time Selena stopped by the house was midsummer. School was out; she was in the middle of packing up their apartment.

Marcus carried a suitcase up the steps, still limping. His foot some-times took a while to warm up. "Give me that," I said and dragged it to Betsy's room. (She was staying with a friend in Bloomington and working for Habitat for Humanity. When she came home, Marcus moved in temporarily with me, until the semester started and she moved back to Ohio.) He didn't know whether to follow or not. Everybody was just hanging around the kitchen.

Mom had made iced tea and a tray of blondies. "Why don't we all sit down and cool down," she said, having dressed up herself for the occasion. I mean, she actually wore a dress. With her red Irish hair, which she couldn't keep straight, she sometimes looked like something she wasn't, relaxed.

Selena wore adidas track-suit pants and a gym-rat tank top, so you could see the straps of her bra, unless she adjusted her shirt, which she kept doing. She said, "I still got a lot to do."

"Give yourself a break." My dad picked up a blondie. "Moving is like a marathon, you need to keep eating and drinking, you need to keep your energy levels up."

"I really gotta go."

Marcus wore jeans and his Members Only jacket, even though it was ninety-eight degrees outside. I guess when you're packing you just kind of put stuff on. Selena pulled at his sleeve and he let her, like a boy and a girl at a dance, where he doesn't like dancing and she's trying to get him on the floor.

"Let's not make this a big deal," she said. They were talking only to each other.

"It's no deal."

"I'll come back in a couple weeks, see how you're doing."

"I'll be fine."

"And if you want to call me, you call me. That's what I got you the calling card for."

"I got it."

"When we get settled you can come for the weekend. I'll send you the bus money."

"Okay."

"Anytime you want."

"Okay."

"Watch out for that foot. You don't want to overdo it."

"Mom."

"Listen to me. I'm a nurse. This is what I do."

"Okay."

"Okay okay?" and she bent down to look up at him. "Okay."

My dad finally cut in. "We're all just standing around here, let's sit down," and Selena said, "I really gotta go, no point dragging this out," and she kissed Marcus on top of his head (after pulling him by the neck with two hands so she could reach him) and then had to walk the length of the hall to get out the door.

My mother followed her out.

"Good luck," she called through the screen door, as Selena got in her car. Then my mom turned around and said, "That was a dumb thing to say, I don't know why I said that." She looked at Marcus. "Do you want to unpack? We can help you settle in and then have some lunch."

"Maybe," I said, "we should just go to the park and shoot around."

So that's what we did.

16

On the flight from LA I wrote a first draft of the piece:

For Jabari Moore, it started out as one of the best days of his life.
You show up at Pauley for a summer workout, and guess who's
warming up, Marcus Hayes. You're a nineteen-year-old kid, and
you don't know what's what. You want to guard Marcus, you want
to be able to tell people afterward that you guarded Marcus Hayes,
that you held your own. You want to call your mom. And the first
time down-court, you see him come off a high screen and plow
into the lane. You slip your man and meet him at the rim, and when
the shot goes up, you pin it against the glass. Goal tending, Marcus
says, and because he's Marcus Hayes that's what it is. But now
you've got his attention. You want to show him what you can do.
So when he picks you up at half-court, nobody calls out the back
screen, and you cut hard and the ball is where you need it to be,
and the next thing you know, you're hanging on the rim. It's going
to be the best day of your life.

But it's like the man said in *Blazing Saddles*, the old Mel Brooks'
movie—if you shoot him, you'll just make him mad. Marcus calls
for the ball, and he calls for you, and dribbles slowly up court. Just
to show he doesn't have to break sweat, he pulls up from twenty-
five feet and the shot touches nothing but net. And then the next
time down he does it again. And the next time down he does it
again. Welcome to the big time, kid. Now get off the court. Game
over. Who's got next?

——

When I pulled my wheelie suitcase up the porch steps it was six o'clock in the late summer afternoon and Dad and the boys were sitting on the couch and watching *Sesame Street*. Because of the angle of the sunshine you had to close the curtains over the side window, otherwise you couldn't see the screen. They were sitting in semi-darkness.

I was entering again the cocoon, airless, lightless, where real life happens and things matter. The contrast struck me, because what I was doing in LA was messing around with people who play games.

Later Betsy came home and roped me into making dinner. I have a limited repertoire but it's mostly kid friendly. Hot dogs and beans, which my dad used to make; meatloaf . . . spaghetti with tomato sauce . . . I cooked spaghetti. After the kids went to bed, my sister and I sat on the porch while she smoked a cigarette and I drank a beer. My dad was inside, watching TV. You could hear the television from the porch. He didn't like to see Betsy smoke, it upset him, otherwise he might have sat with us. But he also basically preferred the television—the Astros were playing.

"Do you feel like maybe we haven't exactly grown up yet?" I said to Betsy.

"This for me is a nice break. I'm not such a fan of growing up anyway. What's wrong?" she said, after a while.

"Nothing. I found the whole experience in LA . . . I snuck into the gym where he was working out and Marcus watched the security people take me away. He didn't say anything, he just watched."

"He's not the kid who slept in my bed anymore."

"I thought, what am I doing, why am I chasing around after this guy?"

"Because you're a sportswriter."

At night, to save on electricity bills, Betsy let the air-conditioning go off, and the whole atmosphere changed. The AC unit (a big brown metal box) sat in a pile of leaves between the house and garage, about five feet below us. It was like turning off a car, the engine shuddered and went quiet.

"I feel subservient."

"Look at you, what are you talking about." There was a Frisbee on the porch she used as an ashtray; I could see her stubbing out the cigarette. "Magazines fly you out to LA, they put you up at a fancy hotel, thousands of people read what you write. When I tell people we're related, they say, I know that guy, I've seen him on TV. My big-shot brother."

"Yeah, well. That's not what it feels like."

"Whereas I come home and argue about whether the broccoli touched the tomato sauce. I haven't had a date in ten years. I wouldn't know what to do."

"Nor me," I said.

Afterward, Betsy walked down the steps and emptied the Frisbee on the asphalt by the curb. All of this was part of her ritual.

Dad was asleep on the couch when we came in; Betsy turned off the television. "Should we wake him up?"

"Come on, Dad. Let's go to bed."

"All right, all right."

Everybody had lights out by ten o'clock. Except me—it was like being a teenager again, where you live in the small hours, because when people are asleep they leave you alone. Anyway, I was still on LA time; my dad and I shared a room, I couldn't even read at night without keeping him awake. So I sat on the couch with the TV on mute and watched SportsCenter roll over into the night. Before going to bed, I sent the piece to Joe Hahn.

A few days later I got in touch with Quinn—I didn't even know her last name. But the semester had started; you can find these things out. She played on the volleyball team, which made her easy to track. There's a roster page on the website, you can click on her name, Quinn Riley, and look up her bio and stats. Highland Park High School in Dallas . . . rated seventh on PrepVolleyball's top-ten senior aces . . . led the Lady Longhorns with 204 kills last season. That kind of thing.

To sit at the computer in a dark house where your sister, father, and two nephews are already sleeping, clicking on various links, involved a deep dive into male shame, where going deeper was also an attempt to overcome it, like one of those dark underwater tunnels or caves you can only get through by holding your breath. The first email I drafted said, *I see from your volleyball page that your birthday is coming up, you're about to turn legal. Can I buy you a drink?* But this struck me as creepy so I deleted it. In the end I wrote, *Quinn, is this you? We met at the Palace on a weird night a few months ago, with Marcus Hayes. I've moved back to Austin but don't really know anybody anymore. So I thought I'd look you up. Let me know if you want to hang out.*

I closed my eyes and sent it.

Marcus had bought a house in Austin, in the Mount Bonnell area, one of those lakefront properties that seem to be computer-generated at the edge of the water. The *Statesman* described it as a Venetian villa modeled after the historic Grand Canal. J. P. moved in while Marcus was in LA—to oversee alterations. Who knows what two people are supposed to do in eleven thousand square feet, maybe avoid each other? But that's not quite fair, there were always people around. Lawyers, agents, shoe reps, guys like Jerry de Souza. J. P. also came with a large entourage. But you can't write about J. P., that's rule number one.

I don't really want to either. But I drove out to Mount Bonnell to check out the neighborhood and failed. Once you reach the island, which is what they call it, you have to pass security. In the middle of a country road, at the foot of a hill, with nothing visible in the distance or the immediate foreground aside from trees, there's a guy sitting in a security booth between a couple of gates. So I got out of the car and looked at the booth and got back in the car. If you really want to see the neighborhood you need to take a boat along the Colorado.

This is how I spent my time. Driving around, talking to people on the phone, checking Twitter. These days the NBA season, from a reporter's point of view, ends in mid-July after the Vegas summer league and begins again in late September with training camp and preseason. Just following social media is a thirty-hour-a-week job. I spent a lot of afternoons sitting on my computer in the kitchen and trying not to let the kid noise bother me.

Joe Hahn emailed to suggest some cuts. Basically, the first paragraph. He didn't want any reference to Jabari blocking Marcus's shot or cutting backdoor and dunking on him. So I wrote back: You understand these are things that happen all the time. There's no shame in getting back-screened at a pickup game in late August, when you're running with college kids who don't know what they're doing. Anyway, from what I know about Marcus, it's the kind of story he likes, since it involves cold-blooded payback. Look, Joe emailed, you asked me my opinion so I gave it to you. Cut the graph. We had a little back and forth. Is that what Marcus told you to tell me? Does this come from him? Marcus pays people like me to look out for his interests in ways that he does not want to bother with—he also expects people who benefit enormously from their association with him to understand what his interests are.

So I figured, let him stew for a while and didn't respond.

Fred Rotha broke a story—that free-agent Eddie Roundtree had signed with Austin. It was a win-now move. Eddie would turn thirty-three in December, and though big men like him, savvy, heavy-footed, strong as an ox, age pretty well, even the first year of the deal was over market price. The League had shifted away from guys like that. But Eddie used to play for Boston, and Rotha thought Marcus was repeating the mistakes that Jordan made in his second comeback, surrounding himself with former-glory yes men.

In other news, he added, tongue in cheek, Todd Steuben has resigned from UCLA to take a job with the Sonics under Coach Kaminski. Battle lines were already being drawn in the locker room, between the

Hayes camp and Mmeremikwu's guys. Fred wrote, this isn't a battle Marcus can win.

I also got in touch with Lamont, Coach Caukwell's nephew, who still lived in Austin and worked for ACC—the community college near House Park. We met in his office and walked along the side of the football field to the Tavern on North Lamar. House Park is where Burleson used to play; we could see it behind a chain-link fence, the green-green grass, carefully lined and numbered, stands rising up like the wings of a spaceship, floodlights at the corners. Lamont was on the football team, too. He said, "I loved basketball, but I was only really good at hitting people."

We sat at the bar, and he showed me pictures on his phone—two kids, a younger wife, and a ranch house in Round Rock. He was digging out a swimming pool in the backyard, putting in the work on weekends.

Eventually I said, "Marcus told me he gave your uncle some money. For a hip replacement. Do you know anything about that?"

"He had a hip replacement, but I didn't know about the money."

"Was anything going on between them? Marcus asked me not to write about him. He said Mel used to play the ponies."

"He liked to go out to Manor Downs. Sometimes he took me along, when I was a kid. But he usually made money, Mel knew what he was doing. Why are you asking me?"

There was a baseball game on TV, above the bar, and the sound of the ball game was part of all the other bar sounds. I had finished my beer but Lamont was nursing his. He had a long drive home through rush hour traffic though the longer he waited the shorter it got.

"Did they keep in touch?"

"Look, I don't know. Marcus Hayes is not a big part of my life, I got other people to worry about. A few years ago Uncle Mel invited him back to Burleson. And Marcus came, they named the gym after him. I went along to that; it was a nice day, he gave out a couple of scholarships. Some us went out afterward for pizza, we played a little pool, too. That's the last time I saw him, until the funeral."

"What do you think about Marcus Hayes?"

"What do you mean, what do I think?"

"You must have some kind of opinion about him."

"He's a good basketball player. But if you ask me, do I want to be like Marcus. No."

"What about in high school?"

"What about in high school?"

"I mean, what did you think of him then?"

"Look, Brian. In high school I was like, I just wanted to have a good time. I figured everybody grow up soon enough. And Marcus was like, he had a stick up his ass. I thought basketball was fun. I don't know what Marcus thought it was. But I was like, where do you think you're going, the NBA? Wake up. I guess he's awake now."

He finished his beer and put his wallet on the bar.

"I got this," I said. For some reason I didn't want him to leave. "What did you think about me? Do you remember?"

"Just what everybody thought."

"What's that?"

"That you was Marcus's whipping boy." But he said it like he was kidding around, he laid the accent on pretty thick.

Dad was asleep on the couch when I got home. Al and Betsy were already in their rooms. Sometimes she dozed getting Troy down and didn't bother getting up again. Or lay beside him reading on her phone. Anyway, I woke Dad up and pushed him off to bed, like a toy boat on a quiet lake, toward shore . . .

By ten o'clock I had the house to myself and sat computer-on-lap in front of *SportsCenter* (on mute). I made some notes about the conversation with Lamont, then rewrote the story about Marcus Hayes at Pauley the way Joe Hahn wanted me to write it, and sent it to Joe Hahn. Ten seconds later, an email came through . . . from Quinn. She said, *I remember you. You're the guy who doesn't like naked women. Why don't you come to my birthday party—every-body will have clothes on.* And she sent me the details: somebody's house on Nueces Street, behind the Drag, a few blocks from campus.

17

Since Mom worked at the university we had access to the same doctors and equipment and physical therapists that Longhorn athletes had access to. She must have added Marcus to our insurance, because he started going to the Whitworth Training Facility in Cooley Pavilion, on Red River and East 15th. Sometimes I rode along to keep him company.

The physical therapist was a woman named Megan Adez, whom my father referred to as the sexpot. Brown hair, brown eyes, she used to be a swimmer and still had big shoulders and highly developed muscle tone in her arms. Her baseline facial expression was a smile, like a dolphin. She also had a slight . . . not a lisp, but a softening of the sibilants, which made her seem more childish than she was. One of Marcus's exercises, when the cast came off, was to stand on a kind of rolling round-bottomed disk, on his injured foot, and try to balance. Later they upped the degree of difficulty, and Megan threw a medicine ball at his chest, which he had to catch. Physical therapy is very social and intimate; we used to tease him about Megan all the time. I think we all had a mild crush.

Part of the rehabilitation process was to engage in high-resistance, low-impact exercises, to strengthen the foot without putting it under unnecessary stress. This meant a lot of water work. There was a pool at the Whitworth, but we also had one right outside the house, where I still lifeguarded several times a week for teenage minimum wage.

Marcus didn't like swimming, but sometimes in the early morning before the shallow end filled up with kids we walked out barefoot across the road and through the park and past the playground to the pool. Then we jumped in, and Marcus made me climb on his back for the extra weight—so he could push hard off the injured foot through the heavy water up and down from one side of the pool to the other. I kept slipping off his wet skin, he grabbed me around the thigh and told me to hold on. Afterward there were scratch marks on my legs and his shoulders. When I got bored, I tried to pull him over into the water, but he was like a running back, impossible to bring down. "Come on, Brian," he said. "I mean, come *on*."

When my sister came back from Indiana, virtuous and annoying from spending part of her post-freshman summer building homes for the homeless of Monroe County, Marcus moved in with me. Her hands were chapped with hard labor, you could see the tan lines on her shoulders from her bra straps, because she often wore tank tops in those days. She was never particularly pretty but she was fun and healthy and at that time, at least, physically and socially confident, so it didn't really matter if she was pretty or not, she attracted male attention. And liked it, and kind of liked making fun of boys who showed her any sexual or romantic interest for being, like, weird.

It was also fraught with potential embarrassment for two teenage boys to share a room. My whole policy, when it came to embarrassment, was to expose myself as much as possible. So if I had a wet dream and needed to get up in the night to go to the bathroom, I made a joke about it. But Marcus really didn't want to talk about any of that stuff, he tried to blank it out. It didn't help that we had only one bathroom, and to get there, at least when Betsy was living with us, he had to walk past my bed. If I saw anything going on, I said something. He used to lie under the covers and wait for me to go first.

At the end of August, a few nights before she went back to school, Betsy cut his hair. She said, "You're looking scraggly." Marcus at that time wore a box top; it made him look taller. But one day he was complaining there weren't any barbershops in Hyde Park.

"What about Unique Boutique? It's only like five blocks away."

"They can't cut my hair."

"Why not? I'm pretty sure they have scissors or some kind of sharp implements."

"They can't cut my hair. That's like a—"

"That's like a what?"

"That's like a lady salon. Forget it. No way I let them cut my hair."

"I don't understand. You think women's hair is easier to cut? This is not something I've heard before."

"Don't make me say it," he said.

"Don't make you say what?" And then she looked at him. We were in the kitchen, eating ice cream—it was like four in the afternoon, when it's basically too hot to go outside, and you have to live indoors, in like the space station, like you're living on an alien planet. "Like, white people have easy hair to cut?"

"It doesn't like . . . do anything, it just like—lays there. On your neck."

"Say that to me again," Betsy said. "Look at this mess and say that to me again."

Betsy had our mother's hair, which was more cloud than hair, especially in Texas heat. Then the air-conditioning dampened it again, sort of wetted it down—I don't really know. It's not something I paid attention to. The only thing that mattered to me is that whenever we had to walk out of the house you had to factor in an extra ten minutes for Betsy, so she could stare at herself in the mirror and feel anger and disappointment.

"You may be like an exception," Marcus said.

"What's that supposed to mean?" But she was only pretending to be mad. She said, "Get me some scissors," and for some reason that's what actually happened.

Betsy told him to make his hair wet, and he said, "That's not what you do," and she said, "Trust me," so he went to the bathroom. Just because, I don't know, she was telling him what to do. Maybe if you don't have sisters, you think you have to listen to women. And for an hour I watched them . . . interact like this, in the kitchen, where he sat on one of the chairs with his head down, and she delicately hesitantly snipped away, making noises like, Ooh, mmm, and laughing, and he said, what, what, let me look, but she wouldn't let him look. Not till I'm done. Meanwhile the floor, which was cork matting, got covered in little black curls. And I watched them, and sometimes commentated, until Betsy told me to shut up, you're not being helpful, and felt . . . left out.

When he woke up the next day, he looked ridiculous. Even Betsy had to admit—she put her hand over her mouth when she saw him. I'm so so sorry, oh my god. The flat top she tried to confect with micro-scissoring just did not exist. It was like somebody stuck his hand in the socket.

"I think maybe you shouldn't have made your hair wet," Betsy said. We were all just staring at him at breakfast.

"That's what I told you, that's what I tried to tell you."

She touched him on the head and he . . . flinched. Marcus was not a touchy-feely person. But she pulled on his hair to make it line up. "This is not the haircut I gave you," she said. "There's no way—I mean," and she was laughing again. "Nobody would intentionally do this to you. Not even me. I mean, it's like . . . everything shrank."

"I told you," he said again. But I think the whole thing was moderately upsetting to him. It's like, I'm living with white people, and this is what they do to me.

Betsy maybe got the point because she stopped laughing, even if she was only laughing out of embarrassment. She did the girl thing where girls make it up to you by stroking your ego. "I'm just kidding," she said. "It actually looks okay. I was just messing with you. It looks fine, it looks good . . . You look like one of those models where they blow wind in your hair, just to get that look. It just takes a little getting used to."

Even when she was apologizing there was this little sting of teasing or flirtation. But it didn't matter because she was about to drive to

Ohio with my dad, so maybe she thought, this is just something stupid and fun, and I can say what I want because tomorrow I'm going away.

At least when she left we didn't have to share a room. Marcus started sleeping in Betsy's bed. I mean, we changed the sheets, but it was still like her room, with all her shit on the walls, so when you go to sleep there and wake up in the morning, you can't help being aware of her intimate absence. The other thing he did was bike over to East Austin by his old apartment, and go to the barber he went to when he was living with his mother. This time he asked for cornrows, which is the way he always wore his hair afterward.

18

If you spend any time covering Marcus Hayes, what that really means is, you end up hanging out or communicating with Amy Freitag.

It doesn't hurt that she's five ten in stocking feet and sat on the bench for four years at Tennessee, under Pat Summitt—which means she can probably beat you at one-on-one . . . that she wears red-framed librarian-style glasses, cuts her blonde hair short, complains openly about her skin if she has a pimple, talks about gas, makes ugly faces as if she doesn't care what she looks like, looks like Jamie Lee Curtis, like one of those fun-friendly people who nevertheless you don't want to cross or disappoint. Most of the beat writers I know have a crush on her, but she's also someone who remembers their wives and kids. The truth is, you never get near her, and the people she respects are the ones who understand this.

When she first met Marcus, she was a twenty-three-year-old intern at CAA, which is where Sheldon Fitch worked. Fresh out of college, living in New York, having a good time. Then Sheldon broke out on his own, and Marcus cherry-picked Amy because of all the people at CAA he had to deal with, she was the one he chose to deal with. It meant moving to Boston and spending half the year on the road. At that point her life became essentially suspended. She's thirty-four now and nothing has really changed in the past ten years, apart from the fact, I guess, that she has salted away a substantial amount of money that she doesn't have time to spend.

Anyway, Amy called. She said Marcus wanted to see me, and I should come by the house. The security guy would let me through, I just had to email her my license plate number. But don't be late—there's a window of opportunity, she said.

So that afternoon I drove out to Lake Austin. Marcus lived on Water's Edge Drive, where every property has its own inlet. Bushes flowered against a high stone wall; there was an electric gate and a red brick circular drive behind the gate, with a palm tree in the middle and a kid sitting in the shade of the palm tree and playing with a dog.

"Kind of hot to be sitting out here," I said to the kid, after parking. The bricks had been baking all day.

"Amy told me to play with him."

Maybe he was eight years old, pale-dirty-faced, sweaty-haired. He had a tennis ball and was throwing it against the tree for the dog to chase.

"What's going on in the house?"

"I don't know." Then he said, "Rocco was annoying everybody."

J. P. opened the door when I rang. Her hair was wet, like shower-wet, and she wore Lycra leggings and a *Sopranos* T-shirt, which I guess she worked out in, because her face was red enough you could see the soft dark hairs against her skin.

"Is Marcus around? Amy said this was a good time."

"Excuse me, do I know you?"

Her accent was low-key Southern, but with money behind it.

"I'm sorry, I should have said. I'm Brian Blum. We've met before. I'm writing a book about Marcus."

"You must have mistook me for J. P. I'm her sister." And she called out to the kid: "I want you to come inside now, you need to cool off." But the kid didn't come.

"He's pissed at me because he let the dog eat my bran muffin," she told me confidentially. "So I said, take the dog outside, if you can't control him, and he said, it's not my dog. But you're looking after him, you're responsible, so he went outside and now he won't come back in. And I'm still hungry."

She laughed. Her son could hear her, she had an audible voice, but it didn't make any difference.

"Who did you think *I* was?" I said, when she let me in.

The entrance hall had bright marble floors and a double-height ceiling, with weird tubes hanging down over your head, like wind chimes or something, but like light sabers—they were LEDs. If you want to spend money there's nothing to stop you, you can spend money. And, actually, the whole time we were talking there were noises of construction going on, drilling and banging, outside or inside it was hard to tell. The house was big enough even distant sounds could be internal.

"What?" she said.

"When you opened the door, you looked at me like . . . you expected somebody else."

"I thought you were the lawyer."

She'd only spoken to him over the phone. Bernadette, that's her name, had split up with her husband and wanted to move to Austin, where her sister had just bought a big house. She was the kind of person who talks openly in front of strangers about the intimate practical details of her life. From a legal point of view, she said to Jerry de Souza, who was also hanging around, one of the things she had going for her is that Eric sometimes beat her up.

"I told him, you get your lawyers and I'll go get Marcus's lawyers, and we'll see who wins. Because Marcus's lawyers are going to be better than yours."

But when J. P. walked in she went quiet. Bernadette was younger by a few years, which you could see when they stood next to each other. Anyway, she was sweating, and J. P. always looked very put together. Skirt and jacket, even in the house.

"Hello, Brian," she said. You could feel the temperature change.

Jerry was making a pitcher of virgin mojitos, juicing limes, crushing mint leaves, pouring syrup. Shaking it all up with ice. He knew his way around the kitchen. Amy Freitag appeared. She asked Bernadette, "Is Rocco part of the solution or part of the problem? I don't want Connor to feel like he's stuck out there," and Bernadette said, "He doesn't listen to me anyway."

Amy also gave me a hug. She said, "Come with me."

Her office was a closet off the utility room, which she showed me with a certain weird pride. I've seen other people in her position try to emphasize their level of authority.

"What does Marcus think about living with his sister-in-law?"

"He likes having kids in the house."

She wore a black jumpsuit, like grown-up OshKosh, and high-heeled sandals, and a necklace that sort of flung itself from side to side. Sometimes when she was thinking she put it in her mouth. She said, "Let me just . . . let me just," and I waited for her to write an email. Then she looked up at me, stopped, breathed, and put her hands to her head. "There was something I wanted to tell you," she said. "I said to myself, when you see Brian, tell him . . ." And she made her eyes big, like, who knows. "We're just so excited that you're going to write this book. It's going to be a great book. You're the only one who could write it."

"I haven't actually talked to Marcus yet."

"Of course," she said, but we didn't go anywhere. Her office desk was covered in Post-it notes and printouts. Rocco had a basket in the corner of the closet, a kind of tweed cushion, so the whole room smelled of dog. "Are you comfortable with the story?" she asked. "I mean, do you have an angle on it? Do you know what you want to write?"

"Sure."

"I fought hard for you, you know," she said.

"What do you mean?"

"There was a discussion. Everybody was there, everybody who cares about Marcus. Joe and Sheldon and Ted Myers and J. P. It was a legacy conversation and the question came up, who should write this book, and I said, everybody here in this room knows, there's only one person who can write this book."

"Thank you."

"So if anything goes wrong, I said, blame me."

She stood up and we proceeded to the next stage of business. "All right, okay. You didn't come here to talk to me. Marcus is just working out, but I'm sure you don't mind seeing him sweat."

And I said, "So do you live here, too?"

"Please. I've got the teensiest little duplex in Travis Heights; we're talking like six hundred square feet. But it's got its own front door, it's got a little porch where I can sit out and get chewed every evening. It's got somewhere for the dog to shit. I'm happy."

I followed her down the corridor and through a glass atrium into another part of the house, where the air-conditioning seemed less all-pervasive. The vibe was more seventies original, linoleum floor tiles, wood-paneled walls.

"We call this the Swedish sauna," she said. "Marcus likes it hot."

There was another kitchen, and then a gym at the back with a view of the water—the old dining room. Marcus lay resting on the bench; Brad Weldt stood over the bar. For years he worked as a trainer for the Celtics, and after Marcus retired set up a fitness consultancy and wrote a book that gets described on his website as a best-selling motivational book. But when Marcus came back, as a personal favor, Brad resumed his old role.

He lifted and lowered the bar and Marcus took the strain of the weight.

A stain of sweat had spread across his shirt. Part of what looks strange about watching Marcus lift is the length of his arms—the bar just keeps going up. He was doing two-twenty-five, with a high rep count and by the end his chest heaved like something inside was trying to get out of the cage. Through clenched teeth he said, "Don't let me cheat," and Brad touched a finger underneath his left elbow, just to give him a boost. Marcus said, "I got this, I got this," but he was hard to understand. The level of effort was extreme. Brad helped him guide the bar back onto the rest and Marcus lay with his head back on the bench and his chest still sucking in air.

Amy waited, then she said, "Brian Blum is here."

But Marcus was in non-response mode. Brad had a towel in his belt and took it out to give Marcus, who wiped his hands and then his forehead, and threw it back, with his head still flat on the bench. He looked different than he looked in Los Angeles. His retirement fat was gone. Loose skin lay on his muscles; his armpit hair had gray curls in it. When he sat up, he had to duck his head under the bar, which he did very suddenly, and took a long pull of water from the plastic bottle on the floor.

He said to Brad, "I want to get twenty-five."

"Maybe tomorrow."

"What was that? Twenty-three?"

"Twenty-three."

"I needed help on my left side. My left side needs to get stronger."

Amy said, "I'm just going to leave you boys . . ."

"Brian doesn't mind watching," Marcus said. "He can wait."

Workout guys are nerds, they're like the grammar-buffs of sports, everything has to be done a certain way. So for an hour I watched him carefully put himself through pain, and like a weird kind of pain, where he had to strain to make it happen. But he was also polishing a beautiful thing. With every rep, another set of muscles stood out distinctly.

At some point, Connor showed up. He just walked in and stood there; Marcus saw him in the wall mirror and looked at him like you look at a deer in the garden. Marcus called out, "Amy, Amy," and I guess there was an intercom somewhere, because a minute later Amy appeared.

"I said I don't want to have to deal with him, that was the deal."

"Marcus, he's just a kid, he's not doing anything."

She put her hand on his hair.

"Get him out. This is grown-up time," and Brad stepped in.

"Connor," he said. "Not now." Then, to Marcus: "I promised to show him how to use the weights."

"Why are we still talking about this?" Marcus said, and Amy took the kid away.

The room stank, even with the windows open. It was mostly Marcus's stink, and it was mostly Marcus's presence that filled the room. Eventually he finished and lay back with a towel over his face. Brad cleaned up around him. By this point in his life he must have been worth like two, three million dollars, but still he wiped down the benches and put the weights away. "How you doing?" he said to me. I never had any problem with Brad Weldt.

"Well, I moved back home. I'm living with my sister now. What about you?"

"I've got an apartment downtown. But it's just somewhere to sleep. Somewhere to put my stuff. I don't have much stuff."

Marcus didn't move, and eventually Brad said, "I'll leave you guys alone."

When he was gone, Marcus said, "Everybody acts like I don't know what goes on in this house. I know." He still lay on the bench, slack, post-exertion, but he pulled the towel off his face and looked at me. "I don't always care but I know."

"What are you talking about?"

"Brad and Bernadette."

"I don't understand."

"Why you think she moved to Austin? J. P. is like, what's it got to do with us. If it makes her happy. But when you step in someone's dogshit, then it's your dogshit, too. Now it's like, Marcus, can I talk to your lawyer."

"Joe Hahn."

"Joe Hahn doesn't . . . This is Pee Wee League bullshit for Joe Hahn. He doesn't play Pee Wee League." He took another drink of water. "What do you want to do now? I can give you half an hour." When he stood up, long-armed, bowlegged, bone-tired, he stretched his neck, once each way, and I could hear it crack. "You want to shoot hoops?"

They were building a court next to the boathouse. That's what the construction noise was; you could see exposed foundations, cinder blocks, a cement mixer, the usual mess, when we stepped out into the backyard. The light watery breeze hit me in the face, but the temperature was still high nineties—late September afternoon, accumulated heat. A Spalding Pro Slam portable hoop stood on the helipad, just a circle of concrete in the middle of the lawn, which stretched out on an artificial spit of land into the lake. If you threw up a brick, it might get wet. A ball lay in the grass.

I reminded him that the last time we played, I beat him at H-O-R-S-E.

"You never beat me at H-O-R-S-E," he said.

"How about a rematch?"

But then he passed me the ball and slapped the ground with his hands. "Come on, let's see what you can do."

It used to be a recognizable form of human interaction when we played one-on-one. But not anymore. Basketball is one of those professions that works like Dungeons & Dragons. You start out at first level and can't do anything but eventually become ten or twenty or thirty times more powerful. Or in my case, stick at first level. So it's hard not to wonder if you play against Marcus Hayes: what has happened to both of you where this is now the difference. I mean, like, what have you done with *your* life?

If I tried to shoot, he put up a hand and blocked it. Even in slow motion, he could ease past me and dunk—like that scene in *The Matrix* where they operate on different frame rates, and Neo moving at ordinary speed is calmly two steps ahead of everybody else. Marcus had been lifting weights for several hours and didn't have any energy but so what. The number of calories he needed to beat me you could get from a carrot. The whole thing lasted a minute; it was totally pointless.

"What do you think of Mmeremikwu?" I said, after we gave up.

He was shooting around now, little lazy set shots, leaving his hand out on the follow-through, working on form; and passing me the ball, too, so I could shoot. Like we used to do in high school, during zero hour, in the empty gym. It was almost seven and the sun had started to drop behind the trees across the water—casting long shadows toward the hoop.

"He's a big piece of the puzzle. He's one of the reasons I signed up to this team. The main reason."

"Big piece of the puzzle" was Marcus's set phrase—I'd read it in a piece by Fred Rotha.

"We just have to find out where to put him," he said. That was in Fred's piece, too. And Fred commented like, I'm not sure that's how Mmeremikwu sees it.

"Have you been in contact?"

"What do you mean?"

"Have you like, worked out at all?"

"It's a long season, we got time."

But then for some reason he started talking about Isaac Brown. "Do you remember Isaac Brown?" he said.

"Sure. I ran into him a few years ago, at Shipe. He works for Terminix now. He was playing in one of those green Terminix polos and kicking everybody's ass."

Marcus loved that. "Terminix. I should get in touch, I need to reach out. Maybe I just show up some day. Remember how I did him, junior year. Everybody's like, watch out for Isaac Brown, he's D-1 material."

And I just kept feeding him the ball, letting him talk. It all happened twenty years ago. The kid we were talking about never made the big time, dropped out of Ole Miss, came home, and started working for a pest removal company. I don't want to make out like this is a sob story, maybe he has a great life. Those Terminix guys earn decent money, thirty, forty thousand dollars a year. It's all good. But Marcus Hayes was Marcus Hayes; if he wanted to move to Austin, he could buy a ten-million-dollar house on Mount Bonnell Shores, he had four championship rings. So what pleasure should it give him that when he was in high school he hounded Isaac Brown off varsity. But it gave him pleasure.

Against the dying light, J. P. came out to watch us play. The sun was in her eyes, she had her Ray-Bans on. "Marcus," she said, "Marcus"— she was standing in the fresh-mown grass.

"What?"

You could smell the water in the air, as the evening cooled; a boat went past, with its buzz of noise. But there were also pleasant echoes across the surface of the lake—coming from a house party on the opposite shore.

"I want to talk to you."

Her flat face under the shades was hard to read.

"I'm working here," he said. "I'm talking to Brian."

"I'm sure Brian doesn't mind."

"Let me just make a few shots, just give me a minute," he said, and for the first time all afternoon, my heart went out to him. She watched him and then turned away and moved slowly across the lawn to the glass double doors. "Five straight," he said to me, so I stood under the hoop and passed him the ball until he made them.

Afterward, he walked me around the side of the house to the front drive. We stood by the car, and I opened the door to let the hot air escape. I got the sense, Marcus was in no hurry to go back in.

"It's good to see you, Baby."

"Did you see me at the gym in Pauley, when security kicked me out?"

"They kicked you out?" He was smiling, with his tongue pushed up against his lip. "No, I didn't see you."

I looked at him; for once he wasn't wearing sunglasses, and eventually he said, "How's your sister?"

"What do you expect? She's getting divorced."

"Is there something I can do? What does she need?"

"A date. She has two small boys, she's living with her father and brother. None of this is a picnic for her, but who's picnicking?"

"Brian," he said, and I said, "What."

"It's gonna be all right." But I didn't know who he was talking about.

19

By senior year, I made varsity, too, which would have happened anyway, but somehow it felt like I was just hanging onto Marcus's coattails. There was a weird vibe in school about the whole thing. People knew he was living with me. Even friends like Mike Inchman felt pushed away. I was aware of conversations going on around me that I used to be part of.

On Saturdays, Marcus played AAU ball or we headed over to the court at Eastwoods Park or lifted weights. He started lifting seriously while rehabbing his foot, so I did, too. We got phone calls each week from college recruiters, who also showed up at games. For some reason he wanted to go to Duke, but Mike Krzyzewski hadn't been in touch. If he had a good game, he might say to me, maybe Duke's gonna call. Do you think Duke gonna call? I bet Coach K knock on my door . . . And I listened to him and said . . . whatever he wanted me to say.

I don't know why he was so hung up on Duke. He worried that maybe he wasn't Duke material, because of the cornrows and where he came from.

Sometimes we even talked about going to college together. He said, Does Duke have a good journalism school? What about UCLA? He thought I could write about the basketball team, because that's what we did at Burleson. By senior year, I was deputy editor of the *Round Table* and covered all our games from the front-row perspective of the team bench.

It wasn't only recruiters who started calling at the house. Girls called, too. Once or twice a week I took a message from some girl saying,

umm, hello (laughter in the background), this is . . . (more laughter)
Melissa Danbury calling for . . . calling for . . . Marcus Hayes, who I
think lives there . . . and leaving a number for him to call back.

We even got some minor media buzz—a three-minute item on the
KXAN six o'clock news, which meant a van parked outside in the
school lot one afternoon and middle-aged guys wandering the halls
with heavy cameras on their shoulders. Kids talked about going to
State, so that on Friday nights Weizenkamper Gym was completely
packed out, hot and loud. If you wanted to run into your friends and
hadn't made plans, you showed up at the basketball game.

There were also the cheerleaders. I wrote an article about them for
the *Round Table* called "Five Stereotypes about Cheerleaders That
Turn Out Not to Be True." For one thing, about half the squad made
the honor roll. Most of these kids were taking AP classes, they were
high-achieving, competitive girls, which is why they made the cheerleading squad in the first place. If you want to waste an hour online
you can look up famous women who used to be cheerleaders. Some
of them are actresses, which you'd more or less expect, like Cameron
Diaz, but there's also Meryl Streep and people like Diane Sawyer and
Ruth Bader Ginsburg. I mean, it's just one of those future-success
predictors.

One of the girls I interviewed was Shelley Vance. She lived a few
blocks from me on the corner of East 39th and Avenue G—in a very
prominent and beautiful house, Victorian-looking, with a wide wrap-
around balcony on the second floor. Like a little girl's dream of a
childhood home. Her dad was a partner at Baker Botts and her mom
ran the Child Development Center at Hyde Park Baptist Church.

In spite of all that, Shelley was okay. If you saw her from the back,
she looked nicely shaped, light on her feet, with shoulder-length
strawberry-blonde hair, like a shampoo commercial—the kind of
woman where just to pass her in the street makes you sniff the air for
her perfume and feel a little sadder, because, like, what can you do.
But then if she turned around you'd think, oh, nice kid. Her face was

a good face, but she had this skin condition, where it looked red all the time. And she must have known she had this condition but you could never tell from the way she presented her face to you. I mean, she smiled like she was much prettier than she was. She was also a straight-A student who scored 1550 on her SAT (a hundred more than I got). The cheerleading thing was probably some kind of compensation mechanism.

At that time, she was also socially religious and tried to persuade Marcus Hayes to come to church. She worried that maybe without his mom around he might drift away from his faith—the subtext being, of course, that he was living with the Blums, which I actually called her out on. My mom was raised Catholic, you know, I told her; and she blushed, which was sort of . . . charming, given how red she looked anyway.

"That's not what I meant *at all*," she said.

"Anyway, how do you know Marcus is religious?"

"Because he wears that cross around his neck."

Which is true—his granma, his dad's mother, who died before I knew him, gave it to Marcus, and he even wore it when he played basketball, he tucked it under his uniform. It was a nervous tic outlet.

Shelley's interest in Marcus Hayes couldn't totally be explained by any single motive, and she tried to cover it up as much as she could. Maybe what she wanted, in her own quiet way, was to piss off her parents. Who knows—they might have loved it if she brought home a black boyfriend. It didn't really matter, though, because Marcus wasn't interested. On the other hand, I had a big crush and spent half my conscious life preparing casual things to say to her and game-planning my responses if she talked to me.

Cheerleaders practiced three times a week, for a couple of hours after school, which meant that we often hung around the parking lot at six o'clock waiting for our rides home. (Shelley was one of those kids who kept failing her driving test.) One day, when her mother was late, my dad offered to give her a lift. She said no, thank you so much, it was like a physical effort for her to resist, she squirmed on tiptoe, but maybe another time we could carpool. I mean, it's stupid, we practically live on the same block. But then the next day in school she came up to me in the cafeteria and said, is it all right if I get a ride with you tonight, because my mom can't make it. This was obviously something she had prearranged, she made it happen. Sure, I mean that's fine. Just like—sure. Whenever she wanted to get near to Marcus she talked to me.

After that she started coming over. Sometimes after school we did our homework together. I also remember having weirdly intense and humorless conversations with her . . . about our futures. My house is not a big house, and my mom's rule was, if you have friends over, and you're hanging out in the bedroom, then you leave the door open. So the only place we could have these conversations was on the porch, or maybe if we went for a walk. Sometimes the three of us took a ball to the park and watched Marcus shoot around, but Shelley always wanted to play, too. She did this girl thing where she pretended to be serious about working on her jump shot, which Marcus hated, because what he really wanted to do was actually work on his jump shot. But I showed her how to shoot a basketball. I stood beside her and lined up her elbow gently and showed her how to follow through.

She kept saying, "Marcus, like this? Is that right?"

It was all pretty obvious and embarrassing.

Sometimes he teased her by blocking her shot. He said, "Shoot it, come on," and he lollygagged in front of her with his hands on his knees, like he was going to let her shoot. But then when she shot he jumped and blocked it, and she said, "Come on, I mean, come on," and tried to take the ball from him and wrestled him for it. While I stood around like, okay . . .

Marcus got bored, though, and stopped interacting and Shelley and I would sit on the low concrete wall between the court and the swimming pool and talk and watch him work out.

I said, where do you want to go to college?

She was looking at Duke, too, which has an excellent medical program. It was one of those stories in the family that she wanted to be a doctor. Her mom had early-onset rheumatoid arthritis, and Shelley always insisted on giving her the pills. Like, when she was a little girl. She also used to bug her about what she ate, because her mom can't help herself when it comes to dairy and just like, anything fried. Shelley was still obviously caught up in the family dynamic to the point where who you are is really a collaborative product that everybody in the family has to agree on. Especially, in Shelley's case, her father — you could practically see his signature on the back of her neck.

But who am I kidding, right? Twenty years later I'm living with my dad and we sit around and talk sports. If you look hard enough most of us have a signature somewhere, next to the phrase, By the hand of . . .

Where do *you* want to go to college, she asked me, and I told her, Marcus and I have the whole thing planned out. He's going to play basketball and I'm going to write about him playing basketball.

She worried he was putting all his eggs in one basket. One thing my dad says is, nobody's life turns out the way they think it will when they're in high school. Like, I think right now I want to be a pediatrician, but maybe I'll go to med school and really get into ENT stuff, and then that's what I'll do. I'm making her sound dumber or more one-note than she really was, because she also said, maybe I'll just like, really get into noses, maybe that's what I want to spend my whole life studying. Or dermatology, she said, laughing.

Sometimes when I talked to her I felt a trickle of sweat roll from my armpit down my rib. I said, I always wanted to be a sportswriter, I always wanted to write about people who can do things I can't do — explaining myself tenderly to a girl.

At Thanksgiving, Betsy came home and Marcus moved in with me. By that point in the season we were seven and oh, and Marcus was

averaging almost thirty and ten. I mean, the thing had already started, the thing that was happening to him, and Betsy returned to a
situation that had developed significantly from the state of affairs
she had left behind three months before. Recruiters called every
day, Marcus hogged the phone, and the whole house was arranged
around sifting through the various decisions he had to make, and
maximizing the opportunities to which he was being exposed . . .

Also, when Dad picked her up from the airport, it was Wednesday
afternoon, and Shelley had come over. She sat on the couch with me,
watching *The Bob Newhart Show* on TV and stitching "Go Burleson
Go!" onto a pile of stadium-seat cushions for a cheerleading fund-
raiser.

So when Dad showed up with my sister, I thought, Fuck. And
Shelley said Hi and made polite conversation, and just doing those
things put her in a position where some kind of consciousness of
what other people thought was going on, like me and her sitting on
the couch together, had to somehow be acknowledged . . . not that
we acknowledged it.

We ended up in the kitchen and when my mom said to Shelley,
would you like a cup of tea, I have some camomile, Shelley said yes,
please, even though tea-drinking was not a normal thing where I grew
up, except for iced tea. Shelley in cold weather wore soft sweaters and
sat in ways that emphasized coziness—with her knees up and her
arms around her knees. She took a lot of pleasure in small things. I remember thinking, Betsy probably likes her but also probably thinks
she's a little . . . too sweet.

For Thanksgiving dinner, Marcus made his mother's recipe of can-
died yams. He kept on having to call her in Dallas. It wasn't particularly complicated but Marcus had never cooked before (which I
hadn't either), and he wanted to do something for the occasion. To
say thank you.

The reason he didn't go to his mom's is that we had a basketball game the next day. Betsy came to watch; I even got a little PT.

Sometimes if we had a small lead Caukwell sent me in to make free throws in the last few minutes, and that's what I did. Marcus scored thirty-five. And afterward, in the car ride home, there was this double standard where my parents were trying at the same time to say, you know, well done, Marcus, for dropping thirty-five but Brian, that was amazing . . . Which my sister found hilarious. She was like, come on. He made some *free* throws. The clue is in the title, and Marcus was like, it's cool.

On Sunday morning she flew back to Cleveland, where you get the campus shuttle to Oberlin College. Somehow her visit was a letdown. I'd actually been looking forward to it, and then it was over, and whatever I expected to happen or get resolved, or wanted to talk about with her, didn't happen.

Partly because Betsy kept teasing me about Shelley. I can't believe my brother's dating a cheerleader. That's the kind of thing she said. Also, for this one year of my life, when I was seventeen and working out with Marcus, I had a body there was no particular reason to be ashamed of. So when she teased me she was also trying to be, like, nice—to say like, my baby brother is growing up. But that's not what was going on.

I pointed out that the only reason Shelley hung around is because she wanted to hang out with Marcus . . . which he was like, no way, don't pin that on me. And I was like, pin what, pin what? Because what I actually wanted to talk about with Betsy was just . . . the whole thing, the way I was getting swallowed up. But I didn't get the chance.

Marcus had an English paper to write, so on Saturday night, after supper, we all did our homework on the kitchen table. Betsy had some reading to do, too, and sat with us. What's the paper about, she said, and Marcus said, Names. What do you mean, names? And he said, we're doing *The Scarlet Letter* and we have to write a paper about the names. Like . . . Chillingworth and Dimmesdale. And she said, I love that book, and I said, how can anyone love that book, and she said, ignoring me . . . Do you know what nominative determinism means?

It's like this idea that we become who we become . . . because of our names. They just . . . invented this term . . . which is kind of a joke term, but it's also kind of . . . and Marcus said, You mean like Hayes?, and Betsy said what, and I said, Like Elvin Hayes, like that's why he became a basketball player.

But this was really my last contribution to the conversation.

Can I see what you're writing? Betsy said, and pushed her chair over to sit next to him. There was a weird sort of charge in the room, a super-politeness, where Betsy and Marcus were making interesting conversation with each other, like you have to make if you go to your parents' friends' house and there are age-appropriate kids for you to talk to, but you don't really know them well and so you say things like, Is that a good school? But in this case instead of being a cover for boredom this super-politeness was almost the opposite, like one of those snowy winter days where it's so bright and cold outside you feel almost warm . . . a kind of expression of deep interest, from which I was totally excluded.

Mom and Dad had gone to bed. Betsy still had packing to do; it was after ten o'clock at night, but when I said, I'm going to bed, too, nobody really responded, and when I said, umm, good night, Marcus just looked me and Betsy said, "Good night, Brian," and I left them to it. And then lay awake in bed in the dark waiting for Marcus to come in, which he eventually did, maybe a half hour later.

In the morning I got up to say goodbye to Betsy; she had an early flight, but everybody was too tired to talk. Dad drove her to the airport.

20

A few weeks after Betsy flew back to Ohio, the Vance family, Mom and Pop and Shelley and her brother Scott, showed up at our door. They all wore church clothes, including Scott, who was still in junior high but wore a little-man suit with loafers and a blue tie. Marcus was ready for them. He had to borrow a shirt and jacket from my dad, which almost fit, although Marcus had to wear it "English style," as my dad called it, with the cuffs riding up on his wrist. It was a Pierre Cardin tweed with a blue thread running through. My dad said it was a "shooting cut." I don't know where he got this crap from.

The Vances waited outside on the porch while Marcus got ready—he didn't know how to tie a tie. So my dad had to stand behind him, with his arms around Marcus, in the kitchen. Mom invited them in but they didn't want to impose. It was a mild drippy winter morning, where the clouds hung over the trees, like sheets on furniture. Mr. Vance was a tall sort of ass-less presence, one of those men who opts out benignly from family occasions. Shelley's mom did most of the talking.

"Don't you look a prince," she said, when Marcus finally came out. Shelley, in a Laura Ashley yellow dress, which made her red face redder, stood smiling with her hands behind her back.

The whole thing was deeply uncomfortable. Like a weird kind of handover, where we transferred the black kid from one white family to another. Mrs. Vance said, "What's your usual church?" and Marcus stared at her. His only black shoes were his new Air Jordans, which at least were all black, except for the bright red Jumpman logo on the heel. But even when he stood slouching on the porch, in badly fitting clothes, you felt, like, the immanence of grace—just the way he held himself back.

161

He said, "My granma used to take me to Mount Zion."

"Did you like going to church?"

"I liked the cookout."

And Mrs. Vance laughed. "I guess you don't get much chance these days."

Afterward, when we closed the door behind them, my dad said, "Was that a Jewish dig?"

The truth is, I didn't understand why Marcus went along with it. And I felt jealous — because of Shelley. Maybe he liked her more than he pretended to, or maybe in fact even though I couldn't see it, he was drifting, too, homesick and just . . . unanchored. Living with strangers, while his mom shacked up with some guy a three-hour bus ride away, and going through the complicated process of turning yourself into an asset, which is what everybody wanted to do to him. For Shelley it was like coming out of the closet. I don't know what she said to her mom. Maybe she even said, he's living with a Jewish family. Hyde Park Baptist is an evangelical church — they're in the recruitment business, too.

Meanwhile, there were coaches in contact with Marcus's mom in Dallas, and somebody even drove out to Killeen to see Mr. Hayes. I think they dangled an assistant job in front of his eyes, because every time Marcus phoned his dad, they had a conversation about Stephen F. Austin, in Nacogdoches, near the Louisiana border. SFA was offering him a full ride and a guaranteed starting spot freshman year, which doesn't mean anything. Because once they put you on the bench, what can you do?

Todd Steuben was one of the guys who talked to my dad. He was just a kid himself, maybe twenty-five years old, an assistant at UT, and part of what he had to overcome is the fact that Dick Menzes, the Longhorn head coach, didn't think it worth his while to come himself.

Marcus asked him, "Where's Coach Menzes, when do I get to meet him?"

"That's up to me," Todd said. "If I tell him, you need to see this kid."

My mother commented, after he left, "That's the most Texan person I ever met, I mean, just the epitome," but actually Steuben grew up in Long Beach, was voted Mr. Basketball his senior year, ended up going to UCLA, where he turned out to be . . . a really good high-school player. He could shoot in space, he played hard, he knew the game, but he was three inches short and a step slow, and what he knew didn't count for much. Until afterward, when he got into coaching.

I liked Steuben. He was still young enough that the person he became later hadn't totally colonized him. Like Al Pacino before *The Godfather*, where he was still a good actor but hadn't figured out yet how Al Pacino acts.

The first time he came to the house, he noticed the hoop over the garage outside and roped my dad into playing against Marcus and me. They beat us two out of three. I guarded Dad and Marcus guarded Steuben. He was wearing cowboy boots, with hard leather soles, and clicked and slipped on the concrete drive; but he was grabby and physical, too, and if Marcus complained, Steuben said, You gotta be tougher than that. On offense he waved my dad over to set picks and stepped around them and knocked down twenty-footers. I mean, he basically didn't miss, which brought home to all of us a new level of awareness of what the people who take this game seriously expect to be able to do. If he wanted to get Marcus's attention, he got it.

We won the third game because they got tired, and Marcus broke free for a couple of dunks, where he could take out pent-up frustration on the old Rawlings rim. But maybe also Steuben let him win.

Afterward, we sat on the porch and had a glass of iced tea. It was late November weather, sunny and cool. Steuben said, "Let me tell you what's gonna happen for the next six months."

The first signing deadline had passed, a week before Thanksgiving—Marcus was just coming onto the national radar and the general consensus was, he should wait. The next was mid-April; Marcus couldn't technically make a commitment until then. One complicating factor was that legally a parent or guardian needed to sign, too, and for a while my dad even talked about becoming Marcus's legal guardian to expedite the process, but then it just became clear this wasn't necessary. Steuben suggested it because he wanted to contain the number of responsible adults he had to appeal to.

Here's what people are going to say, he said. They're going to tell you, you can't shoot. They're going to tell you, you're just a shooter. Somebody will say, Hayes needs to put on thirty pounds. Somebody else will say, you gotta lose weight. He's a killer, he's soft, he can't pass, he can't handle, he's just a passer, he dribbles too much, he's a second option, he needs to have the ball all the time. He can't rebound, he's just a banger. They're going to say all these things and you shouldn't pay attention to any of them. The reason Coach brought me in is player development. It's my job to make sure that if you come to Texas, when you leave, you're ready for that next level. If that's what you want, I can get you there.

"That's the only thing I want," Marcus said.

"I know we're not your first option," Steuben told him. "Even if we're your best option. But you're gonna wanna talk to Kentucky, you're gonna wanna talk to North Carolina, to Kansas, to UCLA. And all of those people are going to talk to you, and say nice things, they're going to sit on your porch and drink iced tea, and then one day you're going to go four for seventeen and you won't hear from them again. And when that happens, I'm still going to be here."

My dad told me afterward, I bet he says this to all the girls.

21

Marcus gave Betsy a car, an MX-5. She came home from work and it was there—with a ribbon tied to the windshield wipers and the keys pushed under the front door. She kicked them when she walked in, thinking, what the hell. Along with a note that said, "With the compliments of Marcus Hayes," written by Amy Freitag, who added her own PS. "I drove it over here and it's just like . . . I mean, enjoy. Brian says you could use some fun. This is fun with a key." His signature was underneath, which he's signed a million times, and which I used to watch him practicing on the kitchen table.

I checked out the sticker price online: twenty-nine thousand dollars. I mean, it was a totally ridiculous car—it had no back seats. Not even the kind with the folding front seat, so you can squeeze in behind. To give this car to a woman with two small kids . . . I said something like this to Betsy after dinner, after the boys were in bed. We sat on the porch together while she smoked a cigarette. October in Austin is still a warm-weather month, and even at night you can sit outside in your shirtsleeves.

"It just shows he has no clue. What are you going to do with this car? Even when the boys are big enough to sit up front, it's like *Sophie's Choice*—which kid do you take along. He's completely out of touch with how people actually live their lives."

"The point of this car isn't to take your kids to the grocery store."

"That's my point."

"I drove it to work this morning and—"

"Do you know how much it costs? I'm talking about the basic package, I have no idea what the bells and whistles add up to."

"I decided not to look."

"Twenty-nine thousand dollars."

She didn't say anything for a moment but lit another cigarette and stubbed the old one out in the Frisbee. "I'm not sure I can describe how much fun it was to park outside the office, but if you want to say it was twenty-nine thousand dollars' worth of fun, I wouldn't disagree with you."

"Come on, Betsy. It's a midlife crisis toy."

"I'm having a midlife crisis. At least, that was the intention."

But we talked about other things, too. I was moving out in the morning—I couldn't keep sharing a room, or falling asleep on the couch. After six weeks, you get on everybody's nerves, including your own. So we agreed that Dad would stay and help out with the kids, and I should get an apartment in the neighborhood. An editor at the *Statesman* had a place she was looking to rent out. Her kids were grown up, her husband had divorced her, the house was too big and she liked to have a man around somewhere in the background just for peace of mind.

The house was on the same block as Shelley Vance's house, with a garage at the end of the driveway that had a decent-sized studio on top. On one side you looked out on the backyard, on the other you could see parked cars. The conversion was done in the eighties and hadn't been touched since—the woman told me, when the kids were kids, that's where the au pair lived. For the past twenty years it was used as storage and part of the deal was I had to help her clear it out. Old box springs and dead televisions, garbage bags full of mothy clothes, the usual mess. So I hired a moving van; it took a day.

When it was empty, what was left was: wrinkled brown linoleum floor tiles, dirty flowery curtains, a futon, a bookshelf, and a water-damaged tulip table you could eat and work at. But it had a separate kitchen, with one of those old electric ranges where the oven makes a noise when you turn it on like a man falling slowly down stairs. There was a ceiling fan and an air-conditioning unit propped up in one of the windows. It was fine, and I could walk to Betsy's house in five minutes if I felt like

I needed to be around people who didn't in the first instance see me as the lonesome male.

Quinn's birthday party was a few days later, which was also the opening night of preseason basketball. But Marcus planned to sit out, so I had no excuse to stay home and watch TV.

The first thing I bought for the apartment was a 40-inch Panasonic. I also bought some new clothes. You can't show up at a party with twenty-something college girls wearing Florsheims and dirty chinos and not feel like what you probably are anyway . . . like everybody's least favorite uncle. Betsy tried to make me get blue jeans. She said, they're cheaper than a convertible, and we spent almost an hour online looking at Levi's and Lee and Wrangler . . . But jeans on me either slip below the ass, so I have to keep hitching and pulling at the belt, so the crack doesn't show, or if I buy them high enough make my butt look inflatable—like somebody who might tip over backward in the pool.

Betsy said, "Come on, you're not that fat. You're heavy set."

"Call it what you want."

"You're a catch."

"Whatever."

"What are you talking about? You're a nationally syndicated sportswriter. You're six foot three. And you're a nice guy. Any woman who sees you with my kids will think, marriage material."

I hadn't told her, the girl's in college. She said, "It's not like high school anymore. There are women out there making reasonable decisions."

"Well, I haven't met them."

But even she admitted, you have to try jeans on, you can't do this kind of thing online. And I hate the whole staring-at-yourself experience, the little cubicle, the unsatisfactory curtain, the hook for your old clothes, the public display of misplaced vanity, where you have to go to the sales clerk, who is probably young, who is probably good-looking, and say, I just want to try these on. Like it's going to make a difference.

In the end, I settled for new Dockers and a pair of retro Jordan high-tops, the black on reds, and drove over to Nueces Street on Friday night. You could hear the party noise from half a block away. Fred Rotha was in town for the Sonics media day, and I'd persuaded him to come along. "I'm an old married man," he said, getting out of the car. "I have a kid, most of my conversation is shit and sleep related, I'm going to bring the atmosphere down. Like, this is what awaits you."

But he agreed to stay for a drink.

We didn't want to show up early so it was ten o'clock before we pushed through the open front door and walked up the stairs, feeling like, these are the stairs that lead you back in time. The music volume was an act of violence. It sort of darkened the senses. Like, under cover of this, all deeds are possible—except of course an actual conversation.

It took me a while to find Quinn, and for the first half hour we didn't try. Nobody seemed to notice us anyway. I said to Fred, "Did you tell Sarah that you were going to some campus party?" and he said, "Of course." Sarah is Fred's wife; I've met her half a dozen times in LA, after Lakers games, when a bunch of us go out to dinner. It was loud enough that after every statement or question you had to gather your thoughts and think of the shortest and clearest way of expressing yourself. But sometimes these pauses also lead to confusion. Like, maybe he was offended. But then he said, "I told her, Brian needs a wingman, and she said, do me a favor, tell me what the kids are playing these days."

"What do you mean, playing? Like Donkey Kong?"

"Like music, like a playlist. She thinks my taste in music is twenty years out of date."

The beer was in the bathtub, which was filled with ice; and for a while we actually stood around the toilet, drinking. The music was some synth-y shit that you could feel in your jaw. *All that I needed . . . was the one thing I couldn't find*—this was the refrain.

Fred wore what he always wore, jacket and tie, and looked like somebody's semi-hip TA. These were the parties I never went to when I went to UT, and here I was fifteen years later trying to make up for lost time. Eventually we gave up trying to talk and Fred looked at me, like, sympathetically. He made a motion with his head, so we pushed our way out and found the kitchen, which had a fire escape running off it for the smokers. But there was also a kind of platform where we could stand around in relative quiet and taste the outside air, cool and nicotine-y.

"The presence of twenty-year-old women makes me unhappy," I said, when we could hear each other.

"So what are we doing here?"

The fire escape overlooked a parking lot. It was a real nothing neighborhood, student-ville, and the party noise bounced out into the low night sky like some aural equivalent of fire in a wilderness, the revelry of people on the fringes of civilization, in a makeshift landscape. Alcohol intensifies my sense of metaphor.

When I didn't answer, Fred said, "Are you okay?"

"I'm fine."

"How's the book?" And after a minute, "Are you getting what you need?"

"I feel like all my life I've been subservient to this guy because he can play basketball better than I can."

"You realize that what you have is like, ridiculous-level access."

"What do you mean *access*. I grew up with Marcus, for ten months he slept in my sister's bed. You only say that because you don't expect him to be an actual human being . . . Why are you smiling? You've heard me say this before."

"I've heard you say it."

"Oh, well." And then: "How about you?"

"How about me what?"

"Have you found anything good?"

There was always, underneath the sportswriter camaraderie, a little competitive friction—like high school buddies who also pay attention to each other's grades. But Fred had already filed; it went online in the morning, and like a lot of journalists he was happy to repeat himself. You get used to it, it's part of the job.

"There's a story going around that Marcus and Mickey got in a fight in practice, and Marcus broke a rib. This is why he decided to sit out preseason. He didn't want to make the mistake Jordan made, by coming back too soon . . . What started the fight, I don't know. One account was, Mickey set a back screen that Marcus didn't like. So afterward he took a shot; they started throwing punches and had to be pulled apart."

"These things happen."

"Maybe. But three years ago, if Marcus didn't like something, he let you know in ways that meant he didn't have to repeat himself."

Somebody was making cocktails in the kitchen, mixing and shaking. At first I couldn't tell if she was a girl or a boy, she had one of those *Leave It to Beaver* haircuts, with a snub nose and freckles; she wore blue jeans and a collared shirt and was making daiquiris. "Do you want one?" she said. The back door was open and there were rows of plastic champagne coupes on the counter, which she had been slowly filling up. So I took one, and she asked, "How about you?" but Fred shook his head.

"Listen," he said to me. "I don't know how much more of this I can take."

"It's okay."

"I don't want to leave you alone with these people but my flight's at like eight in the morning."

"It's fine. I'm just going to try to find this girl who invited me and then I'll go home."

"What are you doing here?" he said again. It was one of his roles to worry about the people he knew.

"My apartment is somebody's garage. I really don't have a whole helluva lot to go back to."

"Brian," Fred said.

"What? I'm having fun. I'm footloose. Isn't this what you married guys are supposed to dream about?"

"All right, all right, I'll leave you alone." And that's what he did.

So then it was just me, standing on the fire escape with a yellow fla-vored drink in my hand. At some point I ran into Quinn. She wore a Chinese kimono, deep red, and green Moroccan slippers that kept fall-ing off her feet, so when she moved she didn't really lift them off the ground, she glided or shuffled. "People keep stepping on my shoes," she said to me. But the first thing she said was "Hey, you" . . . I never know what that means—if it's intimate or one of those things you say that is meant to sound intimate in a generic way, so it doesn't mean anything. But she took me by the hand and introduced me to people.

Apparently the party had a theme: dress like your parents. Which explains why so many guys were in drag. "Is that really what your mom dresses like?" I said to Quinn, and she smiled at me and shook her head. All of her expressions were somehow slow-moving. "My dad's job means he gets to travel. He bought it for me when I was twelve years old. I put it on and it was like—I didn't have anything to hold it up. Twelve was my last year of girlhood, I was like a coat hanger. Before my womanly growth kicked in. But now it's like my party dress, I love it." And she held out her arms in a curious pose, which made the rich red fabric hang down like a flag. But then I real-ized The Bangles were playing, and she was dancing—walking like an Egyptian. For a second I thought she was using it as an excuse to get away from me, but then she took my hand and tried to pull me along.

"I can't—I can't dance," I said.

"This isn't dancing, it's walking. You can walk, right?"

And I tried to follow her, feeling, you are a foolish lonely sex-sad man, as she dragged me through the crowd. People were looking at her and looking at me. Somebody said something to her, which she acknowledged with a very restrained motion of the head—she was still doing the pecking thing with her free hand. When we got to the kitchen, she let go of me and said, "You're right, you can't dance. It's like towing a boat."

"I'm sorry."

"You're not having a very good time, are you?"

"That's what you said to me the last time, too."

"And yet you keep coming back . . ."

She used a funny voice when she said it, a sort of Elvira: Mistress of the Dark voice. We looked at each other for a minute, and she picked up one of the daiquiris on the counter and drank it suddenly. "Come on," she said. "Let's get out of here." And then: "Take a drink." So we took two more daiquiris and went out on to the fire escape again. People were sitting outside the kitchen, sitting and smoking, but we walked along the balcony (which was made of metal grating that shook underfoot) to the steps on the other side. Even there the music was loud enough you could feel it in your sternum.

"You have a lot of friends," I said.

"Most of these people I have no idea who they are."

"So why did you invite them?"

"It's a party."

"Who are the ones you like?"

"You sound like my dad."

"I'm just trying to make conversation."

"Why?"

And she looked at me and eventually I looked away.

"Is that your apartment?" I said at last, and she laughed.

"No way I would live here. This is a shithole."

There was a Taco Cabana across the road—painted dull brown and bright pink, and even at midnight you could see a lot of foot traffic. Friday night munchies. College kids on college time, people with nothing to get up for in the morning. I didn't have much. "What are you doing with me?" I asked.

"Right now, I'm not doing anything."

"I mean, why would you even want to talk to me?"

"Who said I wanted to talk?"

She had on glossy red lipstick, what I think of for some reason as maraschino cherry flavor. Her face looked reddish, too, under the glare; there was a streetlight in the parking lot outside the building. Also, I remembered, drinking had this effect on her complexion. But she didn't sound drunk; she sounded cold. The temperature had dropped in the past twenty-four hours. Fall was coming, it was a clear night, there weren't any clouds to hold in the heat of the day. The silk thing she wore felt cool to the touch. Who knows what's going on in her private life that makes this a reasonable thing for her to do. But you don't find out by not doing it. I bent over to kiss her (Quinn was sitting one step down) and she let me and then she said, "Did you enjoy that?"

I was a little taken aback. "Yes."

"It's just that you never seem to be having much fun."

"I didn't know if you wanted me to."

"It took you long enough. I was like, when's he going to make a move."

But when I bent down again, she stood up. "It's freezing out here," she said. "Come on. I want to party," so I followed her inside.

After that we kept bumping into each other and separating. At one point she told me a story—something weird happened that night they went back to Marcus's hotel room. He had a suite at the Four Seasons, with a view of the river, just water and lights and trees, and when we got there Marcus ordered more food and champagne. There was a huge TV on one wall and somebody turned it on; it was showing music videos, and people started dancing. Marcus didn't dance, he sat in one of the armchairs, looking at his phone. And then it rang, she was watching him, and he went out onto the balcony to talk, because it was too loud inside, and when he came back in he kicked everybody out. Kyla said she knew who it was. Someone in her sorority went to high school with this girl, and she was just like this real . . . stuck-up kind of . . . super Christian, which I don't have a problem with, but like, come on, if you're going out with Marcus Hayes, don't act like . . . and Kyla was at the party now, too, and telling the story, but also saying, at least, that's what my friend says. I don't know.

At two in the morning I went to find Quinn and say good night. Goodbye and thank you for having me, like a good little boy. I didn't want to be a burden to her but couldn't spend any more time talking to college kids. The guys were easy enough, we just talked about sports, but eventually you think, what am I doing this for, why am I here.

When I told her I was leaving, she said, "Oh."

"I mean, I don't think . . . people aren't going anywhere, even if . . . I'm pretty tired."

"It's only . . ." and she looked at her watch, after pulling up the broad silk sleeve. "Two."

"I'm an old man. I need my beauty sleep."

And she said, "Go get your beauty sleep, old man."

"I just wanted to say . . ." But I didn't know what I wanted to say.

"Did you have a good time?"

"I had a very good time."

And thought, you creep, you loser, retreating down the stairs afterward, with the noise of the party receding slowly . . . and stepping out again into the streetlamp-lit night, feeling like, returning to reality, and also like, I'm too drunk to drive. So I ended up walking home, down the Drag and then over at 27th Street, through the seminary grounds, toward Speedway and Hyde Park, under the stars, watching the cars surge past. It took me almost an hour; it was after three when I opened the garage door, by which point I was totally sober and cold and wide awake.

22

Menzes was a Texas lifer; he'd had the job for twenty years, the old boys' network loved him because he was one of the boys. *Basketball's a simple game. You find the kids with talent, and you let them show it, you get out of their way.* That's the kind of thing he said. He had the reputation as a players' coach, because talent liked to play for him, but somehow nobody who came through the system ended up sticking in the NBA.

Like a lot of basically corrupt backroom-operator types, he had a manner that suggested integrity—so that even while nepotizing or doing deals, he could persuade you that he was acting in good faith and even occupying a kind of higher ground. By shaking your hand, looking you in the eye . . . He also kept in touch with a long list of acquaintances on a daily basis, even people who had ceased to be useful to him.

He showed up about a week before the end of the regular season, which must mean, late February. Just a miserable Saturday afternoon, pouring with rain. The yellow grass in our yard had a sort of gleam rising in-between like it was going to float away. Marcus and I were watching *Columbo* when the doorbell rang and my mom said, "Can somebody get the door?" and we didn't move, and eventually she came out of the kitchen to answer it herself.

"You don't know me," he said, "but my name is Dick Menzes, and my guess is the boys on that sofa have a pretty good idea who I am."

Marcus whispered, "Turn off the TV. Come on, turn it off."

By that point I was sick of the whole process and wanted to see the end of the program, but I turned it off anyway when Dad walked in. Marcus on the weekends if he wasn't playing basketball basically didn't get dressed. Sometimes he even went out to shoot in pajamas and high-tops, and maybe a hoodie in winter if it was cold. So he excused himself to go to the bathroom, and when he came back again he wore jeans and the J. Crew shirt my sister gave him for Christmas. He looked preppy and said yes sir and no sir when Menzes asked him questions.

Questions like, You excited about the playoffs?

Yes sir.

I think you folks got Reagan coming up in the first round.

Yes sir.

I wouldn't take them for granted.

No sir.

That kid Anderson is pretty quick.

Yes sir.

But you probably think you're quicker.

Yes sir.

Good, good, that's what you *should* think. Doesn't make it true, he said, and laughed, and everybody laughed. I thought it was hilarious, and my dad said quietly to me, when he got the chance, Brian, don't be an asshole.

What, what?

You know what I mean.

I honestly don't.

But after that I kept quiet.

My mother offered Menzes something to drink, and he asked for any kind of pop—that's the word he used. "I'm on my feet all day and need a little sugar rush now and then." Dad's a Mountain Dew drinker, so Mom filled up a tall glass of Dew, and we moved to the kitchen and sat around the table. It was like having a second cousin around, who was coming through town on business and decided to look us up for the sake of the family.

So everybody made conversation.

He complimented my mother on her home. To my dad he said, looking through the back-door window, "At this time of year at least you can let the lawn take care of itself."

In general his policy was, let the kid come to you. It was part of his trick not to look like he wanted it too much. At some point, with Marcus sitting right next to him, Menzes turned to my dad and said, "Is he a good kid? Does he keep his nose clean? Does he do the dishes and take out the trash? Does he stay out of trouble?" and my dad for some reason started telling the story about the yam and pineapple casserole Marcus made for Thanksgiving dinner. He spent an hour with his mom on the phone, writing down the recipe. But the thing he wrote the recipe down on . . . got a little sticky with molasses and pineapple juice, and whatnot. You could have pinned it on the fridge if you wanted to, that's how sticky it was . . . and Marcus kept calling his mom, after every step . . . while my wife was trying to get the turkey out of the oven . . .

I actually looked at my Timex, because it was one of those conversations where you think, the only thing that's going to get me out of this is just, like, the fact that time is linear. Eventually my dad said, "And he was so proud of himself that he practically ate the whole damn thing by himself."

"It was good," Marcus said, and my dad said, "He's no trouble at all, unless he tries to help out."

I thought, Menzes probably listens to this stuff all the time.

Afterward, he shook Dad's hand and promised to "keep tabs on the boy," and my dumb father, who was always impressed by men who operated in the world and got things done, believed it. He said, "I've got an instinct about that guy that he's not a shit."

Later that night, we had a fight about him. My dad came to my room to say good night, he sat on my bed. I was trying to read and ignored him, and Dad let me read for a while, then he said, "Put down the book for a minute."

"What."

"I said, put down the book."

"Why."

"Because I want to talk to you about something."

So I put down the book, and he waited, and eventually I said, "What? You said you wanted to talk."

"I'm trying to think how to phrase it."

"Can I read while you think?"

"I want to phrase it so that it doesn't seem like a criticism, but just . . . something you could think about next time."

"What do you mean, next time?"

"Because this kind of thing is going to keep happening."

"What kind of thing?" But then I said, "If you mean, the whole embarrassing display this afternoon . . ."

And my dad said, "Display?"

"Whatever it was you and Mom were trying to prove. Although I don't know why I'm lumping Mom in with this, because she at least had the decency to . . ."

"To what?"

"Forget about it."

"What did she have the decency to do?"

"At least she didn't actually get down on her knees and start . . ."

"Brian, please. This is upsetting to me."

"It was upsetting to *me*. Just to watch everybody fawning over this guy, just because . . ."

"I like to think you're somebody who understands . . ."

"It was embarrassing. You were embarrassing yourself."

"I wasn't in the least embarrassed."

"Well you were embarrassing me."

"I like to think that you're somebody who understands . . . that there are times or occasions, when what's happening to someone else is more important than what's happening to you."

"What does that mean?"

"You know what it means."

"I know what it means, but that's not remotely an accurate description of what's going on here."

"Why not?"

"Because there are no times or occasions . . . there's just . . . all the time, all occasions, when what's happening to Marcus is more important than what's happening to me."

"Brian . . ."

"Are you actually going to dispute that?"

"He's your friend. You asked us if we could help him out, you wanted him to live with us, and we said, okay. But that entails—"

"Do you actually believe that's what happened?"

"At this period of his life, a certain amount of obligation, to see him through what must be an extremely trying period, with a decision he has to make, which will . . ."

"I never asked you to let him live with us. I never asked you that."

"Brian, you did."

"Coach Caukwell asked me to pass on the message, that's all."

He looked at me for a minute. "That's not my recollection of events."

"Because you weren't paying attention."

"If you think, for a second, there's any question . . ." He was almost in tears.

"What? Because if the question is, who gets most of the attention in this house, who do we talk about and think about all the time . . . that's not even really a question."

"Brian, this is his opportunity. Right now. This is his chance. If he screws this up, what's he looking at . . . what kind of future. You will have hundreds of opportunities in your life. I'm not worried about you."

And that was really the end of the conversation. I picked up my book again and Dad said, "I want to come back to this, when we can have a reasonable conversation about it. But I want you to know, I've heard you. You've been heard. I hope you heard me."

What Menzes said about Dai Anderson got under Marcus's skin, which is what he wanted it to do. Marcus knew Dai from AAU ball, they came up against each other from time to time. In a town like Austin there are a limited number of alpha-dog high-school ballers.

Dai's father was actually Reggie McWilliams, who played wide receiver and special teams for the Detroit Lions, until he busted his knee, so that Dai always had this cocky rich-kid attitude and drove a Dodge Viper to games. He was quick, though, he really was. He had this whole slow-slow-fast-slow kind of style, where he didn't seem to be doing anything, he was just dribbling around, and then he suddenly slipped past you in a long slippery stride and by the time you knew where he was he was like, at the rim. His jump shot looked streaky, it looked a little pushy, his elbow stuck out, and like a lot of lefty shooters he didn't really jump, he relied on surprise. But if his shot was falling, watch out; there wasn't much anybody could do.

This is the kid we were playing against on the Friday after Menzes showed up. Something else that bothered Marcus afterward—the way he said yes sir and no sir, which is sometimes how he reacted to white men in positions of authority. That's not how he talked to Coach Caukwell. After Menzes left, my dad said, "He seems like a straight-up kind of guy to me," and I said, "Dad, you have no idea."

"What do you mean I have no idea?"

I said, "This is a guy whose whole personality is designed so that you think, *this is a guy I can trust.*"

"What did *you* think of him, Marcus?" my father asked.

"He was like, one of those people you say yes sir no sir to."

And my dad considered for a minute. "Maybe he was a little like that."

I couldn't sleep the night before the game. At six a.m. I saw the digital readout of my clock radio blinking at me and a few minutes later heard Marcus come out of his room and go to the bathroom. So he couldn't sleep either. When I saw him at breakfast he had gone into totally private mode, which is also the mode you go into after a red-eye flight where all you can think about is, just get me through the day.

We wore jackets and ties to school. There was a pep rally at lunch-time; the whole student body assembled in the gym, where the band set up and tried to drown out the noise of a thousand kids with brassy instruments. Just the usual game-day bullshit, but in this case, I think Marcus had the added sense, which is partly what makes a profes-sional athlete a professional athlete, that my whole life is about to be put to the test. Whereas in my case, if we lost, at least the season was over, and I didn't have to do this stuff anymore.

Coach Caukwell told us to go home after school and eat what-ever we wanted to eat but preferably something simple, a plate of spaghetti, cottage cheese and crackers, a bean burrito, whatever, and then stop eating and come back to Burleson around six o'clock for the shootaround.

My dad made Kraft mac and cheese and steamed broccoli and gave us a bowl of Blue Bell ice cream afterward, and then we just sat around watching *Jeopardy!* Shelley came by to wish us luck, but Marcus wasn't in a state where he could interact with people. That old loose wire in his leg had started acting up, so Shelley sat on the sofa next to me and watched, too. I could feel her sweater, which was a cloud of blurry lilac wool, against the back of my neck. She always had an unusually clean, slightly detergent-y smell. Then she said, "I guess I better get ready, too," and kissed her hand and touched the top of my head, and kissed her hand again and touched Marcus on his hair, which for some reason seemed more intimate than my hair. Then she left, and eventually we got our stuff together and Dad drove us back to Burleson. The parking lot was already filling up.

Before tip-off, Marcus and Dai Anderson did the handclasp and stiff-arm embrace at center court. A gesture that wasn't particularly affectionate but more like some masonic acknowledgment that they belonged to the same fraternity . . . like X-Men making themselves known before battle. One thing I forgot to mention about Dai was that he had signed a letter of intent with Michigan. If Coach Fisher had said, Come to Michigan, I think Marcus would have come.

The cheerleaders set up behind the baseline, so Shelley stood twenty feet away. I tried to make eye contact, but she already looked totally engrossed in cheer-mode, which is a really weird mode. It's like a layer of emotion all over your face, as thick as makeup, which she wore a lot of, too. Partly to cover up her skin condition, but also so people in the nosebleed seats could see the expression on her face, which was like a painted-on expression of good cheer. Like *Go, Knights, Go!* For two hours she kept this up. I found it annoying that she had access to so much superficial enthusiasm, but the truth is, she also looked really pretty. She looked like a cheerleader, with long strong legs under the pleated skirt, and her strawberry-blonde hair pom-pom-ing up and down, whenever she kicked and jumped and lifted her arm in the air. Anyway, I should talk about the game.

Dai started off hot. He hit a three off the tip, then he picked Breon's pocket coming up court, and it was Dai Anderson 5 and Burleson 0 after thirty seconds of play. Caukwell didn't want Marcus to guard him, because Reagan ran him through a lot of screens, a lot of off-ball action, and Coach didn't want to wear Marcus out or get him into foul trouble. Our offense was fine if Marcus had the ball. There were guys who could fill in around him, hit jump shots or clean up the glass, but when Marcus sat down it became pretty clear: we were a limited offensive team. Gabe could do a little damage from the post. Breon was streaky, and sometimes, if his jumper was popping, could cause trouble one-on-one, but other than that . . . I could knock down free throws if somebody fouled me. That's not an offense. Anyway, we needed Marcus, and Coach didn't want to use him up. But in the end, he had no choice: Dai was killing us, and after the first quarter, the score was Reagan 19 Burleson 12.

He held out anyway. Marcus in the time-out said, "Come on, Coach, let me take him, I got him . . ." but Marcus already had two fouls. He picked up one climbing the back of the six-eight Reagan power forward, Shawn Dyche, to tip in a rebound, which made everyone stand up in their seats until the ref blew the whistle.

And Caukwell said, "You need to cool off, you're rushing," and actually sat him on the bench for the first couple minutes of the second quarter. So Marcus moved to the end of the bench next to me.

"Lot of time left," I said to him, because it seemed like the kind of thing you say.

"What the fuck you know?" he asked.

We were down ten before Caukwell sent him in. The other problem was, for some reason, his shot wasn't falling. The line was true, the release, the rotation, it all looked good, but everything front-rimmed or back-rimmed or rattled out. Maybe he was too pumped up and kept overcompensating, and then trying to compensate for the overcompensation. He was too much in his own head. That's not a bad time for a coach to say, just D up, which is what Caukwell eventually said. Forget about your jump shot, just shut your man down.

"I want to take Anderson."

"You got him," Coach said.

Lamont actually had a pretty good game. He was one of those kids where it wasn't really about skill. Playing basketball for him was like . . . something you do in the park. If you told him what to do, or how to do it, he sucked. But when he had fun, he was good. Once he pulled up for a three-point shot on the fast break and Coach said, No, no, no, until the ball dropped in. Caukwell started him in the second half because Shawn Dyche was killing us on the boards, and even though Lamont was only like six one, six two, he had a big barrel chest and football thighs and if he wanted to be an immovable object, he *could* be, and if he wanted to be the irresistible force, he could be that, too. Sometimes refs choke on their whistles when it's a small guy pushing around a big guy.

And Marcus took Dai out of the game.

It was like Copperas Cove all over again, Marcus's first JV game, where he was too hopped up to shoot and ended up putting the cuffs on Cyrus Millhouse instead. They used to call Gary Payton the Glove, because if he was guarding you, that's what it was like—you *wore* him. Everywhere you went, he got there first. I love this kind of talk even though it's mostly bullshit, because what actually happens is, guys miss a few shots, they turn the ball over, what you see is just a . . . variation in the probabilities. But there *is* a psychological element. Guys feel beat and the other guy feels like, I got you. Sometimes, at each new level, each increase of pressure or raising of the stakes, people revert to certain habits, and for a while I used to think, this is what Marcus is like, this is who he is. In the biggest games of his life, when the pressure is on, he chokes on offense but turns into a shut-down defender. Anyway, in the second half, Dai scored three points.

With a minute left, we were up two, and for a second I thought . . . Coach might even put me in the game. Just to hit free throws and ride out the win. But then Marcus finally knocked down a triple (he end-ed up 2 for 9 behind the arc), and it was game over. He finished with thirteen points, less than half his season average. Dai had twenty-one; it didn't matter.

Afterward, Marcus went to find him and did the thing I've seen superstars do on TV, when they chase down the star on the other team and whisper sweet nothings in his ear. Even in high school, this kind of thing goes on. It's basically a power play. But it's also true, even though basketball is supposed to be a team sport, that the real intimacy on court is what happens between the two best players, go-ing at each other.

Dad tapped me on the shoulder on my way to the locker room. He was sweating like a pig, hoarse-throated, happy. I was sweating, too, just from sitting on the bench.

"For a minute I thought he might put you in," he said.

"That's what worried me."

When I came out of the showers, there was some kind of reception committee. A lot of middle-aged men were standing around. Caukwell introduced several people to my father. One of them said, "I hear you're the man to talk to," and Dad told him, "Marcus is an old friend of my son. His mother had to relocate for work reasons, so Marcus is living with us, because at his age, at this stage of high school, it didn't seem like a good idea to disrupt his education."

"That's one way of putting it," the guy said. He was an assistant at Michigan. "I really came down to see Anderson but you can always use a lock-down defender."

My father said, "He had an off shooting night."

"Do Dai and he have any kind of a relationship? Sometimes it can make a difference to these kids, coming up together. It's a security blanket."

"You'll have to ask Marcus."

"Well, I'm in the line."

Representatives from Texas Tech, SMU, Rice, Arkansas, and a few other places had made the trip to Burleson High.

Marcus when he finally appeared wore jeans and unlaced vintage Air Jordans, which he never played in; a collared shirt and his Members Only jacket. He liked to go to the barbershop before a big game and always packed a travel kit of products in his gym bag, which included a shower cap. Sometimes I caught him checking himself in the mirror and taking one of the braids in his hand and wringing it out. It was a very patient process, and even though everybody could see him doing it and staring at himself in the mirror, he took his time.

When the guys in suits talked to him, he never said much, but he didn't hurry either. He waited for them to ask questions and then he answered them with a yes or no or maybe a short sentence. "You like your chances next round?" somebody said.

"I always like my chances."

He was a conversation killer, but people hung around anyway. They laughed even when he wasn't joking.

At one point my dad said, "Maybe we should wrap it up, Marcus needs to get something to eat," and then Shelley was there, and she said, "I can give him a ride."

She wore a long coat over her cheerleading outfit but looked like maybe she'd washed her face and put on fresh makeup.

"I don't mind waiting, I just thought—"

"Some of us thought we might . . . go out and celebrate a little. Some of the girls."

"Marcus?" my dad said, and he lifted his head. "You want to come home with us? Shelley says she can give you a ride."

"Brian, you coming?" Marcus said.

The gym was starting to empty out, and the floor had a gritty feel underfoot from all the street shoes. One of the guys from custodial was pushing back the bleachers against the wall. It felt like a party after the music stops and the lights come on and people have to shift gears before going home. There were three or four cheerleaders by the double doors that led to the parking lot waving at Shelley.

My father actually asked, "Is that okay with you, if Brian comes?"

And Shelley said, "Of course it is."

23

We met in the parking lot and ended up taking three cars. One of the cheerleaders had a brother who went to UT and worked shifts at El Camino on Burnet, where he could usually get you in underage, especially if you came with a group of pretty girls. Marcus and I rode with Shelley and another girl, named Briana, who sat in the back with me. Shelley drove an Acura Legend, which she'd bought from her dad ("yes, I bought it—he made me give him actual money") when she finally passed her test. It was her baby and she was a fairly nervous driver, which I noticed even though she pretended to be relaxed and like she was having a carefree good time.

Marcus kept leaning between the seats to ask me questions. "What did Coach Howe say?"

"Who's Coach Howe?"

"The guy from Michigan. I saw him talking to you."

"He said, everybody can use a lock-down defender."

"What do you mean? I average like thirty points a game . . ."

"I'm just saying what he said."

"I killed the game with that three. Maybe I had an off night, but I hit the shot that counts."

"That's what my dad said."

For a while, he turned around again and stared at the traffic. Burnet is one of those long Austin roads that's really part of a highway, with a couple of lanes going each way and a lane in the middle, stoplights every few blocks, so that at night in the dark the cars surge and slow. Most of the restaurants and car dealerships and gas stations have wide parking lots along their storefronts, and lit-up signs sticking out of the pavement. It's like a car culture kind of road, where you think, people live this way, this is how they go shopping, but if you actually live there, it's fine, you drive to where you need to go, it's easy, and when you get there, it's pretty nice—even if you can still hear the low continuous noise of cars, coming and going.

Marcus said, "So what'd he say?"

"What did who say?"

He was leaning again between the seats.

"Coach Howe."

"What'd he say when?"

"Are you guys going to talk like this all night?"

It was Briana. She had short curly hair, around shoulder-length, and was still in her cheerleading outfit, which is why Shelley turned the heating up—her arms were bare.

"I just want to know what he said."

"He asked me if you and Dai get along."

"Why'd he ask that? Why'd he want to know?"

"He thought maybe Dai could get you to come, too, if you guys were friends."

"Is that what he said? I mean, exactly what did he say?"

"Jeez," Briana said. "You're like a bunch of girls."

"You should go to Duke," Shelley told him. "That's where my dad wants me to go, too. They've got a good basketball team."

"They do," Marcus said.

But it was the wrong thing to tell him. A few days ago Coach Krzyzewski finally called, and they had a half-hour conversation, where I had to turn down the volume ultra-low, so instead of listening to the TV I listened to them. We had one of those phones you hang on the wall, next to the kitchen. Marcus stood in the doorway. He said a lot of yes sir and no sir. Coach K promised one of his assistants would show up for the Reagan game, but nobody did. Marcus obviously wasn't a tier 1 prospect for them, but maybe if he made a deep playoff run, that could change. Programs like Duke sometimes keep one or two scholarships back in case someone stands out after the dust settles.

"We should totally go to Duke together," Shelley said. "It would be fun. Even when we got there, we would know somebody. I could tell people, I know Marcus Hayes. We went to high school together." She thought she had found a way of talking to him about something he was interested in and didn't realize it stressed him out.

"I don't know about Duke. They got like, a certain way to play, and you have to play their way."

"Didn't they win the national championship last year?"

"Yeah."

"Aren't they like the number one team in the country?"

"Yeah."

"Come on, let's go to Duke! I will if you will." Then she said, "If they let me in."

But she was parking the car by this point, and he didn't have to answer.

Even when we got to the bar she seemed . . . high-energy. She was really determined to have a good time, to like cut loose. Most of the time she was an honor-roll kid or a dutiful daughter or a youth minister at Hyde Park Baptist Church. But now she was a senior in high school, seventeen years old, a cheerleader for a team that just won its first playoff game in about ten years, and a bunch of other teenagers were heading out to some bar where some guy had a brother who could get them in, and on some level she must have thought, if not now, when.

In those days a place like El Camino didn't have to showcase thirty years of Austin history, it was just there, on Burnet, and you could sit in the window and look out over the parking lot and the highway and the Subaru dealership across the road. There was a TV over the bar, but that's it, so if you wanted to watch it you had to sit on one of the tall stools. It was Briana's brother who worked there, and she had a fake ID, according to which she was twenty-three years old. She actually looked like somebody who is always going to look like she did in high school, even when she's a mom with two kids. Anyway,

Briana ordered a pitcher, and Shelley had a beer and I had my first illegal beer, and Marcus ordered a Coke.

"I can't be messing around right now," he said.

"Come on, it's just a beer. It's Friday night."

But he ordered a Coke and a bowl of chili.

There were nine of us, and we were sitting at two tables. Marcus and Breon were the only black kids there. All the cheerleaders were white. There was a round booth, where people had to squeeze in, and everybody introduced themselves and Breon said, "Briana, that's such a beautiful name," and she said, "Breon, that's such a beautiful name," you know, like, making fun of the fact that they were young and good-looking and sitting next to each other. And I said, "What about Brian, is anybody gonna tell me my name is beautiful?"

And Shelley said, "Brian is such a beautiful name," and put her arm around me so I could feel her hair on my face.

She was already a little drunk, after one beer. Usually I thought of her as a reasonable person, somebody you could have a reasonable conversation with. But the stuff everybody talked about was dumb. Briana started asking, what's the most, like, token black character in an American sitcom? I mean, are there even any black characters on *Cheers*? I think she was trying to say to Breon, I'm on your side, or let's talk about stuff that you have to put up with . . . but the way it came across, at least to me, was, here I am talking to a black kid, so let's talk about black issues but from a kind of ironic point of view. I can't explain why I found it annoying. I don't even know if Breon cared. He probably just thought, she's cute.

He said, "How about *The Cosby Show*? Are there any black characters on *The Cosby Show*?"

"That's mean," Briana said.

"What? What?"

"What do you mean, are there any black characters on *The Cosby Show*?"

"I'm just asking." And then, "What do you think I mean?"

"Just because, I mean, just because, he's like a doctor . . . and they live in . . ."

"What do they live in? A nice house?"

"You're being mean. You're trying to make me say stupid stuff."

"I'm not trying very hard." But he was flirting with her, too. "What do you think my dad does?"

"I don't know."

"Go on. What do you think he does?"

"What about me? What do you think my dad does?"

And Breon looked at her. "Let me see your shoes," he said.

"Why do you want to see my shoes?"

"You can tell a lot about people from their shoes."

But we were all squeezed into a booth; it wasn't easy for her to get her leg out, she had to kind of twist and almost stand up and then, when she got it out, there was nowhere for her to put it, so she put it on his lap.

"Come on," he said. "These are my clean jeans."

"You asked for it."

This kind of conversation was going on all around me, and Shelley kept laughing and trying to join in, and not quite getting the timing right. I felt bad for her. I felt like, you don't have to make these people like you.

At one point, a couple of guys came up to talk to us because they knew Briana. Or they knew her brother, who worked at the bar. They looked like typical UT students, a little overweight, but also like they worked out. The bigger guy was maybe six three. He wore jeans and a black leather belt and a T-shirt that said, "ASK ME ABOUT MY WOLF." The other guy was shorter and had a goatee. He said, "Hello ladies, you having a good night?" even though half the people at the table were guys.

Briana said, "Fuck off, Mason."

And the guy in the wolf shirt said, "You boys don't look twenty-one to me."

What I remember is, Breon and Marcus didn't say anything, or even look at anybody, and it was like something was going on at a different tone or frequency than I could hear.

"Somebody gonna answer me?"

"Don't be a dick, Josh."

Marcus said, "I'm just having a Coke and something to eat."

And Josh said, "I'm just playing with you. Oh my god, you should see your faces." And then, in a kind of TV voice, like, For all you kids out there, he said, "Have fun, kids," and they left us alone.

"They're such assholes," Briana said.

"How do you know those guys?"

"I don't really. They're my brother's . . . I don't even know if he would call them friends. It seems like if you're a guy there are just these guys you know. Mason keeps asking me out. It's kind of gross."

"Oh my god, you like him." This is the kind of dumb conversation I was listening to.

Shelley kept trying to talk to Marcus about Duke. She said, we should totally go there together. Marcus didn't say much. I don't really know why he was there. He kept his jacket on, even inside. He used to chew the collar a little, which is one of the things my mother tried to get him to stop. She didn't always know what to do with Marcus, or say to him, they were kind of awkward together in the house, in a polite way, but when he chewed his collar, she knew what to say. She said, "Don't chew." So when I looked at his jacket I saw this little damp patch on the collar.

At one point, when he got up to go to the bathroom, and everybody had to get out to let him out, I said to Shelley, "Can I talk to you?"

"What about?"

"I just want to talk."

"Okay," and she looked at me.

"It's too loud in here. Let's go outside."

She made a face, like, whatever, but she went. I felt like, okay, just keep your nerve, it's going to be okay, as we walked outside. It had been raining softly while we were in the bar, and the wet roads made the traffic sound like, shush, but it wasn't raining now.

"What did you want to say?"

I felt like, this is the way I can talk to you, when you sound like this. Not that she sounded happy or anything to be standing outside in the parking lot with me, but just, her tone of voice was the tone of somebody who was actually saying what was on her mind, which was, why am I out here. Her face with the makeup on made me feel sorry for her, because it didn't look good under the streetlight, it looked like . . . just, actual chemicals that you put on your face, but in a way that also made me really like her, because she was trying to be something she didn't have to be . . . Maybe that's what you always feel about somebody you have a crush on, who isn't responding the way you want her to respond. But I was seventeen years old. I didn't know any of this. I hadn't tried any of this before, so I didn't know how it worked.

"What did you want to say?" she said again. "I'm getting cold."

"It's not very cold out."

"Well, I'm cold, I mean . . ." She had left her coat in the bar and was standing outside in just her cheerleading uniform.

"I can put my arm around you."

"You don't have to do that."

"If you're cold."

"I'm fine. Just tell me why I'm standing out here in the parking lot . . ."

"Don't talk to Marcus about Duke, it stresses him out."

It's the only thing I could think of to say.

"Why does it stress him out?"

"Because they're not recruiting him. He can't just . . . go wherever he wants to go. He needs a scholarship."

"Okay. I mean, whatever."

"What do you mean?"

"Like, why are you telling me this?"

"Because I don't want you to . . . I mean, get your hopes up or . . ."

"I mean, like, why'd you care?"

And I tried to kiss her.

"Please," she said, and turned her face away.

We stood like that for, I don't know, I didn't check my watch. Eventually she said, "Can we talk about this later?"

"What?"

"What just happened."

"Nothing happened."

"Okay, but can we talk about it later?"

"Why?"

"Because right now . . . I just want to have a good time tonight. Is that okay? Just tonight. You won a big game, and we're out . . . and I just want to have a good time."

"I don't think you're having a good time."

"What does that mean?"

"I mean, it just feels like you're pretending."

"All right, Brian. I'm trying to be nice about this . . . but right now. Forget about it. You're right. Let's all go in and pretend to have a good time."

"I don't want to go back in there."

And she said, more gently, "It's fine. I won't say anything."

"I don't know. I don't know what's wrong with me."

"Nothing's wrong with you. You're a normal boy, and I'm a normal girl, and everybody's normal. Now let's go inside. I'm getting cold."

"Just leave me alone for a minute."

But she didn't leave me. "Well, what are you going to do?"

"I don't know. Go home."

"You don't have a car."

"There are taxis, there are buses."

"Come on, Brian. Just come inside. Then we can all go home together."

"When?"

"I don't know when. When people want to go home."

"I don't really want to be around you right now. With all those people."

"Why not?"

"When you're like that."

"Fuck you, too," she said, and went inside. And I actually started walking home by the side of the wet road, with the cars going past. I wanted to feel all the things you feel when you're seventeen years old and some girl just turned you down. Or even if I didn't want to, that's what I spent the whole time thinking about, which just increased those feelings. The sidewalk is intermittent, you have to cross a lot of parking lots, and then actually a bus came by, which I got on, and which took me into campus. From there I could walk home. I figured, probably by the time I get back, Marcus will be back. It was eleven o'clock at night when I reached the front door. The lights were out, except for the light in the kitchen that Mom always left on. For a second, I thought, maybe I should check his room, but I was tired and miserable and just went to bed.

24

Betsy asked me for Marcus's cell phone number or email address, because she wanted to thank him for the car. I said, I don't have those things. She said, How do you get in touch with him? And I told her, I don't really get in touch. There are media events, to which I'm sometimes invited. This shouldn't surprise you, I said, when she looked at me funny . . . I'm not *surprised*. You don't have to be angry with me. I feel like, for some reason it annoys you that he bought me a car . . . Even after I moved out of the house, we still got in these arguments. Eventually I said, If you want to reach out you can contact Amy Freitag, who is professional and nice.

After a while I realized they were emailing several times a week, and sometimes even speaking on the phone. Amy had this ability, which isn't always standard in pretty women, to make women like her. She was especially good at showing interest in their kids, and at some point, Betsy must have said, my son is just starting third grade at a new school and having a hard time. She said the same thing to me.

School isn't supposed to be fun, I told her. It's something you put up with.

According to Betsy, he was being bullied. I don't know what counts as bullying these days, almost any kind of meanness. In which case, my whole childhood was one long bully-session. Look at the man it made me. She said, he cries when he goes to school, which he never used to do—he was her smiling happy life-is-good little man. Anyway, Betsy started driving him in the convertible, letting him sit in front, so when they pulled up the other kids could see him in this beautiful red sports car. And if anyone asks where we got it, she told him, just say Marcus Hayes is an old friend of your mom's, and he gave it to us.

But the kids didn't believe him. They thought it was one of those lies a weird kid tells, to make himself look less weird, even though it's actually one of the reasons he's weird.

So Amy arranged for Marcus to visit his class. Then she let me know about it, which is how I found out. Because she thought I might want to put it in the book.

Betsy asked me to meet them at the school. There wasn't room in the Mazda. So I walked instead, the same way I walked when I was ten— cutting through Hancock Park past the public golf course.

The school itself is one of those beautiful brick buildings, pale midcentury pink, with columns of tall windows, which you never notice or think about when you're a kid, because you're just a dumb kid. It's just a school. Mr. Rincon, the principal, decided there should be an assembly first, so the whole student body got to see Marcus Hayes, and then he would make an appearance in Al's third-grade class. His teacher was a woman named Mrs. Wallace. Betsy was very pro this teacher. Among other things, she once said, "I'm not sure his friendship with Noah is actually helping him settle in." Noah was becoming a kid toward whom Betsy harbored irrational feelings.

I showed up early and waited around for the red convertible. Betsy had work, so she handed over Albert without leaving the car. I had to get a pass from the office, so said goodbye to him in the hall, where he disappeared in the sea of other kids. Then the bell rang (those bells! still ringing) and I made my way to the auditorium.

The last time I walked in that room was twenty-five years ago, but still it had this strong charge for me. Every day I used to sit on a plastic folding chair, which afterward we had to stack against the wall. When we first moved to Austin I was eight, just a fat unhappy kid, and going to school was like entering an indoor swimming pool, where everything echoes and drips, the tiles are slippery underfoot, and because of all the sound-distortions, your head feels like ... where am I. And to some extent these feelings returned. The auditorium was really just the school gym, with dark leathery wooden floors and brick walls, and those pull-out baskets attached to the walls, which most of the time lie flat against the brickwork.

On one end, a temporary podium had been set up. The windows behind it must have faced west, because at nine in the morning all they let in was secondhand light ... a little greenish from the live oak trees outside. For PE class we played dodgeball in that gym. I was one of those kids who if kids are mean pretends like he hurt himself, or somebody pushed him, and sits down and bawls until the teacher comes over. And I knew they didn't have much sympathy. But I also knew they have to come over if you cry and ask what's wrong, are you okay. It was a deal I was willing to make. It's hard to believe, sometimes, that these things actually happened, and you were stuck in that time and that self the same way you are right now ... even though you eventually escape.

But I misremembered about the folding chairs, because the kids when they filed into the auditorium, by grade and class, actually sat on the wooden floor, cross-legged, and the chairs were for parents and teachers and other grown-ups, like me.

Radko, Marcus's bodyguard, grabbed one of them and carried it to the stage. Marcus sat down; that's when I realized he was there. Even in the dim light he kept his Oakleys on. I saw him say something quietly to one of the teachers, who walked away.

Then Mr. Rincon stepped onto the podium and tested the mic. He wore a bow tie and a denim shirt, like your friendly neighborhood authority figure, but also looked like someone who had gone through recent health issues—pale and stubble-headed. "This is a very special day for the Roadrunners" (that was the school mascot), "because we've got a very special guest ..."

Meanwhile, I looked for Albert's head. He had brown normal hair, he was kind of normal height. Sometimes I thought I found him, and then the kid would turn around and say something, and it wasn't him. For some reason I had a feeling of panic growing inside me. Like a dumbo, I hadn't taken off my coat before sitting down, because it was cold outside. But now with all the heat of childish bodies the auditorium started to warm up. You have to get out of here, that was the feeling.

After the principal finished, Marcus took off his jacket. He said, "Let me get out of all this fancy Dan . . . attire. Make me feel old."

He stepped off the stage, with the jacket in hand, and then dropped it on one of the kids in the front row. Everybody laughed. Marcus said, "Where's he gone?" and picked up the jacket and handed it to Amy Freitag, who waited in the wings. "I'm sorry," he said to the kid. He had done all these things many times before.

Someone passed him a basketball, and then Radko stood up and reached one of the baskets stanchioned against the brick wall—he pulled at the net, and the hoop swung around.

Marcus said, "I just need a volunteer."

A hundred hands shot in the air, and Marcus looked blankly at the crowd through his dark sunglasses. Amy came over and whispered in his ear, and Marcus called out, "Where's my old friend . . . Albert Blum. Come on, Al," and a kid rose out of the line (there he was) and picked his way through the other kids to the front.

"Just stand under the basket and pass me the ball."

Albert didn't look happy or nervous, he looked like a kid who was doing what somebody told him to do.

"Y'all think I'm gonna miss?" Marcus asked, and took off his sunglasses (which he gave to Amy, too) and pulled out the hems of his shirt. "You know what the magic word is, to get what you want?"

A few kids said, "Please."

"Work. *Hard* work. Everybody here can do this if they put the work in."

And he turned to shoot. For a second I thought he might miss. My hands were actually sweating at the thought of . . . making a fool of yourself in front of all those kids, but the ball dropped in and the rim made a kind of clank, from the tug of the net, as it shifted against the wall. Al caught the ball and passed it back to Marcus, who shot again. Another swish. Then another. And another—I started counting and then stopped. He missed one in the middle, which Al had to chase down, but it didn't matter. Everybody in the room was completely silent, three hundred kids watching him shoot.

Afterward, a few of the kids stayed behind to fold up the stacking chairs, including Al. I wanted to say something to him, but he was in school mode. It was like looking at somebody with his face two inches under the water. He just wanted to stack the chairs. You forget, at that age, life is a series of small dumb tasks. But his head also seemed to me like some kind of crucible, inside of which chemical reactions were taking place at great heat. I waited for him to finish, then we walked together to Mrs. Wallace's room, where I sat at the back at one of those tiny desk-chair combinations. We could hear Marcus talking to somebody in the hall, probably Mr. Rincon, and then there was a knock on the glass window of the door, and Marcus and Amy came in.

He had to stoop in the doorway, and his presence in the third-grade classroom was . . . like one of those pictures where everything is normal except for one thing, like a floating hat or an upside-down moon, which makes the rest ridiculous. There were kids' hand-paintings on the wall, and a map of the United States, and a potted palm tree, and for some reason a big piñata hanging from the ceiling, shaped like a dinosaur, and Marcus Hayes leaning against the edge of the teacher's desk.

Albert sat next to Noah, in the front row.

Marcus said the stuff he always says, about hard work, and having fun, and listening to people who got something to teach you. It's not all about winning, it's about getting better. I missed a lot of shots, I lost a lot of games. Find something you're good at, it doesn't have to be basketball. Find something you love to do. It keeps you out of trouble. It kept me out of trouble.

"Can you still dunk?" a kid called out.

"I can still dunk. How high is this ceiling, Mrs. Wallace? Do you think I can hit my head on it?"

"I'd rather you didn't."

"Come on, come on . . ." But he reached up and lightly touched the paneling.

"How many kids do you have?"

"I don't have any kids," he said.

"Are you married?"

"I have a beautiful wife."

"Is that lady your wife?" They meant Amy Freitag, who stood by the window next to the potted palm, and suddenly laughed.

"She's my assistant," Marcus said.

"Don't you want kids?"

"Maybe when my career is over. Right now my focus is, just playing basketball again."

"Couldn't your wife look after them?"

"All right," Mrs. Wallace said. "That's enough of that."

"How come you always wear sunglasses? Something wrong with your eyes?"

"All right," Mrs. Wallace said again.

"It's fine, I don't mind." And he unleaned himself from the desk and bent down to one of the kids in the first row, who asked the question.

"What's your name, son?" he said.

"Noah."

"You wanna take them off?"

And Noah, because that's the kind of kid he was, reached over and took off the Oakleys.

Marcus looked at him—his face was about a foot away.

"Is something wrong with my eyes?"

"No." And then: "Can you put them back on?"

I reminded myself to tell this story to Betsy. Then it was over (Albert gave me a dutiful hug, with his arms around my belt) and Marcus, Amy and I walked back through the empty shiny corridors to the car. It was a suddenly ordinary Thursday morning in October. Plastic slides stood in the front yards; soccer nets and hoses; unclaimed newspapers. Marcus said, "Can I give you a ride?" And I said, "I live about five minutes away," but for some reason I got in the Hummer anyway and sat in back with Marcus while Radko drove, with Amy up front beside him. The day darkened outside through the tinted windows.

"This where you went to school?" Marcus said.

"For about three years. They used to call me Cryin' Brian."

"What's your nephew's name?" He had forgotten already. It was no longer necessary information.

"Albert, Al."

"Does Albert Al like it here?"

"Not much. He's not one of those kids who fights back."

"Well, he'll learn."

"I don't know. Did I learn?"

But this part of the conversation was over. Marcus stared out the window in his sunglasses and didn't answer. I guess this is where he grew up, too. For a year of his life, these streets were his home. Part of me thought, he's got a game on Tuesday night against LA, his first professional game in three years. And you're alone in a car with him. This is the time to ask questions. Instead what I said was, "You did a nice thing today," and a minute later they dropped me off at my apartment.

25

The League scheduled the Lakers for opening night, maybe because that's the last team Marcus beat when he was a Celtic, in the 2008 Finals. Shaq had retired but Kobe was still there. They were on the downhill but still good, still a big-ticket draw. The spread gave them three points, even on the road.

My dad wanted to come, so I contacted Amy Freitag, who arranged a guest pass. Even setting off an hour before tip-off, we got stuck on Red River in a bumper-to-bumper jam. In the end we had to crawl under I-35 and join the overflow parking at Disch-Falk, the baseball stadium, then walk back over the highway on MLK, itself a six- or seven-lane road, cars inching along, people pushing past each other on the narrow sidewalk . . . while autumn sunset shone directly in our eyes and the Erwin Center loomed like some concrete silo or windowless spaceship in the distance. And all of this traffic and all of these people had converged because Marcus Hayes decided to play basketball again.

A father and son stood in the shuffle ahead of me.

"You were too young when Marcus retired. You probably don't remember."

"I remember."

"Anywhere he wants to get, that's where he goes. Can't get in his way."

"Kobe's gonna punk on him."

"Like he did in oh five?"

"Come on, Dad. He looks fat. Somebody should've got in his way when he went to Taco Bell. Only time Marcus scores is if Kobe lets him, because he feels sorry."

"Let him score fifty-three in game six."

"That was, like, ten years ago."

A press pass gets you access to the locker room—they shut the doors forty-five minutes before tip-off. It was hot inside, and Dad was already sweaty from the walk over. His face shone under the lights. We ran into Fred Rotha, who introduced himself.

My father said, "Have you ever seen my son shoot a basketball? He can really shoot."

"Dad, come on."

The Erwin Center was not built to host Major League professional sports. Laycock got a promise from the regents to upgrade the home locker room (let the other team sit in drafts and shower on moldy tiles), but it was still a work in progress and you could see construction tape blocking off an unfinished lounge area, and the carpeting underfoot was that temporary stuff they lay down to protect the floor. Even so, Marcus Hayes had a space to himself, with a black leather armchair and a massage table in front. Mmeremikwu had a similar setup at the other end of the room, while the rest of the guys had to arrange themselves on plastic fold-out chairs. Most of them had headphones on. There was a strong smell of manliness, and also a kind of collective impression of manufactured internal space.

"Mickey" liked to talk though. He got his juices going by making fun of the reporters. He said to one of them, a *Sports Illustrated* guy: "You been working out? You look like you had a good off-season. You lay off starchy foods. Got to keep away from those complimentary muffins." (There was a buffet table of free food pushed up against the wall, with breakfast muffins and grapes and melon slices and a coffee urn.) "Can you do a one-hand pushup? Come on, you look like you can do a one-hand pushup. You want me to show you how?" By this point in his pregame process he wore only undershorts. His almost painful-looking stretched-out body was all muscle and bone. So he got down on his hands and knees and started doing one-hand pushups, and every muscle stood out. "Come on, Kenny Albrecht. It's your turn."

And Kenny, in his Perry Ellis suit, slowly bent over.

All of this is just the brief occasional release of air in a situation that is trending heavily toward greater and greater tension, like one of those blood-pressure straps that tightens and tightens then releases a little and then tightens again.

Mickey came late to basketball and part of what made him scary is that he still seemed to be learning and growing. In high school you get major college or NBA-quality prospects who make the rest of the league look like . . . teenagers, and Mickey had done the same thing to the NBA. He was a kid, he moved like a kid, gangly and high-energy, not totally in control, but somehow next to him other NBA players, big powerful highly skilled veterans, looked like the junior varsity. If on top of the physical tools he developed a working jump shot, the feeling was, forget about it. Put four guys around him who can shoot, space them out along the three-point line, and let Mickey go to work. Then if he learns to pass out of double teams, it's game over. Marcus could shoot but nobody expected him to accept being one of those guys.

I don't know what it does to you where your basic experience of growing up is that everybody else, at every stage, is like your kid brother. You're bigger and faster and stronger and better than they are. Even when you reach the NBA, the elite league in what might be the most relentlessly competitive human activity in the world, you look around and think, why can't these guys do what I can do? Why can't they keep up? Maybe you try to tell yourself every day how lucky you are. But that luck is *you*, it's who you are, and after a while even gratitude turns into self-gratitude, and counting your blessings is just another kind of showing off. Mickey came across as a nice guy, but that's partly because he treated everybody like his kid brother. He put his hand on your head, he liked to joke around. It was important for him to think of himself as easygoing, which sometimes made him a tricky person to deal with.

Not that Mickey had it easy. His parents were immigrants from Enugu, and Mickey grew up stateless for most of his childhood. He used to sell watches, cheap Rolex knockoffs, at the Marché du Prado in Marseille.

At some point I should say something about the other guys sitting between Marcus and Mickey along the locker room wall. A basketball team is fifteen highly ambitious and successful young men who for complicated reasons are willing to accept a rigid social hierarchy. But the hierarchy also has to be enforced, game after game and day after day—in the locker room, too. Eddie Roundtree sat closest to Marcus. About six eleven, he had the kind of fat on his shoulders and arms that he knew how to use, although Eddie was actually pretty chilled out. Before games he liked to eat a couple of candy bars, so people (fans, staffers, reporters sometimes) gave him unusual candy bars to try, and he always had a big selection to choose from.

Mickey's best friend on the team was this mixed-race German kid, Dieter (Diet) Crawford. His dad was US Air Force, stationed in Ramstein, but they moved back to Florida for high school. He was a sort of jitterbug two-guard, a streaky shooter, and one of those basketball players who didn't totally define as a basketball player. He wore dreads and hats and David Bowie T-shirts. There were two other foreigners on the team: Jan Stepanik, a big from Slovenia, who showed up to training camp thirty pounds overweight. But he knew how to play, could handle and shoot from anywhere so coaches let him get away with it. And Tony LaMarca from Argentina, skinny as a beanstalk, seven foot one, who could run and jump but not much else. A project, in other words. Also, an extremely unhappy homesick kid, as we later found out.

The other bigs were Jason Mulroney from Duke, a solid backup player, very low ego, who only did what he was supposed to do: rebound, set screens, swing the ball. He wanted to go into coaching afterward. And Alfonso Jenks, a rookie out of Louisville, the number sixteen pick, who wasn't expected to play much. Before the game it was his job to fill the water bottles. Also, he had to carry his stuff around in a pink My Little Pony backpack, with the words I BELIEVE IN UNICORNS written in diamond lettering across the back. The other rookie was a white kid from Gonzaga, Zach Ballatyne, a real bouncy kid, good-natured, who got on everybody's nerves. His backpack said SPECIAL PRINCESS and he had to bring Krispy Kreme donuts to every practice.

But for the veterans it wasn't a game anymore, just business. Ramon Neves had bounced around the League because he signed a long-term contract that underpaid him, which basically turned him into a trade asset. He got lumped in with a lot of other deals. But the contract was about to run out, Neves was thirty-one years old; if he wanted to cash in, this was his chance. Ty Jones was another gym rat. He once got recruited to play running back for Michigan but chose basketball instead. At six one, he could bench more than anyone else on the team. Very Christian, very upright, very disciplined. But his confidence came and went. Sometimes he could shoot, sometimes not. You had to start him because otherwise his game went to pieces.

In addition to the players, you had twenty or thirty journalists milling around, making small talk, drinking coffee, and eating the muffins. From all over the world: China (CCTV), Germany (RTL and *Die Zeit*), the BBC. The atmosphere was vaguely like a convention center, apart from the steadily growing sense of . . . not disaster, but something as sudden and significant as disaster. It's a weird scene. These big dudes, most of them black, who show up in five-thousand-dollar suits, are slowly getting changed around you, going through their routines, listening to music or playing Beat Sneak Bandit on their phones. While at the same time a bunch of middle-aged reporters (mostly guys, mostly white) are having a kind of office party or conference.

Marcus lay on the massage table getting a rubdown and then sat back in the leather armchair and let them tape his ankles. When someone from *El Pais* started taking pictures, Radko stepped in.

"No photographs," he said.

"Come on," the photographer said to Marcus. "For your fans in Spain."

"What paper you from?" Marcus asked, without lifting his headphones off his ears.

"*El Pais.*"

"That's Madrid, right?"

"Yes! Yes!"

Marcus had a lot of interactions like this, where what counted as intimacy from him or curiosity about other people was just these very basic informational transactions. Sometimes he might say something like, "You can have a good time in Madrid," and the response would be eager and flattered. Even dumb comments like that were an invitation, so he had to be careful.

"I like your headphones," the photographer said. Marcus didn't answer, and eventually the guy went on, "Focal Utopia," and took another picture.

"Don't make me the bad guy here." Radko stood between them.

"Come on, man! I'm just doing my job."

"Me, too."

These things happened all the time.

At one point, Marcus noticed my father at the buffet table and called out, "Mr. Blum, I didn't see you," and my dad walked over to him with a slice of cantaloupe dripping in his hands.

"Please," my dad said. "You used to call me Arthur."

"Brian still causing you trouble?"

"He'll grow up eventually. You look good, Marcus. It's good to see you back."

"Time to get real." Then he said it again, louder. "Time to get real." Then he shouted across the room: "Hey Mickey, what time is it?"

"What?"

"What time is it?"

"Six . . ."

Mickey was getting taped up now, lying on his belly with his legs sticking off the end of the massage table. He had a watch on his wrist but had to reach his arm out to see it.

"Time to get *real*. I said, What *time* is it?"

Mickey didn't answer.

"What time is it?" Marcus said again.

"To get real."

"Time to get real." Each time louder, and this time Eddie Roundtree joined in. "Time to get real. Time to get real." It was embarrassing, like drunk guys at a bus stop. A few minutes later Coach Kaminski walked in, one of these short tough gray-faced ex-military ex-point guards, and they kicked us out of the locker room.

So my dad and I wandered behind the home basket and waited for the players to come out.

"Do you think I can sneak out and take a shot?" he asked. Carts or racks of balls stood at various intervals around the court.

"Better not."

And then three or four Lakers ran out in T-shirts or warm-ups and started working through various routines. It's like an OCD convention. All these guys going through the reps, anxiety protocols, and other guys, lower-tier coaching staff, facilitating or enabling—passing the ball back, standing in certain positions, pretending to play defense. Sometimes two or three stooges for each player. It's all very low-key but at the same carefully orchestrated. You have to bounce two balls back and forth ten times. You have to make a shot before you move on. Just . . . a hundred different tics and comfort habits on display. And all for what? So you can face going out there later under the lights in front of sixteen thousand people and act out a play where the lines keep changing and other guys are trying to stop you from saying them anyway.

My dad said, "Can we stay down here the whole game?"

"Probably not. It's more comfortable upstairs anyway."

Tip-off was a half hour away, so we walked up to the press box to see what was going on. Already the floor was tacky with spilled soda. As the arena filled, so the tension increased. Noise, lights. It was like a high-pressure front moving in. You could feel it like a headache. Cheap tables or desks were lined up inside a cordoned-off section of the stadium, with electrical outlets underfoot so reporters could hook up their laptops and file and watch at the same time. Before each season, the team puts out a kind of program guide (there's a whole publishing and media-production side to running an NBA club) and you could pick up a copy from the stack on one of the tables. Most reporters ignore it but my dad was in free-grab mode. Marcus and Mickey were both on the cover, under the title "Different Journeys."

What made me look is the picture of Su Casa apartments. The article said he grew up with his mom in East Austin and went to Burleson High, but the truth is, almost half of that time he lived with us in Hyde Park. Selena was part of the story, too, a single mother who sacrificed her life and career so that Marcus could become what he became—which on some level was obviously true. But I was also like, she moved back to Dallas when the married guy she was going out with got divorced. It was *my* dad who picked us up after school and dealt with recruiters and everything that happened senior year.

After a while, if you get famous enough, your life takes on the quality of cliché. It becomes less real. The slightly intense high-school kid who's new in town and spends his lonely single-parented hours shooting around at the parking lot hoop of his local church and dreaming of becoming a professional basketball player . . . is a person it is possible to sympathize with. But somehow if he actually *becomes* a pro basketball player, if all of that self-imposed loneliness turns out to be . . . efficient behavior, the kid becomes . . . a little harder to like.

By tip-off, the stadium was full. A capacity crowd of sixteen thousand seven hundred and thirty-four may be the second smallest in the League, but that's still a lot of people. At a certain point the background noise becomes foreground. Every conversation you try to have is peppered with what, what? My dad doesn't hear so well these days anyway. He held the program rolled up in his hand and waited for the performance to start.

All the players had come on court now, running through layup lines and last-minute shooting drills—Marcus worked his way around the three-point arc, while Coach Steuben stood at the free-throw line and fed him balls. Somebody said, "What do you think he's gonna shoot?" and somebody else said, "You starting a book?"

"Give me an over under."

Kenny Albrecht asked, "What did Michael shoot his first game back?"

"Which first game?"

"Both."

Everybody has phones these days; such questions are answerable. We sat in rows like kids at school, so the conversation bounced around without anybody looking at anybody else. The stage lay thirty rows below us, and part of our attention was occupied by watching the flight of balls, and thinking, in, out, in, in, in, out.

Stacey Kupchak, the guy from the *Boston Globe*, got there first. "Seven for twenty-eight."

"What about with the Wizards?"

A minute later: "Seven for twenty-one."

"So how should we do this?" Kenny said. "Do we want to go by shooting percentage or points or what?"

"Field goals made."

"No way he gets seven buckets. I mean, look at him."

"He looks all right."

"He looks like a thirty-five-year-old guy who retired three years ago."

Fred Rotha weighed in. "Five for twenty-one, six rebounds, six assists. Seventeen, eighteen points. Six turnovers."

"He looks good to me," my father said.

Overhead, and all around, a voice from the PA system called out the Lakers' starting five . . . it was hard to imagine an actual five-foot-something human being sitting somewhere with a mic in hand. Like the Wizard of Oz behind the green curtain. The *Statesman* actually ran a piece about this guy, Larry Winfrey, who played one of the deputies in *Pale Rider* and had bit parts in other eighties Westerns, because he really could sit a horse and rope a steer. Then he got sick of LA and came home to Texas. His voice was one of those voices where you think, how do you even use it in private life. Kobe Bryant ran out in breakaway sweats (*"From Lower Merion High School . . ."*), and then the lights went dark and we couldn't see our hands. It was hard to type, even with the lit-up computer screen. The ceiling seemed to open outward to the night sky, and you were aware of vast spaces and concentrations of people, and a kind of nervous restless undercurrent spreading through the crowd.

A dozen spotlights swept around the court, scattered like stars and formed again into the shape of Texas . . . *And now for your hometown Austin SUPERsonics . . .* Winfrey stretched the word out so it sounded like a plane taking off, and then the PA system played "Texas (When I Die)," and sixteen thousand people started clapping to the beat.

I'm almost ashamed to admit, my eyes filled. For a second I wondered who would claim the honors and come out last. Then Mmeremikwu loped on (*"All the way . . . from Marseille FRANCE"*), followed by Eddie Roundtree, Ramon Neves and Ty Jones. There was a pause, until Winfrey rolled out the phrases . . . *"All the way from . . . East Austin, from Burleson High, from the University of Texas, three-time NBA Finals MVP . . . Marcus Hayes"* while Tanya Tucker's voice broke through the music:

> When I die, I may not go to heaven
> I don't know if they let cowboys in
> If they don't, just let me go to Texas, boy,
> Because Texas is as close as I've been . . .

And when Marcus walked slowly on court, everyone stood up and the spotlight followed him, and his childhood was my childhood, and there he was, twenty years later, still playing . . . while Tanya Tucker sang on, *New York could not hold my attention, Detroit City could not sing my song . . . If tomorrow finds me busted flat in Dallas*, . . . all good NBA towns . . . and then abruptly went silent. The ordinary stadium lights switched on and suddenly ten guys were lining up around a circle, waiting for a man in a black-and-white shirt to throw a ball in the air.

26

At six o'clock, in the half-light, the grackles woke me up.

Something Betsy once said kept rolling around my head. She said, you know, it's really not that hard to kiss somebody. It's really not that big a deal. In movies they make out like, it's something you have to be good at. But nobody's that good. It's really kind of a stupid thing to do. What I mean is you don't have to worry about it, if you're worried. You'll be fine.

But I couldn't remember if my lips touched Shelley's lips before she turned away or not, or if maybe I just kissed her cheek. It was like lying in bed and going over some dumb layup you missed in a game. You can't believe you missed it and no matter what your imagination wants, it doesn't change the facts. And actually you can't even imagine anything better, because your thoughts keep going over and over the thing that really happened. "Please," she said. She meant, please stop. She was trying to be nice. Sometimes even in the dark when you're completely alone you have to physically close your eyes against other people's points of view.

When I woke up again it was after eleven. I put on shorts and wandered into the kitchen half-naked and drank a glass of juice. Only Mom was up. I said where is everybody, and she said, "Your father has gone to the police station to pick up Marcus."

Afterward I heard various accounts of what happened, but this is what the *Statesman* reported a few days later. "Burleson High Basketball Star in Barroom Brawl" ran the headline:

Marcus Hayes, a senior at Burleson High, was arrested last Friday
night after an altercation at the El Camino Tavern on Burnet, a few
hours after leading the basketball team to victory against Reagan
High School in the first round of the 4A playoffs. Hayes was in a
group of Burleson seniors including at least one other player and
several cheerleaders. All of them had been drinking. Also arrested
were Mason Kruger and Josh Haldeman, both juniors at the
University of Texas. Haldeman was taken to St. David's Medical
Center with a collapsed lung and is in a stable condition. Doctors
expect him to make a full recovery.

Hayes, 17, has been listed as a "blue-chip" prospect by
Basketball America, and one of the top-fifty high-school point
guards in the country.

The story got a number of facts wrong. Marcus wasn't drinking
that night and he isn't a point guard.

A little after lunch, around two o'clock, my dad's car pulled into
the driveway and I waited out on the porch for them to come up the
steps. Marcus wore what he wore the night before, his red-and-black
Air Jordans and the Members Only jacket, which maybe he'd rolled
up as a pillow, because it was covered in dust. He didn't look like
he'd slept much. A bruise on his cheek had already scabbed over, and
you could see the veins in his eyes. If you saw him on the street, you
might cross to the other side.

"Hey, Marcus."

"Where'd you go last night? I was looking for you."

"Home."

"You left me hanging," he said.

But he didn't want to talk; he wanted to go to bed.

My dad staged an inquisition in the kitchen. He even closed the
door, after Marcus disappeared into his room.

What the hell happened, Dad said. I don't know. What do you
mean you don't know. Shelley drove us with this other girl to this

place on Burnet where we got something to eat. Were you drinking. No. Was Marcus drinking. No. What happened then? Nothing; I went home. Alone? Yes. Why'd you go home alone? I don't know. I didn't want to be there anymore. Why not? Did you have a fight with Marcus? No. What was Marcus doing when you left? He was inside. I mean, when you saw him last, what was he doing? Eating chili.

The coffee pot was on the counter by the sink, half-full, and my dad poured himself a cold cup. He put a tablespoon of sugar in, too, and Mom gave him a look, and he said, "I couldn't get back to sleep last night. After the phone rang." His shirttails were pulled out; his pants were also the pants he gardened in. Then he started up again.

"What time'd you get home?"

"I don't know. Not late."

"What does not late mean?"

"Eleven o'clock."

"Shelley drove you?"

"No, I . . . took the bus. Then I walked."

"Why didn't Shelley drive you?"

"She wanted to stay."

"Did something happen? Did you have a fight?"

"*No*. No."

"So why did you get a bus home by yourself at eleven o'clock at night when all your friends were sticking around?"

"They weren't my friends."

"What are you talking about? Marcus, Shelley . . ."

"Apart from them."

"Something happened you're not telling me," he said.

"What are you bugging *me* for? I told you. I must have left around ten o'clock—Marcus was still eating. It's not my fault."

"What's not your fault?"

"Whatever you're accusing me of, which I don't know what it is."

Mom said, "Nobody's accusing you of anything. We're just worried, that's all."

"I don't see what the big deal is. So he got in a fight with some guys, it happens."

"This could have consequences for someone in his position. We're just trying to figure out what to do."

"All right, leave him alone," Dad said.

Later that afternoon, Shelley showed up. I was in the living room watching TV. "Is Marcus around?" she said, when I opened the door.

"He's in his room. I think he's still sleeping."

"Does he want to see me?"

"I don't know. Let him sleep." Then I said, "Do you want to go for a walk? I need to get out of here."

The sidewalks in our neighborhood are pretty unreliable; you have to walk in the road half the time, which doesn't matter, because there aren't many cars.

Shelley said, "I should have just kissed you when you wanted me to, then none of this would have happened." She started crying.

"Do you want to sit down somewhere?" I asked, eventually.

"I don't want anybody to see me."

"Nobody can see you."

"Of course they can. We're in the middle of the road."

"They'll think we're just having, like . . . a teenage disagreement."

Eventually we walked back to the park. The swimming pool was still empty and full of leaves, but the water fountain worked, and Shelley sprayed her face and took a long drink. Then we sat on one of the benches next to the chain-link fence. The truth is, I felt kind of happy. I felt like, you're in the middle of something here, something real. It was cold enough, she sat with her feet under her butt and leaned against me.

"What happened last night?" I said, and she told me.

Around eleven o'clock, Marcus said he wanted to go home, so she offered to drive him. She'd only had a couple of beers, she didn't feel drunk. But then in the parking lot outside the bar she tried to kiss him and he pushed her away. He said he needed to concentrate on basketball right now. I need to do everything right. That's what he said. But then those guys from the bar saw him pushing her away. They must have thought . . . I don't know what they thought, she said. Maybe that it was the other way around. Anyway, they told him to leave me alone, and he said, what? And they said, Excuse me. Say excuse me, or something like that. It was just . . . horrible. I didn't know what to do.

"What did you do?"

After a minute she said, "I don't think I did anything. I was just standing there. I was kind of . . . in shock. About everything. I was pretty upset. I mean, even before those guys showed up . . ." and she looked at me. "Maybe I was a little drunk. I think I did say something. I don't know. I think I said, like, it's all right, it's okay, just . . . But also I was like, he wanted me to drive him home. And so I tried to pull Marcus away and he pushed me off again, and then one of the guys punched him."

"Which guy?"

"Josh, I think. I don't really know them, I never met them before. They're Briana's friends. Or not even her friends, her brother's."

"Where was everybody else?"

"They were still inside. But then Breon came out and after that . . . I just tried to get out of the way. It didn't last very long. I don't know how long it lasted. And then a cop car pulled up, and everybody ran."

"What did you do?"

"I ran, too. I didn't want . . . I was drinking and it was my car."

Somebody was spreading gravel in the park, along the paths. He had a rake and a little cart full of gravel. You could just about hear the sound of metal on stone. It was a quiet afternoon.

"What about Marcus?"

"He was on the ground with one of the guys. In the parking lot. But when the headlights hit them, they just lay there."

"What happened after that?"

"I don't know. We didn't stick around."

For once, Shelley wasn't wearing makeup so when she cried, it sort of opened out her face; she looked nice.

"I'm getting too cold, I have to keep moving," she said. But in the end she just walked me back to my house and went home.

In the morning, Coach Steuben showed up. I don't know how he heard about it; the story hadn't hit the papers yet. Maybe Caukwell called him. The first thing he said was, "I had to pull up behind the Olds. Let me know if you need to get out."

On Sundays, because of the church, there was nowhere to park.

His cowboy boots clicked on the wooden floor. Mom offered him a cup of coffee, and he said, "Black, two sugars, thank you, ma'am." Then we all sat down at the kitchen table.

"Is Marcus around?" he asked, and I said, "He's at the court."

My dad told me to get him, so I had to put on my shoes. As I walked out, Steuben said, "Maybe it's just as well if we talk first."

Marcus was shooting around by himself, in jeans; sometimes when you watched him from a distance it looked like, he's just messing around. With his head down, shuffling a few steps, feeling the ball in his hands. But a lot of time he was working on footwork. Two steps right, then hesitate, and go right again, but lead with the left foot, to put your body in the way . . . over and over again. Then when you shoot you have to plant left-footed, too. But from the outside it doesn't look like much. It looks like a kid who wants people to leave him alone, which is also what it was.

"Coach Steuben's here."

"What does he want?"

"You."

"What does he want with me?"

"I don't know, Marcus. I'm just the getting guy."

You could still see the bruise under his eye, but the blood had washed off.

When we got home, nobody asked me to sit down at the kitchen table, but I sat down anyway. Steuben said, "You got a nice shiner coming along," and Marcus said, "Yes, sir."

"So what the heck happened Friday night?"

"I don't know, sir."

"What do you mean, you don't know? You were *there*, right, when those guys beat the crap out of you?"

"Yes, sir."

"Did you start the fight?"

"No, sir."

"I need to know what kind of trouble you're in, so I can figure out what kind of trouble *I'm* in if I stick my neck out for you. *Did you pick a fight with those boys?*"

"No, sir."

"You were just minding your own business."

"Yes, sir."

"Were you drinking that night?"

"No, sir."

"The El Camino is a bar, right? They serve alcohol there?"

"I just wanted something to eat. It was after the game—I get hungry. I don't know what anybody else was doing."

"You don't know if anybody else was drinking?"

"No, sir."

"Can you see out of that eye?" Steuben asked.

"Marcus, why don't you tell him what happened," my mother said.

"I told him. I don't know."

"Something must have happened for those boys to pick on you."

"Brian, maybe you can enlighten us," my father said.

"I went home early."

Steuben took another sip of coffee. He had big hands, like baseball gloves, and could barely fit his finger through the handle. "How do those boys look now? You make 'em feel you?"

"There was two of them," Marcus said.

"Sounds like a fair fight." And that part of the conversation was over.

Later, Steuben said, "The phone's gonna go quiet over the next few weeks. All those recruiters who say they love you gonna get real quiet. There's nothing you can do about that. The only thing you can do is play basketball, if they let you. I've already had a word with the Blums about getting a lawyer. Let the lawyers do their thing but you've got to stay ready to do yours. I'm talking about Friday night. Maybe if you win a few games, if you make it to State, the phone starts ringing again. But when it does I want you to remember something, I want you to remember who knocked on your door the day after."

It was really two days ago but who's counting. "Will you do that for me, Marcus?" Steuben said, and then he stood up and shook everybody's hand, and walked out, slipping a little on his hard-heeled boots. We watched him from the living room, backing out carefully onto the road in a shitty dirt-white Chevy Beretta with California plates. He was twenty-five years old and this was his first real job.

After he left, Dad said to Marcus, "Have you called your mother?"

"What do you mean?"

"I mean, have you called her. Have you told her what happened?"

"I got in a fight. I don't know what the big deal is. I got in fights before."

"The big deal is, if this affects your recruitment. Marcus, she's going to find out. Maybe even from the paper. She should find out from you."

So Marcus pulled the kitchen phone into his bedroom on a long cord and closed the door.

On Monday, after school, Coach put Marcus and Breon on the B team, with me and a couple of other stiffs. So Marcus and I played together; he never passed me the ball, not once. But he didn't really pass to anybody. He took every shot and we won every game.

Dad came to pick us up. Caukwell wanted to talk to him so after practice we met in his office, still sweating and juiced up.

"When's the arraignment set?" he asked, and my dad told him, "Next Monday."

Marcus had been charged with a class A misdemeanor, which carried a maximum sentence of a year in jail and a four-thousand-dollar fine. The Haldeman kid might have died; his lung collapsed several hours after the fight, which can happen sometimes. At three in the morning, he felt these stabbing pains and thought he was having a heart attack. They took him to Dell Seton Medical Center, where they shoved a tube in his chest and reinflated him. Josh got off with scratches and bruises. The boys claimed they were just messing around with a bunch of high-school kids, you know, for being where they shouldn't be and doing what they shouldn't be doing, and Marcus jumped them in the parking lot afterward. Apparently, it was a he-said he-said problem—there were no other witnesses. So far Shelley's name hadn't come up.

The good news was, they Breathalyzed the boys in jail. Marcus was sober and the other two were drunk.

My dad did the accounts for a small law firm named Bettis and Gau, which specialized in criminal law. Anyway, Brandon Gau said the prosecutor was unlikely to ask for jail time. In Texas, they try seventeen-year-olds as adults, but it was Marcus's first offense, and my dad said, "If it's a question of money, don't worry about the money."

What Marcus wanted to know was, could he play? UIL rules don't actually specify anything about criminal charges. Basically, if you get the grades, if you're under nineteen, if you live where you say you live, if you're not in prison, you can play. It's the school's decision if they want to suspend you. In other words, it was up to Coach Caukwell, who had just demoted Marcus to the B squad.

"You need to be thinking about something other than basketball right now."

"We got a game Friday night," Marcus said.

"I know what's happening Friday. You need to be smarter about the situations you get yourself into," Caukwell said.

"I didn't get myself into nothing."

"What that tells me is you're still not thinking straight. It was Friday night, you were at a bar. The people you were hanging out with were drinking . . ."

"I had a Coke."

"It doesn't matter what you did or didn't do. Anything that goes on around you is your mess. You need to understand that. Because you're the one who has to clean it up."

"So who decides if I get to play or not?"

"Don't put this on other people, Marcus. What happens to you is what you *choose* to happen."

"Then I choose to play."

"I didn't say that."

"Anyway, Brian was there, too."

"I'm not talking about Brian. He didn't end up in Travis County jail."

"Come on, Coach. I mean, come on. You know what that's about."

"I know exactly what that's about. And whatever it is, you got to learn to deal with it."

On Tuesday morning, the story broke in the *Statesman*. Our copy arrived in a slim blue plastic bag and lay in the wet grass of the front yard until Mom stepped out in her bathrobe, coffee in hand, and picked it up.

"Arthur," she called, coming in. "Arthur. I think you should see this."

And so the day started.

Dad sometimes let us take the wheel when we drove to school. Since junior year, I'd been bugging him to get the test, but Texas state law means if you have a license the head of household has to put you on the insurance, and my father didn't want to pay for it. Still, we got our learner's permits and used to fight with him around the quiet streets of Hyde Park. Slow down, slow down. But they're riding up my butt, etc. That morning he let Marcus drive. This doesn't really have anything to do with anything, but sometimes I think it's funny, when I see him pulling into some parking lot on TV, in his Lexus LFA (with personalized plates), that he learned to stop at all the stop signs with Arthur Blum. A stop means a *complete* stop, Marcus. You're rolling.

At lunchtime I sat with Mike and Andy and Jim DeKalb in the cafeteria, and the first thing Jim said was, "Did you hear about what happened to Marcus?"

"What?"

"He got in a fight at some bar Friday night after the game. The cops had to break it up."

"I know. I was there." Even for something like this, you can't help bragging, and hearing yourself brag, and feeling ashamed.

"What happened?"

"Well, I left a little earlier. I didn't actually see it."

A pimple was blooming just below my bottom lip, where it hurts like hell but the pain is almost sweet and you can't stop picking at it. All day long I had a fat lip.

In practice after school Coach made us run. Three on two, two on ones, and then when he got tired of that, straight suicides. He said, some of you guys still need to work off your weekend, you need to sweat it out.

Afterward, when Marcus hit the showers, I said to Coach, "Can I talk to you for a minute?"

"Okay, talk."

But when I didn't say anything he led me to his office. Every time I was alone with him I felt . . . small, as my granma used to say. Like, that was small of you. His arms were bigger than my legs. To look like that, you have to spend years in the weight room, pushing yourself to the limit of your pain. To look like me you just have to eat.

"What can I do for you, Mr. Blum?"

"I wanted to talk to you about what happened Friday night."

"Well, talk."

"Are they gonna let Marcus play?"

"Sit down, Brian," he said.

"I really have to go—my dad is picking us up."

"Sit down."

His office had a couple metal folding chairs stacked against the wall, so I pulled one out and sat down.

"Is that any of your business?" he said.

"I think they should let him play."

"Why's that, Brian?"

"Because it wasn't his fault, what happened."

"He put himself in a position, which someone like Marcus can't afford to put himself in."

"But he didn't do anything."

"He went out drinking with a bunch of high school kids."

"But he didn't drink anything."

"Brian, I appreciate what you're trying to—"

"He didn't start any fight, either. What happened was . . ."

But I didn't really know how to say it. "There was a girl," I said, "who wanted him to . . . but he didn't want that. And when those guys saw him, with a white girl, they . . ."

"How come you know all this?"

"Because I . . . know the girl, too. She told me. The only reason they picked on him is because he's black."

"I know why they picked on him, Brian."

My face felt hot; I could feel it in my lip. Eventually I said, "Are you gonna let him play Friday night?"

"I was always gonna let Marcus play. Otherwise we get our asses kicked."

"Thanks, Coach."

"Got nothing to do with you." Then he said, "Have you told your dad . . . about this girl?"

"No."

"You should tell him," he said. "The lawyers might want to talk to her. And Brian," he called out, because I had started to leave. "You're a good friend to Marcus. He's lucky to know you."

In the end, they dropped all charges—against Kruger and Haldeman, too. My dad got in touch with Shelley's parents; I don't know what she told them, because we didn't talk about it again, but the Haldeman kid turned out to be fine. His lung was only partially collapsed (the medical term is a pneumothorax), and apparently you can recover from these things in a week or two without treatment. If you're young and basically healthy, which he was. But Steuben was right about the recruiters. They stopped calling.

Marcus played on Friday night and scored thirty-three points on twenty-one shots, with seven rebounds, four assists, three steals, and a blocked shot.

We won.

27

Fred Rotha won the pool. He came closest to Marcus's final stat line: seventeen points on five-for-nineteen shooting. Seven rebounds and four assists. Eight turnovers. But the stat that everybody picked on afterward was his three-point numbers: Marcus went two for nine. People assumed the percentage would improve, but the worry was that he took so many. It suggested a guy running out of options. He couldn't get separation, he couldn't get to his spots. All right, so it's game one, what can you tell. He's thirty-five years old, he hasn't faced competitive NBA defenses in three years. Let him play his way back into shape.

The Sonics lost in a blowout, and Marcus sat the last five minutes.

In the locker room afterward he faced reporters with ice on his knees. He said what you'd expect him to say. I'm just happy to be back. It felt good to be out there, under the lights . . . just a little rusty. I did what I wanted to do, sometimes the ball doesn't drop. And then: It's an adjustment for the other guys, too. They have to get used to playing with me. We'll figure it out.

They lost the next game at home against Memphis, a tough loss, low-scoring, where Marcus took twenty-seven shots and played forty-five minutes. Mickey struggled, too. Nobody could put the ball in the hole. It was the old grit and grind, no fast breaks, high ball pressure in the half-court. Rough justice under the basket, a lot of post ups, a lot of free throws. Then they got their first win against Minnesota on the road two nights later in a walkover.

Meanwhile, Marcus kept shooting threes. On *SportsCenter*, Tim Legler (a former three-point champ himself) broke down the way his shooting motion had changed. Analytics from his last NBA Finals in 2008 showed that his average vertical was twenty-nine-and-a-half inches at the point of release. He rose up, then he waited, then he shot.

"But look at him now," Legler said. "He's become a quick-trigger guy—the ball starts low, right off the dribble, and he jumps into his shot instead of waiting to come down."

"Is it better, is it worse?" Alana Sissons asked. These people are all vaguely friends of mine, having on air the conversations we would have anyway, in semi-private.

"It's different. If you know it's coming, it's going to be easier to block. But it's also harder to predict. This is what happens when you're thirty-five-years old. You have to adapt."

I used to watch the show in my hotel room while going to sleep, and then catch the rerun in the morning, before the breakfast buffet. It's on a rolling cycle. All night long this kind of analysis goes on, and you can dip your toe in whenever you want. But the river keeps flowing.

They lost against Dallas next. In the postgame locker room, I ran into Shelley Vance, who wanted to thank Marcus for inviting her and her husband and their daughter to the game (they waited outside). At first, I didn't recognize her; she was hovering in the background with the other reporters and nervously fingering the access pass around her neck. Her skin was still bad, but looked harder now, like a mask, and she covered it up with foundation. Even in the crowded locker room I could smell her perfume. She'd put on weight, too, maybe thirty or forty pounds. After a few minutes, though, I got used to her again. She still looked like Shelley, the high-achieving high-school cheerleader . . . but it was also like, some terrible thing had happened to her, twenty years of adult life, and then I remembered that it had.

Her son died of leukemia a few years before. I knew about this because Marcus Hayes gave a million dollars in his name to the Cancer Is Not For Kids Foundation, and the charity afterward came under a certain amount of scrutiny. Sixty percent of all donations went toward operating costs.

We had a short conversation. Shelley was an anesthesiologist but had recently stopped working to look after her daughter. Her husband was an employment lawyer; they lived in the Meadowbrook neighborhood of Fort Worth.

"It's so funny to see you here," she said. "But I guess, where else would you be, right?"

For a minute I thought she might invite me to join her family for dinner, but she seemed distracted by all the tall naked men around her, stepping out of showers, putting on suits, listening to music, while various NBA insiders wandered past, staffers, ex-players, broadcast journalists, kids, wives, friends. That night, lying in the over-starched sheets of the Marriott double bed, I tried to remember whether my lips had ever made contact with her lips outside the El Camino bar eighteen years before, feeling, you stupid, lonely, stupid man. Just the ordinary hotel blues. This is my suitcase, this is my life. Falling asleep in front of the television.

Three or four days a week, I drove out to Bergstrom, parked in the lot and boarded a commercial flight to some mid-level American city, Milwaukee, Portland, Denver, Cleveland, rented a car at the other end, checked into a hotel, drove or walked to the ballpark, fought the traffic and crowds, watched a basketball game, and went back to my hotel room to write it up.

What did I write about? The Sonics' problems on transition D. Is their bench deep enough for a playoff run, or are they still a trade away? What kind of assets can they sell (Stepanik, Crawford, Tony LaMarca, who led the League in blocks per minute) and who should they be in the market for? (Another shooter.)

Anything to take the heat off Hayes, because I could feel Joe Hahn and Amy Freitag looking over my shoulder. The Sonics started the season four and seven, but two of those wins came when Marcus sat out the second night of back-to-backs. He was shooting 41 percent from the field, the lowest mark of his career. And even though his three-point numbers were ticking up, he couldn't get to the line anymore.

Fewer than five a game, when his career average was close to nine. In postgame interviews, when reporters asked him about his shot chart, he always said the same thing, You got to take what the defense gives you. I'm trying not to force anything. Just stay in the flow. He was scoring twenty-five a night, neck and neck with Mmeremikwu, but needed six more shots to get there.

It's coming, Marcus said. I can feel it.

Three weeks after the season started, the sports page of the *Austin American Statesman* headlined with a quote from Mary Chapin Carpenter: "It's So Hard Admittin' When It's Quittin' Time." The point of the article was to ask, are the Sonics worse with Marcus Hayes than without him? *Sports Illustrated* put him on the cover under the simple title "The Homecoming," and actually started with a long reference to the Pinter play. There's a power struggle going on, Kenny Albrecht wrote, and Hayes is losing it. He just doesn't have the legs anymore, and it's becoming a question of when, not if, Mmeremikwu takes over the team.

A few nights later, after another loss against the Clippers, Alana Sissons asked Coach Kaminski, "It seems like you're having trouble in the second quarter, and when Mickey sits at the end of the third. Would you consider bringing Marcus off the bench, to help that second unit?"

Kaminski said, "No."

Everybody laughed, but it was hard to tell afterward where the joke lay. He was the kind of guy, people say, who doesn't suffer fools gladly. Which always makes me think, what a dick.

You had to be careful asking questions about Marcus Hayes. Because if he didn't like your questions, he didn't talk to you. And for much of that year, Marcus *was* the story. So everybody had this line to tread. The people who crossed the line first were not beat reporters, but local columnists like Roy Mears on the *Statesman*, who had nothing to lose, because he didn't have any real access anyway, or big shots like Rick Reilly, who didn't care. The rest of us were too embedded. Even Fred Rotha, who doesn't usually pull punches, came out firmly on the fence. The jury's out, he said. The guy hasn't played in three years. The season is two months old. I'm not willing to abandon Marcus Hayes Hill quite yet. This is how we talked—like high school kids, sitting around the cafeteria table.

But people were slowly drifting to the other side of the fence. Kenny Albrecht's story opened the gate. Then Michael Leahy wrote a piece for the *Washington Post*, comparing Hayes's second comeback to Michael Jordan's disastrous two-year stint with the Wizards. And so on. Journalists like us make our living offering small expert adjustments to the consensus, but what that really means is, we're totally dependent on the consensus and get in line behind it, once the line forms.

Except me.

One summer, my sister invited her French pen pal to spend a month at our house. I was thirteen and superconscious the whole time of the presence of a teenage female, sharing our bathroom and leaving her hairs in the shower. This girl (Ottilie) was an averagely attractive kid, whatever that means: hair, eyes, nose, legs, arms, all in the usual places. I don't think we really had the tools to say anything insightful or sympathetic about her real character, because her English was just about like Betsy's AP French, and who you are in that kind of language is the nice girl in class who sweats over her grammar and talks about the public transportation options, and not a full human being.

Anyway, for four weeks I obsessed miserably about Ottilie. Texas gets hot in July, and she wore little green Jean Seberg shorts around the house, and one of those tops or blouses that doesn't need straps, so you could see her shoulders. Which got badly burnt after two days; she was pretty pale-skinned and used to lie in the scratchy grass of our backyard, on a towel, reading a book and getting bitten by ants.

On the last night of her stay, to show appreciation, she cooked us a meal. Some kind of yellow soup, some kind of brown stew. It was like a hundred degrees outside but I finished my bowl of this soup and wiped the stew off my plate afterward with HEB's Primo Pick French Baguette Bread. And after every spoonful or mouthful, I looked at Ottilie and said the one French phrase I felt almost totally confident was appropriate to the occasion: *C'est delicieux, c'est delicieux. Ottilie, c'est delicieux.* Afterward, when she left (and Betsy was glad to see her go; they'd been sharing a room for a month), my sister took out her frustration on me. We still had a lot of summer to get through, she was suddenly bored. Whenever I did anything, or said anything, like thanks, Mom, for making French toast, Betsy turned to me in a supersweet, embarrassed and embarrassing teenage-boy-voice and said, *C'est delicieux, c'est delicieux* until my dad finally told her to cut it out.

In addition to working on the book, I wrote a weekly column for ESPN called the Hayes Report, and for two months it felt like the only thing I could say, even while the losses piled up, was *C'est delicieux*. Just to have him back, playing the game he loves. To watch him now was like confronting your delusions about some past life, when you were younger, healthier, and happier. And what my readers wanted me to prove to them was this: you suck, modern world, because Marcus Hayes can still kick your butt. Almost every night, he did something to remember him by. A sudden run of midrange jump shots in a meaningless second-quarter stretch. An up-and-under that makes the defense eat air. A thirty-foot teardrop as the clock runs down—even before it slips in, he starts to turn away, because he knows, he knows. *C'est delicieux.*

I didn't write about the bricked layups or missed boxouts or lazy transition D . . . Or the way he tugged on his shorts, every time somebody got fouled, or pounded the ball up court after rebounds to catch his breath. Hayes used to be a lockdown defender; there were seasons in his mid-twenties where you really couldn't dribble the ball anywhere near him. His idea was, it's my ball, I'm just letting you play with it. (This is a line from a Fred Rotha column.) But most nights Kaminski let him guard the three and sometimes even stretch fours.

With his extra weight, Marcus was hard to back down. He still had quick hands. But he couldn't track the speed bugs anymore.

Once at the end of a game in Miami (which the Sonics lost in OT), he switched on to LeBron, and LeBron, as he sometimes does, settled for a turnaround fifteen-footer and missed. Afterward, a three-second clip of Marcus pushing him off his spot, and stretching a long arm up, up, up into the King's face as he faded away, went viral. Old man still got it. But the truth is, I don't think it bothered James much. He just missed.

Shortly after Thanksgiving, the Sonics had a game in D.C. and Kaminski organized a training session at Alumni Hall in Annapolis — about a forty-minute bus ride from the Capital One Arena. It was basically a publicity exercise. Kaminski played for the Naval Academy and got his first coaching job there. Anyway, a few reporters came along to write the usual story and afterward they laid on the usual buffet, too, in the hospitality center, which had a wide-windowed view of the basketball court. Practice was in session. I carried my Styrofoam bowl of clam chowder and Keebler oyster crackers over to the window and watched.

Last night they played (and won) in Charlotte. Tomorrow they would lose against Washington. Just another early season road trip, an off day, a scrimmage at the end of a light workout, before they hit the showers and checked into another hotel and figured out how to waste an evening in D.C. In other words, it didn't matter much. Maybe they were just messing around. Maybe Kaminski was trying out some combinations. From my vantage point, fifty feet up in the hospitality center, I couldn't hear a squeak — they played in total silence. Mickey and Dieter, Ballatyne, LaMarca, and Jenks wore the blue practice jerseys; Hayes, Roundtree, Stepanik, Neves and Jones were in red. I started counting score but it wasn't close. The young guns ran them off the court.

Mickey guarded Hayes, spreading his legs wide, waving his long arms around, and Marcus started calling for Roundtree to come off the block and set picks. Everybody on his side of the court deferred to Marcus, waited for him to make something happen. LaMarca was quick enough to show on the screen and still track back if Roundtree rolled into the lane. Stepanik couldn't get open and Jones didn't want to shoot, so Marcus started pulling up from farther and farther out. He even knocked down a couple long threes, but every time he missed, the blue team ran: LaMarca to Crawford to Mmeremikwu. Or Mickey just took the ball himself. Often the only guy back was Marcus, because he never made it past the three-point line. In his day, he could blow up a fast break by himself—jump out to stop the ball while keeping a strong foot back to pivot at the last second into the passing lane. But you couldn't stop Mickey on the fly, and by the end they didn't even try.

I saw Marcus say something to Kaminski, and Kaminski shrug. Maybe he was trying to make a point. This is what happens if you pull off the handbrake. You need to adapt to these guys and not the other way around.

But then a Sonics staffer saw me watching and pulled me away. She said, "You really shouldn't be seeing that."

"It's just a scrimmage."

"Well, anyway. I'm going to have to ask you to come away from the window."

"Is this okay?" I said, standing a few feet back.

"A little farther."

Somehow I always end up being the problem.

28

Quinn Riley let me take her out to dinner. I always paid, she was on a pretty tight budget. We went to Zoot on the first date but after that started going to cheaper places. Not because I cared about the money, I didn't, but it made me feel less creepy to sit in a booth in Hill's Cafe and eat chicken fried steak and potato salad. Also, it's far enough down South Congress that not a lot of students go there. I really didn't want to run into any of her friends and have to explain myself.

I liked her. She could eat. In those days she was practicing five days a week and burning a lot of calories.

Hanging out with Quinn meant hearing stories about people she knew. For example, Annie, her housemate, was going out with this guy Ryan, and they had very loud sex, which seemed to involve uncontrollable crying afterward. Annie cried and Ryan just said, I know, I know. You imagined him stroking her hair. They lived in a fifties apartment complex with cheap partition walls, and Quinn lay in bed and listened to them because, A, she couldn't help it, and B, the truth is, she was kind of curious.

"Maybe I should say something to her," she said. "But, I mean, it's none of my business. And I guess if she really doesn't like what's going on, she doesn't have to let him come over. Because the rest of the time she's totally . . . they're like brother and sister."

Later she said, "This is what I don't like about myself. For some reason I judge her more than him."

The first time she stayed over at my apartment, I felt very . . . not just nervous but exposed. I thought she would think that the sportswriter she was going out with had a more grown-up life than I actually had. But from her point of view, my setup seemed pretty sweet.

I had my own kitchen and living area. You could hear birds from the front window, it was a nice neighborhood. She could walk back to campus in the morning through quiet streets, with Volvos in the driveway and kids' bikes in the yard, and remember what it was like to be normal.

I got the sense from her that I was a special-occasion guy, a once-in-a-while guy, when she needed a break from the rest of her life. Not a serious proposition. In bed, though, she was very . . . relaxed. She could tell how much it meant to me and that didn't bother her.

As a last-minute thing, when really I had been planning how to say it for several days, I said, Why don't we fly out to Boston together next weekend? The Sonics are playing on Sunday afternoon, they'll put me up at the Ritz Carlton. I used to live in Boston; I could show you around. We can do some Christmas shopping.

One reason she said yes was that her volleyball team had just gotten knocked out of the second round of the NCAAs, by Kansas State, a mild upset, and she needed something to fill the suddenly opened-up volleyball-free space in her life.

Quinn turned out to be a fun person to fly with. ESPN only covered coach, but I cashed in some air miles and bumped us both up to business class. She said yes to all the drinks, put on the complimentary socks and snuggled up in the plastic-wrapped blanket. I think she must have told herself, if you're going to do this kind of thing, just enjoy it.

It was nice to sit next to her, even if I had things on my mind. The day before we flew out, I pissed a little blood. Just a hard fleck, like a red scab, which disappeared into the bowl. My first reaction was, let's pretend I didn't see that. But my mother died partly because she spent the last three years of her life ignoring mild abdominal pain, so after twenty minutes googling blood in urine on my phone, I called the Austin Regional Clinic. They said, just show up. Then I sat for an hour on a hard-plastic chair with the background noise of MoPac traffic just audible through the windowless walls.

The doctor who eventually saw me was heavily freckled and pregnant, very skinny and pretty.

After a few questions she sent me to the bathroom with a cup, and I had to piss in the cup. It was a cold early December afternoon. Since I came in the car, I wore a wool sweater but no jacket, and for some reason didn't take off the sweater while waiting on the hard chair. (There were sweat patches on the armpits of my shirt.) But the clinic was extremely well heated and there was nowhere to put the sweater in the bathroom—no hook on the door, and hardly enough room to stretch your arms out and take the damn thing off. I managed in the end and finally wore it around my neck. Thinking, it's gonna slip off, onto the wet tiles, while dick in one hand and cup in the other, I stood over the toilet and hoped the flow would run out before the cup filled up. It didn't, I had to pull away and pissed a little on my fingers. Then screwed the lid on and stood at the tiny sink and tried to rinse it off, soap and wash my hands, dry everything with paper towels, while the sweater slowly eased loose behind me . . . In this state I returned to Dr. Henschel's office and gave the pretty woman my cup of piss.

It looked clear. I've never felt more unattractive or middle-aged, and my bar for both of those conditions is high.

She tested it on the spot for protein levels, which were fine, but also found microscopic traces of blood. She wanted to send the sample away for further testing.

What are you looking for?

Signs of infection. That's probably all this is. A urinary tract infection.

And what do you do for an infection?

We give you antibiotics.

And if not that?

Then we'll do more tests.

I told her that I was flying to Boston tomorrow for work. Is there any point in taking antibiotics now, just as a precaution. Because it might not be easy to find a doctor over the weekend.

She said, That's a good idea, and wrote out a prescription.

But still I didn't want to leave. This trip, I said. There's sometimes a social element to my work. I mean, people around me will be having a few drinks. I'm actually . . . taking a friend.

It's fine to drink a little on the antibiotics. Use your common sense.

I nodded and looked at her. With my hands on my lap, holding the sweater, and feeling now like a ten-year-old boy. So the best-case scenario is, this is a urinary tract infection, right, and the antibiotics clears it up?

That's right. And I had to go.

It was dark when we landed, East Coast winter dark, and twenty degrees outside, clear-skied and dry as powder. We caught a cab to the Ritz Carlton, dumped our bags at the hotel, and wandered into the night, looking for somewhere to eat. I wanted to show her the North End, about a mile away, and Quinn said she was happy walking, in spite of the cold. Her stride matched mine, hip to hip. I've sometimes seen girls walk like this together, when they're in the mood. Like, look at us, we don't care, and she took my arm, too—we were out on the town.

29

At some point during my senior year, Mom was promoted to executive director for the Office of Student Affairs. I was a kid; I didn't really pay attention to her life. But it meant a certain amount of new-school nervousness, which filtered down to me.

Anyway, a few months after starting she invited a colleague and her husband over for dinner. This was around March, in the middle of the basketball playoffs, and while all this other stuff was going on. For Christmas, Dad had bought her a clay pot, because she was in an ethnic cooking phase, and that night she made moussaka in it, which I don't think anybody liked. Marcus picked out the beef and potato until all that was left was a kind of eggplant yogurt goop, and Dad told me quietly to finish my plate but left Marcus alone.

My mother's colleague was named Brenda Peters and her husband Tom was a partner in Bluebonnet Equity, a venture capital firm. Brenda was actually slightly junior to Mom—at least that's the impression I got from the way she behaved at dinner. But Tom was obviously richer and more successful than my dad, so you had these crosscurrents of people trying to impress and defer to each other, which as a high school kid I was supersensitive to. Tom brought a bottle of expensive wine that he walked straight through to the kitchen to put in the fridge. Also, he wore those tan wire-framed sunglasses that I associate with *CHiPS*, the TV show, and took them off only when Brenda nudged him at the dinner table. After the meal, he asked Dad if he had any single malt and my dad found a bottle of Laphroaig in the cupboard where we kept the wedding china. Then they sat on the living-room sofa getting drunk until about eleven o'clock.

There are two reasons I mention this dinner. One is that Marcus and I had practice in the morning, which was a Sunday, because next week was the State Championships—Semis at one-thirty on Friday afternoon and the Finals if we made it on Saturday night. So we needed to get some sleep. And Mom obviously wanted these people to go home. The other is that Tom started telling dirty jokes; somehow he seemed in charge of the conversation. Where you from, son? he said to Marcus. Where your folks at? You heard the one about . . .? He kept trying to get a reaction from him. Marcus didn't say much but you could tell that Tom had his . . . full attention. The women disappeared into the kitchen.

By this stage, the recruiting visits, the phone calls, the letters in the mail, had all dried up. Marcus hoped that if we made it to the Finals, which tended to attract a lot of Div 1 scouts, some of the big-time programs would start knocking on his door again.

Whereas I . . . had been accepted by Texas, my safety school, and wait-listed at Brown, my first choice. Andy was going to MIT, Mike Inchman had a music scholarship to Rice (he played trombone), Jim DeKalb was following his brother to Swarthmore, Max Strom was headed to Georgetown. Basically, they were all cruising to the finish line—most of their grades were in, SATs were behind them, all they had to do was pass and graduate. Play cards, hang out at each other's houses in the late afternoons, perfect the art of stupid conversation. When the season ended I could join them.

But not till then. Caukwell wanted our lunch hour for extra practice and kept us late every day after class. Football is king in Texas but our football team sucked, and so for those three weeks of our playoff run, being on the basketball team was like . . . a taste of celebrity. I don't know; not really, but sometimes girls stopped us in the hallway and said, good luck. Especially if you wore your varsity jacket, which I never did. Mike and Andy started up a fan club for me, and even sold T-shirts in school, which initiated a lot of stupid conversations.

Because nobody understood the shirts. Who are the BB Gunners? They are supporters of BB. Who is BB? Brian Blum. Who is . . . oh, that guy. I mean, he never gets off the bench. Is it, like, an ironic thing? It is not ironic, it is totally sincere, Andy said. We are full of admiration for his accomplishments.

The tournament was at the Erwin Center, a real step up from our previous playoff games, which we played in some high school gym. All Burleson students got Friday afternoon off. That made us even more popular—school buses were booked to take kids from campus to the game. Guys on the team got to skip morning classes, too, so we could hit the gym and run through our final sets. Then we ate lunch together in a cordoned-off section of the cafeteria. Caukwell made a big deal about this lunch, for which the chef printed extra menus, but it tasted just like every other school meal. After that we set off for the stadium.

In other words, the whole day was designed to ratchet up tension. Marcus had the added stress of getting tickets. Harvey wanted one, Don wanted to bring his new girlfriend . . . Selena got in touch and asked if we could put her up, which would have meant somebody (me) sleeping on the sofa. In the end her partner came and they went to a hotel. She offered to stop by for an early breakfast, but Marcus didn't want to see his mom before the game, he didn't want the distraction. And my dad negotiated that conversation, too. Students at Burleson had a certain number of tickets reserved, at half-price; and players on the team could buy two extra tickets at the same price for friends or family. So there was a lot of talk about swapping tickets. I'm not actually sure what the big deal was, because the arena was only two-thirds full.

Langham Creek, our Semifinal opponents, drove in from Houston the night before and stayed at a hotel, which maybe made everything simpler.

I actually wrote a story for the school paper about their coach, Chris Mackey, a former high-school star. Eddie Sutton recruited him out of

Fort Smith, but by the time he showed up in Fayetteville, Sutton had taken the job at Kentucky, and Arkansas had just hired a young coach named Nolan Richardson to replace him.

Mackey had a pretty good freshman season on a team that lost a lot of games. Then Richardson started bringing in his kind of player, fast and long, guys who could run all day and jump out of the gym. He had realized there was a large supply of medium-skill, super-athletic types, especially in the football-crazy Deep South. If you recruited enough of these guys, and whipped them into shape, you could push the pace to the point where all the high-skill players everybody else wanted couldn't keep up. Mackey happened to be one of those players. His numbers declined, and by senior year he was lucky to get ten minutes a game on a team that went twenty-five and nine. He was basically superannuated by an idea. His response to that fact was to have huge respect for the power of that idea.

After graduating, he bounced around overseas for a while, including two seasons at Hapoel Tel Aviv, then came home to marry his college sweetheart, who grew up in Houston, which is where they settled down. Langham Creek High School had opened a few years before and Mackey took over the basketball team. The kind of style he instituted was the kind of style he would have hated as a kid—they pressed full court and ran all day long. He recruited a lot of football players, too, kids you didn't want to mess with, and called their defense "Thirty-two Minutes of Hell."

I actually spoke to him on the phone. He had one of those deep burnt-sugar Southern voices and gave me an hour of his time. I told him I was on the Burleson team, and he said, "Good luck to you, then," and I said, "You don't have to worry about me. I ride the pine."

"You never know," he said.

The previous game ended at one o'clock, at which point we could walk on court and warm up. My dad always complained that I warmed up wrong. He wanted me to practice the skill sets I might actually use in a game. Free throws, midrange jump shots. Short bank shots from the block, etc. But I was seventeen years old, on the varsity of my high school basketball team, in the Semifinals of the State Championships, and shooting around under the high bright lights on the court where the University of Texas played. So I took a few twenty-five footers, and when one went in, turned to look for him in the crowd . . . but saw instead, three rows up behind our bench, a banner (or series of large pieces of paper crudely stapled together and held up by taped-on drumsticks) with the name BB GUNNERS felt-tipped across it. Mike and Andy lifted it in the air and I raised my arms in triumph to acknowledge them.

Then Coach Caukwell ordered us into layup lines, and the clock overhead started ticking; I felt my breath shorten. You could see the Langham Creek guys on the other side of the court in their strawberry and cream uniforms. Los Lobos, with a wolf stitched into their jerseys. About six of them could dunk, the rim never stopped shaking. Afterward, we took turns shooting free throws, and I noticed that Marcus was missing. Apparently (this is what Breon said), he went to the bathroom to throw up. I made both of mine, then Marcus ran out and we huddled around him, touching hands. Lamont called out, Knights on one, KNIGHTS!, the horn sounded, and I wandered over to the bench to take a front-row seat.

It was the after-lunch crowd, people coming back from the concession stands with hot dogs or popcorn or 16 oz. sodas. But the Burleson High section was right behind us. Most of the students wore oversized Prussian blue GO BURLESON GO T-shirts, which someone must have handed out on the buses. They made a big bright block of color. From the tip-off, everybody stood up and didn't sit down again until halftime.

The game seemed faster than normal, even Marcus looked puffed. At the first time-out, I saw a crust of salt around his mouth. His skin had that badly lit, pale muddy quality. I thought, thank God I don't have to play.

Langham Creek doubled him every time he had the ball. If he passed off, he never got it back. We were down thirteen seven after one, and twenty-six sixteen at the half, but it didn't really feel that close.

Five of us hadn't played a minute—me, Blake Snyder, Tony Chua, Ben Silliman, and Josh Ramirez. Our sweat was nervous sweat and stank like old laundry. I could smell myself in the locker room. Caukwell's idea was to let Marcus play point and make Gabe and Lamont set screens for him in the backcourt. "I want you to hurt some people," he told them. "I don't care if they call fouls. Make 'em feel you." He had a smash-mouth football understanding of the game; Caukwell was an old SEC guy, after all. Hand off to your running back and block like hell. To Marcus he said, "Don't give it up unless you have to. It's your ball. It's your game."

Mackey was trying to do to us what Nolan Richardson had done to him, and everybody else the Razorbacks played against. Run 'em so hard that nothing else matters except how much you can run.

At halftime, Marcus took a shower. He had a spare pair of socks but not underpants, which he must have forgotten—they were so wet he had to wring them out. But he looked fresh, for about ten seconds, with the towel around his waist, and then the sweat started showing through. Caukwell had some clean shorts for Marcus, but no extra jersey. It was dripping when he put it on. The horn sounded when he was still tying his shoes.

It was our ball to start the second half, and Marcus beat the double team around the corner and drove the length of the court for a layup. Twenty-six eighteen. The next time down he did the same thing but dumped it off to Breon on the block for a six-footer. Then he pulled up for a three. Caukwell burned a couple time-outs in that third quarter just to give Marcus a breather, which is one of the things he got asked about afterward. What could I do, he said. The kid's going all out both ends. I wasn't gonna sit him.

With three minutes left, down two, Marcus missed an eighteen-footer and Lamont picked up the rebound. Lamont was giving up six inches, but he had an ass and could use it. Just wait till your man leaves his feet, and nudge—I don't care how big or strong he is. If he's in the air, you can move him. Then Marcus cut down the lane, took the backdoor pass and rose up one-handed with the bounce of the ball. When someone got in his way, he dunked on him.

It was a kind of fuck you. They'd been beating up on him all afternoon.

The building was filling up for the 6A Semifinal, and the noise level had started to thicken around us—you could feel the weight of the crowd in your ears, like the buildup to a summer storm. By this point in the game I was almost pure spectator . . . I say this, from a distance of almost twenty years, to explain what happened next. We traded misses, then Marcus released after a long rebound, streaked in for the layup, got fouled hard and lay there by the side of the court.

At first I thought he must have reinjured the ankle but mainly he was just exhausted. Dehydrated, too. The Erwin Center's an old building and the air-conditioning had broken down. They actually brought out a stretcher to carry him off, but when it got there he waved them away. Eleven thousand people rose to their feet when he stood up, if they weren't standing already, and watched, while he made the foul shot. With a minute sixteen on the clock, we were up by three.

Then they scored, and we missed, and they missed; there was a scramble for the rebound and one of the Langham kids knocked it out of bounds, under their own basket. You forget, these are high school games. A lot of what happens happens because things go wrong. Caukwell signaled to the ref that he wanted a substitution, then called out, "Brian!" from the far end of the bench. I pretended not to hear. He must have got up and started walking down the sideline, because eventually he stopped in front of me. "Brian," he said again. "Check in for Lamont."

I couldn't look at him.

"Tell Gabe to inbound. Run stack two. Line up next to Marcus, they're gonna double him, which means you should be free. Then hold on till they foul you. Do what you do."

Nothing.

"Come on, son. This is your chance."

The main thing that worried me, because I knew I wasn't going out there, in the middle of that stage, under all those lights, to shoot free throws, was how many people could hear this conversation. It was pretty loud in the arena, but the Burleson section was right behind us, which is why I didn't want to look up or give any sign that Caukwell was addressing *me*. Ben Silliman, who I knew from six years of Hebrew school, sat on one side; and Josh Ramirez on the other. They were the guys I talked to during games.

"Brian," Caukwell said again but changed his mind. We were out of time-outs otherwise he might have had a chance to do things differently. "All right, Ben, get out there."

Silliman was a decent shooter, a stocky six-foot point guard, who also played backup safety for the football team. Anyway, he came in, they doubled Marcus, and Gabe threw him the ball. Then Silliman missed both free throws. Langham got the rebound and someone released at the other end—for some reason, we didn't have anybody back. Just one of those dumb things that happens if you don't have a time-out. They got a layup and we had three seconds left to go the length of the court and score. Breon used to play quarterback in Pop Warner and took the inbounds. Marcus was running around like crazy at half-court but they put three guys on him. At least we got a shot off. Gabe Hunterton had a twenty-footer at the buzzer, which hit the backboard first and almost went in. And the game was over.

Afterward, Coach made us take the team bus back to Burleson. There were parents in the crowd who could have driven us straight home, but he said, we need another half hour, just us, to let this sink in. "They can pick you up from school. For most of you guys, for the seniors, this is the last time y'all will be together as a high school basketball team. This may be the last time you can call yourself a basketball player. You had a great run. It may not seem like that now, but there will come a point in your life when you wish you were back here again, so you could do it all over."

Nobody wanted to shower. I didn't know who knew about that inbounds play, apart from Josh and Ben, but I didn't want to wait for anybody or walk with anybody, so I got to the bus first and sat where I always sit, front left. Coach Caukwell came in behind and didn't look at me. Marcus usually sat with me, but he actually waited for Ben Silliman, who kept his head down, too, and they sat together a few rows back. Marcus had his arm around him. I felt so . . . jealous, until Dad met me in the parking lot and Marcus had to come with us.

30

After college I worked for a sports website called A Fan's Notes, which was later bought out by ESPN. Danny Liebling dropped out of MIT to set it up. The office was basically his kitchen/living room in Central Square. It overlooked one of those neighborhood playgrounds that got used by the local Montessori a few blocks away. For an hour in the morning and an hour in the afternoon, if you opened the windows on a hot day, all you could hear was the sound of screaming. Danny wanted us to remember what it was like to care about sports when we were kids. Like, when everything was a competition, and the point was to show that other kids were wrong, or dumber than you, even if you had to do dumb stuff to prove it.

Marcus Hayes was the reason I got the job. I spent three years at Texas writing about him, until he came out junior year, when the Celtics made him the third pick in the draft, like Jordan, like Len Bias. After he won rookie of the year, I sent the sports editor at the *Boston Globe* a stack of my articles about Hayes. A few weeks later he wrote back and suggested I get in touch with Danny. At the time, he really didn't have any accreditation, or insider access; he just watched a lot of TV and wrote about what he watched. They talked about pop culture, too.

Alana Sissons was there when I arrived. We overlapped for about six months. Somehow her presence turned the whole thing into a kind of debate team boondoggle, where the nerds were delighted to have in their presence a fellow girl nerd, until she got hired by the *Times* and moved to New York.

I lived on the first floor of a rundown building three minutes from Porter Square. My first job, my first grown-up apartment, my first taste of real life. At the other end of the street, among the grand old Cambridge colonials, was Raymond Park, which had a couple of basketball courts. I heard Larry Bird liked to shoot around there but never saw him. Sometimes, after work, if it was still light out, I put on my high-tops and grabbed a ball from the house and walked over to the courts.

In those days, Marcus didn't need an escort to go out in public. Once or twice he even came over for dinner—we'd order pizza and watch a ball game on TV. Or wander over to the park and shoot around. Then the kids would figure out who he was and ask for autographs, and he'd dunk a little, just to show off, and I'd stand on the side seeing the whole thing unfold and finally take a ball and shoot over on the other basket by myself, until he got bored. My landlady called him, "That nice young man with the interesting hair."

Quinn and I actually saw him that first night in Boston. There was a crowd outside the Daily Catch on Hanover Street, which is one of the places I thought of taking her to dinner. But there's always a line, and it seemed a pretty cold night to spend an hour inching along the sidewalk. Then when we got there we realized it wasn't a line. The restaurant was closed for a private party, but you could see what was going on through the window. Marcus and a young black woman sat at one of the tables, lit by candlelight, eating pasta from a pan.

She wore a long black evening dress, which was just . . . I mean, you shouldn't eat spaghetti, looking like that. Marcus had on a brown suit with oversized lapels, and leaned over the table, all elbows and arms, because he didn't really fit in the chair. Other people were there, too. Rajon Rondo and Kevin Garnett. Maybe also Kendrick Lamar and Mark Wahlberg and . . . Casey Affleck? Mila Kunis and . . . I don't know. Famous people who don't play basketball are not my field. There was a rotation of rubberneckers. People saw the crowd and went over to check out what was going on, maybe take a few pictures, and then move on. It was twenty degrees outside, and you could feel your face because you'd kind of stopped feeling your face.

Quinn said, "I know that girl."

"Which one?"

"The one sitting with Marcus. She's in my psych lecture."

"What's her name?"

"Cheryl something. Cheryl Dillard."

"What's she like?"

"I don't know, she's in my . . . we have these seminar groups, and she's in mine. Kind of stuck-up but smart. Smarter than me."

In the morning, the papers were full of Marcus Hayes. I asked at hotel reception to get the *Globe* and the *Times* and picked them up outside my room while Quinn slept, then climbed back into bed and read them while she lay beside me.

It was front-page news in the *Globe*: "The Prodigal Returns," by Stacey Kupchak. The last time Marcus suited up in Celtics green he lifted the Larry O'Brien trophy over his head, and then, which is what he always did, laid it against his cheek and seemed to slow dance with the cold gold metal against his face. They had a photo of that, too, on court at the Staples Center after the Finals. But the article itself was mostly about the Sonics' current struggles. They were eight and thirteen coming into the game; Marcus was shooting the lowest percentage of his career. Stories about locker room tension had started to emerge, with Marcus on one side and Mickey on the other. Every minor game-time interaction between them, caught on camera, had become a subject of minute analysis. There were rumors that Coach Kaminski was about to get fired.

Meanwhile, the Celtics had their own problems. Garnett was getting too old to carry a lot of minutes—on the downslope, hanging on. Sometimes big-body guys can stretch out a career long enough for you to forget what they were like when they were actually good. They look great on the lineup sheet, but there's a difference, and eventually it shows. Young guns like Avery Bradley hadn't broken through yet and maybe never would. The Celtics were twelve and nine, just keeping their head above water. This is the kind of game that can make or break a team, in the long dead stretch of season between Thanksgiving and the All-Star break.

Of course, reporters have to say stuff like that, to keep selling papers. The art of sports journalism is to combine the memory of an elephant with the attention span of a goldfish—what they really care about is the next six seconds. Which doesn't mean they're not right, some of the time. Kupchak wrote, "This may turn out to be one of those classic late-career encounters, where all of the drama ends up being unconnected to the real implications going forward: Mmeremikwu is the future of the League, but this isn't his moment."

There was even an article about me, which I pushed across the table when we finally went down to brunch. About the sportswriter who grew up with Marcus—it called me the Hayes Whisperer. I knew it was coming because the journalist asked me for a quote.

"I'm having such a good time already," Quinn said.

"What makes you say that? I mean, I'm happy you're happy. Me, too."

"I'm sitting at the Ritz Carlton in Boston with this famous guy who used to live here and is gonna show me around."

The truth is, I don't know how much I showed her. The game sat like a big lump in the middle of the afternoon. But we walked around the Common and little specky snow began to fall. Not enough to stick but enough to . . . blur the cloudy sunshine, like an etching . . . to make it look like what was happening had already happened and wouldn't be forgotten. I showed her the metal ducklings waddling out toward Beacon Street. They were already wrapped up for the season in Santa hats and red-and-white scarves, but Quinn didn't know the story, so I had to tell her. What I could remember. Some cop helps them cross over from Beacon Hill. My mom used to read it to me. Now I read it to Betsy's kids.

"And later, when we get back to the hotel, you can read it to me."

But she was kidding and looked kind of filthy when she said it, which was part of the joke.

Amy Freitag managed to get me a comp for Quinn, which she described on the phone as an A1 favor, because tickets were hard to come by. You owe me, she said. The things I do for other people's sex lives. It was one of Amy's long-standing jokes that she couldn't get a date, a way of flirting with you and putting you off at the same time.

We had lunch in Chinatown and afterward walked to the game. It's a nice thing; I always like walking to a ballpark and seeing the city converge, like ants on a watermelon rind. Everybody in a good mood, the way you tend to be when you've already spent the money on something you're about to enjoy. I saw kids wearing Marcus's old Celtics jersey, the famous 11, and even a few Sonics green-and-gold number 4s.

A few minutes before tip-off, the lights brightened and the heat increased, and I noticed an ABC crew setting up on the sidelines to interview somebody sitting in the front row. It was Don Hayes, Marcus's dad, who wore sweatpants and loafers, and a Bat City Sonics sweatshirt. You could see his face reproduced in quadruplicate on the jumbotron in eight-foot by eight-foot pixelated lights. Some people in the crowd must have recognized him because there was a scattering of applause, and then he stopped moving his mouth, the camera shifted, and Selena said something, because she was sitting next to him—brightly made up, in kiss-me red lipstick.

When she heard the clapping she sat back smiling and clapped back, and I thought, I guess he knows they're here because Amy must have gotten them the tickets, but when Marcus walks on court to play basketball this kind of thing will be going on, whatever this is. So far as I knew Don and Selena were barely on speaking terms.

But then they killed the lights, and the screen showed a picture of Marcus Hayes rising up to shoot over Derek Fisher in the '08 Finals . . . "My Time" started playing over the sound system: *My life has been a movie all the time, every single night . . .* while Eddie Palladino, the Celtics PA announcer, crooned . . . *At guard, six six, from the University of Texas, Marcus Hayes . . .* and out of nowhere the spotlight chased him on court and it was like a snarl of high-voltage wiring blew up, the place exploded in static sound. For a full minute Marcus stood shifting from foot to foot, singled out by a beam of light, while a montage of his Celtics highlights flashed overhead.

After that he had to play basketball.

There's always a weird transition moment when the light show ends, and you realize you're just in a crowded hangar-like space, while a dozen or several hundred feet away, in the middle of a relatively small area, a few guys have started to play basketball. Marcus couldn't make a shot, maybe he was too pumped up; or too tired, which can also happen after an adrenaline surge. But Mickey kept them in the game. He blocked KG at one end from behind, then took the ball the length of the court and dunked over Avery Bradley like he didn't see him. The way Mickey ran the floor was like nobody else. I can't describe it, he ran like somebody with eight legs—like a lot of separate limbs were racing each other neck and neck. He looked angry, too, but that was just cartooning for the cameras.

Bradley was another Texas guy; he and Marcus had a connection. It's funny how these NBA players carry the torch for their alma maters. They look out for each other, too, there's an old boys' network. I saw Bradley say something to Marcus a few minutes later, coming out of a time-out. And Marcus looked at him, like, I know. What can you do. These are the things you notice from the third row center court. Bradley guarded him most of the time and did a pretty good job. Marcus couldn't get anything going and finished the half with four points, on one for nine shooting. The only bucket came when he didn't track back after a long rebound and cherry-picked a layup after Crawford stole the ball. His physical expression was totally recognizable to anybody who has ever messed around on a basketball court. Like, finally. Then he jumped up and pulled on the net, as if to say, okay, there *is* a hole in the middle.

The Sonics were down seven at the break. It was a high-scoring game, very loosey-goosey, more like pickup basketball. Marcus had already started pulling his shorts in the free-throw lineups, sucking wind. But things tightened up in the second half, when Marcus took over the point. They started playing big, Marcus, Mickey, Stepanik, Roundtree and Neves. A lot of long arms, and three of those guys could switch one to four. So you couldn't pick them apart, and you couldn't pass your way through, and when the Celtics tried to establish Garnett in the post, Mickey was quick enough to double down and help out Roundtree, and then get back for his rotations. It was like playing in mud. The third quarter score was nineteen sixteen Sonics.

Even when Marcus sat down, and Jones came on at the start of the fourth, the pace didn't shift. It was more like playoff basketball. At a certain point, if everybody starts really trying, the number of guys on court who can actually score turns out to be surprisingly small. Jones never trusted his jump shot in tight games. Stepanik couldn't get free. Roundtree had a couple of putbacks but both teams were more or less treading water or holding the fort, whatever you want to call it. Even Mickey couldn't score. The Celtics packed the paint. The only shooter they had to worry about was Stepanik, and Bradley took him out, it was almost like a box and one. Anyway, they dared Mickey to shoot jump shots, and Mickey accepted the dare and missed.

Then with six minutes left, Marcus came in. At that stage he had ten points on three for thirteen shooting. They switched Bradley back on to him, so Marcus, pounding the ball at the top of the key, called Stepanik up to set a pick. Even from where I was sitting I could hear him say, *Come get me, Step.* Bradley just moved his eyes for a second, to see where the pick was coming from, and Marcus, from twenty-five feet, knocked down a three. Garnett made one of two free throws at the other end (after a hack by Roundtree), and then

Marcus called the same play again. This time Stepanik slipped the screen, and Marcus hit him with the pass and cut down the middle, and Jan bounced it back. Marcus pulled up from the foul line and knocked down another.

In the row behind me, someone said, "I've seen this movie before."

The Sonics were now down three. Whenever Marcus hit a shot, a subset of fans clapped or cheered but most of the crowd wanted him to lose. People were on their feet, so Quinn and I had to stand up, too. I said to her, "What do you think?" And she said, "What?" So I shouted, "What do you think?" tasting the heat of my own breath in her ear. And she said, "Feel my hands," and I held her hand, which was warm and damp with sweat. She didn't let go. I thought, you're a nice kid, to let yourself get caught up.

After that they traded misses, and then Bradley broke free for a fifteen-footer on the baseline (Marcus had doubled down to help on the block), then Mickey drove and kicked out to Stepanik on the wing, who hit a three, and the Sonics were down two with twenty-seven seconds left. The Celtics called time and the air leaked out of the balloon again; everybody just kind of sat around until the commercials ended for all the folks watching at home on TV. Then ten guys walked out again to the middle of the court and nineteen thousand five hundred and eighty people stood up to see what they were going to do.

What happened next happened quickly. The Celtics tried to run the clock down, but Crawford, who was back in the game, forced Rondo toward the right sideline, maybe ten feet from where we were sitting. Mickey was fronting Garnett in the post but suddenly abandoned his position and ran out to trap the ball. Rondo swung it to Bradley at the top of the key, who lofted a pass toward Garnett . . . Roundtree came over from the weak side but too late. KG had an easy layup, until Mickey, with two ridiculous strides, flew in from behind and blocked his shot hard against the backboard, then caught his own block and started sprinting the other way.

Kaminski wanted to call time-out but nobody saw him. Mickey never really had control of the ball. It was like a broken-field play—Rondo stood at half-court, but Mickey pushed the ball beyond him and kept running. The Celtics had another Frenchman on the roster, a wing named Pietrus, very long, very quick, who knew Mickey from the national team. They'd played together for years. Anyway, he held his ground, and when Mickey tried to spin around him, going full tilt, he lost his balance and threw the ball at the rim before falling out of bounds. There he lay, with his long arms stretched wide, waiting for the whistle, but it never came.

Roundtree picked up the loose ball, he really had a hell of a game. As soon as Mickey started running, he started chugging after. But Pietrus bodied up to him from behind, so Roundtree kicked it out to Marcus at the three-point line, and Marcus caught the ball like it was shooting practice and released. The horn sounded while it was in the air, the red light over the backboard flashed on, and by the time the ball dropped through the net the game was over, and the Sonics had won.

Their bench emptied out while Marcus held his right arm in the air, and a few people from the crowd spilled onto the court. It was half a celebration and half a collective sigh. One of the guys running toward him was Don Hayes, who almost stumbled over a front-row chair and tried to grab his son by the shoulder. Don by that point was seventy-five, an old football player, top-heavy, but Marcus at the same time had started to turn toward half-court, like he was looking for a face in the crowd . . . and when his dad tried to hug him, or just hold on, Marcus seemed to shrug him off. The guy almost fell down. His glasses swung around on his neck and his momentum carried him past, in short shuffling steps . . .

This is the clip they showed on *SportsCenter* that night, after the game-winning shot. Over and over again.

"Ouch, that hurts," the commentator said.

31

Quinn and I watched the seven o'clock edition in the hotel room after the game. I felt wiped out. We were lying in bed together, fully dressed. She said, "What do you want to do tonight?"

"We could get room service and watch a movie. It's Sunday night, we've got an early flight."

"Bri-an," she said, like that. Bri-*an*—which is something she'd started to do, and I couldn't tell if the voice she was putting on was like a bratty kid sister voice, or like my mom, calling me in to dinner. But it meant the same thing—come *on*. Shape up.

"So what do you want to do?" I asked her.

"We could go out with Marcus and Cheryl."

"What do you mean?"

"Why don't you give him a call? Whatever they're doing is probably going to be more fun than something we can come up with."

"You can't just call Marcus."

"I thought you used to live together."

"That was in high school. He's not a person I can just call on the phone and say, hey, what's up. You want to hang out."

"We hung out with him before. I don't see why not."

"He's not a person like that anymore. If he wants to see you, he lets you know."

"How do you know?"

"What do you mean?"

"How do you know he doesn't want to see you? Do you ever call him and ask?"

"No."

The truth is, I was beat. I don't sleep well after alcohol, and we'd had a pretty late night the night before. Sometimes like a cold coming on you can feel depression starting to settle in, even though I told myself, this is not the time, with this warm body lying next to you, to feel these things . . . but you feel them anyway.

"So call him," and I had to say, "I don't have his number."

She turned on her elbow and looked at me. Her long red hair lay between us like this extra thing, like a cat or something—whenever she lay down she had to arrange herself around her hair.

"So how do you get in touch with him?"

"I don't. If I need something, I call his assistant, Amy Freitag."

"So call her."

"Quinn, it's Sunday night. She works all the time but at the same time, I try to respect the fact that all these interactions for her are work. What's going on? What's this really about?"

"Aren't you supposed to be writing a book about him?"

"Yes."

"I want to help you. I want to be a part of it."

"It's nice for me just that you came along."

"We can do better than that," she said and got out of bed.

"What are you doing?"

She was looking at something on her phone.

"Texting my friend who knows Cheryl." And then we just waited around for her phone to ping. By this point it was almost eight o'clock. She said, "Bri-an, come on. You may as well start getting ready."

"Getting ready for what?"

"To go out."

The number came through, and Quinn called it, standing by the window—she pulled open the curtains and looked out. On nothing much. Boston at night. The snow had stopped, it was overcast, and the clouds held in the light pollution. Nobody answered.

"What are the ten best restaurants in Boston?" she asked me.

"What do you mean best?"

"Like fancy . . . like if you want to have a good time. Forget it," and she started tapping on her phone. Then she clicked a number and put it to her ear. "Hi, this is Amy Freitag," she said. "Calling about the reservation for Marcus Hayes . . . okay, thank you." And hung up.

"You can't do that."

"Do what?"

"You can't . . . Anyway, none of these guys use their real names."

"Come on, Brian. Get your dancing shoes on. We're going out." Then, after a minute, "So what name does he use?"

"I don't know."

"What name?"

"I don't know! Superhero alter egos . . . guys they played with when they first came into the League, who nobody heard of again . . . I don't know." Then I said, "Isaac Brown."

"What?"

"Isaac Brown. It's the kid who beat him on to the varsity at Burleson in his sophomore year."

Five phone calls later she found the reservation at L'Oseille. You can walk there but I promised to get a cab—Quinn wore three-inch heels and a nothing green dress, with only her North Face puffer over the top. I could tell that she had decided to have a good time and was going to use whatever materials she had on hand, which included me.

L'Oseille is one of those places where they put tall dead branches in a glass vase on the grand piano. Couples huddle intimately around packed-in tables, like they don't want anybody to hear what they're saying. In which case, they should stay home. But it's true, when you walk in somewhere like that, and have to put up a front just to approach the maître d', it gets your blood pumping. You figure, screw it, and take out your wallet.

Even on Sunday night the place was full. But we could get a drink at the bar, which is what we did, and Quinn sat with her long legs hanging off the high leather stool. I don't usually get to sit in a place like that with a girl like that. Everybody probably figured I was her dad, or rich. Near the bar, a booth with yellow sofas was separated from the rest of the tables by a black-and-yellow screen. Six people could sit there comfortably, but I only saw the top of his head—tight cornrows. Copley Square is not a cornrow kind of scene, so I figured, Brian, get off your ass and say hello.

"Come on," I said to Quinn, and we carried our cocktails with us. I had an old-fashioned, Quinn was drinking manhattans. Neither of us had had anything to eat.

"Fancy meeting you here."

And Marcus glanced up and for a second gave me the look he gives a hundred strangers a day, like, is this where the threat comes from? Is it happening now? The girl he was with was the woman in the cocktail dress from last night. When she saw Quinn, she said, "Oh my god, I can't believe there is someone I actually know in this place. I've totally forgotten your name. You're in my psych class."

"Quinn."

"Are you stalking me because of Marcus?"

I said, "We used to live together in high school."

"Where are your manners, Mr. Hayes? Tell them to sit down. I want to hang out with normal people."

"Who have you been hanging out with?" Quinn asked.

"Matt Damon."

And Marcus said, "It's okay," not to any of us, but because Radko appeared behind me.

"Hey, Radko, good to see you."

So we sat down, sliding into the other side of the booth.

"Lookee, lookee, lookee," Marcus said when nobody else said anything. "It's the Hayes Whisperer."

"Did you read the article in the *Globe*?"

"People tell me things."

Then the waiter came and we ordered. Quinn looked at me, and I said, "Whatever you want." The cheapest entrée was in the forty-buck range, although you could get a plate of pasta for half that.

"You using me to get girls?" Marcus asked, because Quinn and Cheryl were talking about college stuff, and not really requiring input from the two of us.

"I always used you to get girls."

"Yeah, well. You never had any girls."

"Whose fault is that?"

"I'm not your fucking pimp, Brian," he said.

From time to time people approached the table to say something to Marcus. Great game, nice shot, good to have you back at the Garden. You wore the wrong color uniform. You killed us out there tonight. Fat men hiding their guts in double-breasted suits; women in pearls. I'm sorry to disturb your dinner. I just wanted to say . . . If they asked for an autograph, or took up more than ten seconds of his time, Radko stepped in. But Cheryl also talked to them. She said, "Oh my god, this is such a nice restaurant. Most of the time I'm eating, like, dining-hall baked ziti."

Marcus didn't say much. After a game, he always looked a little drugged, like he was coming down off something . . . The main human quality expressed by his personal interactions with the public was patience. Also, he was thirty-five years old, he had just played thirty-nine minutes that afternoon; at that age, you pay for every one. Until the food arrived, he nursed a Chivas Regal—he swilled the ice around his glass, sipped, and put it down. I don't think Cheryl was drinking. A bottle of Perrier sweated in front of her.

Quinn said to Cheryl, "We're going dancing later."

"We are?" I said.

"I told you to put on your dancing shoes."

"That's just an expression."

"Oh my god," Cheryl cut in. "I know exactly what I want to do."

"What's that?" Marcus looked at her, amused.

"Late-night bowling."

"We're not going late-night bowling."

"Radko," she called out. "Where can we go bowling around here?"

"What'd I just say?"

"*She's* going dancing," Cheryl said.

"I don't know about that," I said, and Quinn said, "I know."

This is how the conversation went. It was really just the Cheryl and Quinn show. Cheryl said, "You should see our hotel room," and "Where are you staying?" "At the Ritz Carlton." "Us, too. What floor?" "The ninth." "We've got the Presidential Suite, which I guess is . . . the penthouse. I said, if I'm going to fly all this way for your . . . thing, I want a balcony with a view . . . but apparently, they don't have balconies at the Ritz Carlton. But oh my god, the view. You should come have a look. Right over the park . . . just knock on the door." Then: "*He* never sleeps anyway."

Meanwhile, underneath this back-and-forth, I said to Marcus, "What about the house?" Marcus spent ten years with the Celtics and lived for most of that time in Brookline, in one of those faux-Renaissance mansions off Woodland Road, between Dane Park and the Country Club.

"We're selling it."

Then the food arrived.

Cheryl had said, I want to try everything once, which is why, when she saw the menu, she ordered foie gras. I had the cauliflower soup and Quinn chose the wild boar gnocchi. It was that kind of place. Marcus had a Cobb salad, which he picked at but didn't really eat. Anyway, the foie gras arrived, just a slab of paste-colored . . . stuff, it looked like meat-substitute, with a soft half-pear on the side and shavings of black truffle on top. Marcus looked at it and looked at me and said, "Shit or stick," which was a game my dad used to play, if he saw something brown in the grass.

It wasn't really a game, it was more like a joke, like pull my finger. My dad was famous in my circle of friends for saying stuff like that. Anything he could do to embarrass me.

Cheryl said, "I can't eat that now."

Her mood had suddenly shifted; she was disappointed with her order and not having such a good time. This is what happens when you hang out with people three years out of high school.

"So don't eat it."

"Now you ruined it for me. We can't just throw it away. That's expensive food."

"I know. I'm paying for it."

"So you eat it."

"Come on, baby," Marcus said.

"You eat it. I don't want to throw it away. A goose died for that plate of food."

It was a lovers' spat, public and private at the same time.

"You know I can't eat it," he said gently. "You know I can't eat rich food."

"Why not?"

"It gives me gas."

"I don't want to throw it away."

"So eat it."

"I don't want to now, it's spoiled." And eventually he pulled her plate across the table and ate the goose, and she kissed him—on the cheek, like Daddy had just bought her a new dress.

"Always got to have her way," he said. "I'm gonna pay for this later, you know that, right. You will, too."

And we had to sit there and watch.

Later, though, after the meal, he put his foot down. Cheryl wanted to go bowling, and he said, "Not tonight." You never sleep anyway, she said, we just sit around that hotel room. That's why we got a nice hotel room. Then she turned to Quinn. "Why don't you come, too. We can watch *SportsCenter* on the fifty-inch TV. We can watch you make that shot all over again, right, baby?" And she snuggled up against him, with her head in his armpit. But Quinn really wanted to go dancing, so Cheryl got excited about trying to figure out the best place to go. She said, "Radko knows, or he can find out. Radko knows everything." And so he got involved, too. In the meantime, I went to the bathroom to take another pill—to stare at myself in the mirror over the gold-plated faucets. What are you doing? I said to the face I saw. Why is this your life?

When I came out again, decisions had been made. There was a club called Tunnel about five blocks away.

"We're not walking anywhere tonight," Quinn said.

"Tunnel sounds like just my kind of scene."

"It's fine, Brian. It's totally . . . for grown-ups, it's in the basement of the W Hotel."

"Is that what I am?"

Marcus when we left took my hand and kind of snapped his fingers against it . . . and looked me in the eye like, you and me both. And as we walked out into the night, Cheryl called out again, "You have to see the view from our hotel."

It was snowing again, coming down soft and heavy, so that the car lights cast little polka-dot shadows on the road. But in her high heels, Quinn's feet stayed perfectly dry. She said to me, "What do you think of Cheryl Dillard?" while we waited for a cab.

"I think she's crazy."

"Good crazy or bad crazy?"

"I don't know. I think I feel sorry for her."

Then a cab pulled over and we went dancing. Who knows when you fall in love. Everything that happened that night happened because Quinn had the energy to make it happen—she pulled me along. The club is not even worth describing; it was too loud for normal descriptions to mean anything. You were just in a world of sound. They played "Blow Me" and "Scream" and "Die Young," and I don't know what. In the strobe lighting Quinn's pale skin and green dress flashed like a fish in a fish tank. I was totally aware that everywhere she moved other bodies gravitated toward her, and that she closed her eyes and hung her arms around me so that I had no doubt of her allegiance . . . which was clearly, on some level, like she was saying, I give you this gift.

Then around one in the morning, they were playing "Halo" and I bent down to shout in her ear, "Can we go home now? I want to go home with you now," and she nodded.

The snow had stopped when we stepped outside—about a foot lay on the ground. Under my shirt, the sweat cooled instantly. Quinn was still hot enough to leave her puffer unzipped. A cab came and took us back to the hotel.

32

In her rolling suitcase, Quinn had rolled along with her for this dirty weekend a file of notes and half a dozen textbooks, including *Learning, Memory and Conceptual Processes*, by Walter Kintsch, which I actually remembered from my own psych seminar fifteen years before. Of course, she barely cracked them. That first morning I picked up the Kintsch and started reading it in the big king-sized bed until she came out of the shower and asked me to stop. "You're totally freaking me out," she said. One of the things I liked about her is that she said it and then forgot about it.

But after we cleared security at Logan, while waiting at the gate . . . reality could no longer be ignored. So she sat around texting people about how screwed she was.

I went to the bathroom and for some reason called my voice mail. Like, I've got my own life, too. There were a couple of messages, one from my sister about Christmas plans and another from the Austin Regional Clinic. My urine sample came back negative for infection. I needed to book a kidney and bladder scan. Then I bought a bag of Fritos and the latest *Sports Illustrated*, which is what I always read on planes. On the flight home, Quinn read *Psychology*, by David G. Myers, one of these Yellow-Page-style doorstoppers, and I tried to figure out, why kidney and bladder.

We landed in Bergstrom and eventually walked out into the winter afternoon, fifty-eight degrees and sunny, and crossed the underpass to the garage where my car was parked. I dropped her off at the Orange Tree Condos on Rio Grande, got out to carry her suitcase to the doorstep, kissed her once in a casual way, and said, "Do you want me to come up?"

"That's nice, Brian. I had such a nice time. But I need to get in the zone. Just for this week."

"Then it's Christmas."

"I'll call you before I go home."

Then I kissed her again harder and she let me. There was nothing else I could do but drive off.

When I got home, I had an email from Amy Freitag. *What a game, right. I hope your friend had a good time.* But that's not really why she was writing. The Sonics had one of the best analytics departments in the NBA, and she thought I might like to see some of the data.

Taffy Laycock was an early adopter. He believed in nerd power and actually invested in one of the startups that lost out to Second Spectrum. Anyway, this is what Amy wanted me to see: the Marcus and Mickey pick-and-roll numbers, which weren't great. The problem was, Mickey couldn't shoot threes, so defenders slid under the screen. It worked better with Mickey as the roll man, but the most efficient pick-and-roll numbers on the team belonged to Stepanik and Hayes. Either way, defenses had to fight over the screen, and Marcus was still quick enough with the ball in his hands to force you to pick your poison—a layup for him or a lob to Mickey in the dunker spot. Sometimes Stepanik slipped out for open threes. They were scoring a ridiculous 1.21 points per any pick-and-roll involving both of them.

I shouldn't really be showing you this stuff, Amy said. (In those days it was harder to get hold of such information; the teams that had it kept it to themselves.) But I get sick of reading that Marcus is holding Mickey back. If you cut out transition, their numbers look pretty similar. Where it gets interesting is when you look at *team* offense, in the half-court. And she attached a screen shot: the Sonics were scoring 1.03 points per possession whenever Hayes was on the floor without Mmeremikwu. That dropped to 0.94 when it was the other way around. Just watch the games, Amy said. Defenses are scrambling to stop him from taking threes, leaving everyone else wide open. The only reason Mickey's numbers look better is because of fast breaks, and we all know what happens in the playoffs—you don't *get* fast breaks.

This isn't the kind of thing she usually emailed me; it felt like calling in a favor.

All of this stuff is technical. If it doesn't mean anything to you, ignore it. But here's why I care or find it interesting. Professional basketball players are unusually successful people, and part of what makes them successful is an ability to sift through complex data and produce instant decisions. Shoot or pass. Switch or stick. Drive or pull up. They are people who can negotiate reality faster than the rest of us and get what they want from it. If you think being an athlete is just a set of physical tools, you never played sports. Marcus Hayes was quicker than me, he could jump higher, by senior year in high school he could bench press twice as much, but he could also think faster—he could process information, see patterns and respond to them on the fly better than I could. The analytics was really just an attempt by nerds, with millions of dollars of technology behind them, to see what he was seeing in real time.

And what Marcus had figured out is this: he could make up for lost foot speed by taking more threes. He also started shooting out of different situations—pulling up on the fast break, driving around screens. He couldn't get as high on his jump shot but the ball barely touched his hands. If you watched the games closely, you could see him talking about it, too. Marcus liked to keep up a running conversation with his defender. You better get up on that. Too late, baby. It's too late, baby . . . Whenever he scored, he let you know about it. All day long I had nothing to do but sit around in my apartment watching games on NBA League Pass. Rewinding if I saw something interesting, making notes. Eating lunch in front of the TV. Wondering if I should change out of my pajamas.

After the Boston game, he went on a little tear—against Milwaukee, New York, Brooklyn and Washington. A lot of mid-tier teams fighting for the same playoff spots. Marcus scored twenty-six, thirty-three, thirty-one and thirty-nine in those games. He shot 43 percent on threes—I used to scribble out the math on the sports page of the *American States-man*. Defenses started picking him up at half-court. Sometimes, just to find an open look, he pulled up from thirty feet out—and it's true, you could see that he was soaking up attention. The Sonics got a lot of offensive rebounds. But they split the rest of the road trip, and the verdict in the media was, Marcus is shooting too much. He can't get to the rim anymore. You can count on two hands the number of dunks he's had this season. There's something not right with this team, and Hayes is the problem. He needs to hand the reins to Mmeremikwu. Accept a supporting role. Mickey was shooting in the mid-fifties but his usage rate had dropped. When Marcus sat, the team started running more. Everything opened up.

The first available radiology appointment was Friday afternoon.

For the rest of the week, *not* googling "urine in blood, possible causes" was almost a full-time job. Even on the flight to Austin, with Quinn sitting next to me and totally absorbed by the panic induced by her exams, I felt rising in me this deeper anxiety. The phrase, *This is what dread is*, kept coming back to me, and I had stupid conversations with myself, which were actually conversations with Betsy, and went something like this. *I kept thinking, this is what dread is* . . . in the past tense, describing my feelings to her . . . in the desiccated air, with dry nose and throat, and my mouth tasting of cheap sour orange juice, while actually still sitting on the plane.

Several times I almost said to Quinn, *Something weird happened to me a few days ago*, but I didn't want to be the older man in her life with prostate or urinary troubles. Also any kind of sympathy would make it real.

Meanwhile, every time I pissed I checked the bowl for blood. Nothing, but I felt twinges and tweaks of pain all the time and started

groping my balls for lumps as I lay in bed. One of them was notice-
ably larger than the other. So I called the clinic again and eventually
spoke to Dr. Henschel. She said, "Urine in the blood . . . is not a
symptom of testicular cancer."

"Is it normal for one ball to be much larger than the other?"

"Nobody's perfect, right? Yes, it's normal." Then she said, "How
much larger?"

"About twice as big."

"If you're feeling anxious, come in."

"Also, can I stop taking the antibiotics?"

"What?" she said.

"The pills you gave me. For the infection. Can I stop taking them?"

"Yes, yes," she said. "You don't have an infection."

So after lunch, I got dressed and drove back to the Austin Regional
Clinic—and parked in the lot, with the sounds of MoPac tearing away
below me, across the winter afternoon. To calm down in the waiting
room I looked at the Sonics data Amy sent. It was like being a kid
again, where to get through school I took along the box scores from
last night's game and studied them at quiet moments in class, preparing
stuff to argue and talk about with my friends.

Then they called me in. Dr. Henschel was very nice again, still very
pregnant and tight as a drum. When she shifted in her seat I could feel
the pain in her hips.

I said, "How do we do this?"

The office had one of those tables with a mat on top and a strip
of blue paper over the mat. She told me to sit on the table and take
off my pants and underwear. Then she pulled on a pale blue medical
glove and felt my scrotum, for about a minute, with cold tacky rubber fingers.

"You can put on your clothes," she said afterward and started typ-
ing something on her computer.

"How are my balls?"

I was sweating again, in spite of the air-controlled climate.

"Normally, if something was wrong, I'd expect you to feel a jab of pain—enough to make you yelp. Did you feel anything like that?"

"No, just . . . tenderness. But no."

"One of your testes is larger than the other. But that's not unusual. If you're anxious about it, we can book you in for a scan."

"Okay." And then, "How are you feeling? When are you due?"

"Oh," she said, surprised. "Fine." Like most pretty women, she had a smile she could use to put an end to a conversation. Anyway, she had other things to do.

When I came out again, it was almost five o'clock. The sun cast long shadows across the empty parking lot; the temperature had dropped to the forties. It was a week before Christmas. I had no kids and lived in the garage apartment of someone else's house. My girlfriend was still in college and spending it with her parents. The things I cared about hadn't evolved a hell of a lot since high school, watching basketball, talking about sports, but what used to be a social activity had somehow turned into a job. I was thirty-five years old and going through tests for various kinds of cancer.

It's a short drive home, unless the traffic sucks, and I spent it trying to explain to Quinn in my head, you reach an age where all the stuff you like to do . . . is just stuff you like to do and doesn't add up to much. And you think, how many more years do I have left of this stuff? Does it really matter? But I was also talking to my sister, and saying, *This is what dread is*, so she could say something back, like, you're in a phase.

The only time Quinn could see me was Friday afternoon, after her last exam. A guy she knew from high school was driving back to Dallas and offered to give her a ride.

We met at the Spider House bar and coffee shop on Fruth Street, just off West 29th, one of those pockets of Austin that looks like old Austin but wasn't actually around when I was a kid. At two o'clock direct sunlight on the patio was still strong enough to make wearing a dress and Havaianas a reasonable thing to do—maybe Quinn got changed after coming out of class. She carried a JanSport so full of books clothes whatever that it was only partly zipped up, and wore sunglasses, and the way she walked into the patio garden it was like, nothing matters anymore so what's the hurry. It still seemed ridiculous that this girl with waist-length red hair flip-flapping coolly along the crazy paving was looking for me. In fact, I had to call her name a couple of times to get her attention, and when she sat down she didn't take off her shades.

She was in relax mode and acted like she had ear buds in and was listening to music, but she didn't—I looked at her ears. I said, "How did your exams go?" And she said, "Fine. Well, not fine, but they're over now, it doesn't matter." But she seemed in a good mood. She seemed happy and I couldn't tell if it was happy to see me.

I ordered iced tea and she had a frozen margarita, which gave her a brain-freeze when it came so she didn't want any more and I actually finished it. Thinking, what the hell. My scan was later that afternoon. It wasn't easy getting her to talk so I gave up. There's a lot of people-watching you can do at the Spider House, various Austin types, and the patio was decorated with Christmas lights and other kinds of ironic and cheerful ornamentation—a Pabst Blue Ribbon neon sign shaped like a guitar.

Eventually she said, "What's wrong?"

"What do you mean?"

"You're just like . . . being weird."

"What are you talking about?"

"Not saying anything. Is something bothering you?"

"No." And then, to change the mood: "I'm gonna miss you."

"When?"

And I stared at her, but she laughed.

"I'm not . . . it's only for a couple weeks. It goes by like . . . I mean, it's Christmas. It's just something everybody has to go through."

"Don't you like going home?"

"What do you mean? I love going home. I love my family."

"That's not . . ." but I gave up.

The whole thing lasted less than an hour, which is when this guy showed up. She introduced me to him, formally. Lloyd Tolliver meet Brian Blum. Brian Blum meet Lloyd Tolliver. He looked like a swimmer, about six four, clean-shaven, short-haired, long strong arms that kind of hung around when he walked without doing anything. He wore Bermuda shorts and a friendship bracelet on his wrist. When he came, she took off her sunglasses, and he said, in the undertone you use when parents or teachers are around, "You ready to head out?"

"Yes I am."

I didn't know if I should stand up or not, or what she wanted me to do. But I stood up and suddenly she kissed me on the mouth in front of him. Our lips were still cold from the margarita.

"Okay, I'm ready." But she didn't move; her arms were still around my neck. Then she said, "Just give me a minute, Lloyd, okay?"

"Whatever. Do what you need to do."

"I'm sorry," she told me, after he left. "This week has been kind of a disaster, which I don't really want to talk about. I love my family but I have to . . . protect myself against them. My father has an unbelievable talent for picking on your weak spot."

"I wish I could be your protection," but it was a stupid thing to say.

"You're sweet." But I was being managed; she gave me a little squeeze before letting go. "Anyway, Lloyd really wanted to meet you. He reads all your stuff."

Maybe she said that to make me less jealous. It takes about half a minute to leave the patio, there isn't a direct exit. You have to walk up the steps to the bar; there's a veranda, too, and the whole time I could see her, with her backpack slung over one shoulder, like any other student, before she got in Lloyd's car—a Jeep Grand Cherokee, which was parked on the street outside. It was like watching a past-self drive off with your girlfriend, although when I was in college I never had a car like that or a girlfriend like that.

Then I had another half hour to kill before my appointment. The doctor had said, you need a full bladder, so I asked the waiter for a glass of water, drank it, and asked for a refill, and drank that, too, and sat there feeling the weight of liquid slowly build.

The imaging center was out in Westlake, off one of those quiet seven-lane highways you get in the hills. I felt fine sitting in the car but after walking around the parking lot with a water balloon hanging between my legs, all I could think about when I sat down again was the balloon.

There were three other people in the waiting room: an elderly couple, where I couldn't figure out who was waiting with whom and who came along for moral support. The guy looked pale and wore a large khaki dress-shirt loosely tucked into his pants. The woman was more elegant but too skinny, cancer-y brittle; she had a thermos of something and thick sunglasses. They communicated almost imperceptibly, like ball-players on the bench trying to hide their mouths from the cameras. The other guy was this twenty-something Asian kid with a chronic cough. From the minute I got there to the moment the nurse called me in, he coughed and spat what he was coughing up into a paper cone. Once it filled up and he threw the old cone away and replaced it with a new one from the water dispenser. I thought, these are the people I now share a demographic with . . . this is the category I belong to.

The radiologist who saw me had taken off his wristwatch and put it face-up on his desk; he seemed tired, it was the end of the week. We talked briefly about my referral and I repeated what had almost become a formula: last Friday I pissed blood and afterward the doctor found microscopic traces of blood in my urine but no sign of infection.

He told me to take off my shirt and unbutton my pants. He said this might feel a little cold and spread a gel across my stomach down to the elastic lining of my briefs. Then pressed what looked like a microphone against my skin. The whole time he had his eyes on a monitor, which I couldn't see. He didn't say anything. After a minute, he said, okay, you can go now and relieve yourself and gave me a paper towel to wipe the gel off. He had to tell me twice where the bathroom was but I managed to find my way through the reception room with the coughing kid to a unisex stall just beyond the front desk. Then stood holding my dick gently in hand and feeling sweet pain when after half a minute the blocked-up piss flowed loudly into the bowl.

When I came back, the radiologist was still looking at the screen and I could see what he was looking at: a green faintly pulsing pix-elated image with a bright red gout or swathe of blood pooling in the middle of it. I sat down again, lifted my shirt, unbuttoned my pants, and he reapplied the gel.

I said, "Is that blood?" and he said, "What?"

"Is that blood on the screen?"

"No, no," and he turned the monitor toward me. "That was urine," he said. "And now you can see it's gone."

And it was—only the green was left. He'd have to write a report, which he would send to my doctor. But there was nothing to worry about. The bladder was clear. It had drained completely, he could barely find it after I went to the bathroom. There was an age-related cyst on my left kidney, that's all.

"How do you know it's age-related?" I asked.

"I've been doing this a long time."

"I was supposed to have a testicular scan, too," I said, but there was nothing in his notes about that. In any case, he had other patients to see.

Okay, I told myself, relax, when I got in the car again. Another dying winter afternoon. Four days until Christmas. The sun was still bright enough that the car had a nice warm greenhouse stuffiness, warmer than the outside air, which I was glad about because I could feel underneath my skin the chill seep away. Sometimes you have to *hear* good news, you have to make yourself believe it. Bee Cave Road, which I rode all the way out to Route 1, was almost empty, and on either side, the tree-lined side streets, wooded crescents and convoluted backstreets where the rich people lived flashed past, and I wondered if Quinn would be home by now, if Lloyd had dropped her off in Highland Park.

33

Betsy invited me to spend the night on Christmas Eve. She said it would be nice for us all to wake up together, like a family, so I packed my backpack and carried one of those semi-shapeless Ikea bags full of wrapped presents the four or five blocks from my apartment to her house.

When I got there everyone sat down to mac and cheese. Except Dad, who was on one of his diets where he wouldn't eat anything. Well, he ate a watermelon—or the stump of one, which he took out of the fridge still sweating into the Saran Wrap bandage. He looked pale, and not skinny but like his flesh was loose. Mom always hated these diets. She thought they were a comment on her.

Even before the meal was finished, Dad started clearing up. He soaked the pot and put dishes in the dishwasher. Then he announced to the table, "I'm retiring to my chamber, if there's nothing else useful I can do. And even if there is."

Betsy gave me a look, like this is what I deal with. She thought he was depressed and should get help—one of our ongoing disagreements. I'd say, I lived with him for five years, this is what he's like. And she'd say, What he's like is depressed. You just don't want to see it.

Good night, Dad. Good night. Good night, son. Thank you, he always said at the end of an evening.

After getting the kids to bed, Betsy took out the sheets and comforter from the hall closet and started making up the sofa in the living room. Let me do that, I said, standing helplessly aside, knowing that she was in full flow and actually taking some kid-brother comfort from the fact that my sister was in charge again. She tucked in the corners and smoothed down the comforter and shook the pillows into their cases with a snap.

"What can I do tomorrow to make your life easier?" and she said, "Take the boys to the park."

"What about Dad?"

"Him, too. Just get them all out of my hair."

"What about Greg?"

"What about him?"

"Does he see the kids at all on Christmas?"

"He gets them for New Year." Then she said, "Come sit on the porch with me and breathe secondhand smoke."

So that's what I did. It was cloudless and cold enough for an overnight frost. Betsy spent a few minutes draping blankets over the potted plants. "Are you seeing somebody?" she asked.

"Yes, maybe. I took a girl to Boston with me last weekend."

"Who is she?"

"A college girl. I met her in a roundabout way through Marcus. She's twenty-one, on the volleyball team. Right now she's back at home with Mommy and Daddy in Dallas."

"You dirty old man," she said.

"That's what I feel like."

"Is that what you feel like?"

"Not really. I feel like, for some reason she's being nice to me."

"Why do you live like this?"

"Like what?"

"In that shitty apartment. You make good money, you can live like a grown-up."

"What do I need a nice apartment for? Mostly I just sit around watching basketball."

"To impress girls," she said, but I didn't want to talk about it. Then she sat down next to me on the top step, where we could look out over the quiet neighborhood street, lit up by Christmas lights, and the park beyond it, gloomy under the trees. You become aware over time when you have these intimate conversations of a certain amount of repetition. Betsy and I go over the same ground, intimacy is a habit like anything else. I mean, it relies on a lot of go-to moves, stuff you've said before, but sometimes in spite of that you push the conversation along a few inches.

"I still don't totally understand what happened to your marriage. Greg seemed like a nice-enough guy."

She took out the Frisbee and laid it beside her and lit a cigarette.

"There are complicated ways I can answer that question but there's also a totally simple one. We stopped having sex."

"Did you want to have sex with him?"

"Not really."

"So what's the problem."

"He used to bug me about having sex, which I resented, but then it got to the point where he stopped bugging me."

"But you just said you didn't want to."

"I cook, I clean, I do the laundry. Wanting to have sex was *his* responsibility. It was just like, another one of those man-jobs he didn't want to do or know how to do. Like dealing with the car."

"That's a pretty old-fashioned view of all this stuff."

"What can I say, I'm an old-fashioned girl."

"You realize that nobody tells us these things," I told her. "You realize that."

"Well, you have to figure it out for yourself."

We sat there for a few more minutes, while she finished her cigarette. Betsy or Dad had strung the porch roof with white lights, which blinked on and off, so the shadows shifted around us.

"Are you seeing anybody right now?" I asked.

"Who am I gonna see? I have a relationship with my Mazda, which makes me happy. It's a very nice car."

In the morning, Dad and I took the boys to the park so Betsy could make Christmas dinner. They had already opened their presents. Troy got one of those balance bikes without pedals that you can ride

Flintstone-style by running sitting down. Be careful with him, Betsy said, but Troy at that stage was a nice fat uncomplaining kid who bounced. Your typical bowling ball, my dad called him. For Albert I bought a junior-sized official NBA-licensed Marcus Hayes Number 4 Austin Supersonics jersey, signed by Marcus himself. Amy Freitag set it up, and Marcus actually wrote BLUM next to HAYES on the back of the jersey.

He put it on without a T-shirt or anything underneath and insisted on walking to the park like that, even though it was fifty degrees outside. You could see his skinny little arms.

Dad said, "Brian, show him how to shoot a free throw."

"He's seen me shoot before."

"Come on, show him how it's done."

So to please my father, I stood at the foul line and lined up an underhand shot, dipped my knees and let go, and watched the ball slip through the net.

Albert was now old enough and socialized enough at school to find any kind of nonconformity lame. Since I moved out, we had stopped going to the park together.

"You shoot like a girl," he said.

"If that's how girls shoot, we should all shoot like girls," my dad told him. "Brian, do it again."

So I flipped in another underhander. "You try it," I said to Albert, but he wouldn't. When he shot, he had to hoist it from his shoulder, like someone bracing himself against the recoil. My dad tried to tell him, start small. Start with what you *can* do. Do it the right way and go from there. But Albert wanted to take fifteen-footers. "I had the same argument with your uncle," my dad said. He could be very patient in this mode. When I was a kid he could watch me practice the same shot a hundred times and get the ball each time and tell me what I was doing wrong, if I was doing something wrong, or offer encouragement, if that's what he thought I needed. For him this never got boring. It's how you learn.

Meanwhile, Troy rode his bike into the creek, which was mostly mud. He was fine; this is how the morning wore on. Afterward, when we came back to the house, Betsy changed Troy's clothes and dressed him in a checkered shirt and long pants, but Albert wouldn't take off the Hayes jersey. Then we sat down to eat—meatloaf and mashed potatoes and biscuits and gravy.

But I don't want to talk about lunch. All of these family scenes remind me of my mother, and the fact that I'm just a guest on this show. The Sonics were playing in the second afternoon game, against the Heat, and I said to Betsy, let me do the clearing up now because I need to get back to watch the game. And she said, there's no hurry, you can watch the game here. So at three o'clock I sat down on the sofa and turned on the TV, and Albert and dad joined me. Betsy said she would come in a minute, she wanted to get a start on the kitchen. Troy was Mommy's little helper, he liked to put things away.

"I said I'd do it." And she said, "I'm just making a start."

The Heat came into Christmas on a five-game winning streak. (A month later, in Toronto, they started a twenty-seven-game run.) While the Sonics were still trying to turn things around . . . and playing on the road, on national TV, against the reigning champs.

At halftime the score was tied at fifty-seven. Mmeremikwu was having a great game, with twenty-three points, running every chance he got. Marcus had nine. You could see him telling the Frenchman, slow down. Mark Jackson, who was doing color, said, "The worst-kept secret in the NBA right now is that those two guys don't get along. It's just an alpha-dog fight to see who's gonna run the pack. Right now Mickey is winning."

Albert sat next to me, still in his Hayes jersey, which almost came down to his knees. Betsy walked in and Dad stood up to make space on the couch, but she said, "Don't bother. I'm just going to fall asleep anyway."

"What are you talking about, I can take the desk chair." And he wheeled it over and Betsy sat next to me on the other side, with Troy on her lap. Then all the Blums were watching the game together.

In the third quarter the Heat ran away with it. Bosh hit a three, LeBron hit a three, Mickey drove wildly and missed and LeBron picked up the board, turned in one motion and threw a quarterback pass to Wade at the other end for a dunk. The camera zoomed in on Marcus, who was still in the backcourt, sucking wind, waiting for the play to play out. Then LeBron said something to him and smiled, and Marcus, who wasn't looking at him, didn't react, and LeBron said something else. Mike Breen, the play-by-play announcer, said, "I wonder what that little exchange was. Oh to be a fly on the wall of *that* conversation," and Jeff Van Gundy said, "I know what he said. Is this what you came back for? Welcome back."

Betsy said, "Why are they talking like this? What are they talking about?"

"This is just what they do. They have to say stuff."

"Are they even watching the game?" She was suddenly indignant.

"They're watching the game."

"What was Marcus supposed to do? That play had nothing to do with him."

It turned into a blowout. Marcus rested at the beginning of the fourth quarter and had no reason to come in again. Mickey tried to bring them back single-handed but ran into a lot of dead ends, one-on-three fast breaks, two-on-fours. By the end the expression on his face was French disgust. When Kaminksi pulled him with seven minutes left, he kicked a water bottle into the front row and walked past Marcus without looking at him and sat down by himself at the end of the bench.

To keep things lively, the announcers got in an argument about the Sonics—there wasn't much else to talk about. Jackson said it was time to hand over the reins. This was Mickey's team, and the Sonics couldn't sort out the mess they were in until Mickey took over. Van Gundy said, "Tell that to Marcus Hayes." That's a coach's job, Jackson said. That's what they get paid for. "I'm not disagreeing with you," Van Gundy said. "But . . . you tell him."

"Why do you let them say these things?" Betsy asked me.

"What am I supposed to do?"

"I thought you knew these people."

"Not these guys."

When the game ended, I went into the kitchen to finish the dishes but the dishes were done. Albert was in his room, with the door closed, and Betsy shouted at him to come out and say goodbye to his uncle. So he dutifully appeared and gave me a hug, hiding his face against my shirt. He wasn't wearing the jersey. Dad lay asleep on the sofa. I picked up my backpack and walked out the door, into the cold night. The neighborhood streets were lit here and there by Christmas decorations and the glow from living-room windows, and I thought, all of this buildup of family life is also an accumulation of frustration and unhappiness and disappointment, which you can just walk out on.

In the morning, I wrote a long piece for the website called "Marcus Hayes Is Not the Problem," which used the data Amy sent me to argue that the Sonics were better as a half-court team and needed to rein in or trade Mmeremikwu if they wanted to win. It got a lot of play. That same day, the Sonics fired Kaminski and made Todd Steuben interim head coach, and Josephine Patrice Hayes filed a petition for divorce.

34

After the State Semis, for complicated reasons, I decided to come off the wait-list at Brown and accept the offer at UT. Maybe not so complicated. I went into a hole and couldn't face the thought of a six-hour flight to start over again in a place where I didn't know anybody. Also, if I went to Texas, I could live at home.

During this time, I entered into a more or less constant state of argumentation with my mom, who went to Brown herself and wanted me to go there, and suspected that my decision was somehow connected to my obsession with basketball and this idea I had of following Marcus Hayes. Which I denied. Why spend the money to go to some fancy Ivy League school when I can live here for free and get a first-rate state education? Don't you want me living at home anymore?

"Of course, I want you . . . but that's not the point. You're not supposed to want to, you're supposed to want to get out of here."

My dad let it play out.

In fact, Marcus and I talked a lot about going to Texas together. Or I talked to him about it. When the season ended, we started going to the park again and shooting around. For fun, we used to practice alley-oops. The rim on the court at Shipe was a couple of inches low and Marcus could almost hit his head against it. If kids saw us coming they climbed out of the pool and lined up still wet against the chain-link fence. Marcus worked himself into a sweat. His hands were covered in calluses, with pixels of dark blood buried under the skin.

Sometimes he teased me into trying to dunk and stood aside, while I took a ten-step run-up and grabbed . . . fistfuls of net. Touching rim was the closest I got. Afterward, I said, Did you see that? I touched it. I totally touched it.

Naw, naw, I didn't see it. Do it again.

Once after class, after the school bus dropped us off, we were messing around at Shipe and Marcus started rapping, *I got no father, I got no mother, How come I got stuck with this white-ass brother?* He was dee-ing me up, and every time I tried to shoot or drive past him, he knocked the ball away and waited for me to get it. Beating me at basketball was like an expression of affection, it made him happy. Anyway, he kept rapping the whole time, even though he really couldn't rap. It was just one of those things kids at school did, sitting around the hallways with scraps of paper. Eventually he gave up looking for rhymes and started dunking. *Let's go to Texas!* he shouted, hanging on the rim. *We're going to Texas!*

The other reason was, I wanted to take control of this ridiculous process where people who didn't know me, college administrator types, made important evaluations and decisions about my character and potential. Which I thought, screw that. So I wrote to the Brown Office of Admissions and said, no thank you. And I called up Texas and said yes.

For weeks my mom barely looked at me. She just couldn't talk about it. Finally she said, "I feel like, about ten years ago, maybe when we moved here, I made this decision just to . . . accept that your father came first, which seemed fine at the time, because he's a great dad, but I feel like now, this is the price I paid and now you're paying it, too."

The funny thing is, one of the best things about the whole setup turned out to be going to work with Mom. Her office was in the Sánchez Building and she could park in the lot outside. Most of my classes were a few blocks away. The first day we drove in together, she said, This is what I listen to, meaning, that's how it is, and put in one of her opera cassettes.

We never played this stuff at home. It was another example of how her interests ran parallel to ours. Sometimes, while the rest of us sat on the sofa and watched TV, Mom retreated to her room and if you knocked on her door she wouldn't answer. The lights were off, and she lay with the music in her ears. But every morning on the ride to campus she made me listen to it.

For the first time I had a sense of her as somebody with private thoughts, which her kids had nothing to do with. We talked about her job, about my professors, whatever was happening that day, and then ten minutes later got out of the car.

I didn't see much of Marcus. For a while we discussed living together freshman year and even looked at a few apartments over the summer. But then he got a room at Jester East, near the stadium, where a lot of athletes lived. Including guys from the basketball team. So I stayed home and saved money. We didn't take the same classes or know the same people, although sometimes I ran into him at Dobie Mall, where we both liked to eat at Subway. Usually when I saw him he was hanging out with other ballplayers.

At that time three or four senior classmen on the basketball team were brothers of Kappa Delta Nu, and Marcus told me he wanted to pledge in the spring. That was Jordan's fraternity, too.

The *Daily Texan* is the student newspaper. They have a pretty good sports page, so I got in touch with the editor, Alex Barber, and sent him some of my clippings from the *Burleson Round Table*. He turned out to be a she, who said, the best thing you can do is just go to some games. Write 'em up and send 'em in; we'll see if we can use them. So that's what I did. UT's first game was against the Mean Greens of North Texas (broccoli, kale, spinach?) in one of those walkovers they schedule before the real season starts. I hadn't been back to the Erwin Center since the Semifinals. Hayes played nine minutes and scored three points—nobody watching had any reason to notice him, and I didn't mention Marcus in the write-up. But I made a lot of pre-Thanksgiving detox diet puns and the piece got printed.

Ninety-five was a transitional year for Texas basketball. B. J. Tyler had graduated, and Terrence Huckabee took over most of his scoring. Not a bad time to be a freshman—Coach Menzes had minutes to fill.

His motto was, let the players play. Guys know who's got game and who doesn't; they can sort themselves out. Which meant you could earn playing time by tearing up one of the starters in a scrimmage.

In those days, anybody could walk into varsity practices. Nobody had cell phones, nobody cared, and I used to go over to Gregory Gym in the afternoons and watch.

Years later they interviewed Huckabee about freshman Marcus Hayes.

After the first captain's practice, we're talking late September, it's still high nineties outside and the gym was like a steam room. Huckabee had run them hard for two hours—it was his first season as captain, and he wanted to make them feel it.

I'm about to hit the showers, he said, when this kid comes up and challenges me to a game. Son, I tell him, we got a long season ahead of us. This is day one. But he doesn't really say anything, he just looks at me like, whatever. Like I'm scared. So we start to play.

Did you beat him? (You can see the whole interview on YouTube, with Bob Costas.)

I beat him. Huckabee is laughing. I beat him. At that time Marcus was only like, hundred and seventy, hundred seventy-five pounds. I was two-thirty. In those days, it was two hundred thirty pounds of muscle. I beat him. He was too quick for me but I could back him down. Maybe I swung my elbows, maybe I caught him once or twice. He wasn't gonna call foul. We played to eleven, win by two. You make it you take it. I think the final score was eighteen sixteen, nineteen seventeen, something like that. I beat him. But I tell you something else. (Still laughing.) I never played him one-on-one again.

You could see it in practice—nobody wanted Marcus to guard him. But he struggled on offense, he kept rushing. Spots didn't open up on the floor the way he was used to. What you need is a few simple repeatable moves, which you can apply in recognizable situations. Turnaround from the block. Jab step jump shot. He didn't have those yet, he needed to play in the flow. Sometimes he broke free for dunks off a turnover or pulled up for a three—or cut into the lane after a switch. But mostly he looked like a kid who had too much sugar, running around at someone else's party.

Menzes said to him, "Slow down, Hayes. It's not a race. You win by scoring points." He said stuff like that to everybody.

Gregory Gym has a few bleachers courtside, and a low upper tier, with maybe fifteen rows of seats. I used to sit at the edge of the balcony, leaning over the rail. Nobody else was around; the floor squeaked, I could hear the coaches talking to each other on the sideline. It gave me something to do, if I didn't have anything else.

Mom once said to me, "Do you ever see Marcus? You should give him a call."

"Not much."

"Why not, Brian?"

"He's on the basketball team. He hangs out with basketball players."

"He can't play basketball *all* the time," she said.

A few days later I actually ran into Marcus outside PCL. He was coming out of the library with a couple of teammates, I recognized them from the gym: Shay Gilmore, Bernard Meeks. Instead of introducing me, he sort of nodded at them and they kept walking, across the plaza toward 21st Street, and he strolled over. He dressed different now, even his walk had changed. His jeans hung down and his laces were undone. In high school he had kind of a preppy look and buttoned up his shirt all the way. First few months of college, I guess everybody tries to remake themselves. Or almost everybody. His cornrows hung down to his shoulders, and he carried a backpack by one strap.

"What up, Big Baby," he said.

"You didn't want to introduce me to your friends?"

"What are you talking about?"

"Those guys you were with."

"They're not my friends."

Something about the whole business had annoyed me. Maybe I was still sore about the apartment.

"Why do you only hang out with black kids?" He just looked at me. "Every time I see you it's with a bunch of black guys."

"Man, you don't even know. I just hang out with guys on the team. That's all we do. Play basketball."

"Mom says hi," I said.

But then the season started, and things got better. I began to stop by the *Daily Texan* office in the basement of HSM, two blocks from the Drag. The editors went to Thundercloud for lunch or drank at the Crown & Anchor Pub, if they were old enough to drink. Even if you weren't, you could eat. I liked these kids, they were real news brats. Most of them came from out of town or out of state. I attained a certain street cred just by being native Austin. They let me write food reviews, too.

A couple of weeks after this conversation with Marcus, I tried to make it up to him—in print. The Horns had just beaten UT-San Antonio in a shootout. Marcus scored twenty-one, coming off the bench, and the copyeditor let me write the headline: "Freshman Phenom Has Breakout Game."

The next day in practice I sat in my usual seat. Some of the guys were ribbing Marcus, calling him phenom. Everybody was in a good mood. Wednesday morning, after an early season win. Watch out for the phenom. Don't let the phenom shoot. Some of the coaches, too, including Steuben. I think it actually started to piss Marcus off. At one point, Steuben looked up at the stands in my direction, squinting a little, with his hand over his eyes. "Who's that guy who always sits up there? Is that a *reporter* from the *Daily Texan*?" He knew who I was.

Marcus looked up. "Aw, he's all right. That's just my sidekick."

A week before Christmas Mom baked a loaf of zucchini bread, which she said Marcus loved. She carried the pan to the car and told me to give it to him. "Do you know what his holiday plans are? Because I want him to know, he can always come here. He's very welcome. I want him to know that."

"Where's he gonna sleep when Betsy comes home?"

"He can sleep in your room."

"What am I supposed to do with this zucchini bread? Carry it around all day?"

"You're supposed to give it to him. You get home-cooked food every night. Not everyone's so lucky."

"Yeah, lucky."

"Don't start this conversation again," she said. "I'm delighted to have you at home but you know perfectly well what I think about *that*."

"All right, whatever." Later, when we got out of the car, I said: "I really don't see him that much."

"Brian, it's not five minutes on foot from here to his dorm."

"He's probably at practice."

"So leave it by the door, with a note. And don't forget to invite him for Christmas."

"His mom lives in Dallas. You can get a bus."

"I imagine his situation at home is not easy. There's a stepfather now, and other children, who may take priority."

"Whatever," I said again but figured I may as well get the cake off my hands and walked away.

The only time I'd been to his room was when he moved in. I had to drive his stuff over from the house. He didn't have much, just a suitcase, but my mom gave him a couple of towels and some sheets and pillowcases and a microwave that we never used anymore, that kind of thing. It was now mid-December, gray and mild. To get to his dorm you pass the Clark outdoor basketball courts, and the playing field, with Waller Creek at the bottom, which is the same creek that runs through Shipe. At every gap in the buildings, the football stadium looms above you.

When I knocked on his door, a woman answered. It took me a minute to remember her name—Megan Adez, his physiotherapist. She wore short red nylon running shorts, the kind girls sleep in, and a PROPERTY OF TEXAS LONGHORNS T-shirt. She had long pale legs.

"Marcus is in the shower," she said. "He'll be out in a minute." Then she recognized me. "Brian Blum."

Marcus came out with a towel on. It was nine in the morning. His body had already started to change with the college weight program. You couldn't see his ribs anymore; they were covered in muscle.

Megan said, "I've been helping him study for finals."

"Team pay for that too?"

Then my face went red. I just wanted to break the ice, but maybe she didn't hear me.

Marcus said, "Let me put on some clothes," and went out again. He had one of the rooms at Jester with a private bathroom.

I gave the cake pan to Megan, because we were just standing around. "My mom baked it. She said Marcus likes zucchini bread. I don't even know if that's true."

"We can have it for breakfast."

A table stood under the window, which looked out on the street and Waller Creek Park. Megan rolled over the desk chair so three of us could sit, and I sat, butting my knees against the drop-leaf.

The cake was actually pretty good; you could hardly taste the zucchini. I had a couple of slices and told Marcus what my mom told me to tell him. "She says you're welcome to stay with us for Christmas, if you don't have plans. Betsy's coming back but you can sleep in my room."

Megan looked at him, and he said, "I told my mom I'd go home."

"Well, that's what I said to her. I said he's got a family he can stay with. His actual mother."

"I told her I'd go."

Megan said, "If you stayed here . . ."

"What?" He wasn't angry, he wanted her to finish the sentence.

"I could see you. On Christmas."

"I told her."

"You should go," Megan said. They were very gentle and polite with each other.

Eventually I stood up to leave. Megan said, "Let me clean out the pan for you," and ran to the bathroom, which left me and Marcus alone. You could almost hear the clock tick. Every time you stood alone in a room with Marcus you felt, like, his physical self-restraint. Just the way he moved. He said, "It's good to see you, Brian. We don't really . . . see many people, usually. We just kind of do our own thing."

"You know I don't talk about your business," I said.

Then Megan came back with the pan.

35

When the Celtics drafted Marcus in '98, they hired Steuben as assistant coach. Almost certainly because Marcus asked them to; he liked having familiar people around, people who were also grateful to him. You can see Steuben sitting on the bench as the Celtics won the title, that first strike-shortened season—a young white guy in a suit, already getting fat, with the paychecks, with life on the road, and wondering, how the hell did I end up here?

I don't know where he'd be today if he hadn't knocked on our door in high school . . . to recruit Marcus Hayes. He was another one of those guys that Marcus carried along on his coattails. But that doesn't mean he was lightweight or hadn't somehow internalized his success. Because if you met Steuben now, you'd think, don't mess with him. He's been around powerful people for most of his adult life and figured out how it works. You identify the boss in any situation, you identify how much pushback that guy wants, and give it to him; and everybody else can kiss your ass. Anyway, Steuben was now a head coach in the NBA again, because Marcus Hayes wanted him back.

There was no question, then, who ran the team. And you could see it in their first game after Christmas, an eighty-one to seventy-eight loss to the Knicks at Madison Square Garden. Marcus had thirty-one, he hit five three-pointers. Mickey almost had a triple double. They put him in the post, where he hated playing, as a kind of point forward; or shifted him to the dunker spot and isolated Marcus at the top of the key. Dieter Crawford played seven minutes, mostly in the second quarter. Ty Jones started, because he muscled up on D and did what he was told on offense—bring the ball up court, so Marcus doesn't have to. Set the offense. Slow it down. If you can hit a few open shots, that's gravy.

For the first few games, Mickey did what he was asked to do but didn't look happy about it. One of his nicknames was the Beast . . . and fans started showing up at games holding signs that said *Unleash the Beast*. There was always something uncomfortable about the way people talked about Mmeremikwu, like he was some freak of nature, instead of a talented guy who worked harder than other people. But Mickey played up to it, too. I think he liked the idea that he had this raw force that couldn't be contained . . . Anyway, the Sonics tried to contain it.

Already the basketball commentariat had started to sharpen their knives, middle-aged white men were shouting at each other across TV-studio coffee tables. This is the kind of thing they love, an argument where you can give, like, names to the data, and turn a technical question into a fight between personalities. Here's what they said. Marcus is telling Mickey, this is *my* team, and you can get in line with everybody else.

On New Year's Day, a receptionist called from the Austin Regional Clinic to book me in for another scan; and a few days after that, I drove out to Westlake again so someone could look at my balls. A part of me thought, don't go. You're fine; don't go. This kind of thing only leads to trouble.

It didn't take long. The radiologist this time reminded me of my sophomore year roommate, Martin Zwicker, who quit the cross-country team fall semester because organic chemistry was kicking his ass. He had sandy-blond hair, pimples, just a nice serious kid. In the middle of these boring, tense situations you get odd associations.

A nurse prepared the bed and drew a curtain around it while I pulled down my pants and boxer shorts. She said to lay the penis pointing up across your stomach, and gave me a cloth to fold over it. Then she came out and the Zwicker guy came in. He didn't say much but applied the gel to my scrotum. "This will feel a little cold," he said, and pushed the microphone thing against it, and moved it around, and looked at the screen, and moved it around again.

"The right testis looks fine," he said, after a few minutes. "There's some . . ." and he used a word I didn't recognize. "Basically, like varicose veins. Not unusual to find them . . . as you get older. They may cause some discomfort."

"I haven't noticed anything."

He spent a little longer on the left testis. Eventually he said, "Okay, you can get dressed," and I sat up.

"Did you see anything?"

"I'll send the report to your doctor, which you should get . . . in a couple of days."

"Is there anything to worry about?"

And again, the guy was my roommate, Martin Zwicker, who hated to intrude himself on the conversation. Late twenties, maybe it was his first residency. I don't know how often you have to give bad news, or at what point you develop strategies for it. He said, "There's something there . . . I don't know what it is," and turned the monitor toward me so I could look. "These are cysts," he said, but then he pointed to a black spot on one of the small . . . orbs, glowing gray against the gray background. "I don't know what that is," he said again. "It's not vascular, which is a good sign."

"What's the next stage? I mean, will I need another procedure?"

He gave me a towel to wipe the gel off my scrotum. But you can't really wipe that stuff off; anyway, you feel like an idiot, dabbing around between your legs.

"I don't know; maybe."

"What kind of procedure?"

"Another exam . . ."

"Surgery?"

"Maybe, I don't know." And then, as I pulled on my shorts and

pants, "It's nothing to worry about." He opened the curtains and
stepped out into the room beyond, and closed the curtains again, so I
sat on the table in the artificial half-light for maybe a minute alone. By
the time I put on my shoes (I didn't bother tying them, just squeezed
each foot under the tongue of the Rockports and let the laces drag),
he was back at his desk, looking at the computer. He had other problems. I felt like the guy at a party who doesn't know, should he say
goodbye to his host or just go.

Dr. Henschel gave me a name to call at UrologyAustin, which had
more specialized facilities. So I called and made an appointment.
Meanwhile I tried to get on with my life. Classes at UT started up on
the 14th and Quinn came back on the Thursday before.

We'd had two slightly awkward communications over the break.
On Christmas she sent me an email with a photo of herself standing
next to the tree in a new dress. I can't really describe dresses, but it
looked like a prom dress or a bridesmaid's dress, it had frills and folds
and fell away from one shoulder. Her father gave it to her.

I had the feeling something intimate was being communicated but
didn't know what. Was the point that she looked nice in this dress
and wanted me to see her in it? Like a Christmas present, all wrapped
up. Or that her dad had no clue, and for two weeks she was stuck at
home pretending to be Daddy's little girl? I remember what she said
at the coffee shop, that she loved her family but sometimes had to
protect herself against them.

My phone makes a ding when emails come through, which sometimes wakes me up. So I lay in the dark of my rented apartment and
looked at this image. Quinn wore her hair down, all brushed and heavy
and long, and it's almost like the real person I was looking at wasn't
the person in the photo but somebody else who took the photo and
wanted to show it to me. But I didn't understand it. In the morning I
sat over my computer for half an hour, writing and erasing a response,

which in the end I cut down to, I'd send you a picture but nobody got me a dress. I miss you. There was more after that but that was the gist.

The second communication was worse. On New Year's Eve, I called her cell and her brother picked up. She must have left it lying around. Anyway, I got flustered and said, "Is Shelley around? I mean, Quinn," and then after a minute she came on the phone. But I was still flustered and she was just on her way out to a party, which her brother was driving her to, because it was his friend from high school who was throwing the party. We had a two-minute conversation, because they were already late and in the background I kept hearing him say, Quinn, let's go, Quinn, come on, let's go. The person I was talking to seemed totally incapable of the subtleties or intricacies I had been trying to read into her photograph. She seemed straightforward and young, and like somebody who had a party to go to on New Year's Eve and was already excited about it.

"I'll call you when I get back," she said, and I didn't know if she meant, after the party, or when she returned to campus. But that's what she must have meant because I didn't hear from her again.

There's a kind of understanding among beat writers that you don't talk about the players' private lives. But occasionally something comes up that it's your job to ask them about, which is a category that included J. P. filing for divorce. Nobody wanted to do it, so Alana Sissons took one for the team. She actually said beforehand, you owe me guys, because we had a conversation during the game about who would do it and she volunteered. "I don't know *what* you owe me," she said, "but some day, *and that day may never come*, blah blah blah. But it's gonna be good, that much I know."

It's one thing to joke about it in the press box, but it's another to look Marcus in the eye and ask him something you know he doesn't want to talk about. The Sonics had just beat Denver ninety-seven to eighty-three, which was their best win since Kaminski got fired.

Marcus had scored thirty on twenty-two shots, and after the game, in his brown Armani suit, he faced the usual bouquet of microphones outside his locker.

When the questions dried up, Alana cleared her throat and said, "Do you expect the divorce proceedings to have any effect on your preparations for the second half of the season?"

It was a softball pitch, the softest she could throw and still have it get over the plate. Marcus looked at her, still sweating from his shower. The room had filled with steam and people; the atmosphere was what my mother used to call close.

"Alana Sissons," he said. "Alana Sissons."

He liked to repeat people's names, to stall for time and show he remembered them. Every day hundreds of people said hello to him, whom he'd never met before. So if he knew your name he liked to use it, because for a lot of the people he said hello to, that made their day.

"You've known me since I came into this League," he said. "Have I ever let my personal business get in the way of playing basketball?"

There was a silence; everybody waited for him to go on. He leaned forward into the bristle of microphones with their various logos and symbols: KXAN, FOX7, KEYE, CNN, ESPN. Most of the reporters who held them out were a head shorter than Marcus, and just to carry the weight of the mics wore them down. After a few minutes if you looked closely you could see their arms beginning to tremble.

"I asked you a question," he said.

In the end there was nothing else she could do. "No," she answered quietly.

"Next question."

Afterward, when we stood outside in the parking lot and argued about where to eat, she said again: "You guys owe me."

I emailed Kyla, Quinn's friend, to see if she could put me in touch with her sorority sister—the one she told me about at the party, who went to Burleson and knew Cheryl Dillard. In the end I offered to buy them both lunch.

We met at Kerbey Lane Cafe on Guadalupe. Just an old house with a porch and a couple of front windows overlooking the Drag. When she saw me walking up the steps, Kyla said, "Notice anything?" and gave me a big smile. I stared at her. "My braces are gone. Don't you remember. I had these braces that made me feel about ten years old."

Her friend was called Tash, a dance major, one of these big-boned, skinny women, where you could keep loose change on the shelf over her collarbone. It's lucky that Kyla came along because it meant the two of them just talked and I could listen in.

Tash played basketball in high school. Caukwell didn't coach the girls' team but she knew him anyway. He got along pretty well with Coach Sanders, and sometimes they had to share the gym. What happened with Marcus Hayes was . . . Caukwell asked him to talk to the school, and they had this big assembly in the gym, and Cheryl played piano and for some reason they asked her to play for the assembly. They dragged out this grand piano onto the middle of the court. She played "Clair de Lune." She was really pretty good, but it's a long song, and while she was playing Marcus Hayes started spinning a basketball on his finger. I don't know why it was funny. Marcus was looking at Cheryl, and spinning the ball, and people started laughing. Not to be mean or anything, but just because it was funny. Maybe you had to hear the music.

Anyway, Cheryl didn't know what was going on. Her piano teacher, Mr. Hammenasset, kept turning the pages but then Cheryl heard people laughing and looked up and saw Marcus spinning the ball. Honest to God she had no idea who he was. I guess she thought the whole assembly was gathered together just to hear Cheryl Dillard play "Clair de Lune."

So she stopped and people laughed and then everything got quiet and Cheryl said, "Do you have to do that?"

I don't know if he was embarrassed or just pretending to be

embarrassed. But everybody was laughing again, and Marcus said, "No, ma'am," and she said, "Thank you," and waited for people to settle down and then actually finished the song. I mean, she just started playing from where she left off. That's how they met.

A few weeks later there were these rumors that Marcus Hayes and Cheryl Dillard were going out, but I didn't believe them. Then I saw this guy in a black suit waiting outside a Hummer after school, and Cheryl getting into the car. That's really all I know for sure.

But Coach Caukwell was really upset about the whole thing. He really didn't like it at all. Even if—I mean, Cheryl was seventeen years old. She was not somebody who did anything she didn't want to do. But she was also just . . . extremely competitive. About everything. And if she went out with Marcus Hayes then I figured, that's because she made it happen. But that's not how Coach Caukwell saw it, and that's not how Coach Sanders felt about it either. But teachers always think, kids are so innocent, especially girls, where, when you actually go to class with these girls, you know what they're really like.

I don't have any problem with Cheryl, we got along fine. But she was not somebody I trusted. Not because she lied or anything or was phony, because she wasn't. But because she was one of those people who just doesn't care what anybody thinks about her, because she thinks she's better than they are, or holds herself to a higher standard. That's how she comes across anyway. Like someone who doesn't expect other people to live up to her standards— not like, she's disappointed in them, but like, that's why she's nice to them. Anyway, she can keep it to herself.

The rest of what I heard is just what people said about her, because Cheryl was somebody everybody talked about anyway, especially after she started going out with Marcus. Then she stopped coming to school. After that, I did worry about her for a bit. But she must have made alternative arrangements because she graduated with everybody else. It was our last semester anyway, we just had a few months left. What I heard was, Coach Caukwell talked to her family, and talked to Marcus, and had to kind of negotiate between them. But that's just what I heard. There was a story she got pregnant, and Marcus paid the Dillards to have an abortion, which they wouldn't want to do. Her family is very Christian. But I don't know about that. Cheryl's dad is pretty rich, he owns a lot of property in East Austin. But then the crash came and I heard they had money problems, too.

People were not as nice to her as they could have been when she showed up at graduation. But she used to annoy them beforehand anyway. She looked like a model, even in high school. All the guys wanted to go out with her, and she wasn't that nice to them about it. And people took their side, I mean, the guys'. And then it's like, the first guy she goes out with is Marcus Hayes.

My phone was on the table the whole time, in record mode—between the syrup pitcher and the coffee pot. But this is a condensed version. Kyla asked a lot of questions, too.

I told Tash, "I don't believe she didn't know who Marcus Hayes was."

"Well, you don't know her," she said. "Anyway, he's not like Michael Jordan."

Lunch lasted about an hour. It was funny paying for them afterward, because they were both super-polite about it, like kids. Like, thank you very much. You're very welcome. I couldn't help myself, before she left, I said to Kyla, "How's Quinn? Have you seen her lately?"

And she said, "I don't know. I think she gets back tomorrow. You should give her a call." So for the rest of the day, I wondered what that was code for, if Kyla had some kind of inside information.

Some of the stuff Tash said I could verify. The Celtics' Texas road trip that year came in the middle of March. They played at San Antonio, Houston and Dallas, with a day off after the Rockets game.

It's less than a three-hour drive to Austin from the Toyota

Center. An appearance at his alma mater might get a mention in the *Statesman*, which is where I found it—along with a picture of Marcus in a suit and tie, with a basketball in his hands and a crowd of kids filling the bleachers. Off to one side, you can see the outline of a grand piano.

The financial element was harder to track down. Caukwell was dead. And I didn't feel like asking Charles Dillard about it either. But some of his company's transactions were a matter of public record. CDC Development LLC filed for bankruptcy under Chapter 11 in February 2008, just as the Economic Stimulus Act came into force. That summer, the court discharged the case; Dillard had paid his debts. Their portfolio included Su Casa Apartments, on the corner of Chestnut Avenue and East 17th. Dillard tore it down and built a row of clapboard and corrugated-metal single-family homes on the site. That's where the market was heading before it collapsed.

Anyway, none of this gave Marcus much time—from March 19, when he showed up at Burleson to do Caukwell a favor, to Friday July 4, when Stacey Kupchak announced his retirement in the *Boston Globe*. Three and a half months, and for most of that time he was on the road, playing basketball. He never had more than four days off, until the season ended; but maybe he didn't need much time. He was looking for a reason to quit. Did he take her out to dinner the day they met? When did Radko pick Cheryl up in the Hummer—in the break before the playoffs started in mid-April? Did they sleep together then? She was a teenage girl, who presumably had to explain to her parents where she went after school and what time she got home.

Did they talk on the phone every night, like high school sweethearts?

If Cheryl got pregnant, the media attention would have made ordinary life for her impossible. Even if it became public that Marcus Hayes was going out with a seventeen-year-old girl . . . Maybe he quit to withdraw from the public eye, so he could pursue the relationship. It made as much sense as anything else. But in that case, why come back? Because he figured she was old enough now for them to get away with it?

Kyla over lunch told another story about them. Cheryl lived in Prather Hall, which has a restricted visitation policy. So if Marcus came over after dinner and wanted to stay the night, they had to go downstairs to register his presence at the 24-hour desk. Maybe he wanted to live like a college kid again and sleep in a dorm. Anyway, what Kyla heard was (because a friend of hers lives in Prather), one night they must have had a fight because her friend saw Marcus standing in the hallway knocking on Cheryl's door, saying, "Come on, baby. Let me in." The security guard had to escort him from the building. Marcus went quietly; apparently, the guy asked for his autograph, but all of this is thirdhand information.

I still hadn't told anyone about the blood in my urine or the unknown black spot on one of my testicles. My dad would only worry, and at his age, you don't want to have to think about the mortality of your son.

Meanwhile the whole prognosis progressed almost comically slowly and sporadically. Dr. Henschel referred me to Dr. Kleinman at Urology Austin, a sixty-year-old Jewish Friar Tuck type, with a roll of fat under his chin and a wrinkle of fat on his bald head.

When I came into his office, he said, "So you've got a lump on your ball."

"Do I? I don't know." All of these conversations made me feel like you do when the curtain comes down across your computer screen, because a virus has hit or it's running out of power. Outside forces are taking control of your intimate life. "The radiologist just said there was something on one of them, he didn't know what it was. He said it was non-vascular, which he said was a good sign."

You find yourself arguing with these people, as if the explanation makes a difference—like the cancer is listening, to see who's right.

Kleinman asked me how often I went to the bathroom. To piss? The normal amount, I said. What's that? Six, eight times? Probably more than that. How's the flow, do you get a strong flow? That depends, I don't know. Sometimes it's better than others. How long when you stand in front of the toilet does it take for you to make water. Do people measure this, do they count the seconds? Just give me an estimate. Ten, fifteen seconds? Is that a long time? It's longer than normal. I don't really know, I said, and tried to explain myself. I work at home, I sit around all day, I watch TV. Sometimes, when I don't have anything else to do, I get up and take a leak. It doesn't mean I have to go.

The whole conversation lasted about five minutes, which I had been nerving myself up to face for the last five days. On the way out, he told me to get my blood tested, and I sat in one of those soft-upholstered chairs with my sleeve rolled up and a nurse looming over me. It was hot in the office, and I was under the air vent. At first, the nurse couldn't find a vein but then I felt the needle go in. After a minute, when I looked back, the tube was only half full.

"I don't know what happened," the nurse said. "It just stopped. Let me try the other arm," and she rolled up my right sleeve, too.

I remember saying, "If it's all right with you, I think I'll just go to sleep," and closed my eyes.

When I opened them again, I had no idea where I was. The ceiling light was an iridescent tube, fixed to those pock-marked panels you get in offices. A woman's eyes looked down into mine, too close for me to focus on her face. Then the face retreated and I could see her again. I thought, in a minute, you'll know, you'll figure this out. Keep calm until then.

The woman said, "Let me get you a glass of water." She came back with the water and I drank and felt the temperature of the liquid passing through my system. "I guess you must have been pretty tired."

"Did I pass out?"

"No, you just fell asleep," and I didn't argue with her, because I thought she might not let me drive home.

"Did you get enough blood?" I asked.

"We'll manage."

I noticed cotton balls taped to the inside of each of my elbows.

There was a vending machine in the reception area, and with shaking hands I pulled a dollar bill out of my pocket and bought a Snickers. When I reached the car, which was parked just outside, I sat there with the window open, eating the chocolate and feeling a slight headache coming on from the sugar rush. It's only about a fifteen-minute drive to Hyde Park from there, but some of it is on the highway. Merging on to MoPac took all of my concentration. I had the feeling that I wasn't processing information normally, but these things are hard to measure. There's a lot of information in the world, which most of the time you don't even think about.

Then it was just . . . another Tuesday afternoon. I worked at home, I sat around all day, I watched TV.

36

The Sonics went seven and three after Kaminski got fired. For the first time since opening day, they reached .500. Steuben had slowed the pace, which suited vets with middle-aged knees like Marcus and Roundtree and Stepanik, but not young guns like Crawford and Mmeremikwu. The problem for Mickey was he liked to see himself as a get-along guy. Which meant he didn't want to complain, at least publicly, so he let his agent do it for him.

Mickey's agent was Chris Hutchence. He and Sheldon Fitch more or less divided the A-list talent between them. Fitch was old-school, Jewish, he had a law degree from Cornell. Hutchence played point guard at Morehouse. Fitch gave him his first break, when he hired him at CAA. Then Fitch split off and started his own agency and a few years after that Hutchence split again. There's still a certain amount of bad blood between them, because he took with him many of Fitch's clients. Not Marcus, although Hutchence made a pitch. (That's partly where the criticism started that Marcus surrounds himself with white associates.) In other words, behind the scenes, people were making decisions about who played where and when, people with their own agendas and complicated personal histories, which most of us never get to see.

Actually, one of the ways that Hutchence differed from Fitch is that he had a public personality—he had a brand. And Hutchence started saying in the media (on *SportsCenter* and *Around the Horn, Inside the NBA*, anybody who would give him air time): *Mickey wants a trade, he wants out of this situation*, which Mickey if you asked him about it always denied. He said Hutch has his own way of making his opinions known, which are different from mine. That was his denial. Mickey was the seventh pick in the '09 draft and had two years left on his rookie contract, which paid him six million a year. His market value was probably four times that amount, depending on where the salary cap ended up. But to max out his earning potential, he needed to put up big numbers.

So when you write a piece, as I had done, arguing that the Sonics were better with Marcus running the show, and Mickey taking fewer shots, some people who read it would have a financial incentive for disagreeing with you. About a week after my lunch with Tash and Kyla, I got an email from my editor at ESPN, Steve Winnikoff. Hutchence wanted access to the tracking system I used for my article, otherwise he threatened to sue. "How do you want me to respond," Steve wrote, so I got in touch with Amy Freitag, who put me through to Joe Hahn. Joe was one of those important people who replies in the subject heading. This is not serious, he wrote. Ignore it.

But the thing wouldn't go away; it took up a lot of my expandable free time. Eventually, Hutch started writing me personally—my email address is listed on the website. When I'm finished with you, you'll never work in this business again. Your friends will pretend they don't know you; your girlfriend won't answer your calls. Shots in the dark, although the bit about Quinn hit home. When I couldn't sleep I sometimes wondered if Marcus paid her to keep me happy. But these are stupid thoughts, you shouldn't even say them.

He sent these messages at two a.m. In the middle of the night, we lay there thinking of each other.

The tracking system data belonged to the Sonics, not Marcus Hayes. Something didn't add up—maybe Laycock was just stirring the pot. Sometimes he liked to use freshman-psych-style motivational tricks. Anyway, it was proprietary technology; they wouldn't let me play around with it. Mickey had recently signed a big deal with Mercury Shoes ("Wear Wings"); they were making a push into the NBA, trying to eat away at Nike's market share. If something cost Mickey money, it also cost them. At a certain point, if you get famous enough, your problems become so complicated and involve so many people that they're not even really your problems anymore. I was just one of the people.

In the end, nothing happened; or almost nothing. I got an email from an editor at Deadspin, in case I wanted to correct or challenge any of the facts in an article they were running. Called *Just Write It: How Marcus Hayes Controls the Media*. It was partly about me. Apparently, Amy Freitag had sent the same data set around to a number of journalists, she pitched the same piece, and one of them noticed the overlap with what I eventually wrote.

When it came out, I sent the link to Winnikoff, who was reassuring.

Nobody cares about this stuff, he said. It's inside baseball. Anyway, talking about it only makes it worse.

But for months it was something else hanging over my head.

One day at the end of January I picked up the phone.

"Listen," I said. Quinn was always good about answering her cell. "I've got a favor to ask you," as if we were in the middle of a conversation.

"Hey Brian." In the background I could hear coffee shop noises. "I need to talk to you, too."

"But first I want to say, how are you doing. How was Christmas."

"I have some news," she said.

"Good news or bad news," and she laughed, but not like happy laughter.

"Let me just go outside, I can't talk in here."

For a minute I listened to various sounds, loose change on table sounds, somebody putting down a phone, talking to the waitress, and while this was going on, I sat on the sofa in the garage apartment with the curtains drawn, because it was sunny outside, cold and clear, and the sunshine blurred the television screen.

"Hey, Brian," she said again, and the space sounded different around her. She was walking. "What is it?"

"What is what?"

"The favor."

"You said you had some news."

"You first. You called me."

"I've been having some medical issues I didn't want to bother you with. Basically, about a month ago, I pissed a little blood. And the doctors have been trying to figure out what's going on. There are other complications I won't go into. But next Friday I'm having what's called a cystoscopy. They stick a camera up my penis. It's supposed to be painful but not a big deal. But you're not supposed to drive afterward, at least it's not recommended, and I wondered if you could give me a ride."

She didn't say anything, and I went on: "I haven't told anybody until now. I don't want to worry my dad. Betsy could drive me, but she has work and the kids. I didn't know who else to talk to about this." She still didn't answer. "I just want you to be there. This whole thing has kind of thrown me for a loop."

"Of course, Brian," she said. "Let me just . . . I can't have this conversation standing up."

She must have found a bench because I heard her sit down.

"I'm so sorry."

"It's not a big deal, it's just an unpleasantness. That's what my dad always says about these things. I'm sorry to dump it all on you." And then, laughing: "This is what you get for going out with a middle-aged guy."

"You're not middle-aged."

"I'm thirty-five. I feel fifty."

"Yeah, well," and then she laughed, too.

"What's your news." She didn't answer, so I said, "You said you had some news."

"Brian, I met somebody. I mean, I knew him already, but you know what I mean."

"I figured it was something like that. Is it Lloyd?"

"What? No . . . who's Lloyd? No. It's not him."

"Can I ask who it is, or is that none of my business?"

"What's funny is the whole time I really wanted to talk to you about it. I keep almost picking up the phone. I feel like, you're the only person I can talk to who will understand."

"I'd like to understand," I said, opening the curtains a little, for something to look at. My landlady had just come home and parked her Camry in the driveway; she was carrying out paper bags of shopping.

"He's a family friend. He's my dad's best friend. It's been going on, off and on, for a couple of years. At Christmas he told me he's getting a divorce, which is something they both wanted to do for years but now is the time because Miles is out of the house. I know his kids, too. He has two sons. We went to a New Year's Eve party together. I told him about you and he asked me if I could stop seeing you because he was ready to see if this could be a real thing. We still haven't told anybody."

"What do you want me to say. Do you want me to talk you out of it?"

"You don't have to say anything."

"Is there anything I can do?"

"Just don't hang up," she said.

We talked on the phone for two hours. She wanted to tell me all about him. For some reason I listened. His name was Daryl Farnham; he was a pilot for American Airlines—DFW is their hub airport. When Quinn was a kid whenever the Farnhams came for dinner, he brought her and her brother airline gear, AA pins, or even, when she got older, a uniform once, or stuff he picked up from airports around the world: a Paddington Bear from London Harrods when she turned thirteen, an Eiffel Tower key ring from Paris. He gave her brother stuff, too, a cricket ball, a wallet from Rome. It wasn't anything kinky, it was just nice. Sean (that was her brother) played on the same Little League team as Miles's brother Roy. The Farnhams were basically like everybody's best friend. When this came out, Daryl was worried, Quinn's dad would never speak to him again. They might both be cut off.

For her eighteenth birthday, over Thanksgiving, Daryl flew the whole family to Hawaii—he got them discount tickets, and he was actually the guy who flew the plane. He let her sit in the cockpit, he put his hand on her hand and let her touch the controls. It was the first time he ever did anything like that. I mean, he never did anything inappropriate until then, I don't think he even thought about it, she said. Nothing really happened until that summer, and he didn't want to ruin what he called my college experience, he wanted me to be free. So for two and a half years we just saw each other over the holidays and not usually more than once or twice. Sometimes he had to work, it was hard for him to get away. But then Miles went to Notre Dame and his whole thinking about his life started to change. He just felt like, I've got this limited time left to live the way I want to live.

I told him about you. He was very jealous. He's a huge basketball fan, he knows all about Marcus Hayes. He made me promise not to see you or get in touch and for the past three weeks that's what I've been doing. I kept hoping that you'd call, so it wasn't on me.

What could I say to her? He sounds like bad news. But was I in a position to make this point? Somebody else should really do it, but nobody else was having this conversation with her.

I said, "Does that mean you don't want to drive me next week?"

"Of course I want to drive you. I want to see you. I want to help."

"Will you tell him about it?"

"I don't know yet."

She was still in tears when I hung up.

37

University policy expressly prohibited consensual relationships between "intercollegiate athletics coaches, affiliates, or athletics employees and student-athletes" unless "the person in the position of
greater authority or power notifies appropriate University offices
and a mitigation plan is put in place." I guess in this case Megan was
"the person in the position of greater authority or power." She was
thirty, Marcus was eighteen, although maybe they started going out
when he was in high school.

Megan was only part-time at UT. The rest of the time she looked
after her mother, who had MS. This meant she didn't travel with the
players but still treated or worked with Marcus's teammates.

I never saw them kiss or hold hands, not once. But guys must have
been aware. Sometimes I sat with Megan during games, she wanted
somebody she could talk to about Marcus. Because this is what you
want when you're in love, and the person you love is going through
a complicated transition—from somebody his friends know to somebody strangers stop in the street.

By the end of the season, Menzes had put him in the starting lineup. Steuben was working with him in practice. He taught a lot of
European techniques, jump stops, two-dribble pull-ups . . . his heroes
were guys like Drazen Petrovic. Eventually the tournament came
along. Down one to Michigan with five seconds left, Marcus picked
up a rebound and started pushing hard against the clock, like a grey-
hound chasing a mechanical rabbit—people on both teams kept falling away. Then three things happened at once: the buzzer sounded,
he fell down, and the ball dropped in.

Okay, so it was a meaningless first-round game, and Texas ended up losing to Wake Forest two days later. Just one of those highlights they save for One Shining Moment, where part of the poignancy comes from the fact that the kid probably went home that summer and made five bucks an hour mowing lawns and nobody heard from him again. Except that the kid turned out to be Marcus Hayes, and this was the first real imprint he made on the national conscious-ness—running, as if for his life, to put the ball in the basket before time expired.

At the end of the semester, Marcus got in touch. He still had a few bags of stuff in our garage and wanted to pick them up. Players kept their access to the rec center, and some of the guys planned to stick around and work out together. Marcus said he was moving out of Jester into an apartment; I don't know who with and didn't ask. Megan still lived at home, to help with her mother. That wasn't a situation where Marcus could add himself to the mix. But maybe he also wanted a place of his own so she could come over. I never talked to him about Megan.

Anyway, one Sunday afternoon he biked over to my house, which used to be his old house. It was Jordan's first full season back, game three of the Finals. Marcus left his bike on the porch and came in— you could see the TV through the picture window. The Bulls got off to a fast start, and Marcus, sitting next to me on the couch, said, "I can't watch this. Man, I can't sit here watching this. I need to play." At halftime the lead was twenty-four. "Come on, man," he said. "This game is over." Michael had like twenty points, a couple of threes, he was tearing them up. Marcus kept saying, "He ain't no glove," talking about Gary Payton, who was guarding Michael.

When the commercials came on, I put on my Air Jordans and we went out to the garage to get the ball. It needed pumping up, but I found the pump. Marcus looked for his stuff, too, which was in a black garbage bag, and carried it inside the house.

"What the hell do you have in there?" I asked.

Mostly old basketball shoes, clothes, a 1985 Rolando Blackman jersey, from when his dad took him to a Mavericks game. It even had a few signatures on it, Blackman, Mark Aguirre, Derek Harper. "Blackman could play. He was *nice*," Marcus said, his favorite praise-word at the time. "People forget." He must have been nine years old when he saw that game.

"What are you going to do with it?"

"Sell it."

"What about the shoes?"

"Sell those, too."

He read somewhere you could make money selling old Nikes and he needed all the money he could get. For part of the summer, Marcus was helping out at Coach Caukwell's basketball camp. He also had a job washing cars at East Side Car Wash, three blocks away on San Bernard.

We walked across the park together, under the trees and past the swimming pool. School was out and the pool was full. Even the basketball court next door was occupied by a bunch of kids, messing around. They looked about twelve.

"You could do some stuff would make them tell their parents about it," I said to Marcus.

"Let's just shoot in your driveway." So that's what we did.

Marcus wanted to play one-on-one, so for a couple of minutes I let him beat up on me. He wore gray jeans and an Abercrombie & Fitch maroon T-shirt, and I tried to grab his shirt, which pissed him off, so I stopped. Anyway, it was ridiculous but not in a fun way, just dumb.

"Don't dunk on the rim like that," I said.

"Why not?"

"It's old, it's already a little messed up."

"I'm not hanging on it."

"Just leave it alone. My dad gave it to me. You're really not supposed to dunk on it. He gave it to me for my ninth birthday, and there were these instructions, and that was one of the instructions."

In the end I suggested we play H-O-R-S-E. "A dollar says I win," which he couldn't resist. I think we both felt, like, a slight uptick of intensity. His first two shots were jump shots from the grass. I made one out of two. Then he hit a three-pointer from the road, where you have to compensate for the dip in the driveway. I missed that, too, and he got a little cocky. He tried a hook from the free-throw line, from the same strip of Celtics green that my dad painted in ten years before. Over the years the front rim had bent a couple of inches, mostly from Marcus dunking on it. Anyway, his shot hit the backboard and rolled off the lip.

After that, I just lined up free throws, calling "underhand, Rick Barry style." He didn't complain the first time, which set the precedent. I made the first one and he made the first one and started talking shit. Then I made eleven straight, and he missed five of them. Game over.

He didn't want to pay up but eventually took a dollar bill out of the front pocket of his jeans, where he kept a small wad. "I should really get you to sign this," I said. "Sign and date it—To Brian Blum, who beat me at H-O-R-S-E on this day, Sunday, June 9, 1996. So I can take it out and show people when you're rich and famous."

But of course I spent it a few weeks later, I just forgot. Before he got on his bike, I said, "Some of the guys are coming back this summer. Andy and Mike and Frank and Jim." We could all get together, if he wanted to join us. Frank was talking about setting up a D&D campaign.

"Maybe, let me know."

It was about ninety-five degrees outside and five o'clock in the afternoon, the mosquito hour. My shirt had stuck to my back, which was covered in sweat. Leaf dust or something had gotten in my eyes, which already stung with the salt and itched from hay fever. We stood in the driveway and didn't know what to do; I think Marcus patted my shoulder. Then he rode off down the street with those live oak branches arching overhead, moving in and out of shade and carrying the black garbage bag over his shoulder like a sack.

The next couple of years we drifted apart. I heard about him the way everybody else did, by reading his box scores in the paper and watching him on *SportsCenter*. I still covered the Longhorns for the *Daily Texan* and even stopped by Gregory Gym from time to time. But our relationship was basically a professional relationship, and other reporters stepped in to take my place, guys from ESPN and *USA Today*. They knew his name, and he knew their names back. Even around campus he attracted a crowd. To get to him you had to push through hangers-on.

Almost every year there's a Cinderella team that makes it to the Final Four. The schedule bounces their way, somebody gets hot. All you have to do is win four games. This year it was Texas, and Marcus was the guy.

He scored twenty-nine against Wisconsin in the first round, against a slow-it-down, pack-it-in Big Ten bully. You couldn't score inside against them, so Marcus went outside and finished with five threes, including a twenty-four-footer with a minute left that put the Horns up six. Afterward, he kissed his hand and blew the kiss toward somebody on the Wisconsin bench. A reporter asked him about it in the press conference, and he said, "We just been having a little back-and-forth. All game long. I wanted to show him my appreciation."

Against Coppin State, another Cinderella team, with the Horns down one and three seconds left, he hit a leaner from the left block with two guys hanging on him to win the game.

Billy Packer from CBS Sports asked him in the postgame show, "Can you talk me through that last play? Is that how Coach Menzes drew it up?"

Marcus leaned into the microphone and said, "Not exactly."

He was figuring out that it isn't hard, if you're in control of a situation, to make people laugh. What matters isn't being funny, it's being in control.

Texas faced Louisville in the Sweet Sixteen, which had a week to prepare for him. Denny Crum, the Louisville head coach, started with a full-court press. Menzes let Marcus bring up the ball, because you couldn't trap him in a corner, he was too quick. But that cut his scoring in the first half, and the rest of the Horns struggled, too. In the second half, he stopped passing. Sometimes it's easier to attack a defense when you come from the backcourt with a head of steam. Even if they throw another defender at you, it's a guy running toward you while you're going the other way. He finished with thirty-six.

When the horn sounded, you could see Marcus pushing through the crowd toward the Louisville bench. Denny Crum put an arm around him and Marcus said something in his ear.

A reporter asked him about that, too. "What did you tell him?"

"I told him I always wanted to play for Louisville. They had the Final Four in Dallas when I was in fourth grade, so I got to stay up and watch. That was the year they won it. Milt Wagner, Billy Thompson, Pervis Ellison. Never nervous Pervis. They had some great players, I loved Milt. They beat Duke."

"So how did you end up at Texas?"

"I guess Coach Crum didn't want me."

More laughter. You could see him becoming a public person, without giving anything personal away. Maybe that's what it means.

By the time they faced North Carolina, Texas was Marcus's team; they'd live or die by his sword. Even in the press conference afterward, in the layup lines beforehand, in the locker room, in the cafeteria, in the hotel, on the team bus, they deferred to him. This is the role he was comfortable in, with other people—it's the role he played with me. In December, in Honolulu, when they met on New Year's Eve, the Tar Heels beat Texas by six points. But Texas got their revenge and it wasn't close.

The Final Four that year was in Indianapolis, but I didn't have the money to fly out. Plus, I had class. So my dad and I watched the game at home—sitting on the couch where Marcus used to watch games, too. Texas faced Kentucky, the defending champs. Marcus played fine. He finished with twenty-two points, nine below his tournament average, and they lost.

One minute you're on national TV in front of a hundred cameras, and the next day you're back at school with all the other kids. There are five weeks left in the semester and you have homework and final exams.

Coach Menzes gave me an interview for the *Daily Texan*. He said the things you'd expect him to say. Marcus Hayes is a very mature young man, he really stepped up and accepted the responsibility. To be honest, he said, we're a little ahead of schedule, I didn't expect to make that kind of run. Next year there's gonna be a target on our back.

38

Quinn had borrowed her housemate's Impala; she pulled into the driveway a little after seven o'clock. They like to get these minor surgeries out of the way early. I went out to meet her in a soft rain.

"I can't believe I'm making you do this."

"Of course, Brian."

"I can't believe I'm asking you to see me like this."

"Like what? It's just nice to see you."

At that hour, college students don't have a lot of conversation in them. I don't either. She took MoPac and we sat in commuter traffic; you forget, if you have a job like mine, that this is people's lives.

"Did you bring some work? You may have to wait a while."

"I've got my phone, it's fine."

"You're not missing any classes, are you?"

"I don't have anything until this afternoon. Don't worry, Uncle Brian."

We stared at the rain coming down over the highway, and on top of the cars, moving at half-speed. By the side of the road, beyond and below us, the tree canopy spread out. Sunrise was half an hour ago but the cloud cover kept lightening and you had the feeling, day breaks, everything starts again.

The clinic was a low-rise building, peach-colored, with parking directly outside. Nobody in Texas wants to walk up stairs anymore.

We went in and sat down. Most of the other people waiting were middle-aged men, alone or with a wife or girlfriend. Forty, fifty years old, otherwise healthy-looking, but their presence itself was like an admission of guilt.

When the receptionist called my name, Quinn said, "Do you want me to go with you?"

"That's all right."

"Sometimes it helps to have somebody else to remember what they said."

"I think this is just prep . . . I'm sorry to have dragged you into this."

"Don't be stupid."

"I'm not usually somebody who asks people for help, at least . . ."

"Go, just go."

I saw Dr. Kleinman for a couple of minutes, who explained the procedure. His manner was always the manner of somebody having a good day. You didn't want to disappoint him by having a bad one. First we apply a numbing gel, he said. What does that mean? We put it into your penis, so you don't feel anything. Does that hurt? What we say is, that it's uncomfortable . . . that's the official line. Afterward, if you want to disagree, you can disagree. And he laughed, not mean-ly, but just to show—none of this is really a big deal. Then we stick a camera in and have a look around. Sometimes it pinches a little, but I've done a lot of these. I've got a pretty steady hand.

Afterward, for a few weeks, you may notice a little blood in your urine. That's normal. We also have to watch out for infection. If it starts to burn, if you get a fever, anything like that, we'll put you on antibiotics.

The whole time I'm sitting there, I have a full bladder, because they tell you to tank up before the procedure. That way the camera can scuba dive through a sea of urine and not pinch against the edges of a dry sack. So everything he says goes right to the groin.

"Can I have sex?"

Dr. Kleinman looks at me. You expose yourself to these people, but whatever you say is something they've heard before.

"See how you feel. Maybe give it a day."

He has other patients, my time is up. A nurse leads me into a room where I can get changed. I take off my shoes, my jeans and underpants, my shirt and undershirt, and put them in a plastic bag, which they give you. They also give you one of those light blue wraps or dressing gowns that you tie at the back. It's like stepping into a bed sheet. Everything is loose, everything hangs free. What you feel is, totally unprotected.

There's another waiting room outside, where the guys in gowns are already lining up. You can sit down, but it feels weird sitting down, you feel the weight of your scrotum on the vinyl chair. A TV bolted to one of the walls shows a breakfast talk-show: a man and a woman, both heavily made up, drinking coffee and making public-facing conversation. Intimate but also social. It's like the good mood you have to be in with friends of friends.

Part of what stresses me out is the thought of leaving my wallet and phone in a plastic bag. So I tell the nurse, I'm just going to give this to someone, and walk down the end of the hall, where a door leads on to the reception area. Then I open the door and lean out. Quinn is sitting there, looking at her phone. She's wearing a pleated skirt and green tights and lace-up leather boots with a modest heel. She got dressed up for this, she wanted to look nice. Her face is one of those pale Irish faces where a little red lipstick really stands out. Whenever she sits down she has to adjust for her hair. When I was in high school, I always thought the girls with superlong hair had some kind of damage; it's like they needed a security blanket. But I don't really know what girls are like.

"Quinn," I say. "Can you take this for me?"

I don't want to come in the room because the only thing keeping my butt from hanging out is a loose knot, which I tied blindly. So she has to stand up and come to me.

"Everything okay?"

"Fine. Nothing's happened yet. My wallet's in here, I don't want to leave it lying around."

"Should I take the whole bag or just . . ."

So for a minute I dig through the tangle of clothes and find wallet

and phone and give them to her, while propping the door open with
my shoulder. She takes them from my hand, and I say, "I haven't even
asked you yet, how you're doing. I mean, how's it going with . . ."

"Maybe now is not the time," she says.

A lot of guys have had this procedure. It's like a whole world opens
up, of middle-aged manhood, and you enter the club. They don't
need to read about it and I don't expect anyone else wants to either.
So I'll keep this short. Dr. Kleinman did to me what he said he was
going to do—he shoved a handful of numbing gel up my dick and
waited a minute for it to take effect. Then snaked a camera down the
opening; don't ask me how, I wasn't looking. I lay on my back on the
blue roll of paper and watched somebody who was good at his job
controlling the controls.

But this is what I thought about. When I was a kid, the first home
computer we owned was an Apple IIe, which Betsy got when she started junior high. It came with a monitor and you could attach a joystick
to it and play a few limited games. One of those games was Tharolian
Tunnels. The premise was, you had to steer a kind of underground
spaceship as it descended through various interconnected caverns into
the heart of the world. Sometimes the caverns fed into each other and
you could maneuver the ship so it didn't touch any of the walls; but
occasionally the opening was too narrow and you had to blast your
way through, using Space Invader-style bombs. If the ship hit the walls
or got too near to one of the explosions, you lost a life but kept going
until all your lives ran out.

Anyway, this is the game that Dr. Kleinman was playing in my
urinary tract. He dived into the urethra and passed through the
prostate into the bladder, trying as much as possible not to touch
the sides, while at the same time looking around to see what he
could see. There were a few explosions, nudges and bumps against
those delicate internal skins not designed for contact, but mostly

he did fine. Afterward he said, "It all looks good. Your prostate is impressively large, but I didn't see anything to worry me."

The whole conversation lasted about five minutes.

"So why did I piss blood?"

"Who knows. Maybe a kidney stone, maybe a UTI that cleared up before we tested it."

"Does that mean I'm in the clear?"

But he wanted to have another look at my balls before signing off. Come back in a couple of months, he said. We'll see if that tumor is doing anything it shouldn't be doing.

The nurse wouldn't let me leave until I passed water. So I stood in the bathroom and held this thing in my hands and tried to ease the pressure hanging between my legs. Counting out the seconds, one Mississippi, two Mississippi, three, etc. like I was waiting to rush the quarterback in some pickup game of flag football. A trickle came out and turned into a stream. It was like pissing through someone else's dick, I couldn't feel a thing. Except a thin wire of pain, like a memory of something that used to be there.

When I came out, the nurse asked me, "Any blood?"

"I don't think so."

Then I could go. The plastic bag was in the changing room and I put on my clothes and went to see Quinn.

"Well?" she said, standing up.

"They didn't find anything."

"What does that mean?"

"It means good news. They were looking for cancer."

"That's great, Brian . . ." She had a backpack over one shoulder but tried to put her arm around me.

"I'm sorry I dragged you out here for nothing."

"What are you talking about. I had fun."

Her hair was in my face and one of us had to release first. I didn't want to make her feel like I was clinging on. Keep it light. We stepped outside and I said, "Do you want to get breakfast somewhere?"

"Sure, okay."

It was ten o'clock in the morning, the rain had stopped, and which happens in Austin in the winter, when you tear the cloud away, underneath it like a layer of old wallpaper is a bright spring sky. By the afternoon it would be seventy degrees; already I could smell the sweat in my armpits as I sat in the car, and opened the window, and let the air from Westlake Hills wash over me.

"You had me worried there for a while," she said.

"Well, I have to come back for a follow-up. But so far so good."

There's an IHOP just on the other side of MoPac and that's where we went. In my NBA beat-reporter days I used to eat at places like this all the time. You sit in one of the booths and watch the cars come into the parking lot and the traffic on the highway beyond.

"I shouldn't have made you do this," I said, when the waitress took our orders. "It was selfish of me. I could have driven, I just had a bad experience the last time, when they took my blood. For some reason I had this dumb idea that if you saw me like this it might make you feel closer to me."

"I feel close to you."

"But as soon as we got there I realized, this is not how I want you to see me."

"Like what? Women are used to this stuff, we deal with it all the time."

"You're a good kid," I said.

"I don't know why you call me that."

"Because you did a nice thing today. That's all I mean."

"You don't have to push me away like that," she said.

"Who's pushing away?"

For some reason the tone had changed, but then the pancakes came and we could eat. I had the impression things were moving into another gear or stage. But what that was, who knows, or maybe I misread the situation. She seemed to me suddenly very young, and I was like this guy with dirty hands, where everything I touched you could see my fingerprints. Sometimes I tell myself on dates, talk about what *she* wants to talk about. Figure out what that is. So I asked her about Daryl Farnham.

"What about Daryl Farnham?" she said.

"Does he know you're here?"

"I don't have to tell him every time I eat pancakes."

"You know what I mean."

"No."

"Are you going to tell him?"

"About what? Your prostate problem or whatever. I don't think he's that interested."

"No, I just mean. Have you told your parents yet. About him." She didn't say anything. "I'm trying to take an interest in your life, so that we can have some kind of normal interactions . . . going forward."

"You have a really weird idea of normal interactions."

"I didn't put it very well . . ."

"It's not *normal* to be interested in some other guy I'm seeing, when you go out with a girl. That's not normal."

"No, I can see that."

"Anyway, you don't have to pretend to be interested in anything."

"That's not what I mean."

The waitress kept refilling my water glass. I was drinking too much and worried I'd have to go to the bathroom again. Also, I had a headache from the ice, and a sugar rush, and various other conflicting feelings.

"What do you want to talk about?" I said, trying to be polite.

Quinn looked at me; under the harsh diner light you could see that her very white skin had little irregularities. My mother got them, too. She called it her rosacea, which always seemed to me as a kid a funny kind of intimate and beautiful name for something like that. She put on a cream at night, which didn't do much. I used to watch her in the bathroom mirror. It amazed me that she still cared about what she looked like. Her face was my mother's face, what more could she want. This is the feeling you have about somebody when you fall in love.

"We don't have to talk," Quinn said.

I paid the bill, and she didn't offer. It's the least I can do, I said, which also seemed like the wrong thing to say. But then on the car ride home the silence took on a different complexion again. She didn't seem angry anymore.

Eventually she said, "I was asking myself in the waiting room, what would you do if it's bad news."

"What do you mean, what would you do."

"It's just a conversation I was having with myself."

But it's only a twenty-minute drive—she pulled onto MoPac for about five miles, then came off at West 45th and entered neighborhood streets. Once you reach the park you're basically there.

"Do you want me to come in?" she said, after parking the car. "You're not gonna collapse or anything."

"I don't think so."

I got out of the car, but then she got out too, and walked with me to the front door. There was a kind of side entrance to the garage—my apartment was on the second floor.

"What are you gonna do now?" she said.

"Probably just . . . take a shower, and go to bed. I'm pretty wiped out."

"I don't want to go to the library," she said. "I don't know what to do."

"If you ever need anything, just call me. It doesn't matter what it is. I won't interpret it as anything else." This is a line I had prepared beforehand, lying in bed and waiting for the day to start.

"Okay."

"I don't want to be a problem in your life."

"You're not the problem. I'm just glad everything's all right."

"Thank you, Quinn," and I kissed the top of her head.

"Not many guys can do that to me," she said.

39

Texas entered the season ranked seventh in the AP Poll. Four months later, after winning the Big 12 Conference, they moved up to third and earned the number one seed in the Midwest Regional. The Final Four was in San Antonio, an hour and a half by bus from the UT Campus. They'd practically have home-court advantage—if they made it that far.

A week before the tournament started, Marcus was shortlisted for the Naismith Player of the Year Award, alongside Mike Bibby, Raef LaFrentz and Antawn Jamison.

In the first round, they doubled-up Prairie View A&M—110 to 52. Marcus scored twenty-seven points, even though he sat for most of the second half. Two days later they faced a Bob Knight Indiana team that went nine and seven in the Big Ten and never cracked the top twenty-five.

As hot as Marcus was the year before, that's how cold he got. The opposite of "the zone" is also a zone, which you can't get out of. It has its own kind of flow, even if the beat's a half-second off. Part of what you realize is that there are a lot more ways to go wrong than to be right.

Even so, with thirty seconds left the Longhorns had a chance to win. Down two, Marcus had the ball at the top of the key, drove hard to his right against Bruce Wigmore (who died in a car crash that summer), slipped on a sweaty floorboard or tripped over Bruce's foot, it isn't totally clear, and dribbled the ball off his knee. Somehow Wigmore ended up with it and the only thing Marcus could do was foul him. The kid made both free throws, with twenty thousand fans screaming at him and waving thunder sticks. (The game was played in Columbus, and much of the Buckeye fan base hates the Hoosiers.) And that was it.

Texas stayed at the hotel after the game then flew home to Austin in the morning. It was mid-semester, but Coach Menzes let the players take the day off. Megan called Marcus's apartment in the afternoon, but his roommates hadn't seen him or heard from him. They didn't know where he went; I still don't. Maybe he drove up to Dallas to visit his mom or stayed with his dad in Killeen. In those days, people didn't have cells, and if you wanted to get away, you could do it without making too big a deal out of it. But for the rest of the week, he didn't show up to class.

On Friday Megan called again, and Roy Vaughan, who was a senior, and the starting power forward on the team, said that Marcus had come back but wasn't home. At least, his stuff is on the bed, Roy said. Maybe he went to the Kappa Kappa party.

Did he say he was going, Megan asked, and Roy said, That's what Tark said, I didn't actually see him. Tark was Shawn Tarkington, the backup point guard, another housemate.

Every year at the end of the basketball season, Kappa Sigma Chi and Kappa Delta Nu, which were the two main sports fraternities, threw a party to celebrate, basically, the end of training, so everyone could get drunk. It helped that their houses were catty-corner from each other, on Leon and 25½ Street, about seven blocks from the Drag, toward Shoal Creek. Kappa Chi was the football frat, and traditionally pretty white—they'd had some racist hazing incidents that got them national attention a few years back. Kappa Nu was the basketball fraternity, and black. The Kappa Kappa party was supposed to be like an olive branch thing, to show how times had changed. But it was also famous for being totally out of hand. For a certain subsection of the student body, which included many of the sororities, getting ready for Kappa Kappa involved a lot of time, money and effort.

So Megan put on a dress and went to look for Marcus.

She still had to ask her dad if it was okay to go out on a Friday night. Even though he was semi-retired, Megan did most of the physical labor involved in caring for her mother, which included getting her into bed. He said, what time will you be back, and she said, not later than eleven. She just wanted to see Marcus and make sure he was all right. At nine o'clock she got in her old VW Golf, which she actually bought in college, and drove across the river toward campus.

By the time she parked on San Gabriel, the party was in full swing. It was really two parties and took up most of the block. People came and went between the frats. Kappa Chi had the nicer house, a 1930s stone mansion, with pillars over the front door and a long low extension to the side with big French doors, and railings on the roof, so if some guy climbed out drunkenly he didn't fall over the edge.

I don't think Megan understood the scale of Kappa Kappa when she set out. For the first half hour, she didn't accept a drink—just smiled and pretended she couldn't hear, which was probably true. Megan was partially deaf in her left ear, from chickenpox as a kid, which also explains her slight lisp. Sometimes she even wore a hearing aid, although not on social occasions. At a party like that it would have been useless anyway.

Later, when describing what happened to my mother, she tried to remember as clearly as she could everyone she spoke to or who might have seen her. On that Saturday night, the Final Four was playing in San Antonio. Guys from the team were watching the game—somebody told her to check out the TV room at Kappa Nu. But Megan didn't know where that was. Students took her in hand and then ran into somebody and started talking, and she drifted off again. It was a warm, late March night, still mosquito-free, really the best time of year in Austin, and just humid enough that even if you felt a little cold you didn't mind.

Eventually she started drinking. Sometimes it's easier to accept the cup and sip it and put it down afterward than to keep explaining why you're not drinking.

What was in these cups, my mother asked her. One of her jobs was to deal with allegations of sexual assault on campus. Don't mind me, she said. I'm just going to take a few notes.

I don't know, Megan said. I don't really remember. A lot of people knew me there, and it became like a thing to get me something to drink.

You don't remember what was in the cups?

Beer. Some of the girls on the . . . softball team were drinking margaritas. I don't want to get anybody in trouble. There was a kind of blue punch.

Who gave you that?

I don't know, some guy. He was pretty big, maybe he was a football player. I don't really remember.

Was he white or black?

White.

Could you recognize him again?

I don't think so. There were a . . . lot of guys who looked like that at the party.

This is how the conversation went on. My mother had to strike a balance between expressing sympathy and figuring out what had happened. In some ways it's harder than dealing with these things in a court of law, where the roles and rules are more clear-cut. Of course, you can pass cases over to the city prosecutor but then it's out of your hands, and most universities want to keep them in-house, and my mother worked for the university.

Can you explain why you were there? she asked. Employees are generally discouraged from socializing with students.

I was looking for Marcus Hayes, I was worried about him. I hadn't seen him since the team got back from Ohio.

Why were you particularly worried about Marcus Hayes?

Because of the way he played against Indiana. I hadn't talked to him since that game. Normally we talk every day, but he just disappeared.

You talk every day?

He's my boyfriend, she said. That's another thing. I don't know if he's coming back next year. I mean to school. It feels like all these things are going on with him, and I'm just on the sideline.

Another pause, another tiptoeing act.

You know that . . . it's against university policy for any employee to . . . enter into a relationship with a student without notifying . . . someone from the university?

Yes.

Did you notify anyone?

No.

Can I ask you how long this relationship has been . . . going on?

Do I have to answer that? she asked. Marcus just told me, go talk to Dr. Blum. She'll deal with everything.

I'll do my best. But if you go forward with this, you may have to answer some of these questions.

I know.

Normally my mother was only involved in this kind of incident at a later stage—after the initial investigation. She could have sent Megan down the usual channels but didn't want to hand over the problem to somebody who might turn out to be less sympathetic to Marcus.

Her office overlooked a campus street, shaded by live oak. On her walls, she still hung the pictures Betsy and I did when we were kids, including a crayon drawing I made when I was nine years old, of my dad's head shaped like a basketball. All of the university buildings had gray brown carpeting and seventies-style furniture and metal chairs. The air-conditioning was effortlessly powerful, so that sitting in her office felt a little like being suspended in time.

At some point during the Kappa Kappa party Megan ran into Shawn Tarkington. She asked him if he'd seen Marcus, and Shawn said, Not yet. He said he was coming. But when he left the house he was actually heading to the gym. At least he had his gym bag with him. Megan almost went home then. It was already eleven o'clock, which is when she promised her dad to be back . . . but she was also feeling incredibly anxious and upset, and the noise level and the people and the different kinds of alcohol she had already drunk made it difficult for her to make decisions. She said to my mom, It's like I couldn't . . . make a new decision, I just wanted to find Marcus, even if he wasn't there.

What did you do then?

I don't really remember. It was a party, people kept saying hello. There were some girls who wanted me to dance with them, and I danced for a while. Guys came up and talked to me. I work with the football team, and a lot of guys from the team were there. I started asking everybody where Marcus was, which they acted like was incredibly funny. I had a bad feeling but didn't want to leave. Plus, I thought, if you just start drinking water maybe in an hour or two you can drive home. I really hadn't drunk very much.

What happened next?

One of the guys said, I know where Marcus is. And another guy said, yeah, I know where he is. Haven't you seen him? But maybe you don't want to know what he's doing. And I was like, what, what? Tell me. Because I knew they were just . . . trying to get me to react. But they kept saying, if you want, I can take you to Marcus. I know where he is. Just on and on, and I said, he's not here, he's not even at the party, and they said, well, then, why are you looking for him? These are guys I work with sometimes.

On the football team?

One of them was on the football team. The other was a basketball player. So they said, I don't think you want to know what Marcus is doing. And I was like, what's he doing? And they said, this is a party . . . So I said, you guys are so full of shit. They were just laughing. So I said okay, if you know where he is, why don't you tell me? And they said, I don't think you want that. But if you really want to know . . . It just went on like this. Finally, one of them said, I'll take you to him, but you have to promise not to get mad. Why should I get mad?

You have to promise not to get mad at him, they said. I don't want to get him into trouble. Just take me to him. It wasn't funny anymore. I was really feeling . . . I didn't feel at all well, and I knew I was making dumb decisions but couldn't stop.

So then they said, okay, and started going up the stairs, and I followed them up the stairs, and when we got to the top, one of them said, he's in this room. There was a door in the hallway. I said, what's in that room? And they said, that's where the party is. You have to promise not to get mad. We don't want Marcus to get in any trouble. So I said, what are you talking about, and opened the door. But there was nothing in the room. It was just like an office, with a desk, and a couch, and a filing cabinet. Then they pushed me in the room and shut the door.

Are you okay? my mom said. We can take a break.

I'm so embarrassed, Megan said. It's so stupid. I was just like . . . out of my mind.

You didn't do anything wrong. The people who did wrong things were the other people.

It's not as bad as you think, she said. They were pretty drunk, they thought they were being funny. One of them tried to make me lie down on the couch, the other one was just laughing. But I threw up on him. I don't know what happened, I really didn't have that much to drink. Maybe they put something in it. Then the other guy started laughing even more and I actually just . . . walked out. They let me go.

What time was it?

About one in the morning.

What did you do next?

My purse was in the room, but I just left it. There were some people on the stairs, and I walked past them into the front yard, and there were people there, too. Nobody said anything to me, I didn't have any shoes on. But then I recognized this girl from the swim team named Linda Lawrence. She could see something was wrong. All I told her was that I lost my purse, which had my car keys in it.

Why didn't you tell her anything else?

I just wanted to get home. I wanted to get cleaned up.

What did she do?

She loaned me some money. I said, I don't even have a phone, and she called a cab, and she waited with me until the cab came. She brought me a glass of water and we sat on the curb.

Did you say anything to her then?

No. I was too embarrassed . . . I think she just thought I was drunk.

Did you feel drunk?

No. I had a headache, but I didn't feel drunk.

What happened next?

I went home. My dad locks the front door at night, but you can go around the side to our backyard, and he didn't lock the kitchen door. So I went through the kitchen and went to bed. Actually, I had a shower first. I used the guest bathroom, which is farther from my parents' bedroom, then in the morning when I woke up, it was about eight o'clock. I realized I probably should have gone straight to the police.

Did you tell your parents what had happened?

No. I didn't have any money, and my car was still parked outside the frat house. I had a spare set of keys but couldn't really face going back there. So I just canceled my cards and called Verizon and canceled my phone plan. On Saturday Marcus finally called our home number. I told him what happened, and he picked me up and drove me back to campus so I could get the car.

My mother didn't know what to do. Obviously, she had a very distressed young woman on her hands. But there might not be enough in Megan's story for a prosecutor to work with, especially if the only witness was the other guy. The burden of proof for disciplinary action against the two students was much lighter. Maybe she could get them suspended, or even kicked out. Her job was to report to the vice president, who had his own team of lawyers to advise him. In other words, my mother's actual influence was slight, she was just a link in the chain. But, being good at her job, and generally respected, she could shape her part of the conversation, which can still have an effect on many conversations down the line.

Megan herself didn't want to press charges. Her relationship with Marcus Hayes violated university policy and would have to come out at any hearing, which could get her fired. She just wanted to pretend the whole thing was a terrible dream and forget about it.

So why did you come to me? my mother asked her.

Marcus wanted me to. He blames himself for what happened.

Because he wasn't there to protect you? (It turned out he spent the evening at Gregory Gym, lifting weights and shooting on the empty court, and went to bed around eleven o'clock.)

No. He felt like, a lot of people resented him and knew we were going out, and didn't like the fact that he was going out with a white girl. When he played so badly against Indiana . . . some of the guys at the party must have felt like, he was weak enough they could go after him like this.

They didn't go after him, they went after you.

He says the only thing guys like that understand is power. They respect people who have more power than them. That's the only thing that makes a difference. Because I'm white he thinks the police will be on my side.

If you want to go to the police, that's your decision. That might be a long road. There are other things we can do but it's up to you.

I don't see how anything good is going to come out of it, Megan said.

My mother took me aside after dinner one night; she wanted to know what I knew about their relationship. She said, you can't mention this to anybody, including your father. (After she died, when we cleaned out her office at the university, I found her notes from the conversation with Megan. She always kept meticulous records.)

Did you know they were together? she asked me. I said yes. For how long? I don't know. Did it start when he was in high school? I don't know. Are they still together? I don't know. Marcus doesn't talk to me about stuff like that.

One week later, at a ceremony at the Tipoff Club in Atlanta, Marcus Hayes was named Naismith Player of the Year. I saw him on TV, wearing the Men's Warehouse suit my dad had bought him for our high school graduation. Three years older, it showed a little tight across the shoulders, which somehow added to the general impression of a very self-contained young man. A few days after that, in a press conference hosted by Coach Menzes and staged in the media room at the Erwin Center, Marcus announced that he had decided to skip his senior year of college eligibility and make himself available for the NBA draft.

40

Driving to one of my doctor's appointments I was flipping through radio channels when the *Brandenburg Concertos* came on. My mother used to play them in the car on the ride to school. By this point I was in a state of more or less constant low-level anxiety but for some reason the music calmed me down.

Later I asked my dad if he knew where her tape collection was. He said, try the garage. So I spent an afternoon kicking around in there, with a light bulb dangling from the ceiling on a wire. There was a bookshelf at the back where he kept his handyman tools, shoeboxes of nails and screws, pickle jars filled with screwdrivers, old matchbooks, that kind of thing. One of the shoeboxes was labeled EILEEN. It had her cassettes in it, along with her old Sony Walkman, so I took them back home and replaced the batteries and started listening to her music. She didn't just listen to opera but anything classical: Pachelbel's *Canon in D*, Verdi's *Requiem*, Vaughan Williams, Purcell's *Timon of Athens*, many of these tapes she must have recorded herself, because they were labeled in her careful Catholic-school handwriting.

All through my childhood this stuff was going through her head. It was like wandering through empty hallways . . . My mother didn't care about or value most of the things I was interested in. When I was younger we used to fight about this, but if she were still alive the things that mattered to me would be different, that's undeniable.

What else did I do? I wrote this book.

At one point my editor emailed me for a progress report. Not my editor at ESPN, but the HarperCollins guy, Pete Morgentau—who was basically one of us. I mean a thirty-something sports nut from Bloomington, who played JV soccer in high school and realized he wasn't good enough to make varsity so discovered books. His favorite sports book of all time was *Season on the Brink*, by John Feinstein. Which is also why he wanted to become an editor, because of Jeff Neuman, who published Feinstein and five years later bought *The Jordan Rules* from a general-assignment guy at the *Chicago Tribune* named Sam Smith.

Nobody at the time wanted to touch Smith's book, but Neuman took a punt and it ended up topping the best-seller lists. Part of the reason was the tight turnaround—Jordan won the title in June and six months later the book was on the shelves.

These days, Pete said, the time pressure is even more intense. He wanted me to send him what I had.

It still wasn't clear if the Sonics would make the playoffs; in other words, what kind of timeline we were dealing with. Marcus's season could end in April or in June. It could be a triumph or a flop. Pete thought I should get something ready for the start of the playoffs either way—a teaser, which ESPN could run at the end of the season, to generate interest in the book.

We had a lot of back and forth about it. In the end, I pitched something to Winnikoff about why Marcus quit—and why he decided to come back. A Rosebud story that involved the breakdown of his marriage and the arrival on the scene of Cheryl Dillard. Since the divorce announcement, J. P. had started talking to reporters. She was getting out her side of the story and gave me a great quote. I managed to reach her at the house on Mount Bonnell Shores.

"You know that joke?" she asked me. Her voice on the phone always sounded faintly out of breath. "What's the hardest thing to do in the NBA . . . keep the smile off your face when you kiss your wife goodbye before a road trip."

"I've heard it before."

"Ten years, that's how long we been married."

"That's a long time."

"I never wanted a dog on the leash. You understand what I'm saying."

"I understand." (You say whatever you *can* say that keeps them talking.)

"I been around the game a long time. But you need a baby, to make this work. You need to give them a reason to come home."

"I wondered about that," I said.

"He thinks I knew but I didn't. Anyway, it's over now."

All of this went in the piece, along with Shelley Vance and Megan Adez. At every stage, before going to the next stage, Marcus was pushed—in high school and college; at the end of his NBA career, when he fell in love with a seventeen-year-old girl and retired to get away from the publicity. But there is no next stage for him now; at least, nothing he wants. The only thing left is to do it all over again. After three years of retirement, he realized that the rest of his life was just going to get worse.

The Sonics went twenty-five and ten after firing Kaminski—third best record in the League since Christmas. In February, Marcus Hayes was named Western Conference Player of the Month, with a stat line of thirty, seven and seven, while shooting 42 percent on threes. If the playoffs had started then (I'm talking early March), the Sonics would have been the number six seed. Then Mickey broke his hand.

Apparently, this is what happened. Steuben had instituted half-court scrimmages in practice, to get the team ready for the playoffs, when everything slows down. But the real point was to show the guys that Marcus Hayes was boss, so Mickey would stop complaining.

Even at thirty-five, Marcus was an elite half-court scorer. He could pull up for three off the dribble, find the weakside shooters with either hand and keep you on his hip when he got in the lane. Mickey had a Eurostep, which you can't really use in traffic anyway, and a baseline turnaround jump shot that was mostly for show. Other than that he just kind of scrambled points. You could pack the paint against him and dare him to shoot. There are guys who shoot worse the more you leave them open. What Mickey really liked was flying out on the break. It pissed him off, every time he grabbed a rebound in one of these scrimmages, to walk the ball out past the arc and turn around.

Steuben lined up Marcus and Stepanik and Roundtree against Mickey and Crawford and the other young guns. At the end of practice, Marcus liked to rub it in. Beat me at *this* game, if you want to make your point, but Mickey couldn't.

Then one day Marcus curled hard off a high screen and drove to the basket. Roundtree tried to box off Mickey from the play and gave him a little hip-nudge in midair, which sent him tumbling. When Mickey got up, he punched Roundtree in the sternum and walked off the court holding his wrist.

In the news reports, this is what they call a heated exchange of views. X-rays showed a fractured metacarpal. Doctors said he could be out six weeks.

A few days later I got back to my apartment and found a message on my answering machine. Fred Rotha was coming to town, to work on a story about Mmeremikwu, and wanted me to pick a night so we could have dinner.

All week long, I had a weird kind of nervous anticipation about this evening. For the past two months, I hadn't gone out except to see Betsy and the kids. You get a little inward, it's hard to turn outward again. Also, I figured, I'd have to give some kind of account of myself.

But it's easy talking to Fred, you forget how easy.

Mostly we talked about basketball. I feel bad for Mmeremikwu, he said, this should have been his breakout year. If you had told me at the beginning of the season that Marcus Hayes would not only win the alpha battle but get Kaminski fired, turn Mickey into a role player, to the point where, lashing out, he actually breaks his hand

and has to miss the first round of the playoffs . . . while Marcus ends up third in the League in scoring, and first in three-pointers made . . . I wouldn't have believed you.

"This is what he does," I said.

Fred wanted to write about the legacy implications. I've been calling around the League, he said. Front office guys, scouts, some ex-players. What does this do to his final ranking? Can he leap-frog Bird, Kobe? And now Mickey is out, what if Marcus drags them to the playoffs, does that move the needle? If they make it into the Conference Finals? They can't go further than that, can they? I don't see them beating the Spurs.

But he was talking too much, and knew it. "What are you working on? How's the book?"

"I'm writing something about why he quit," I said.

"Was it the McConaughey thing?" He meant the NBA ref who took bribes.

"No, something else."

And I told him the story. March 2008, his last title run. They had just lost back-to-back games, for the first time all year, including a tight one in Houston the night before, when Marcus went seven for twenty-three. So the next day he gets in a rented car and drives three hours to do a favor for his old high school coach and meets a girl who's never heard of him. These windows open up in your life, where you're vulnerable to new impressions. A few months later he wins Finals MVP and two weeks after that, he quits. Over the summer he starts hanging out in Austin.

"You have to be careful with this," Fred said.

"What do you mean?"

"It's not the kind of thing we write about."

"Why not?"

"Because it's none of our business. Have you shown it to Marcus?"

"Not yet."

"If you write this thing," Fred said, "people may stop talking to you.

I mean people in the League, players, coaches, everyone else. I don't see how you can keep going."

"I don't see why not."

"Come on, Brian."

"I'd rather talk about this stuff than whether Marcus Hayes is the ninth or thirteenth best player in NBA history."

"That's fine. But if you're gonna do it, do it with your eyes open."

The bill came and I paid. This is my town, I said, and he let me, even though it was a couple hundred bucks. I think he figured, Let Brian feel like the big shot, if that's what he wants. What he said was, thank you.

Afterward, I didn't join him for drinks at the Driskill Hotel. Some of the people he was meeting were people I knew—Alana Sissons, Kirk Bohls from the *Statesman*, other reporters. It was a crowd, basically a nice crowd. Not that different from the guys I hung out with in high school. Fred Rotha was like a 2.0 version of the DeKalb brothers, smarter about basketball, probably more popular with girls. A nice guy, too. In the morning he called me from the airport to say hello, just checking in. The friendship I had with him was like these other friendships, but it was also missing something. That feeling of sitting at the back of the class, which is what I missed. When the world was far away and didn't matter.

41

I used to be a Celtics fan, like my dad. For the first twenty years of my life. Sometimes I forget that fact. They won the championship in '76, the summer before I was born, which is why my middle name is David, after Dave Cowens. Dad used to call me Big Red, too. They won again when I was four and too small to remember. But then in '84 they beat Pat Riley's Lakers in seven games and I was allowed to stay up late and watch—that was the last year we lived in Boston. It pissed my sister off to see me on the couch past my bedtime, in pajamas, nestled up to Dad. Larry Bird was Finals MVP.

They won again in '86, the year after I got the Rawlings hoop over the garage door. On a Sunday afternoon, against my home-state Houston Rockets, which made the prospect of going to school the next day, and rubbing it in, all the sweeter. I'm really a Boston kid, that's the point I wanted to make. I don't really live here, I'm just passing through. Six hours after the whistle blew, I was still banging away on the driveway, pounding the ball under the garage light.

Come on in, Brian, my mother called. It's a school night. People are trying to sleep.

I just have to make five straight.

But I didn't actually stop until my dad came out to get me, hauling me in by the neck of my shirt, in a sweaty hug.

Then they lost to the Lakers the next season, and after that, my teenage years were lean years—the Pistons came along, and then Michael came along, and that was that.

So when the Celtics drafted Marcus in '98, part of what I felt was, that's *my* team. But what does it mean, my team. Just because I grew up watching them and rooting for them, just because some of the most *impassioned* three-hour stretches of my life involved staring at their highly paid employees on a little backlit screen—does that make me a sad human being? Okay, then that's what I am. Marcus was just another employee.

Senior year in college I finally moved out of my parents' house and shared an apartment with a couple of guys from the *Daily Texan*, on Pearl Street, four blocks from the Drag. We never had a working TV. After the cable guy failed to show the first few times, we just gave up.

This didn't bother me much because of the NBA lockout. Over the summer, the owners opened up the collective bargaining agreement . . . and the whole thing dragged on. It must have been a weird time for Marcus, sitting around in Boston, a town he didn't know where he didn't know anybody, trying to stay in shape, waiting to play, with money in his pocket for the first time in his life. Once you start this kind of us-and-them the only way out is to let it go on until everyone gets sick of it. Anyway, on February 5, the season opened, and I used to wander over to the Crown & Anchor to watch the games.

One night the Celtics were on TNT, playing the Pacers, and when I walked in I noticed Megan Adez sitting on the veranda with a few friends. Mid-February, not particularly warm, but they had those gas burners attached to some of the wooden posts giving off waves of heat. Megan was smoking a cigarette, which surprised me. I'm slow to react to this kind of thing and just walked on, but when I sat down at the bar and asked the barmaid to change the channel to TNT, the whole time I kept thinking, go over and say hello.

Of course, I just sat there and ordered a burger and cricked my neck looking up at the box. It was the middle of the second quarter. Just a dead time of the game, at a dead time of the year, amid the neon cheerlessness of an almost empty bar. But some of the rookies were getting action, including Marcus Hayes. There he was, in Celtics green and white—I could spot him by the way he moved.

Then Reggie Miller checked in for Indiana and Marcus switched on to him: pointy-out ears, alien bald head, grasshopper arms. Marcus always loved watching Reggie, another six-seven wing, but guarding him was something else because he never stopped moving. He could catch, turn and shoot on a dime, and used to kick out his legs to trick the defense into fouling. Marcus was actually a better athlete, bigger across the shoulders, stronger and more explosive, but Reggie was one of those guys . . . where everybody on the other team had to scramble like crazy to stop him from taking shots that nobody else on the court even wanted. *I Love Being the Enemy*, Reggie's memoir, came out during our senior year in high school, and Dad bought a copy, which we all read. Anyway, when Marcus caught the ball on the wing, there was Reggie, standing in front of him. Crouched a little, with his hands on his knees, waiting for him to do something.

It was a moment he must have been dreaming of all his life and Marcus did what he had always dreamed of doing—and launched himself into a three-pointer that touched . . . air.

Megan said, "Somebody's going to pay for that."

She had come to the bar to order drinks; I could smell the smoke on her.

"What do you mean?"

"Hello, Brian," she said. It almost surprised me that she remembered my name. But it was nice to hear her say it, like I'd been there all along at the back of her mind. "That's just what he's like. If he messes up, he takes it out on somebody else."

"This is a different level. You can't just take stuff out on these guys."

The barmaid came over and Megan asked for a pitcher of Shiner Bock and a basket of cheese fries.

"Where are you sitting? There's actually table service," the lady said, and Megan told her, "There actually isn't."

"You can't just take stuff out on Reggie Miller."

"Who's the worst player on the Pacers right now?" she asked me. "I mean, on the court?"

"I don't know." It was still early in the season, after the lockout. Teams hadn't found their rotations yet. "Al Harrington maybe." Harrington was one of those kids who jumped straight to the pros out of high school. Later he turned into a pretty good player, but this was his rookie year. He was nineteen years old and lucky to get eight minutes a game.

"Marcus told me once, if you want to pick off a pass, just look who's got the most power on the other team, and guys will pass it to him even if it's not a good pass."

"You can't just . . ."

But then Harrington caught the ball on the post and didn't know what to do with it. Walker was on him, and Reggie circled to the corner. Harrington tried to loft it to him and Marcus reached up and took the ball out of the air. Somebody had put a song on the jukebox, "Tecumseh Valley," which was nice and quiet but still too loud for me to hear the announcer.

Megan was laughing.

She waited for the beer and food and we talked while she waited.

"Is that why he went pro? Because of you."

"What do you mean?"

"My mom probably told me things she shouldn't."

"Oh, that," she said. "He wanted me to . . . press charges. That's what he wanted. But I just . . . didn't want to go through all that. He couldn't understand it. Like, why wouldn't you, if you can."

The pitcher came but the fries took a little longer. "He thinks everything is a power play," she said. "He thinks everybody's trying to get an edge on him. That's just what he's like. I used to tell him, some people are just . . . trying to get along, but he didn't buy that."

"Are you still in touch?" I asked her.

"Sometimes about . . . financial stuff. How about you?"

"No."

"The first thing he did when he got his first paycheck . . ." The music was sad and she turned away a minute. "He gave me some money, which he said, he wanted me to get some help for my mother, which is what I did. So she has a full-time carer now."

"You look great," I said.

"Well, it makes a difference. I'm full-time now, too."

"You know what my dad always called you?"

"No." She laughed again, she could move easily between different emotions.

"The brown-eyed bombshell."

"I always liked your dad."

"Can I call you sometime? I don't think I have your number."

"I don't see why you would."

Then the food arrived and she went back to her friends outside.

A version of this story went into the piece. I sent it first to two people, my father and Amy Freitag, so she could show it to Marcus. Dad got the email after breakfast; and then, that afternoon, when I stopped by to see the kids, he didn't mention it. We took them to the park.

The swimming pool closes at the end of summer and doesn't open again until May. It just lies there, full of leaves. One of the water pipes must leak, or maybe the supporting wall needs reinforcing, because you often get streaks of mud spreading out from the bank of grass by the pool onto the basketball court next door. Anyway, it's often empty and the kids can run around.

Albert is just at the age that I was when we moved to Austin. He's strong enough to make a free throw underhand but doesn't want to learn.

"Nobody does it like that anymore, Uncle Brian."

"Nobody did it like that when I was a kid. Who cares, it works."

It's an old argument, and I tell myself, let it go. There are things you can say, which, if acted upon, might make a difference. Take the shots you can make, keep your elbow in. But then you tell yourself these things all the time and where did it get you.

"Let an old man try," my dad said and pulled off his sweater. Even in April, when it's eighty-five degrees, he wears one of the cashmere sweaters my mother used to give him at Christmas, and that Betsy gives him now. He does yard work in them, too; they don't last long.

It's a small court, and all the markings are small in proportion. He stood at the free-throw line and held the ball in his hands, like a pot, by the sides. Then bent his legs and let go and it bounced hard off the back of the rim.

"Give me another shot," he said. "The rim's low. I read your piece."

So we had this conversation, with him shooting free throws and me chasing the ball down and passing it back.

"You going to tell me what you think?"

"I'm choosing my words," my dad said.

"That doesn't sound good."

I'm writing this down line by line, but the conversation actually took about half an hour. The shadow of the swimming pool fence grew diagonally and crisscrossed the court. Grit from the ball got in my hands, and then, when I wiped my forehead, dripped into my eyes. It was hot enough for that. And, of course, when you argue, the kids argue, too. Troy kept kicking the ball into the grass and then Albert took it away and Troy fell down. If you step in, there's grievance, if you don't, there's bloodshed. But they have a long day at school. The playground is really their happy-hour drink after work, where things get messy.

"All day long, I've been trying to figure out why you want to do this."

"Do what?"

"Get back at him like this. And for what?"

"This is my job, to write about sports. If anything, I'm too sympathetic. At least that's what people accuse me of."

"Your head is somewhere you don't see everything right-side up."

Maybe I wanted to have this fight, and expected it. And that's why I sent him the piece. But still when it comes you feel indignation—a heat and pressure rising in your chest.

"Is anything I wrote untrue or unfair?"

"All of it, Brian. All of it. I don't recognize him from this story. You make him seem like a badly damaged person."

"Well, he is."

"If he took up with this young woman, which on the face of it, I can't say I like, still, this is none of our business. And what goes on between two people is not something we can judge."

"I don't judge him. I tell a story."

"But what upsets me most is . . . the feeling that you have some grudge against him, which I don't understand at all."

"Come on, Dad. This is what I do."

"You haven't done this before."

Afterward, when I dropped the kids at home and went home myself, I thought of other things to say. When Marcus plays basketball, he uses whatever he's got against you—he holds nothing back. Yet for most of my life with him I've withheld something, some judgment or insight. Later that night, my dad called. He said, "I've been thinking about our conversation, which I must tell you, I found extremely upsetting."

"Forget about it."

"Maybe it's my fault. I should have addressed these feelings sooner."

"Since I was fourteen, I've been in his shadow."

"That's not true, Brian."

"He never pulls any punches. Why should I."

All day long I had watched the boys fight, and all their fighting was basically a bid for attention. I'm better than you, no you're not. I can do this and you can't. Why should he get away with everything, and not me. Maybe healthy people outgrow these feelings, or just suppress them. Or maybe neither. They just realize certain facts and feel depressed about it, and like there's nothing they can do.

I tried to explain this to my father but he misunderstood me.

"Okay, so he's better than you at what he does. There's no shame in that. That makes you a normal person. Marcus is better at what he does than almost anybody. But you can live a better life, a normal life. That's what *you* should do."

Meanwhile, without Mickey, the Sonics tried to hang on. For once, the NBA was front-page news in Austin. You could hear people talking basketball at the 7-Eleven, where I used to buy Ho Hos for the kids before picking them up from school, or at the Avenue B Grocery, where I sometimes ate lunch. Marcus was usually coy about local advertising, but Ross Mason, who ran the grocery, had put up a signed photo behind the register of the 1995 Burleson varsity team from a newspaper clipping about the State Semifinals. There was Marcus, kneeling up front, with his hand on a basketball; there was me, almost skinny and seventeen years old, standing a little apart at the end of a row.

"Do you want me to sign, too?" I asked, but Ross was ringing up another customer. I don't think he heard me.

In March, the Sonics went seven and ten and dropped to eighth in the West, neck and neck with Utah. They got a big win in Salt Lake, when Tony LaMarca came off the bench at the end of the game (Roundtree had fouled out) and blocked a layup by Mo Williams. This was the first week of April, but then they lost both ends of a back-to-back at the Staples Center, and the Clippers and Lakers put clear water between them. Houston and Utah and Austin were fighting for the last two spots.

For a week, Amy Freitag didn't answer my email, which was almost a relief. I figured, okay, that's something else I don't have to deal with. But then it started bugging me and I decided to call again.

She picked up and I could hear in the background the noise of some kitchen appliance. A juicer, or maybe a vacuum cleaner. After moving out of Mount Bonnell Shores, Marcus rented the penthouse at the Four Seasons Residence on San Jacinto. Right downtown, with views over the water. Then the sonic space seemed to expand in my ear—Amy must have drifted out to a balcony. Even then you could hear the noise of drilling or hammering or haulage rising up from the neighborhood below. Austin was, as the websites like to say, under construction.

"Hello, Brian," she said.

"Did you read it?"

"I read it."

"Did you show it to Marcus?"

"I gave it to him. You should know, I sent it to Joe Hahn, too."

"Can I talk to him, Amy?"

"Come on, Brian. What are you trying to do?"

"My job. Can I talk to him?" She didn't answer and I said, "You owe me that much, Amy."

"For what?"

I meant, getting me in trouble over that article. But there's no point going into something like that. For these people, even the nice ones like Amy, journalists are just a means to an end.

"Is he there now?"

"Brian, he's got a lot going on. Things like this don't help."

"I don't know why not . . . it's very sympathetic. Can I talk to him?"

"If he wants to talk, he'll call you."

And that was it. The sonic vista in my head closed down again, and I was on my own.

Pete Morgentau wanted it to run on the final day of the season, just after the Sonics' last game. If they make the playoffs, great. This sets the stage. If not, that's fine, too, it'll be a nice postmortem. I mentioned my problems with Amy Freitag, and he said, "Brian, this had to happen, right? If not now, when the book comes out."

So I told him what Fred Rotha said. You won't be able to work in this business again.

"People exaggerate these things. Who do you think Sam Smith writes for now? Chicago Bulls dot com. Anyway, judging by the book," Pete said, "I think you're about ready to put this relationship behind you."

For days the sense of something . . . impending had been growing in me, like a change in the weather. I feel these things mostly in my back. A cold coming on or a cold front or even depression activates the nerve running from my butt down the back of my leg. I can't sit in cars, even the driver's seat, without taking a minute afterward to unfold myself. At a certain age you realize that any pain that shows up in one place will probably end up somewhere else. But realizing this doesn't help, you just have to wait.

A nurse from UrologyAustin called to book another appointment—my three-month scan. Just a routine final check, but every time these medical dates approached they absorbed a certain percentage of my desktop capacity. Back pain is one of the symptoms of testicular cancer . . . that's the kind of useless information I mean. Then one day the phone rang and Marcus was on the other end, his famous voice was in my ear.

"You wanted to talk to me," he said. It was four in the afternoon, I must have fallen asleep.

"Did Amy show you the piece?"

"She showed it to me."

"Did you read it?"

"She told me what it was about."

"Did you read it?"

"Come on, Brian. I never read what you write anyway. I don't need to read it. It's always about me."

"You might learn something. It's very sympathetic."

But you can get tired of your own self-defenses; they start to sound different over time. For a while he didn't say anything and I thought he might have hung up, or was maybe looking at his phone or watching TV.

"What makes you think you know me?"

"Give me a break, Marcus. Don't make it like that."

"You don't know my life."

"Who knows you better than me? I remember when you got corn-rows, after Betsy cut your hair. You were living with us . . ."

"Brian, Brian."

"I thought we were friends."

"We had an arrangement. You got what you needed from me, I got what I needed from you."

"This is what people call friends."

"It was always your house, I always had to come to your house."

"Come on, Marcus," I said. "Who are you kidding."

"Oh well." He breathed in heavily through his nose. "Amy said, why don't you call him. That's all he wants, a phone call. So I called you. If this comes out, it's over, right. You know that. No more access. Not now, not ten years from now. We're done."

"I don't see why. This is what I do. You do what you do, this is me."

"Yeah, well. You know the rules." Then he said, because he couldn't help himself, or maybe because it wasn't over yet, and he wanted to talk to me the way we used to talk twenty-odd years ago, when we were kids. About making varsity, every day after school. "Man, I wanna taste the playoffs again. I want to taste it."

"What's so great about the playoffs?"

"People just play hard. When you beat 'em, you really beat 'em."

That was it, he hung up. They had two games left in the season and probably had to win both.

42

I started waking up in the night, worrying about edits. For that last week, I spent all day on the phone, checking email, talking to fact-checkers, talking to lawyers. ESPN wasn't taking chances; the piece went through several drafts. They cut the stuff about an abortion, and Caukwell's gambling, or arranging payments for the Dillard family. Bankruptcy details tend to be more complicated than interesting, and the symbolism seemed strong enough on its own: a girl he met at the high school where he used to play; her father owned the building where he grew up. We tried to make contact again with Marcus Hayes, or at least Joe Hahn. But they weren't returning emails. And at two in the morning, I woke up, thinking, Is it true? Do I believe this version of events? But at a certain point you have to sign off; the story is over.

Winnikoff called me on the cell. They were flying me out to Atlanta when the piece came out. He wanted to go over my schedule, the turn-around was pretty tight. *Inside the NBA* on Friday morning, then the *Jim Rome Show* in LA. After that, back to Bristol, Connecticut, for an ESPN special on Marcus Hayes. A podcast in New York with Alana Sissons. These days you don't just publish a story, you go door to door. The quiet in which I wrote the book was ending. All of my private feelings were going public; it was like coming out of the closet.

Before he hung up, Steve said, "Are you sure you want to do this? We're big enough to take the heat but I'm worried about you. I just want to make sure that you're happy."

He was a funny guy; English by birth, or half-American. He left London to go to Harvard and never went home. In conversation his accent was hard to place. He was hard to read in other ways, too, but I liked him.

"I'm happy," I told him.

I was sitting in the doctor's reception area, waiting for my scan. When the phone went dead I started thinking, if you don't think about your breathing, maybe you'll breathe normally. Which was stupid, which was just a kind of magical thinking. My blood tests were fine, my last three urine samples came out clear. But even if you're fine, it's true: all of your worries are short-term worries, all of your pleasures depend on this idea . . . that nothing more important is going on. If the ambulance waits outside, would you still watch the end of the game? I don't know.

Then Dr. Kleinman called me in and I lay back on the blue strip of paper.

"You know the drill," he said. A nurse draped a blanket over me and I inched my butt off the table, and pulled down my pants and boxers, and positioned my dick so it lay pointing up on the skin of my belly. Then he pulled away the blanket and applied cold gel to my balls.

There's always a pause while they look at the monitor, during which time they have information about the next phase of your life that you don't have.

After a minute, he said, "Sometimes in this job you get to give good news."

"I'm okay?"

"It looks fine."

"How do you know?"

"Because I've been doing this for thirty years."

"But how can you tell?"

"Look, Brian. It's the same as it was three months ago. To the last dot. Cancer doesn't sit around on the couch all day, it changes, it grows, it moves."

"So you're done with me?"

"I'm done with you. Go forth and live."

That night while eating Chinese takeout, I watched the Sonics beat Sacramento at the Arco arena. The Kings had nothing to play for except a lottery ticket, and the game was over by the middle of the third—Marcus sat down and never checked back in.

They flew home afterward and got into Austin around three in the morning, which gave them a day to rest before the season finale against San Antonio. This is a game they had to win to make the playoffs, because Utah defeated the Lakers that night in LA. (I lay in bed in the dark, fidgeting with my phone, checking for updates.) The problem was, San Antonio needed to win, too, to hold off Denver for the number one seed. Otherwise there's no way that guys like Ginóbili, Duncan and Parker would even suit up.

Just keeping up with the news-cycle was a full-time job. For weeks the rumor had been growing that Mmeremikwu might come back by the end of the season. Coach Steuben refused to answer questions about him. He read out a scripted statement each day and left it at that. There were stories that Mickey had engaged in "full-contact workouts" and looked sharp in scrimmages. Taffy Laycock said, "Our priority is his long-term future with the team." But he also said, "Austin needs playoff basketball, that's what we came here for, to bring NBA excitement to the city." What he really wanted was a tax break for a new stadium.

On the day of the game I didn't leave the house. Messages kept coming in, from Fred Rotha and Alana Sissons and Kenny Albrecht. All the guys were in town. They were meeting at five for an early bite at El Chile, which I don't much like anyway. From there you can just about walk to the stadium, under the highway, and show up dripping with sweat, when it's ninety-five degrees out. Or share a ten-dollar cab.

Tip-off was seven-thirty, and the whole day seemed to drain toward the evening. Sometimes it's like that in Austin anyway, it's too hot to go out until the sun goes down. I should have gone to the stadium but couldn't deal with the crowds. Or sitting in the press booth with everybody else, watching and talking and hearing them talk. Once the piece went live, I might have to answer questions about that, too, and face Marcus afterward in the locker room, which I didn't want to do.

So I lowered the blinds and lay on the sofa and put one of my mom's cassettes in the Walkman: *Bach's Concerto Number 5 in F major*, Glenn Gould recording. I wanted to hear the math in it that said, Everything's okay. There's nothing you can do about it anyway. Phone on lap, I kept checking the score. It was like that bit in *The Matrix* where you see the world reduced to binary code—just a series of numbers flashing across the screen. Hayes . . . jump shot 18 ft . . . missed . . . rebound Duncan. 7–4 . . . 9–4 . . . 9–6 . . .

Mickey wasn't playing. Steuben decided to hold him back; Marcus had to do it on his own. At halftime the Spurs led fifty-seven to forty-eight and I thought about calling Quinn. Then the phone rang and I realized I was lying in the dark. The sun had set and twilight fell in gray bars across the room.

Dad said, "Why don't you come over. Everybody's watching the game."

So I walked the five blocks to Betsy's house . . . along the wide Hyde Park avenues, where you can walk in the middle of the road. But when I got there only Dad was up, the kids had gone to bed. It was a little after nine o'clock, on a school night.

The second half had already started, and there he was, the guy I used to share a bedroom with, on TV. After a time-out, Marcus fed Roundtree in the post then ran a split action with Stepanik, who set the flare screen. Marcus popped to the top of the key and Roundtree swung it back to him. Boris Diaw got hung up on the switch and Marcus knocked down the three.

"Come on," my dad said. The Sonics were down four.

He had lost weight since moving in with Betsy, or maybe it just descended to his belly because his shoulders had become these narrow, fragile old-man shoulders. On the soft couch, when he leaned back, you could see his belly like a heap of mashed potatoes, which he rested his hands across. Normally he fell asleep watching ball games, at least that's what he did for much of my childhood, so that Mom used to come in and say, "Brian, tell your father to go to bed." But tonight he looked wide awake.

"Are you packed?" he asked, during a commercial.

"Not yet."

"What time's your flight?"

"One o'clock."

"Where you going first?"

"Atlanta."

Then the game came back on. Roundtree picked up an offensive board and bounced a pass to Ty Jones, who was cutting for the layup. But then Ginóbili went on a mini-run for the Spurs—a three, a spinning drive, a one-hand pass to Danny Green, for another three. The lead shrank and grew again. At the end of the third, Marcus drove hard against Green, who moved his feet to block him off at the foul line. Diaw was there, too; they had started double- and triple-teaming him, collapsing in the lane. So Marcus turned three-sixty and switched the dribble from right to left and found a gap in the traffic. He rose up against Duncan but then ducked under him to finish with the left hand. Behind the backboard, and all around him, crowds stood and chanted.

I must have shouted, because Albert walked in, wearing only pajama bottoms—they had little VW bugs driving across them.

"You woke me up, " Al said.

"Come sit here," my dad told him.

"Mom said go to bed."

"It's a two-point game."

So Albert sat between us. I could feel the heat coming off his bare skin, because the sofa bent under my weight and made him lean against me.

At the start of the fourth, Steuben left Marcus on the bench, to extend the break. Albert kept saying, "Why isn't he playing? Where's Marcus?" and Dad said, "He's resting."

"Why is he resting?"

"At his age, you can't go all out for forty-eight minutes anymore."

"Why not? I can . . ."

So the whole time there was this undertone of conversation and explanation. With Marcus out, the Sonics couldn't score. But Duncan was sitting, too, so was Parker, and Ginóbili went cold. He took one of his long set-shot threes that barely scratched the rim, and lost a dribble off his foot when Jones probably pushed him from behind. But the ref swallowed his whistle. The Erwin Center is really a college stadium, and the crowd inside was like a college crowd, young and loud. I saw a lot of painted faces on TV, people standing on the hard concrete rows, holding up signs.

"It's not too late to change your mind," my father said.

But I didn't answer.

"When does the piece come out?"

"After the game."

Marcus came back with a little over eight minutes left. He hit a three and missed a three, drove hard into a double team, and found Tony LaMarca under the basket for a dunk. The score went back and forth. Albert wanted to get his Marcus Hayes jersey from the bedroom, which he now shared with Troy. But I said, just leave it, we don't want to wake him up.

"But I need it," Albert said.

"Do you want him to sit here, too, and get in the way?"

"No."

"So forget it."

But every commercial break he kept repeating, I just want to get my Marcus Hayes shirt. Maybe it comforted him, to have something to say.

Steuben called time-out, with a minute left and the Sonics down two. Mostly just to give Marcus a breather. He had a couple of foul shots coming and made them both to tie the game. Parker brought the ball up for San Antonio and found Duncan in the post, who reversed it to Ginóbili on the wing. Roundtree had doubled from the weak side, which forced Marcus to switch on to Diaw—anyway, nobody picked up Ginóbili, who hit the three. The Sonics called another time-out. Off the inbounds pass, Marcus caught the ball on the right wing and drove into the lane. Diaw and Duncan converged, but he managed to loft a layup high off the glass and in. Parker brought the ball up again. There were thirty seconds left and the Spurs led by one.

Again, he set up Duncan in the post, but this time Marcus never cleared when Ginóbili cut along the baseline. Duncan had his back to him, and Marcus crept over and brought his hand down hard like a hammer on the ball. There was a scramble for it under the basket but he got there first and slowly dribbled up court. Time was running down and Marcus let it run, bouncing the ball in the glare of lights coming off the hardwood, about twenty-five feet from the basket— while Danny Green watched and waited for him to make a move.

All of this is just more binary code. If he scored, they won, if he missed, they lost.

Sometimes I like to think of these situations as just another problem at work. Down one, fifteen seconds left. Have we got anybody in the office who can deal with this? Well, somebody says, we got a guy . . . he's been thinking about problems like this for the past twenty years. Ever since he was a kid. That's really all he does. His whole life has been one long preparation—middle school, high school, college, his first few jobs after graduation. There's nobody in the world right now with more expertise.

Okay, bring him in.

The analytics people like to tell you, there's no such thing as clutch. Here's what they mean by that. Nobody shoots *better* in late-game, high-pressure situations than they do the rest of the time—at least, not in any statistically meaningful sample size. Even the great ones roll the dice like everybody else. But here's what clutch actually means. That everybody on court can know what you're going to do and you still have a decent chance of doing it. For most guys, even NBA stars, the numbers drop off a cliff. Too much of their success relies on inattention. But for guys like Marcus, the numbers hold pretty steady. And here's what the data tells us: over the course of the season, he made 49 percent of his midrange jump shots, between sixteen feet and the three-point line. An elite figure, but still, slightly worse than your chances of landing on heads if you flip a coin.

And yet, it's true—this is why we watch sports. To feel for a moment the illusion that some guys can control the coin flip, too. That this is their relationship to the world. That for them, unlike the rest of us, it's a perfect medium of self-expression.

Marcus inched forward, bounce by bounce, then took two hard steps to his right and stopped. He stopped dead, and Green went past him. Marcus pulled up from twenty feet and let fly. While this was going on, Albert kept saying, "I need my jersey, let me get my jersey. It's my good luck jersey, I need my shirt, it's good luck," and I said, "Sh, sh, just watch. You may remember this one day." Then Dad said, "Son of a bitch," and tried to get up. "Eileen," he called out, with his hands on his knees. "Betsy! Come see this. You should see this. They'll show a replay in a minute." Albert started screaming and running around, while fans rushed onto the court and crowded the television screen. Marcus didn't move. He stood at the top of the key, while everyone pushed against him, and it was like everything I felt about him for the past twenty years was rushing the court, too, and surrounding him, while he just stood there.